TIME
QUAKE

Also by Linda Buckley-Archer

GIDEON THE CUTPURSE

THE TAR MAN

TIME QUAKE

being Book III of

The Enlightenment of Peter Schock

by

LINDA BUCKLEY-ARCHER

SIMON AND SCHUSTER

The quotation: '*Plus je connais les hommes, plus j'aime mon chien*' is taken from *Textes de scène* by Pierre Desproges, published by Editions du Seuil, France.

First published in Great Britain in 2009 by Simon and Schuster UK Ltd
A CBS COMPANY.

Simon & Schuster UK Ltd
1st Floor, 222 Gray's Inn Road
London WC1X 8HB

A CIP catalogue record for this book
is available from the British Library.

HB ISBN: 978-1-41691-712-0

1 3 5 7 9 10 8 6 4 2

Printed in the UK by CPI Mackays, Chatham ME5 8TD

www.simonandschuster.co.uk
www.thetarman.com

TABLE OF CONTENTS

TO THE READER

The world turns on such seemingly trivial incidents. An argument between a father and son led to a boy travelling up to a Derbyshire farmhouse for the weekend with a girl he did not know. An encounter between the girl's Golden Labrador and a Van der Graaf generator caused the dog to panic and run amok through her father's research laboratory. The frantic chase which ensued led, in turn, to the boy and girl hurtling along corridors and down stairs towards a collision not only with an anti-gravity machine but also with a different century.

The children's accidental discovery of time travel – proof, if ever it was needed, of the relationship between gravity and time – had many serious consequences. One of which, as you will see, was to put the future of one of the world's great nations in jeopardy. It is curious that the fate of so very many could depend on the actions of a single man, yet there are occasions when it takes only one hand to steer the great engine of history – and many more to put it on its right course.

So this, then, is the final volume of the story of Peter Schock and Kate Dyer, two twenty-first century children, whom fate plucked from their everyday lives and dropped into the year 1763. Peter and Kate were swept up in events which no child should have to confront and which ultimately threatened everyone. Yet no adult could have shown greater courage.

The fortunes and actions of two men, seemingly irreconcilable one to the other, are also at the heart of this tale. Gideon Seymour, a reformed thief and an honourable man, came to the children's aid at no small risk to himself. The Tar Man, Gideon's nemesis and, as it subsequently transpired, his elder brother, was a feared and talented villain, who succeeded in establishing his vicious reputation not only in his own century but also in ours.

I have already described how the Tar Man made off with Peter, Kate and the last two anti-gravity machines in existence, and returned to 1763. One of the devices proved to be useless to him, for he had no knowledge of the code needed to make it function, but with the other, he hoped to undo the injustice that had blighted him all his life. In so doing, however, the Tar Man made a rare but calamitous error of judgement: he trusted his master, Lord Luxon, to help him. However, Lord Luxon had plans of his own for this machine that could travel through time, and he stole it, leaving the Tar Man stranded alongside Peter and Kate in 1763.

Lord Luxon's mind was as keen as his soul was unfulfilled. Alas for the Tar Man, he underestimated how much even bad men need to atone for their failures in life; nor did he grasp, until it was too late, the scale of Lord Luxon's ambition.

Since that first time event in a Derbyshire laboratory, the cost of interfering with the universe's fragile time mantle has become abundantly clear. The formation of parallel worlds, the first time quakes and Kate's accelerated fading, were all symptoms of a fatal disease. Perhaps if Lord Luxon had not stolen the anti-gravity machine, it would not have been too late for the scientists to act. But History has always been littered with 'What Ifs?'. Beware of clever men who cannot see the whole picture. For like a boy crawling out along a rotten branch to reach for a last, ripe fruit, Lord Luxon was blind to the dangers inherent in time travel. All he saw, indeed all he *wanted* to see, was one glorious opportunity . . .

When Peter told me that the Tar Man had lost possession of the device to my former master, Lord Luxon, I was afraid. For I knew Lord Luxon's heart better, I think, than any man alive. I understood his parched soul and how far his thirst might take him. He was not always thus. Once, long ago, and for no personal gain, he saved my life. But now Lord Luxon was that most dangerous of creatures, a good man who has turned bad.

Gideon Seymour
Lincoln's Inn Fields, 1763

CHAPTER ONE

Manhattan

In which Lord Luxon takes a
fancy to New York

The sun shone down on the remarkable island of Manhattan, whose thrusting castles – too tall and numerous by far to be the stuff of fairy tales – held gravity in contempt as they vied to be the first to reach the sky. Great alleys of skyscrapers seemed to strut across the city, catching the rays of the dazzling sun and casting vast shadows behind them. It was August, and the air was heavy with an intense, moist heat and those foolish enough to leave the cool shelter of the giant buildings for the scorching street would soon find their shirts sticking to their backs and their hair plastered to their foreheads. More than one New Yorker, turning off Sixth Avenue into the comparative calm of Prince Street, found their gaze sidling over to an individual whose stance, as well as his dress, marked him out, even in SoHo, as somewhat unusual.

The buildings were smaller here, on a more human scale, a mere six storeys high, some of them with iron staircases zigzagging down towards the sidewalks that, mid-afternoon, were already in deep shade. While he waited for his valet to hail a cab, Lord

Luxon stood in front of an Italian baker's shop, its windows piled high with crusty loaves baked in the form of oversized doughnuts, in order to observe his reflection in the dusty window. He adjusted his posture. People were strolling by in various stages of undress, wearing shades and shorts and brightly coloured T-shirts, as they darted from one air-conditioned building to another. Lord Luxon, however, appeared cool and immaculate in an ivory three-piece suit, cut expertly from the lightest of cloths, which skimmed the contours of his slim figure. He assumed his habitual stance: legs apart, one arm neatly behind his back, the other resting lightly on his silver-tipped ebony cane. He consciously lengthened the muscles at the back of his neck so that he held his head at precisely that angle which announced, eloquently, that here was an English aristocrat, born of an ancient line of English aristocrats, and accustomed to all that life can afford, in whatever century he happened to find himself. He observed his silhouette and congratulated himself on discovering a tailor of such exceptional talent in an age when the male of the species seemed to have forgotten both the art and pleasure of self-adornment. And how curious it was that although well over two centuries separated his tailors, their respective premises, on London's Savile Row, were but a few dozen paces from one another.

A middle-aged tourist, his sagging belly bulging over the waist of his shorts, stopped to stare for a moment at this vision in cream linen. Lord Luxon eyed him with distaste and thought of his cedar wood chests in 1763, specially imported from Italy, and the layers of exquisite silks they contained, the frothy lace, his embroidered, high-heeled shoes, his tricorn hats and brocade waistcoats, his dress wigs, his rouge and his black beauty spots in the shape of crescent moons. It was disappointing, he reflected, that twenty-first-century man's sense of fashion had not kept pace with the truly staggering progress he had observed in every other walk of life. Although the current fashion for body piercing, tattoos and hair dyes in the wildest of colours *was* tempting – indeed, it might be amusing to have his navel pierced and a ruby, or perhaps a diamond or two, inserted . . . Lord Luxon suddenly laughed out loud, causing the staring tourist to make even less effort to conceal his curiosity. Faith, he could even have his own coat of arms tattooed on his shoulder! How deliciously unseemly!

Lord Luxon looked around him, still smiling. What a transformation this new millennium had worked on him. Little wonder, he thought, that the Tar Man, his errant henchman, had become so attached to this age of wonders. Deprived of the means to travel through time, Blueskin's own century must now feel like a prison . . . Lord Luxon recalled the Tar Man's expression, his rage and desperation and horror, as he realised that his master had stolen the ingenious time device and that, like the rest of humanity, he was once more limited to his own short span of history. Lord Luxon let a shiver of pity pass over him like a cold draught. And yet, extraordinary though he was, the Tar Man had disappointed him in the end. Just as Gideon had done. But what did that matter to him now?

Lord Luxon closed his eyes and listened to the roar of the city and sensed its throbbing pulse. How astonishing to witness what Britain's wayward little colony had become! Those first American seeds had yielded a crop so bountiful it defied belief! This city took his breath away! It was as if the Manhattan sunshine had burned away the cloud of world-weariness and boredom that in his own time so rarely left him. Here he felt an energy and an excitement and a zest for life surging through him which he could scarcely contain. Here, his convalescent soul was regaining its appetite: sops of bread and milk were no longer enough. Now he wanted *meat*. He believed that he had found his purpose on this earth and if he succeeded in his quest, which, by all the gods, he was determined to do, his name would be shot across the skies in eternal glory . . .

The annoying little man continued to stare at him and Lord Luxon glanced at the tourist's dun-coloured excuse for a shirt, wrinkled and stained with sweat, and decided to acknowledge his presence with a disdainful bow, putting one foot in front of the other and pulling out a handkerchief from his top pocket as he did so.

'Good day to you,' Lord Luxon said. 'Upon my word, sir, your very countenance makes the heat seem less tolerable, if that were possible . . .'

'Excuse me?'

'Why, on an afternoon such as this, it is difficult even to conceive of the notion of ice, or snow – although I heartily recommend that you try . . .'

An angry cloud scudded across the man's red and shiny face and he did not reply, not quite understanding Lord Luxon's meaning but detecting more than a hint of disrespect in his arrogant, peacock's attitude. He scowled and clenched his fists and took half a step towards Lord Luxon, but immediately found himself confronted by a ruddy-cheeked man, with a black beard and pigtail and a chest the size of a small ship, who planted himself squarely between the overheated tourist and his master and proceeded to fold his arms as if it were a threat. The tourist took one look at Lord Luxon's lackey in his worn white trousers and braces, his curious crimson jacket and his bulldog stare, and fled in the direction of Sixth Avenue, unable to decide if he had imagined the low growl or not. When he felt it was safe to do so, the breathless tourist looked back and saw that on each level of the emergency

6

stairs that climbed up the red-brick building behind Lord Luxon, there was a man, seemingly standing to attention, in white trousers and military-style crimson jacket. 'Who are these guys?' he said under his breath, and found that all the hairs had risen on the back of his neck.

CHAPTER TWO

A Spent Rose

In which the party struggles to know what
to do about Kate's affliction and
Gideon brings some promising news

The hot summer of 1763 was drawing to a close and there was something in the air, a quality to the light, that made the residents of Lincoln's Inn Fields cherish every last warm evening before the first chill of autumn sent them scurrying indoors. Only a few streets away, amidst the raucous cries of street hawkers and the incessant thunder of wagons, starving children begged; soldiers, mutilated in the recent war, drowned their sorrows in gin, and, for the sake of a few coins, footpads beat their victims senseless up dark alleyways. But here, in this civilised London square, all was calm and comfort and respectability. Who could have guessed that behind these fine façades could be heard the first rumblings of a cataclysmic storm that threatened to destroy all before it?

Dusk was approaching and the trees in the square were thick with songbirds which trilled and warbled in the rapidly fading light. A blackbird perched, sentry-like, on a tall, wrought iron gate that graced the frontage of an imposing house to the west of

Lincoln's Inn Fields. The sweet birdsong drifted into Sir Richard Picard's first-floor drawing room, carried in on wafts of air made fragrant by the honeysuckle that scrambled beneath the open window. Inside the room were to be found Parson Ledbury and two children from the twenty-first century, although their appearance gave no clue as to the century they called their own – except that, under closer scrutiny, their shoes seemed better suited to a modern-day sports field than the elegance of an eighteenth-century drawing room. Kate Dyer lay stretched out on her belly, on a couch beneath the window, her red hair vivid against her sprigged green dress. She supported her chin in one cupped hand whilst with the other she tugged absent-mindedly at the sleeve of a discarded jacket draped over the back of a chair. The boy it belonged to, Peter Schock, was sitting at a circular table in front of a chessboard. Opposite him, white wig awry, sat a portly man of the cloth who emptied a glass of claret in one gulp and set it back on the table with a bang that jolted Kate temporarily out of her reverie.

In the middle of setting out the chess pieces for a return match with the redoubtable Parson Ledbury, the young Peter Schock glanced over at his friend, a white knight suspended in mid-air between finger and thumb. Kate's eyelids kept sliding shut but as soon as they closed she would jerk them open again through sheer effort of will. Another day spent searching for the Tar Man – and, hopefully, the duplicate anti-gravity machine which Kate's father and the scientist, Dr Pirretti, had built – had left Peter frustrated and anxious. But Kate was utterly wrung out and exhausted – as, it seemed to Peter, she so often was. Gideon and Sir Richard had been keen to continue the search but when they noticed Kate's white face, they had insisted that the Parson take the children home to rest.

'Go to bed, Kate, before we have to carry you up,' Peter said.

Kate shook her head and pushed herself up. 'No. I want to see Parson Ledbury thrash you first.'

Peter stuck out his tongue at her.

'Now if *you* were to challenge me, Mistress Kate, it would be a different matter entirely,' said the Parson.

'All right,' she replied. 'I will. Afterwards.'

Kate laughed and slumped back onto the overstuffed sofa, pulling out the flounces of her dress that were badly spattered, she noticed, with mud and other unmentionable substances from the gutters of Covent Garden. She should really get changed, but not yet . . . not just yet. Perhaps when she had rested for a little longer. The familiar, piercing cry of swallows made her turn her head to look through the open window. As her eyes followed the birds swooping and diving through the air in search of midges she felt a pang of homesickness. How often had she and her brothers and sisters stood in their Derbyshire farmyard and watched swallows build their nests under the eaves. Kate wondered if she would ever do so again but instantly scolded herself for even doubting it. So she forced herself to look out at the dome of St Paul's Cathedral, whose silhouette, rising up into the golden evening sky beyond Lincoln's Inn Fields, spoke to her so powerfully of hope. She sighed heavily and another strand of hair tumbled down over her face.

The Parson beat Peter in three moves but by then Kate was fast asleep and even his victory cry did not wake her. The two players looked first at Kate and then at each other.

'I don't think Kate likes being alone right now,' whispered Peter.

'I do not think it is a question of her being alone,' said the Parson, endeavouring to lower his booming voice a few notches. 'Rather, it seems to me that Mistress Kate is frightened of being separated from *you*. Bringing up the rear of the party, I observed her tagging behind you like a lamb to its mother, growing ever more anxious as the crowds grew denser.'

This was not what Peter wanted to hear. He had noticed it, too. A frown etched itself onto his forehead.

'I saw a few people staring at her today. If she carries on fading at this rate I think it's going to be really noticeable. She can still get away with it – just – but not for very much longer.'

'Alas, I am of your opinion, Master Peter. Her condition has worsened since her return to this time.'

'I don't get why it's happening. I've travelled through time as much as she has. It's not as if she keeps blurring back or anything . . . It's not like the first time. And I haven't blurred once.'

'Ay, the phenomenon is the queerest thing I ever saw and I cannot for the life of me account for it. Upon my word, how you, Peter, continue to be in rude health while your companion droops and fades like a spent rose is quite beyond my comprehension.'

'Do you think she'll get better if we get her back home?' asked Peter.

'I am certain of it, my dear boy,' said the Parson, unconvincingly. 'But for her own safety I fear she must soon be restricted to going out under cover of darkness . . .'

'What! Am I becoming a vampire now?'

Kate was suddenly fully awake. She shot up from the sofa and stood facing Parson Ledbury accusingly. The Parson stared vacantly back at her.

'A vampire?'

'Are you all planning on putting a stake through my heart or something?'

'Don't be daft, Kate!' exclaimed Peter. 'We're just worried about you, that's all.'

'I most humbly beg your pardon, Mistress Kate, I thought you

11

were asleep,' the Parson said guiltily. 'To distress you was the last thing in the world I intended . . .'

'I'm not fading!' Kate practically shouted. 'I'm *not*! I'm still me! I'm Kate Dyer and I have five brothers and sisters and I live on a farm in Derbyshire and I have a Golden Labrador called Molly and my dad is going to come and get me! You see if he doesn't!'

Parson Ledbury and Peter exchanged glances. Peter looked at Kate's pale face, flushed with emotion, and expected to see tears rolling down her cheeks though none came.

'I am a foolish old man who should have known better . . . I hope you will forgive me, Mistress Kate,' said the Parson.

Peter sat down next to Kate on the sofa and slowly put an arm around her shoulders, unsure whether she wanted to be comforted in this way but Kate immediately clung to Peter and put her face into the crook of his neck. She took hold of his hand and gripped it hard. Peter looked down. Kate's flesh was no longer the same as his own. The effect was subtle but unmistakeable. It looked faded and ever so slightly translucent, a little like wax and, if he had not known better, he would have thought there was an invisible layer that insulated his skin from hers. So little warmth radiated from her hand. Peter felt desperate. He badly wanted to help Kate get better, but what could he do?

'I promise we won't let anything happen to you, we'll—'

Kate cut him off mid-sentence. 'Don't. Don't make any promises you can't keep.'

'I shall fetch Hannah,' said the Parson. 'She will know what to do for the best . . . Some smelling salts perhaps, or a drop of brandy . . .'

Parson Ledbury stepped onto the landing and closed the door behind him. Kate and Peter were left alone and, anxious to break the silence, Peter reached into his pocket and showed Kate a worn and very grubby piece of paper, folded up into a tiny square.

'Look. Do you remember this? I'd forgotten I still had it—'

'What is it?' said Kate, peering at it. 'It's not your Christmas homework, is it?'

Peter smiled and nodded. He unfolded it carefully and read:

'Christmas homework. To be handed in to Mr Carmichael on Jan. 8th. Write 500 words on: My Ideal Holiday.'

Kate burst out laughing. 'You showed it to me that first day in Derbyshire. How funny!'

'If I did it, do you think it'd get us home?'

'You'd be handing it in really late . . .'

'Yeah – I'd probably get a detention . . .'

'Probably two . . .'

'And a hundred lines. *I must not time-travel during term-time.*'

Peter put it back in his pocket and presently they heard voices in the hall and the sound of the front door shutting, and then the click of heels against wood as someone bounded up the stairs.

'I trust that Mistress Kate fares better,' said Sir Richard, striding into the room, followed by Parson Ledbury. 'Ah,' he continued, observing her strained, pale face. 'I see that she does not . . .'

'No, I *do* feel a little better, thank you,' protested Kate, who hated people to make a fuss – well, unless it was her mother.

'Then I am heartily glad to hear it.'

'I trust your luck improved after we left you, Sir Richard,' said Parson Ledbury. 'For I grow weary of searching for confounded needles in confounded haystacks.'

Sir Richard beamed. 'Indeed our luck *did* improve, my dear fellow. I shall let Gideon tell you his news in person, but I gleaned a crumb or two of information myself in the city this afternoon. I admit that I was becoming a little dispirited and resolved to take my ease a while in the Mitre tavern in Fleet Street. It was while I was there that I happened upon an old acquaintance, a wealthy merchant from Surrey – and a most happy coincidence it was, for he is a great lover of horses and his country estate adjoins that of Tempest House.'

'Lord Luxon's house?' asked Peter.

'Precisely, Master Schock. And when I asked him if he had seen his neighbour of late, he replied that he had seen him not two days past in Child's coffee-house in St Paul's churchyard. The merchant did not announce himself, however, as he was hidden behind *The London Gazette*, toasting himself in front of the fire. Lord Luxon sat at one of the small tables, in earnest conversation with a gentleman whom my friend immediately recognised as none other than Mr Gainsborough, the portrait painter.'

'Oh, I've seen his pictures at Tate Britain!' exclaimed Kate.

Sir Richard smiled. 'It does not surprise me that his fame will live on – he has a truly remarkable talent.'

Peter shrugged his shoulders. 'Never heard of him,' he muttered.

'My acquaintance admitted that the two gentlemen's conversation was more interesting than his newspaper. Mr Gainsborough, it appeared, remarked to Lord Luxon that he was sick of portraits and wished, instead, to take up his viol da gamba and walk off into some sweet village where he could paint landscapes and enjoy the autumn of his life in quietness and ease. To which Lord Luxon replied that if only he would agree to sell him his present commission and the diverse drawings and sketches of which they had spoken, he would give Mr Gainsborough more than enough gold to retire from society if that is what he so wished. He also advised him to invest his wealth in the American colonies as he himself had been doing, for he was convinced that the country had a great future . . . My acquaintance observed the two fellows shake hands and leave the coffee-house in excellent spirits.'

'So Lord Luxon is still in 1763!' said Peter.

'Or he's returned here,' said Kate. 'If he knows about America it means that he's learned how to use the anti-gravity machine.'

'Which is not such good news . . .' said Peter.

'But what the devil is the fellow doing commissioning paintings?' asked Parson Ledbury.

'That's easy,' said Kate. 'A painting by Gainsborough would be worth millions in our time.'

'Ha! I thought as much!' exclaimed Sir Richard. 'Well, if my Lord Luxon is bent on plundering his past to pay for his future, at least we stand a whisker of a chance of catching the rogue.'

Peter's face brightened. 'Not to mention the anti-gravity machine!'

'I have already sent a couple of fellows to Tempest House and also to Lord Luxon's residence in Bird Cage Walk. If Lord Luxon is still here we shall find out before the night is out.'

Suddenly the drawing-room door swung open and Gideon Seymour's lean and agile figure appeared in the doorway. He looked about the room and his blue eyes softened when they fell upon Kate. He nodded to the Parson, then walked over to the children and knelt at Kate's feet.

'We have promising news, Mistress Kate. There has been a sighting of the Tar Man. At Bartholomew's Fair. He cannot have been able to solve the puzzle of how to start up your device. If we are to stand a chance of catching up with him and the machine we must make haste. Even if you are still not fully rested, I wonder if it would not do your heart good to help run down that foul villain who is the root and cause of your unhappiness. Will you accompany us, Mistress Kate? Shall we capture Blueskin and win back your machine?'

Kate jumped up from the sofa. 'Are you kidding? Of course I'll come! I want to see the Tar Man get a taste of his own medicine for once!'

CHAPTER THREE

A Wolf in Sheep's Clothing

In which the redcoats take to spitting at Orcs
and Lord Luxon contrives to
meet a talented young American

William, Lord Luxon's trusted valet, who had relinquished his liveried uniform for a sober, dark suit, dabbed at his neck with a handkerchief as he perched on the edge of the sidewalk hoping to flag down a yellow cab. The heat and the noise bothered the grey-haired William, as did the uncouth dress of the people who thronged the pavements of Prince Street, and he longed to return to the verdant, rolling hills of Surrey and the cool stone walls of Tempest House with its gardens and fountains and an etiquette which he understood. But William had seen the look in his master's eye and he knew that he would have to be patient until the deed was done.

The sound of sudden, ferocious barking caused both William and his master to look up in alarm. On the second flight of iron stairs one of the redcoats, a short, wiry man, was kneeling down, talking quietly into a massive dog's ear. Then he took something out of his pocket, a piece of raw meat by the look of it, and threw

16

it into the air. The dog, half Irish wolfhound, was disturbingly cross-eyed. It jumped up, snapping shut its powerful jaws over the morsel. The redcoat gave it a rough pat on its head and the animal licked his fingers and sat peaceably at his feet.

'Where did that hideous hell hound appear from, Sergeant Thomas?' called William. 'It has a bark like a six-pounder!'

Sergeant Thomas stood up and his intense gaze met that of the manservant. 'I did not know you'd been near enough action to recognise the sound of a cannon, Mr Purefoy,' he commented good-humouredly.

William's colour deepened. This gruff veteran of numerous military campaigns enjoyed taunting his employer's valet. He could not understand why a man would want to spend his life attending to the whims and wardrobe of Lord Luxon. Only the previous night, as he and the men had supped cold beer together Sergeant Thomas had slapped him on the back and called him a canary in a cage. 'A pretty gold cage to be sure,' he had said, 'with plenty of vittles, where you are no doubt sheltered from the harsh winds of life. But you are a *man* – would you not prefer to spread your wings even if it meant a harder existence?' William's ego was still smarting.

'A valet knows the sound of a cannon, Sergeant Thomas, even if he is not accustomed to firing one. But what of the hound?'

'The bitch has taken a fancy to me and I have a mind to keep her,' the soldier called down. 'As I have said to you on numerous occasions, Mr Purefoy, this building is the devil itself to guard, and for such a task a dog is worth half a dozen gangly youths who've taken the King's shilling. You'll sniff out any intruders, won't you, my girl?'

Lord Luxon raised an eyebrow. Sergeant Thomas and his men were a law unto themselves and he chose to avoid direct contact with them, preferring to leave day-to-day negotiations to William.

'What shall I call her, do you suppose, Mr Purefoy?'

William looked at the dog, and reflected for a moment. Then he smiled. 'Sally,' he said. 'After my sister. She's the ugliest woman in Suffolk but she's got as much bottom as you, Sergeant Thomas, and she'd tear anyone apart who tried to harm her or her abundant brood.'

Sergeant Thomas roared with laughter. 'Then by all means, my friend, her name shall be Sally.'

As if she understood, the dog lifted her head and howled.

'And if she does not behave herself,' said Lord Luxon under his breath to William, 'you'll be slipping poison into the bitch's supper.'

The smile faded from William's face. 'Yes, milord.'

When, at long last, a yellow cab swooped towards him, William hurried to open the door for his master and, sweat dripping from his nose, stood to attention as Lord Luxon lowered himself elegantly into his seat.

'Do you wish me to accompany you, my Lord? Or any of the men?'

'Thank you, but no, William. I scarcely think an assignation with the charming Mrs Stacey and her clever niece should cause you to be fearful for my person. On the other hand, I sense that our red-coated friends are restless. An attack of cabin fever begins to afflict them. We should take yesterday's incident as a warning sign.'

'I conveyed your displeasure to Sergeant Thomas, as you requested, my Lord, and I know that he remonstrated with his men – although I fear it was in a half-hearted fashion. I am given to understand that the men see such incidents not as misdemeanours but rather as the spoils of war.'

'The spoils of war! Fleecing some pathetic fellows who cannot hold their wine? And surely it cannot have slipped Sergeant Thomas' attention that battle has not yet commenced.'

'With respect, my Lord, that is not how the men see it . . . They hope for much out of this campaign; indeed, you have promised them much . . . and, surrounded by the temptations of this city, I fear they grow tired of being confined to camp.'

'A soldier's life is not all action,' snapped Lord Luxon. 'This ragged band should be more sensible of the unique honour bestowed on them . . .'

'And yet, my Lord,' said William softly, 'they come with the Colonel's highest recommendation. Sergeant Thomas says that every last one of them would lay down their lives without a murmur if he asked it of them.'

'Very well, William, very well. Besides, if Mrs Stacey's niece is free with her information they will have action aplenty ere the month is out . . . and it is true that this maddening heat is enough to turn a saint into a scoundrel. Profit from my absence and contrive to divert them in some way.'

'A visit to the cinema, perhaps, my Lord?' suggested William hopefully. 'I could escort them, of course . . .'

'Yes, yes, do so by all means,' Lord Luxon said, waving his valet away. 'Reduce the guard to two for the afternoon and tell the men that when they are on duty they are to refrain from spitting on the pedestrians below.'

William tried not to smirk. It was true that the men's aim was excellent. 'Yes, my Lord.' He clicked the cab door shut and bent down to address the driver, who observed beads of sweat trickling off the end of the valet's nose.

'Hey, buddy, there ain't no law that says you've got to keep your jacket on. Your engine's gonna overheat . . .'

William ignored him and rapped the roof of the cab as if it were Lord Luxon's coach and six all set to gallop up the sweeping avenue of elms that led to Tempest House.

'Fraunces Tavern, if you please, my man, and be smart about it.'

Later that afternoon, William and half a company of English redcoats who had last seen action during the Seven Years War in the autumn of 1762, drank cold beers in a bar they frequented off Sixth Avenue. It was owned by Michael, a shaggy-haired Irishman who – having convinced himself that they were actors on tour refusing to come out of character – now treated them all like long-lost friends. They perched in a line on high stools, hunched over the bar, while Michael showed them photographs of his large family and encouraged them to move to America where, if you worked hard, like he had done, anything was possible. Afterwards they trooped into a near-empty film theatre on West Houston Street where there happened to be a retrospective screening of *The Lord of the Rings* trilogy. It was their third experience of the magic of the big screen and William had bought them generous quantities of cookies. Now they waited in breathless anticipation for the lights to go down and for the next three hours they lived through every last second of the epic story that unfolded before their eyes. As the first episode drew to its conclusion and Boromir, mortally wounded, fought bravely on against the odds, it was all William could do to hold the men back and stop them rushing the screen to help this flawed man whom they instinctively felt to be their comrade. When the noble Aragorn smote his foul foe, the redcoats all leaped to their feet, roaring their approval and embracing each other, and punched the air with their fists. 'Huzzah!' they cried in voices hoarse with emotion. 'Huzzah!' And then, as Boromir died and Aragorn spoke words of comfort to him and told him that he had not failed in his quest, the surge of emotion that the men experienced in this dark, cocooned room in the middle of New York almost overwhelmed them. They gave in to heart-rending sobs. Two teenage boys, seeing the film for perhaps the thirtieth time, looked around in wonder at these burly grown men who clearly felt the same way about this story as they did. They would not have to explain to these guys why they were driven to keep coming back for more and why real life mostly did not match up . . .

William, more restrained, dabbed at his eyes with a handkerchief, all passion utterly spent. He had seen many wonders since arriving in the future, but no invention had impressed him like that of moving pictures. Indeed, he had often felt homesick since Lord Luxon had taken a fancy to New York but how, he wondered, would he accustom himself once more to a life without the thrill of the big screen when, as surely would happen one day, his master would finally return home?

At the same moment as Sergeant Thomas and his lads were resuming their watch on each level of the zigzag of metal stairs in Prince Street, their heads filled with stirring images and music, dreaming of glory whilst spitting at the Orcs below, Lord Luxon was stepping out of an elegant building on the corner of Broad and Pearl. His visit to the Fraunces Tavern Museum, with its many exhibits dating from the American Revolution, had moved the English aristocrat in ways which would have disturbed the museum's curators. As he strode past portraits of America's famous sons, Lord Luxon was put in mind of the portraits of his father and uncles at Tempest House. These proud military men had never hidden their poor opinion of him, yet all their achievements put together would appear insignificant compared to the audacious plan *he* envisaged.

The sun beat down onto his blond head and he squinted in the strong light. He was accompanied by two carefully acquired Manhattan acquaintances, the raven-haired Mrs Stacey, immaculate in scarlet linen and pearls, and, more importantly, Alice, her niece, a research student in the History Department at Princeton. Alice was an elfin-faced young woman in her mid-twenties, with a shining bob of chestnut hair. She was dressed for the heat, her black, tailored shorts revealing the legs of a runner. His guide for the afternoon had surpassed all expectations. Alice's commentary had been as insightful as it was compelling. He had chosen well, Lord Luxon reflected. She had an elegant mind – which was more than he could say, at least from his eighteenth-century perspective, of her outfit. The notion that it was acceptable for a lady to wear shorts still struck him as *surprising*.

'Surely you cannot mean, madam, that this is one of the *oldest* buildings in New York?' asked Lord Luxon with a sardonic smile.

'Now, now, behave yourself, Lord Luxon,' laughed Mrs Stacey. She turned to her niece. 'Alice, I can see it's going to be difficult to impress someone who owns a thirteenth-century castle in Scotland . . .'

Alice's pale green eyes widened. 'A castle?'

'Oh, I rarely stay there. I can assure you, madam, that most caves are more comfortably appointed . . . I am mostly to be found on my estate in Surrey or at my town house in Bird Cage Walk.'

Alice pushed back her hair behind her ears. 'Bird Cage Walk?'

'Yes. The house has a fair prospect over St James's Park.'

'A fair prospect . . .' repeated Alice, taken by the turn of phrase. 'I studied in London for a while. I had a bedsit in GreenPark – I must have walked past your home many times. Bird Cage Walk – what a great address! And I love it that Charles II's habit of displaying his menagerie lives on in the street name.'

'I wish I had as good a head for facts as you, Alice,' said Mrs Stacey. 'I have difficulty recollecting who won the last Superbowl.'

'Sorry, Aunt Laura, I'm being a bore. I'll take my historian's hat off now—'

'Pray do nothing of the kind!' exclaimed Lord Luxon. 'Your reputation precedes you. It is on account of your learning that I have been anticipating this rendezvous with such pleasure – and I assure you that I have not been disappointed. Upon my honour, I count on becoming *frighteningly* well informed in your company.'

Lord Luxon gave a respectful bow in Alice's direction.

'Ah, *such* a gentleman!' exclaimed Mrs Stacey, touching her heart. 'You are a rare breed, Lord Luxon. I hope you don't turn out to be a wolf in a sheep's clothing!'

Lord Luxon let out a resounding howl, startling several passers-by. The two women laughed. This handsome milord was proving good company, even if he did insist on speaking like someone out of a costume drama. Mrs Stacey had already offered Lord Luxon the use of her summer house in the Hamptons whenever he cared to use it. Lord Luxon, however, seemed less impressed by Mrs Stacey's stellar social connections than by Alice's knowledge of American history. Intrigued though she was by Lord Luxon, Alice did not quite *get* him. He had listened, in rapt attention, to everything that she had said about the museum exhibits; his manners were old-fashioned to the point of eccentricity – doubtless an affectation which he cultivated – but she sensed something else going on underneath that cool, Anglo-Saxon exterior. Something she could not quite put her finger on. But, hey, Alice told herself, at least he's not *boring* . . .

'Ha!' said Mrs Stacey, tapping the museum catalogue. '*This* is what I was trying to find. Washington's farewell speech to his men before he left for Mount Vernon and the quiet life.'

'Washington? The name escapes me . . .'

Alice grinned. This guy enjoyed playing games. 'General

George Washington – you know, first President of America? *Big* in the Revolutionary War . . .'

Lord Luxon flashed Alice a smile in return. 'Is that so? Upon my word. Fascinating . . .'

Alice returned his look. '*Upon my word . . .*' she repeated softly.

'And to think,' continued Mrs Stacey, 'that Washington said goodbye to his men in this very building. After such a *resounding* victory against the British . . .'

Alice burst out laughing. 'Now don't you go sparing the feelings of our English visitor, Aunt Laura!'

Lord Luxon admired the flashing of blood-red nail varnish as, with a sweep of her manicured hand, like a gash in the air, Mrs Stacey waved aside the remark.

'Listen: *With a heart full of love and gratitude I now take leave of you. I most devoutly wish that your latter days may be as prosperous and happy as your former ones have been glorious and honourable . . .* Isn't that moving?'

Lord Luxon ostentatiously stifled a yawn and Mrs Stacey tapped him on the back of the hand as if he were a naughty child.

'It *is* moving,' said Alice. 'There can't have been a dry eye in the house after everything they'd been through together.'

'You'll have to forgive me if I do not share your patriotic fervour,' said Lord Luxon.

'Didn't I tell you he's a terrible tease? Take no notice of him, Alice,' said Mrs Stacey. 'A lot of water has gone under the bridge since Britain lost America. But we're all friends again now, aren't we, Lord Luxon?'

Lord Luxon took hold of Mrs Stacey's hand and stooped to kiss it. He glanced up at her and his ice-blue eyes met her warm brown ones.

'Indeed we are, madam, and why ever should you doubt it?

Though would an America still under *British* rule be so undesirable?'

Alice started to laugh while Mrs Stacey wagged her finger at him in mock disapproval.

'Why, Lord Luxon! I am shocked to the core! Here you are, a guest in the Land of the Free – you should feel ashamed of yourself . . .'

'Ashamed, madam? Alas, I gave up *that* emotion long ago. Besides, as my friend De Courcy is fond of saying, shame is so terribly bad for one's posture . . .'

'But *would* you change history if you could?' Alice persisted. 'It's an interesting question – would you have had Britain quash the American Revolution?'

'I am an Englishman, and loyal to King and country. Surely you would not have me harbour treasonable sympathies? Certainly I would. *Indeed* I would!' Lord Luxon's smile suddenly vanished. 'I should have had our redcoats trample your sainted General Washington into the dirt . . .'

Mrs Stacey's intake of breath was audible. There was a prolonged and uncomfortable pause, during which time the sun beat down on the three figures' heads, and Lord Luxon's words hung heavily in the air. Alice tried to make some sense of his outburst. Was this Lord Luxon's idea of a joke? Did he enjoy being provocative? But he calmly returned the women's searching stares without a hint of apology. Then Mrs Stacey's face suddenly cracked into a broad smile, as did Lord Luxon's, and soon both of them were laughing.

Alice studied the Englishman's fine-featured face and smiled. 'I don't know if you play poker, Lord Luxon, but if you don't you should!' said Alice. She wanted to ask him why he had said loyal to *King* rather than *Queen* and country but something made her hold

25

back. For an instant, she realised, he had actually made her believe that, if he could have done, he would have won back America for King George III. It wasn't often that anyone managed to catch her out. Alice's eyes sparkled.

'Daring to say such a thing about George Washington in front of two good American citizens!' said her aunt. 'I am beginning to find you out, Lord Luxon! You are a tease, a *terrible* tease!'

Lord Luxon inclined his head in a slight bow but he was already starting to laugh again, which set off Mrs Stacey and Alice. Lord Luxon pulled out a handkerchief and dabbed at his eyes. 'A tease? On the contrary, good ladies,' he said, barely able to get the words out. 'I assure you I meant every word . . .'

When, last night, after supper, I told Peter that I had a mind to set down on paper the momentous events we had lately witnessed, he became suddenly animated. To my astonishment, he told me that his grown-up self had already given a copy of The Life and Times of Gideon Seymour, Cutpurse and Gentleman, 1792 to his father, a book that I would not complete until after I had seen my fiftieth year! My young friend plainly did not grasp the turmoil that erupted in my heart at this, for he asked me, a most cheerful smile playing on his lips, if I believed that with each second that we lived and breathed we were erasing our previous histories!

Shaking my head, for I knew not what to say, I took my leave of him in order to reflect awhile in the cool of the night. Perhaps it is due to Peter's tender age that he appears so little dismayed at the notion of an existence wiped clean away. Whereas I, more encumbered with the baggage of a life already lived, walked around and around Lincoln's Inn Fields, pursued by a flock of questions that hovered over my head and would not fly away.

The notion that there is somewhere another Gideon Seymour, with the same flesh and hair and appetites, whose heart beats to the same rhythm, who has, perhaps, the same dreams and longings, distresses me more than I can say. Yet what disturbs me more is the notion that this other Gideon Seymour's life could be overwritten by my own in which I become a kind of cuckoo in my own nest.

Yesterday I awoke not doubting the truth of who I am, a truth so evident you could rap your knuckles on it and feel the pain. But today a great crack has appeared in Life's certainties, for is it not in our nature to wish to be on the one hand the same as our fellows, and on the other to be different? For if I am not unique in all the universe, am I not, in consequence, a lesser man?

Gideon Seymour
Lincoln's Inn Fields, 1763

CHAPTER FOUR

St Bartholomew's Fair

In which Gideon is horrified to learn of Lord Luxon's deception and the party pays a visit to St Bartholomew's Fair

The party waited on the steps while the footman and the driver finished making ready Sir Richard's coach and six. The horses were skittish and unsettled and they snorted and pawed the ground. Kate held on to Peter's arm. A procession of billowing clouds, streaked with an ominous red, raced across the pale evening sky, buffeted by a strong south-westerly wind that blew Sir Richard's tricorn hat clean from his head and sent it scuttling over the pavement. Peter broke away to run after it. Kate flinched and stretched out her hand after him as he darted off. She noticed the Parson observing her and let her arm drop slowly to her side.

'The weather has turned,' declared Parson Ledbury, turning to Sir Richard. 'That is the last of the summer, you mark my words.'

Kate was gripping Peter's arm as he walked back to the steps to return the tricorn hat back to its owner. She saw the Parson, a frown on his face, looking first at her and then back towards the empty space next to Hannah where he was sure she had been

29

standing but a moment ago. He looked at Kate again. She knew precisely what he was thinking. How had she passed in front of him without him noticing? The Parson shook his head in puzzlement. Kate stared fixedly in the opposite direction.

Bats flitted about in the twilight above their heads and, far away, a mournful church bell tolled. They all squeezed inside the carriage and breathed in its now accustomed odour of leather and horseflesh. Kate sat between Hannah and Peter, whose hand she held tight in hers. Opposite the children sat Parson Ledbury, Sir Richard and Gideon. Peter reflected that not so very long ago there would have been no way that he would have let a girl hold on to him like this, no matter how upset she was. But he did not pull away and even gave Kate's hand a reassuring squeeze. She looked up at him and smiled.

'Everything will be all right,' he said.

'I know . . .'

Sir Richard's coach and six rumbled out of Lincoln's Inn Fields. The streets seemed curiously empty. Amazingly, theirs was the only carriage in High Holborn and not a single street hawker was to be seen. Hannah said that it must be on account of the great fair in Smithfield. Half of London would be in attendance. The sound of oversized shop signs swaying and creaking in the wind and horseshoes striking granite setts echoed through the streets. Kate watched a pug dog, on the corner of High Holborn and Gray's Inn Lane, mesmerised by some dry leaves whipped into a dancing whirlpool by a gust of wind. The dog backed away, growling. Then it charged helter-skelter up the street, barking a warning to anyone who would listen.

'Silly old thing . . .' Kate laughed, then thought of her own dog. 'I wonder what Molly's doing right now. I hope she's okay. I hope she's not pining.'

Peter stopped himself saying that 'right now' did not actually make sense and gave her hand another squeeze instead. Then he leaned over towards her and whispered into her ear: 'I've been thinking . . . Ought we to tell Gideon about the Tar Man, now there's a possibility they might actually meet each other again?'

'Do we have to?' whispered Kate back to him. 'I mean, it can't be true, can it?'

'But we *should* tell him even if it's not true. Don't you think?'

'He's not going to like it.'

'You think I don't know that! Shall I tell him or will you?'

'You! *Definitely* you.'

Peter took in a deep breath and blew it out again noisily. 'Okay . . .'

'What are you two rascals plotting?' demanded Parson Ledbury.

When Peter looked up, all three men opposite were watching them expectantly.

'Gideon?' asked Peter hesitantly.

'Yes, Master Peter?' asked Gideon with a half-smile on his face. 'You have the air of someone with a guilty admission to make. What have you done, my young friend?'

'No, it's nothing like that.'

'Then what is it that troubles you so?'

Peter paused and then plunged straight in. There was no easy way to say it. 'When the anti-gravity machine brought me and Kate back again to 1763, just before Lord Luxon made off with it and we ended up at Hawthorn Cottage, we heard the Tar Man and Lord Luxon talking.'

'Yes?' Gideon smiled at him encouragingly.

'And obviously we don't know if it's actually *true* or not and you know how Lord Luxon will say anything to get what he wants . . .'

'What did he say?'

'Well—'

'Spit it out, boy, how bad can it be?' exclaimed the Parson.

Peter looked at Kate who nodded her head vigorously. 'Go on, Peter. Tell him.'

'Well, he . . . he . . .' Peter raced to the end of the sentence. 'He said that you and the Tar Man are brothers and that he'd known it from the start.'

Hannah gasped and put her hand to her mouth and then for a long moment the only sound was the creaking of the axles and the *clip-clop* of the horses' hooves. Sir Richard and the Parson exchanged alarmed glances. No one knew what to say. Then Gideon started to laugh.

'What fantasy is this? Lord Luxon lies – although for what purpose I cannot tell. All my brothers are dead – save for my half-brother, Joshua. He knows this. As I have told you, Lord Luxon forever craves diversion – he will have said it to cause mischief.'

Peter nodded. 'I'm sure you're right – I mean, how could *you* and the Tar Man possibly be related?'

'Upon my word,' said Parson Ledbury, 'what a shocking notion! Why, to contemplate the mere possibility that you and that monster might come from the same brood chills my marrow!' The Parson rubbed the white bristles on his chin and continued: 'And yet, in truth, stranger things have happened . . . Nor can it be denied that the Tar Man's motive for coming to your aid in so timely a fashion at Tyburn has long been a puzzle. If he had discovered that the same blood ran in your veins, why, that would be reason enough, would it not? Perhaps we should credit him with some human decency: perhaps his actions demonstrated a desire to save his younger brother—'

'We do not share the same blood!' cried Gideon. 'As I have told you, Parson,' he continued through gritted teeth, '*I have no older brother!*'

The Parson opened his mouth to speak but Sir Richard put his hand on his arm and Gideon stared fixedly out of the window.

'I'm sorry, Gideon,' said Peter. 'I had to tell you.'

Gideon nodded but would not turn around to look at him. The two children exchanged guilty glances.

Darkness had now fallen and the sooty glass globes filled with whale oil that served as street lamps on this main highway were few and far between. Inside the carriage the passengers could not see their hands in front of their faces. Soon, however, an orange glow illuminated the street and they saw a family huddled around a roaring fire stoked up with what appeared to be rafters. The giant bonfire crackled and hissed and great showers of sparks shot up into the night. Behind the fire the party could see that a building had collapsed, leaving a gaping black hole in the row of houses like a smile with a missing tooth. A pungent smell of mould and lime and ashes met their nostrils as their carriage rumbled past. Too slow to catch up with them, a woman clutching a shawl ran after them, her arms extended in supplication. She shouted something at them but her words were carried away in the wind. Sir Richard reached into his pocket, drew out some coins and threw them, rolling, at her feet. Peter leaned out of the window and saw the whole family jump up and start scrabbling around like chickens pecking in the dirt.

'What would make a house fall like a pack of cards?' exclaimed Hannah. 'I have never seen such a thing!'

'Alas, Hannah, it is a common occurrence of late. It is the second house I have seen collapse in less than a month,' commented Sir Richard. 'These dwellings are not well built, and the hot summer has shrunk and cracked the earth in which they sit.'

'Then I pity those poor souls with all my heart,' said Hannah, 'and I am glad that I live in Derbyshire in a house made of stone.'

Kate shivered all of a sudden and loosened her grip on Peter's hand. Peter looked at her questioningly. Kate shrugged her shoulders.

'It's this funny wind. I keep thinking a storm is coming, don't you?'

Peter shook his head. 'No – how can you tell if a storm's coming? I can't.'

On Snow Hill the traffic grew suddenly dense and they found themselves surrounded by chaises, and carts, and wagons full of barrels of ale, all jostling for space on the thoroughfare. Everyone was headed in the same direction – Smithfield Market, the site of Bartholomew's Fair. They proceeded at a snail's pace while they watched the spectacle of two Irish sedan chair-men, so determined to get through the blockade of vehicles that they deliberately rammed a hackney coach, causing the skinny horses to rear up and whinny in terror.

Normally so calm in a crisis, Gideon was becoming increasingly agitated.

'Confound this traffic!' The words burst out of him. 'If the pleasures of Bartholomew's Fair do not hold him, Blueskin could be miles away by now!'

When they reached Cock Lane they decided to continue on foot. The driver was told to wait for them at the bottom of Snow Hill. There was such a multitude of folk, Sir Richard suggested it might be quicker to go a long way round through a maze of small streets which he knew. They could hire a link-boy to light their way through the dark alleys. The Parson was not in favour of such a plan, nor was Gideon.

'Trust me, Sir Richard,' he said, 'for I have cause to know, Bartholomew's Fair is a magnet for all the thieves in the city – Smithfield will be seething with villains lurking in the shadows.'

Suddenly Hannah let out a cry of fright. A man carrying a fiddle, with a pair of donkey's ears strapped to his head, was blocking her way. He pressed his face close up to hers, turned his head coquettishly to one side and crowed like a cockerel. Hannah screamed a second time when a monkey appeared between the donkey's ears on the man's head, reached out its delicate, leathery fingers and proceeded to grab hold of her nose – hard.

'Oh! Oh! Oh!' Hannah screamed, flapping her hands in front of her face as if trying to get rid of cobwebs. 'Get that devilish creature away from me!'

The fool laughed, satisfied with her reaction, and gambolled away. As he lurched drunkenly about amidst the mass of Londoners, he took out a fiddle and bow from the inside of his jacket and began to play a fast Irish jig. People immediately started to sing along and clap in time to the tune and the monkey danced on the fool's shoulders whilst staring up at the night sky with glittering, coal-black eyes.

'Are you all right, Hannah?' shouted Kate.

'Bless you, I am, Mistress Kate, thank you for asking. I never could abide Merry Andrews. Their purpose is to make folk laugh but the principal effect they have on me is to make my flesh crawl. And that monkey will haunt my dreams – why, a person could mistake it for a tiny, wizened old man!'

'Well, my dad told me that humans and apes share a common ancestor . . .'

Hannah looked at Kate, flummoxed, unsure whether she was supposed to laugh.

'Is that so, Mistress Kate?' she replied non-committally. '*My* ancestors came from Yorkshire.'

And so they pressed on, with Gideon and Sir Richard leading the way and pushing through the throng. Kate held tightly on to Peter's hand and both children stared around them, eyes wide with wonder and not a little fear. Soon the din of the crowd grew into a riotous, echoing roar and they all sensed that they were approaching the great open space of Smithfield Market. They heard the pulse of a drum and then the insistent, clanging bell of a street crier. 'Show! Show! Show!' he bellowed. The wind – already troublesome enough to make the men hold on to their hats or wigs and the ladies to their skirts – suddenly roared furiously up Cock Lane so that the party was blown rather than walked into Smithfield. All at once they passed from darkness into light, as countless lanterns and flares of pitch and tow illuminated the vast, heaving, monstrous, stupendous spectacle that stretched out before them: Bartholomew's Fair.

Released from the tight funnel of the street into Smithfield, the crowd was now able to disperse. The party stood motionless for a while, looking around them and getting their bearings, alert to the sounds which assailed them: canvas tents flapped and billowed in the wind, barrow boys rang their bells, hawkers cried themselves hoarse, revellers clapped and shouted and jeered, dogs barked and monkeys chattered, sudden waves of riotous laughter reached them from a nearby beer tent.

'My head is spinning already!' exclaimed Hannah.

Keeping together they started to walk further in. A double-jointed contortionist, skeletally thin and able to dislocate his bones at will, tied his body in knots, eliciting loud *ooh!*s and *aah!*s from an appreciative crowd; a juggler vied with a fire-eater for the attention of fashionable ladies and gentleman whose powdered faces, studded with black beauty spots, glowed a ghostly white in the flickering half-light. A flower girl picked up apple cores and scraps and threw them to a brown bear. The beast was shackled with heavy chains to a stake and sat motionless on his ragged haunches, the expression in his soulful eyes enough to make a heart of stone weep.

'Oh no!' cried Kate. 'How could they do such a thing?'

Gideon guided her gently away.

'Can you smell that awful smell?' Peter asked, wrinkling his nose. 'It's like a butcher's shop. Worse.'

''Tis hardly surprising,' said Gideon. 'Smithfield is a meat market and always has been to my knowledge. This place is steeped in the stink of slaughter.'

The children exchanged glances. A more savoury smell drifted towards them, however, and Parson Ledbury lifted his head and sniffed the air appreciatively. He was watching two bare-chested men, their pronounced muscles gleaming with sweat, slowly turn a giant spit on which two whole pigs were roasting. The fire hissed as drops of grease fell into the glowing embers.

'I begin to feel an appetite,' said the Parson. 'I hope we might make short shrift of running down Master Blueskin, for I declare I should make fine work of a rib or two of pork.'

'We have need of your bottom, not your stomach,' quipped Sir Richard. 'And your stout heart, too, no doubt before the night is out.'

'Upon my life, sir, not a morsel will pass my lips until we've cowed the scoundrel into submission and then, I promise you, I shall sate my appetite and not hold back!'

Gideon smiled. 'Do you see that Up and Down yonder?' he said, indicating a wheel-shaped structure rising up out of the centre of the fair. 'That shall be our meeting place.'

'When I rode on them as a child we always called them whirligigs,' commented Sir Richard. 'But then, I have twenty years on you, at least, Gideon.'

The children looked to where he was pointing.

'Can you believe it? It's a Ferris wheel, for goodness' sake!' exclaimed Peter to Kate.

Sir Richard turned to Gideon. 'Should we divide ourselves into two or three parties, would you say?'

'Three, sir, in my opinion. For surely we must cover as much ground as we can in all haste.'

'Very well. I suggest that Parson Ledbury accompany Hannah and that you, Mr Seymour, take Peter. And, if I might be permitted that honour, I shall chaperone Mistress Kate,' said Sir Richard, not noticing Kate's expression.

Kate tried to master her emotions but a feeling of desperate panic rose up inside her. How could she reject Sir Richard's kind offer? But she *had* to stay with Peter.

Peter felt Kate grip his hand even more tightly and he wondered if he should say something. But it was Parson Ledbury who came to her rescue.

'I believe that Mistress Kate would prefer to have the comfort of her friend at her side, my dear Sir Richard. And, as it is all the same to me whether I go accompanied or alone, I suggest that you escort Hannah.'

Sir Richard, however, would have none of it and ventured forth into the fair by himself, saying that he would search the north end of the square. He told the Parson and Hannah to take the west side while Gideon and the children should take the east.

'Let us agree to meet at the foot of the whirligig within the hour, whether we have caught sight of the Tar Man or no.'

'Stay close by me,' said Gideon to Peter and Kate.

He set off at a rapid pace and his young companions kept up as well as they could. Peter turned to Kate. 'It's not that I mind, Kate, but why is it that you have to hold my hand *all* the time? It's as if you're frightened that I'll go off if you don't. Listen, I *swear* I'm not going to leave you behind. Surely you must trust me by now!'

Kate blushed, which made Peter wish he had not said anything. 'I'm sorry,' she said. 'I know I'm being a pain.'

Kate was already panting with the effort of keeping up with Gideon. Peter glanced at her. She didn't look too good. Kate had not loosened her grip on his hand for an instant. He wondered if it had been such a great idea bringing her along. They passed wooden stalls piled high with gingerbread and puppet shows and games of dice. All the while the threesome scanned the sea of faces that surged around them for a glimpse of a livid white scar and a slim, athletic build and those fathomless dark eyes which all of them now had cause to fear.

'I forgot to say that the Tar Man has whiter teeth now,' said Kate breathlessly to Gideon. 'He's had them done. And I think he must have had treatment for his dodgy neck, too, because he doesn't hold his head to one side any more.'

'Upon my word,' replied Gideon. 'Do not tell me that the brute has turned handsome.'

'Actually,' said Kate, 'he looked pretty good when we last saw him . . .'

'Kate!' exclaimed Peter.

'Well, he did!'

'What miracles your century can work,' said Gideon. But he did not smile.

After perhaps a quarter of an hour of fruitless searching, Kate asked if they could stop for a moment for her to get her breath back. They found themselves outside a canvas tent, its entrance guarded by a burly figure in the costume of a Turk. The man stood erect and motionless, his arms folded across his impressive chest, although when a woman from an adjoining stall brought him a tankard of ale, it was with a Cockney accent that he replied.

'Bless me,' he said in a nasal voice. 'I am heartily glad to see you. I did not imagine that standing still would bring on such a thirst.'

At that moment the door of the tent flapped open. A black-haired woman in an exotic silk dress and with something of the gypsy about her escorted a doe-eyed girl from the tent. The girl turned around and Kate saw her swelling belly.

'Bless me, madam, if I didn't forget to ask you how many children I shall bear!'

'To foretell the future, sweet child, is a terrible burden and costs me dear each time I step into that mysterious realm. But cross my palm with silver and I shall tell you anything your tender young heart desires.'

The girl pulled open her purse and peered inside.

'Perhaps it is best not to know . . . Upon my life, it wouldn't do to go frightening my husband! Fare thee well, madam, and thank you.'

The fortune-teller shrugged her shoulders and bade the girl farewell.

'What am I paying you for?' she snapped at the keeper of the door, nodding at his tankard. 'Three customers a night won't pay for that beer!'

Peter and Gideon continued to scrutinise every face in the crowds that filed past them but Kate's gaze happened to fall on the fortune-teller. The woman, who had been on the verge of re-entering the tent, suddenly stood stock-still and stared directly at Kate without blinking. Then, after a moment she took an uncertain step backwards, putting her hand to her mouth. The colour had drained from her face. It was fear that Kate read in those dark eyes. She pointed a scrawny finger at Kate and then backed slowly into the tent, tugging violently at the canvas door flap to close it. No one else witnessed the woman's reaction. Kate's heart thumped in her chest. The only thought that came into her head was *she knows.*

'Ouch!' cried Peter. 'There's no need to dig your nails in!'

'Oh, I'm sorry,' Kate replied. 'I didn't realise I was.'

Gideon turned to her. 'Do you feel recovered enough to continue awhile, Mistress Kate?'

Kate nodded and Gideon strode on ahead. He stopped again, however, after only a few paces when a booming voice called out to him.

'Mr Seymour!'

Gideon turned to look at a man of majestic proportions advancing towards him with a broad smile on his face. Gideon walked over to greet him.

'Mr Featherstone! It is good to see you! Though I am astonished to find you here! Who attends to your customers at the Rose?'

'The Rose is three-quarters empty on account of the fair, Mr Seymour. So I said to myself, why the devil *shouldn't* old Featherstone seek out a little diversion? Come, will you drink a glass with me?'

'On another occasion with a good will, Mr Featherstone, but you find me in search of a certain person and I must not tarry lest his trail cool.'

'A pity. I should have enjoyed your company. But who is it that you seek, if I might be so bold as to enquire?'

'Blueskin.'

Featherstone laughed out loud. 'In which case you shall be

happy indeed that Fortune caused our paths to cross. I exchanged a word or two with Blueskin not five minutes past!'

Gideon was a good head shorter than the porter of the Rose Tavern but he grabbed him by the elbows and half lifted him into the air.

'You have spoken to Blueskin! Where? Tell me, good Mr Featherstone!'

'Why, in Newgate Lane heading east.'

'Was he alone?'

'Joe Carrick walked with him, I believe, though I did not speak to him.'

Gideon bade farewell to Featherstone and rushed back to Peter and Kate to tell them the good news.

'The Tar Man is but five minutes hence with Joe Carrick. I must run if I am to stand a chance of catching him. Make your way to the meeting place and tell the others there has been a sighting of the Tar Man and that I have gone to Newgate Lane in search of him.'

'I'm coming with you!' cried Peter. 'I'm a fast runner! I've won prizes – well, one . . .'

'I do not have the time to argue, Master Peter,' said Gideon. 'Stay with Mistress Kate. I must fly!'

Peter turned abruptly to Kate. 'I *have* to go with Gideon. If the Carrick gang are with the Tar Man he's going to need help! I'd say that you could come, too, but . . . I just don't think you're fit enough to run a long way.'

Kate looked desperate. 'No! Please! Don't leave me alone!'

Peter turned on her angrily. 'Kate, don't give me a hard time about this! I've got to go. I won't be long. Go to the meeting place and tell the others what's happening.'

'*Peter! Please!* You said you wouldn't leave me . . .'

'And I meant it! I'm not *going* to leave you! Do you really think I wouldn't come back for you? Surely you don't need me to be with you every single second . . . Can't you see that the sooner we catch the Tar Man, the sooner we can get you home and make you better?'

Kate watched Peter's back receding into the distance. Gideon's blond head had already disappeared from view. How long before she fast-forwarded? The cold, creeping fear that was becoming her constant companion made Kate's shoulders slump and her head droop towards her chest. Groups of revellers sailed by: poor and rich, young and old, comely and plain – the whole world, it seemed, was in high spirits except for Kate.

A grimacing fool approached, beating a drum and capering and frolicking about, drawing attention to a mountebank who followed in his wake. The Merry Andrew suddenly threw himself to the ground, performed a perfect somersault and stood up so close to Kate that she could see lice crawling in his coarse hair. In a reflex action she pushed him violently away. The fool staggered back a step then used the momentum to turn a deft back-flip causing the tiny bells sewn to his costume to tinkle. There was laughter and a smattering of applause.

Kate felt someone brush past her skirts and she took a step forward to give the person behind room to pass. But the person did not pass and she felt the warmth of a physical presence at her back. The next moment she felt a hand on her shoulder. She started in surprise. Then a second hand took hold of her and strong fingers squeezed her flesh until she was held in a vice-like grip. Kate gasped with the shock of it and felt her palms grow cold and clammy and the hairs rise at the back of her neck. A sixth sense told her who it was before she even turned around to look. She peered upwards over her shoulder.

'You!'

'Greetings, Mistress Dyer,' replied the Tar Man.

'I don't understand, Gideon—'

'Contrary to what Mr Seymour might believe, he would not be here had *I* not summoned *him*.'

Kate's mind raced. Gideon and Peter would be far away by now. The others were at the other side of this huge fair . . . Should she scream? Run? Shout for help? After a moment's hesitation she craned her neck to one side, sank her teeth into the Tar Man's hand and ground them into his flesh, clamping her jaws together with every last ounce of her strength.

CHAPTER FIVE

High Treason

In which Lord Luxon gets an answer to his question and Alice encounters a dog with bottom

No sooner had Lord Luxon commented that he had taken a fancy to observing the New York skyline from the sea, than Mrs Stacey remembered a pressing, prior engagement and volunteered Alice to accompany him on a boat tour. Alice opened her mouth to object but Lord Luxon seemed so genuinely pleased that she relented and closed it again.

Mrs Stacey flagged down a cab and as she got in she whispered into her niece's ear. 'How many men have you met who can boast a castle in Scotland?'

'Oh, hundreds,' whispered Alice back. 'Enjoy your afternoon, Aunt Laura.'

Mrs Stacey got into the cab and called through the open window, 'I look forward to hearing *all* about it . . .'

'Thank you *very much*, Aunt Laura,' said Alice pointedly.

Mrs Stacey smiled sweetly at Lord Luxon. Accustomed as Luxon was to half the matrons in London throwing their daughters at him, his face betrayed nothing and he merely expressed regret that he was to be deprived of Mrs Stacey's company that afternoon.

Half an hour later Lord Luxon and Alice were seated on slatted wooden benches at the prow of an embarking cruise boat at the South Street Seaport. The rusting vessel chugged into the murky brown waves of New York harbour and, after the stifling heat of the city, a welcome sea breeze wafted their faces. Alice tipped back her tanned face towards the sun and smelled the tang of salt water. She filled her lungs with deep breaths of air and put on a large pair of sunglasses.

'That feels good,' she said. 'I was slowly melting back there in the museum.' She turned to face her companion, still perfectly attired in his ivory suit. 'If you don't mind me asking, how hot does it have to get before you take your jacket off?'

Lord Luxon did not reply straight away and the corners of his mouth turned up in a sardonic smile.

'I should wear a coat in weather hotter than this if the occasion demanded it, madam. It is true to say, I believe, that our attitudes to fashion are . . . *dissimilar*.'

'By which you mean,' said Alice, looking down at her shorts and T-shirt, 'that you don't understand people who think that holidays are too short to spend more than half a minute a day deciding what to wear?'

Lord Luxon was tempted to say: *As much as that?* but thought the better of it.

'No, no, I assure you, I am all admiration,' he said. 'Such a conspicuous lack of vanity can only be judged as . . . *commendable*.'

Alice raised her eyebrows. She resisted the temptation to say that the line between looking fashionable and looking ridiculous was a fine one.

Lord Luxon, meanwhile, tried to imagine Alice in full court dress with a tightly laced corset and petticoats and acres of heavy silk draped over a wide hoop and a high, elaborate wig to complete the picture. His face started to crease into a broad smile at the thought of it. He shifted his position and tactfully pretended to turn his attention to the Statue of Liberty whose colossal form was now looming towards them. If Alice were transported back to his century, he reflected, and dressed in the fashions of the day, she would, he had no doubt of it, swoon within moments. Nor, he suspected, would she possess the self-discipline required to permanently maintain that elegant posture expected of a lady under *all* circumstances. He was acquainted with many women whose years of attendance at court meant that they could stand to attention for longer than any soldier on parade. They could do so for hours at a stretch, even when heavy with child, or grieving for a dead husband or half crazed with the fever . . .

'Actually,' said Alice, 'I'm rather fond of this T-shirt.'

Lord Luxon scrutinised her black T-shirt covered with large red letters in an italic font. He tipped his head to one side and read from it, pronouncing each word with great care: '*Plus je connais les hommes, plus j'aime mon chien.*'

'The more I know about men, the better I like my dog,' Alice translated.

'That being the case, I long to make the acquaintance of your dog.'

'I don't have a dog.'

'Then, upon my word, Madam, your choice of garment is perplexing . . .'

Alice burst out laughing. 'This is all a big act, isn't it? All these *madam!*s and *upon my word!*s. Is it because you know I'm an historian?'

Lord Luxon raised his eyebrows in surprise. 'I cannot understand you, madam!'

This only made Alice laugh the more. 'Whereas I, on the other hand, am beginning to understand *you* perfectly!' she said. 'You're having a little fun at my expense, aren't you? Which is okay . . . I was raised with three brothers – I'm used to being tormented.'

Lord Luxon looked at her quizzically.

'But tell me,' Alice continued. 'Just how old *are* you exactly? You sure *sound* like you're a hundred and three but I'm guessing you're not a whole lot older than me . . . Twenty-six? Twenty-eight? Am I close?'

Lord Luxon stared fixedly at a seagull gliding overhead, its feathers a dazzling white against a deep azure sky.

'Madam, I refuse to admit to being more than two hundred and seventy years old.'

'In which case, *sir*, you look darned good for your age.'

'You are kindness itself, madam.'

'Do you think we might move on to first name terms?' asked Alice. 'All this formality is making me uncomfortable.'

'If you wish, you may call me Edward.'

'Edward . . . Lord Edward Luxon. That's a good name . . .'

'I am gratified that it pleases you. I was named after my father.'

'*I* was named after *Alice in Wonderland*. Though I'm still waiting to fall down that rabbit hole!'

Lord Luxon's expression revealed his confusion.

'You know – *Alice in Wonderland*, the children's novel by Lewis Carroll . . . The white rabbit, the mad hatter . . .?'

Lord Luxon shook his head.

'But you must know – you're English!'

Loudspeakers suddenly burst into life and the tour guide's commentary echoed over the decks of the boat. The guide narrated the story of the Statue of Liberty and Lord Luxon seemed transfixed.

'She's a wonderful sight, isn't she?' Alice commented.

'The dimensions of the statue are so astounding as to defy belief. Although, in truth, I find Liberty rather . . . *ridiculous*.'

'You can't call the Statue of Liberty ridiculous!' exclaimed Alice. 'You'll have us thrown off the boat!'

'On the other hand, this prospect,' he said, indicating the New York skyline with a sweep of his pale hand, 'is *sublime*. I could look at it for ever and never grow tired.'

'Then it's my turn to be gratified that it pleases *you*.'

The boat curved back towards the city in a gentle arc. New York rose up out of the sea like a miracle.

'Who owns Manhattan?' asked Lord Luxon suddenly.

Alice laughed. 'What a question! Everyone and no one. Or are you talking real estate? Could you tell me who owns London?'

'As it happens, there is a gentleman of my acquaintance who owns a great deal of it. He once bet half a street of houses that one raindrop would reach the bottom of a window before another.'

'That's sick!' said Alice but then after a pause asked: 'Did he win?'

'Yes. He has the luck of the devil. But then so, they say, do I . . .'

The tour guide's commentary droned on and for a while it seemed to Lord Luxon that it was not the boat that was moving but New York itself that was gliding by. The cityscape was one of vast blue distances and giant, striving proportions. How he had laughed when Mrs Stacey had called it the Big Apple. He had not seen the sense of it, and yet, looking at the city now, he would have bitten greedily into its flesh, and felt the juice trickle down his chin . . .

The afternoon sunshine sparkled on the choppy water, dazzling Lord Luxon who, in the absence of a three-cornered hat to shade his eyes, put his hand to his brow. Alice rummaged in her large bag and offered him a pair of sunglasses.

'Here – I always carry a spare pair.'

Uncertain at first, Lord Luxon thanked her and placed the sunglasses gingerly on the bridge of his nose. He looked out across the harbour through oval, metal-rimmed lenses.

'They suit you,' she said. 'They make you look Swedish.'

'Upon my word,' Lord Luxon exclaimed, taking them on and off to compare the difference in what he could see. Then he got up and leaned over the handrail excitedly to stare into the greenish-brown water. 'I see shoals of fish!'

'*Upon my word!*' said Alice with a smile. 'Haven't you worn polarised sunglasses before? They're great if you want to see through the surface glare. Keep them if you like them!'

'I could not accept so valuable a gift . . .'

'I got them from K-Mart. Trust me, they're *not* valuable.'

'Thank you . . . Alice.'

It seemed to Alice that it was the first time all afternoon that Lord Luxon had sounded genuine. Her expression softened and Lord Luxon noticed. He quickly returned to his seat. It was the moment, he decided, to risk posing the question that had caused him to seek out Alice in the first place. He began to marshal his thoughts but, as it happened, it was Alice who broached the subject before he did.

'Were you serious when we were in the Fraunces Tavern Museum – about being fascinated by that episode of American history? Is it a genuine interest or were you . . . were you being polite?'

Lord Luxon turned to face her and sensed a sudden unease in his companion. The corner of her mouth twitched.

Faith, could it possibly be, thought Lord Luxon, that this over-educated American was warming to him? He detected the tiniest flutter of an emotion in his breast but was careful to conceal it. Perhaps this would make her freer with her information . . .

'No, I assure you, I have developed a passion for that precise period of history. Although I am sadly ignorant of the detail of it . . .'

'The Revolutionary War?'

'Indeed. And is it not true that you have made a particular study of Britain's errors, military and diplomatic, that led to America gaining her independence?'

'How did you know that?' Alice exclaimed. 'It's the subject of my doctoral thesis. I'm halfway through a book on it. *Please* tell me Aunt Laura hasn't been singing my praises to you!'

'No. She did not need to. But will you permit me to ask you a question, Alice? I doubt that there are a handful of people alive better equipped to answer it.'

'Curiouser and curiouser!' said Alice. 'Sure – what is it?'

Lord Luxon adjusted his posture and stared out over the harbour, dotted with vessels making tracks across the expanse of water. Alice found herself admiring his fine profile and, despite herself, the cut of his jacket.

'If you could go back in time and sabotage the Revolutionary War – so that Britain emerged victorious and America never won her independence – how would you contrive to do it?'

Alice's expression changed from curious to surprised to amused within the space of a few seconds.

'I *like* your question! I'm due to teach my first class at Princeton this fall and that would be such a cool assignment to give to my students! It would be a great test of their understanding of the conflict and the progress of the war . . .'

'The opinion of your students holds no interest for me, unlike your own. How should *you* answer the question, Alice? With the benefit of hindsight and the clear eye of an historian, which American weaknesses might you exploit? Which were the men that fate destined to be the heroes of the hour? What could the British forces do to secure a glorious victory?'

Alice's face lit up. 'You really *are* an enthusiast, aren't you? Though I warn you, I could go on at some length. You might end up sorry you asked!'

'Quite the contrary, I assure you,' said Lord Luxon, taking out a small leather notebook and a gold pen.

Alice looked at him askance. 'But *why* are you so interested?'

'Does not the possibility of an alternative history excite you?'

'History contains enough of its own puzzles without getting sidetracked with counterfactual stuff, too!'

Lord Luxon pointed at the city shimmering in the heat haze. 'Look what America has become. What might it have been if it were still a part of the British Empire? Does it not fan the flames of your historian's curiosity – even a little?'

Alice laughed. 'I guess. More than a little. Though I'm not sure I want to tell an Englishman how he could return America to the yoke of colonial rule!'

'It is but a fantasy, a conceit!'

'True, but I should still be guilty of acting as your accomplice in your treasonable fantasy.'

'Pish pash, it is an intriguing fantasy, is it not? Will you not indulge me?'

'*Pish pash!* Where *do* these quaint expressions come from?'

Alice sat back, closed her eyes and sighed deeply. Lord Luxon waited expectantly, sincerely hoping that she was not about to fall asleep. It seemed to him that several minutes had passed and he was becoming agitated for the young historian had neither moved nor spoken. Abruptly Alice sat up.

'Realistically,' she said, 'I think Britain has only two chances to win a decisive victory. The first being during the harsh winter of the 1776-77 campaign when Washington manages to frustrate the British on two noteworthy occasions. A second opportunity will arise later, I think, during the 1780 campaign. Although I definitely need to think about this some more . . .'

Lord Luxon observed her animated face and smiled. He started to write. He had to write quickly, his pen scratching at the thick paper, for once Alice had started she could not stop. The story of a bitter war poured out of her and he found himself forming unfamiliar words with his fine gold nib: the names of battles and soldiers and politicians. All these names with which he would soon become so intimately acquainted: Washington and Thomas Paine; Clinton and Benedict Arnold; Trenton and Princeton and Valley Forge . . . By the time the boat had docked and the passengers were ready to disembark, Alice's voice had grown hoarse and Lord Luxon's hand ached. Alice had conjured up such a convincing picture that Lord Luxon half-expected to see icebergs floating down the Hudson River and long lines of redcoats and mercenaries carrying rifles and singing as they marched. It was almost a surprise to step back into a New York moist with August heat and thronged with American citizens going about their business in total liberty.

The two figures parted company then, for Lord Luxon declared it his intention to walk back to his hotel, while Alice decided to catch a cab back to her aunt's apartment overlooking Central Park. Both felt suddenly drained and exhausted, as if something mysterious and momentous had occurred.

'I am in your debt, Alice,' said Lord Luxon, kissing her hand as she got into her cab. 'I hope that I might have the pleasure of your company again very soon. And I have so many more questions . . .'

'Sure,' said Alice. 'I'd like that.'

He watched the cab drive away and then, to his fury, he discovered that his pen had leaked and a great black ink stain was slowly seeping through the breast pocket of his ivory linen jacket.

As if some sixth sense communicated her niece's unsettled frame of mind, Mrs Stacey called Alice to ask her how the afternoon had gone. The ringtone of Alice's mobile, the 'Hallelujah Chorus', was so loud it made the cab driver brake. He glared at her in the rear-view mirror and she gave him an apologetic smile.

'Where did you meet Lord Luxon, Aunt Laura?'

'In Bemelmans Bar . . . Why?'

'So Lord Luxon introduced himself to you?'

'No, it was your old history professor – the one who was at Princeton but now teaches at Columbia. What's his name? Steve something . . .'

'Steve Elliot?'

'Yes! Well it was *him* who introduced Lord Luxon to me. And he introduced *me* as the aunt of one of his old students who – with Lord Luxon's particular interests – he really ought to get to know.'

'So he used *you* to meet *me*! Why didn't you tell me?'

'I did! I told you he wanted someone to show him round the Fraunces Tavern Museum.'

'I just thought he was a friend of yours here on holiday . . .'

'Alice! Why all these questions?' Her aunt started to sound alarmed. 'What's happened? Are you all right? What has he done?'

'No, no, I'm fine, Aunt Laura. And actually I like him better than I thought I would. It's just that—'

'It's just that *what*?'

'It's just that I told him how to sabotage the Revolutionary War.'

There was a moment's silence.

'How very unpatriotic of you, darling!' Alice could hear the laughter in her aunt's voice. 'And is *that* what is upsetting you?'

'As it happens, yes . . .'

'Oh, Alice! I think you've spent too long in the sun . . .'

'All right, Aunt Laura, point taken.' Alice felt suddenly ridiculous and ended the call. 'Gotta go . . .'

Irritated with herself as much as her aunt, Alice dropped the mobile into her capacious bag as if into deep water. This heat was horrible. Alice wiped her forehead with the back of her hand. Aunt Laura was right, though, *why* was she allowing herself to get so worked up?

When the cab turned into Sixth Avenue the traffic was at a standstill. It was too hot to be patient and car horns punctuated the street noise in random bursts. She stared absent-mindedly through the window at the streams of people descending into a subway like lemmings. It was then that she spotted Lord Luxon. He had taken off his jacket which he carried draped over one shoulder. He cut a striking figure as he strode through the crowds. The full sleeves of his snowy-white shirt billowed and his tightly fitted waistcoat accentuated his slim frame. Alice noticed how many heads turned to look at him. After a few moments she watched him stop in his tracks and look down. She saw his lips moving. Was he talking to a child? Or perhaps to a dog? Then, holding up his jacket between finger and thumb he suddenly dropped it . . . Alice's gaze followed him as he set off again up Sixth Avenue, his receding white form gradually disappearing into a floating mass of rainbow colours. Once the lines of cars started to move again, Alice opened her window and stared at the space on the sidewalk where Lord Luxon had stopped. A tramp with wild hair and skin the colour of tanned hide held the jacket to his face, stroking the cloth and pushing his fingers into the pockets.

People were swerving to avoid tripping over the old man's out-stretched legs.

Who'd have thought he had such a kind heart? said Alice to herself. Giving his beautiful jacket away like that! On impulse, she told the cab driver to stop, thrust a handful of dollar bills into his hand and started to push through the crowds, her eyes always on Lord Luxon's blond head, hurrying when she could, but mostly struggling to beat a path through the army of shoppers that advanced on her. When she spotted him crossing to the other side of Sixth Avenue, she hurried to do the same but the lights were against her. Alice had to wait, dancing on the spot until she could dash across the street. But by the time she had reached the other side Lord Luxon had disappeared into Prince Street. Alice followed and found herself breaking into a run, her white trainers beating a rhythm on the baking sidewalk. When she saw that Lord Luxon had stopped in front of a six-storey red-brick building, she came to a halt, suddenly feeling ridiculous. What am I *doing*? Alice asked herself. What precisely am I going to say to him if he spots me? Who needs Aunt Laura, I can manage to embarrass myself without any help at all!

She backed away from the street and stepped into a narrow, rubbish-strewn gap between two buildings. She leaned one shoulder against a blackened brick wall and wiped her moist face and neck as she tried to catch her breath. Unable to resist taking a peek at Lord Luxon, she peered out from behind her paper tissue and what she saw made her instantly forget her embarrassment and her yearning to be anywhere else so long as it was air-conditioned. Her jaw dropped. While Lord Luxon waited on the sidewalk below, above him, on every level of the fire escape, Alice saw a redcoat standing to attention. All at once it seemed to her that she was no longer looking at present-day SoHo, rather, she was seeing a

56

fortified castle, impregnable and mysterious. When one of the men let down a ladder for Lord Luxon, in her mind's eye she saw a drawbridge. Alice's spine tingled with the thrill of it. And even though she knew in her heart of hearts that these guys must be into historical re-enactments – mid-eighteenth-century by the look of the jackets – she was in no rush to explain away what she saw. How utterly intriguing!

Soon Lord Luxon had disappeared into the building and a moment later four out of the five redcoats did likewise. She stared up at the last remaining redcoat and suddenly he swung his gaze towards her. Alice immediately hid behind her tissue and dabbed her forehead. When she looked up again he had disappeared. The drawbridge to the castle, however, remained tantalisingly in place. Alice waited for a few minutes and, when no one reappeared, unable to control her curiosity, she darted out from her hiding place and crossed the road.

Lord Luxon climbed up the ladder two rungs at a time and, as he emerged through the trapdoor onto the first level of the emergency stairs, took hold of his valet's outstretched arm. The metal landing clanged as William hurried to hold open the heavy security door for Lord Luxon. Up above, Sergeant Thomas and his men gave a cursory salute, their faces almost as red as their jackets. William observed his master march over to a sink in the corner of the dark, cavernous room, tearing off his waistcoat and unbuttoning his shirt as he did so. William found it difficult to read Lord Luxon's mood. He did not detect any of his habitual languor. Was he excited about something or in a rage? Lord Luxon turned the tap full on, untied the ribbon of his ponytail and held his head under the gushing cold water for a long moment, turning it slowly from side to side. Then he stood up and shook his head like a wet dog and small rivulets of water ran down from his bare shoulders and splashed onto the dusty floor. William was relieved to see that Lord Luxon had a smile on his face. All the Venetian blinds were, as usual, firmly closed; nevertheless fine, gold stripes of daylight forced their way inside, illuminating a gorgeous jumble of artefacts. Choice pieces of satinwood furniture, some inlaid with mother-of-pearl or gold, gleamed in the half-light. Amongst them stood randomly placed statues and silver candelabras and stacks of lustrous blue and white porcelain from Delft. The marble head of a pope seemed to rebuke a troupe of dancing nymphs on a Grecian urn; an equestrian statue charged out from behind a long-case clock; whilst from their gilded frames, and scattered amongst panoramic views of Venice and London, half a dozen pairs of aristocratic eyes gazed out at every movement in Lord Luxon's treasure house. Next to the door, in pride of place, was a life-size oil painting, hung in a simple frame. In fact, it depicted the head gardener's son at Tempest House – except that he was dressed in clothes befitting a prince – and the limpid-eyed boy stood serenely under the broad canopy of a copper beech. A pair of butterflies hovered above his head while in the distance the rolling hills of Surrey receded into a misty blue-green horizon. Mr Gainsborough had added some whimsical touches to hint at the identity of his sitter. A trowel and some boxes of seeds nestled in the roots of the great tree like clues to a murder, and there was a conspicuous grass stain on the boy's white britches. Recently delivered to Lord Luxon by the artist himself, the painting was, by any reckoning, a masterpiece. Lord Luxon glanced greedily at it, regretting, not for the last time, that he was obliged to sell it.

'Find me a chair, William! And bring me some beer before I expire of heatstroke. Pshaw! I love this city but it is even more crowded and steamy than The Bucket of Blood on a hanging day!

And fetch Captain Thomas and the men while you are about it. I have news.'

'Yes, my Lord,' said William, picking up Lord Luxon's shirt and waistcoat from the concrete floor. By dint of rearranging various items of furniture and wooden crates William came across what he was looking for. The huge, gold armchair was too heavy to lift so he dragged it, scraping its legs noisily, towards the centre of the room. Lord Luxon immediately flung himself into it and kicked off his shoes. He retrieved his leather notebook from his trouser pocket and started to read.

When William returned with Sergeant Thomas and three of the men, it occurred to him that the chair did not merely look like a throne, it *was*, in fact a throne. From which court and from which century, he wondered, had his master and the men plundered this particular item. A king might not miss a painting or a clock but it did not seem right to steal his *throne* . . . In the small, dark kitchen at the back of the building, William cooled his cheeks with the bottle before delivering it to Lord Luxon who, like all the men, had developed a taste for ice-cold beer.

The men stood vaguely to attention, relieved to enter the comparative cool of the building, and waited for the bare-chested Lord Luxon to address them. An animated expression played on his face and he tapped the open pages of his book. Lord Luxon drank deeply then wiped his mouth with the back of his hand, continuing all the while to read his notes. The men looked longingly at the bottle of beer, beaded in condensation, that dangled from Lord Luxon's fingers and licked their lips, wishing they were in the cool of Michael's bar, with a fancy coaster and a bowl of salted nuts and their hot hands pressed round a chilled glass. They waited for Lord Luxon to address them. Presently he looked up and met their stares.

'Finally, gentlemen, I see a path through the quagmire of History. I had hoped for much from my meeting with Mrs Stacey's niece today, yet the brilliance of her observation has done nothing short of astound me. She has given *clarity* and *purpose* to our campaign. Already we have made great strides, we have learned to navigate our way through time with ever-greater accuracy, but today this gifted young American has unwittingly betrayed her country in the most complete way possible. Gentlemen, no longer need we stumble lost and directionless through the backwaters of a revolution, now we have a compass and a stratagem. We, gathered together in this place, shall soon be privileged to witness the stillbirth of an independent America . . .'

William felt a shiver run up and down his spine as he observed the fire in his master's eyes. Though whether it was patriotism that he felt, or fear, or horror, he could not have said. He looked over at Sergeant Thomas and they exchanged glances but whatever it was that the seasoned soldier was feeling, he kept it to himself. Suddenly an inner door opened and a fair-haired boy stepped into the room. He seemed agitated but did not dare speak.

'What's amiss, lad?' barked Sergeant Thomas.

'There is a girl, sir. I fancied she was watching us but I was not sure. So I hid for a moment to see what she would do. I fear she is even now a-climbing up the ladder.'

'Did no one pull it up after me?' exclaimed Lord Luxon angrily.

Sergeant Thomas caught sight of William's contrite expression. 'It is my responsibility, my Lord,' he said quickly. 'It will not happen again.'

Sergeant Thomas rushed to the window and nudged down one of the slats. Lord Luxon and the men did likewise. Sergeant Thomas took out his loaded pistol and pointed it at the girl.

'It is Alice, Mrs Stacey's niece!' whispered Lord Luxon.

'Has she provided you with the answers you required?' asked Sergeant Thomas.

'Yes – for the most part, at least.'

'Then it would be as well to dispatch her with all haste.'

'No!'

'Forgive me, my Lord, but this is war. If she has followed you, she clearly has her suspicions. If you do nothing, I fear you may live to regret it.'

'Since when,' hissed Lord Luxon, 'did I take advice from a common sergeant?'

'As you say, sir.'

The shadow of a slight figure passed noiselessly in front of the blinds. Everyone stepped backwards. The contour of a head which pressed against the window was clearly visible. She was trying to see inside. No one moved. Then Sergeant Thomas whispered into Lord Luxon's ear.

'If we do not harm her then we must at least frighten her off.'

Lord Luxon nodded.

A few moments later Sergeant Thomas was crouching behind the door. With one hand he silently turned the door handle. With the other he clasped together the jaws of his oversized mongrel. When he judged the moment was right he whispered something into Sally's ear, flung open the door and pushed the cross-eyed bitch out onto the fire escape. Concealing himself at the back of the room, Lord Luxon caught a glimpse of shining, chestnut hair and Alice's petrified face as the hound knocked her to the floor and stood over her growling, front paws on her shoulders. Alice screamed and kicked and hit the dog hard on its nose with her heavy bag. But Sally would not be put off. Alice leaped up and ran to the ladder, hoping that the dog would not follow. Sergeant Thomas had his pistol trained through the blind at Alice's head as she climbed down. Sally's staccato barks were deafening and all of Prince Street looked up to watch the commotion.

'You only have to say the word,' Sergeant Thomas said to Lord Luxon over his shoulder. 'If not here, I could follow her to a quiet place to do the deed . . .'

Lord Luxon joined him at the window and peered through the blind. He rested his hand on the soldier's pistol and pushed it down.

'No. She may well be the instrument of our victory.'

Sally continued to bark like a mad thing.

'As you wish,' said Sergeant Thomas in a flat voice.

Lord Luxon flinched as Alice seemed to look straight back at him, wild-eyed, as if her gaze had penetrated the blind, before sprinting away towards Sixth Avenue and safety.

CHAPTER SIX

The Oracle

In which it is the Tar Man's turn to bare his teeth and Kate proves her worth

Other than a sharp intake of breath, the Tar Man did not permit himself to react even though Kate's incisors had broken his skin. Instead, with his free hand, he calmly leaned over and pinched a nerve in her neck. The acute, electric pain this simple gesture caused made her cry out. The Tar Man retrieved his throbbing hand and pulled both of Kate's arms behind her back. She felt a cord tighten around her wrists. Kate tried to spit out the taste of the Tar Man. She felt sick to her stomach.

'If you wish me to treat you civilly, Mistress Dyer, I recommend that you mend your manners – although it was scarcely gallant of Master Schock to leave you unaccompanied. Does he not know that Bartholomew's Fair is teeming with rogues who would prey on those such as yourself?'

'What do you want with me?' Kate cried.

'All in good time.'

Kate opened her mouth to scream for help but her cry was instantly smothered when the Tar Man slapped his fingers over her mouth. The fool's antics were still attracting the attention of the crowd and only one man noticed this minor disturbance on the edge of the circle of onlookers. It was the fortune-teller's gate-keeper. Kate, still wriggling like a fish on a hook, opened her eyes wide and looked at him beseechingly. He ignored her silent pleas. The Tar Man, too, fixed the big man with a stare and, with a jerk of his head, indicated that the fellow should remove himself from his sight.

'I believe you have urgent business elsewhere, Mr O' Donnell.'

'Yes, Master Blueskin, indeed I do.' The tall, turbaned figure sidled off as quickly as he could without breaking into a run.

The Tar Man dragged Kate backwards into the fortune-teller's tent. The woman, still shaken from her sighting of Kate, was sitting at a small table and drinking gin from a pewter mug. She looked up expectantly, composing her face into a pleasant smile for her latest customer. The smile withered on her face.

'I'll thank you to hold your tongue, madam,' said the Tar Man, holding the struggling Kate in one hand and the point of his knife to the woman's throat with the other. The woman looked from Kate to her attacker and back again and an expression of such abject terror came to her face that even the Tar Man was taken aback. She pointed a trembling finger towards them and then made a curious sign in the air that Kate could not decipher.

'The Oracle!' she breathed.

The woman's face had turned ash-grey and an instant later she fainted clean away, her head landing with a thump on the table. The Tar Man, who was accustomed to his victims using all manner of ruses to escape his clutches, instinctively questioned the authenticity of the woman's fainting fit. He therefore pushed at the woman's chair with the sole of one foot and continued to lever it over until the laws of gravity caused the woman to collapse out of it like a sack of potatoes onto the hard ground. Kate winced as she heard the woman's head knock against a table leg.

'Oracle?' the Tar Man repeated. 'What did the wench mean?' It was a rhetorical question given that his hand was still clamped over Kate's mouth. He kicked out at the woman's back, without any particular relish, to confirm her unconscious state before diverting his attention back to the matter at hand.

He leaned over, picked up the fortune-teller's chair and pushed Kate into it. He stood looming over her. Kate managed to return the searchlight of his gaze for only a few seconds. She looked away but could still feel his eyes burning into her. The Tar Man's presence was powerful, knowing, unpredictable . . . Joe Carrick, the vicious leader of the gang of footpads, had terrified her, too, in the same way that a mad dog would, but at least she had the measure of him. With the Tar Man she felt that she was floundering out of her depth. Gideon's words came back to her. *I suppose he is fearless because he has faced the worst a man can face and still survived. Most rogues' hearts are not completely black but his heart is buried so deep I doubt it will ever see the light of day . . . Beware of him, children, he is always two steps ahead of you while appearing to be two steps behind.* Surely he and Gideon couldn't be brothers, *could* they?

Why was the Tar Man just standing there, looking at her without saying anything? Kate stared fixedly at her lap, steeling herself for whatever was about to happen. She would be brave. Or at least she would try. A dog barked outside the tent and, for one blissful second, she convinced herself that it was Molly, and that her dad had travelled across time to rescue her. But it was not to be. She was alone, where none of her friends would think to look for her, with Lord Luxon's wicked henchman, who did not care if she lived or died. Who could help her now?

Finally the Tar Man broke his silence. 'I have grown fond of your century, Mistress Dyer,' he said in a half-whisper, too close to Kate's face. 'I had a secret that was the envy of every villain in London. A secret that you and I share, do we not? Each morning I arose to look out over a world where *anything* was possible. I am not a man inclined to fancy, but in truth, I often travel back, in my mind's eye, to my home high above the Thames with all of that other London laid out before me for the taking; I ride in my airborne carriages and fly wherever my desire takes me over land and sea; and sometimes I like to recall the expression on young Tom's face when first he witnessed me fading back into my own time—'

Kate forgot her fear for a moment. 'Tom! Tom who was with the Carrick Gang?'

'Yes.'

'*Tom* is in the twenty-first century?'

'Was. He died there.'

'Oh no! Not Tom . . .' Tears pricked at Kate's eyes but she blinked them back. 'But how?'

'On account of a reckless girl of whom he was overly fond . . . He allowed sentiment to rule his actions.'

The Tar Man paused for a moment, and the frown between his black eyebrows deepened. Kate risked snatching a glance up at him and she wondered what thought was going through his mind. He exhaled heavily and looked at her again.

'And so, in short, I am bent on returning to the century which is now also my own, and, I assure you, I shall balk at nothing until I succeed. Moreover, I desire *you*, Mistress Dyer, to help me in that resolve.'

'How am I supposed to do that?' Kate exclaimed. '*I* don't know how to get back! If I did I'd be there already!'

The Tar Man replied in a voice so low and silky Kate had to

strain to hear. 'But you forget that I have the means to return. The machine is in my possession. It could take both of us home.'

Kate scrutinised the Tar Man. She did not trust him for a second.

'So . . . what do you want *me* to do?'

'Your father built the machine, did he not? With the handsome Dr Pirretti? You were no doubt privy to certain information. I want you to tell me the secret code.'

'But I don't know it!'

The Tar Man put his hands on the arms of the chair and lowered his face towards hers so that she could see every pore of his weather-beaten skin.

'You *do* know it,' he growled. 'Why else would you and your friends come after me like hounds after a fox? You want my machine! But as you can see, I am not about to let you have it! Don't act the fool, Mistress Dyer! I'll warrant you wish to return to the future even more badly than I! Would not your parents be overjoyed to see you once more? Tell me the code!'

'I can't! We were going to worry about finding the code once we'd got back the machine!'

'You lie!' he shouted, so loudly that Kate jumped involuntarily. 'Tell me!'

Then the Tar Man seemed to lose all self-restraint. Never had she seen him in such a passion. He drew his knife from his belt and pushed her roughly forward. Kate felt him untie the cord that bound her wrists. He took hold of her left arm, forcing her elbow open and laying out her hand flat on the table, splaying out all her fingers. He clenched the knife and the fearsome blade hovered an inch above her trembling knuckles.

'You have five chances until I start on your writing hand!'

Kate was so terrified she could not focus, she could not breathe, she could not speak.

'Tell me the code!' he bellowed.

There was an unbearable pause whilst every sinew in the Tar Man's arm tightened as he gripped the knife in his clenched fist. Kate's tongue stuck to the roof of her mouth. She felt the hysteria rise up inside her. The blood seemed to roar in her temples. The blade was pressing into her skin! She felt something trickle down her finger! He was going to do it! She hit out at him uselessly with her free hand. The monster was actually going to cut her fingers off one by one! Suddenly the words exploded from her throat.

'I don't know! I don't know! I don't know!' she shrieked.

The Tar Man stood back and observed Kate's face dispassionately, like a doctor searching for symptoms. He was perfectly calm.

'No,' he said matter-of-factly. 'It appears that you do not.'

The Tar Man lowered his knife and paced up and down for a moment, deep in thought. The adrenaline still pumping through her veins, Kate did not know what to do with herself. She sat panting and trembling and was conscious of her face screwing up into weird shapes as she refused to give in to tears. She squinted at her finger, half-expecting to see it hanging on by a thread, but, in fact, her tormentor had not even drawn blood. He had not needed to. Her own fear had invented the nick in her skin . . . A surge of anger boiled up inside her. But if he'd been convinced that she *did* know the code, would he have cut her finger off, then? Yes, she thought, the Tar Man would not have hesitated for an instant.

'No matter,' said the Tar Man, still pacing. ''Tis a pity. But your father will not refuse me when the time is right . . . And now, Mistress Dyer, please be so kind as to remove your shoes.'

'What?!'

'I desire your trainers. You could not, in any case, call them dainty slippers. You would do well to choose more elegant attire.'

While Kate merely sat bewildered and motionless, the Tar Man grabbed hold of her ankles and pulled at the heels of her trainers. They both dropped to the floor. For a brief moment he paused and looked quizzically at Kate's flesh and then, holding out his hand, compared it to his own. He made no comment, however, and began to push the trainers into his jacket pockets. Kate closed her eyes. Was he going to cut her toes off now? She wished she could faint away like the gypsy woman, and escape into another world where he could not get at her. And when she opened her eyes again Kate found that, in a way, her wish had been granted.

Kate sat down in a heap on the back of an open wagon to nurse her feet which were sore and bleeding after walking barefoot for so long. Newgate Lane – and her friends – were proving difficult to find. She glanced around her at this sterile world scattered with living statues. In spite of her mind telling her that it was the accelerated speed at which she was passing through time that accounted for this state of affairs, Kate still had the impression that some terrible sorceress has passed through the world, blasting all living creatures with her wand and turning them to stone. Next to her, just passing by, was a young lad, younger even than her brother Sam. She guessed that he was a link-boy, hired by the middle-aged couple who walked at his side to light their way through the dark streets. No doubt they were headed for the fair. The man was dour-faced, while the woman – his wife, Kate supposed – wore a shapeless grey dress, and her thin lips were parted, as if she were about to speak. The boy's flaming torch lit up their lined faces and cast a glow on the inside of the wagon. Kate had thought her resting place was empty; now she could see that it was not. The driver of the wagon was nowhere to be seen but a small child, probably a girl, although it was difficult to be sure, lay curled on top of a bulging sack of grain in the corner of the wagon. Her hair tumbled over her face in soft, golden ringlets and she sucked her plump fingers. Kate reached out to stroke the child's cheek but her flesh felt cool and hard, not like living flesh at all.

Kate was not enjoying this practical lesson in relativity. Sighing heavily, she turned her attention to her feet. Why hadn't she made more of an effort to retrieve her trainers from the Tar Man's pockets? But objects were difficult to handle when she was moving so quickly. Everything seemed to resist her touch. Even sounds were now increasingly transformed into a low-pitched, ambient noise which her brain swiftly blanked out. It was on account of this that she was beginning to suspect that with each succeeding episode of fast-forwarding she was moving through the world at greater and greater speeds.

She had not been conscious of treading on anything sharp but when she examined the sole of her left foot she saw that it was split near the heel and dirt was becoming engrained in the wound. Kate decided to ignore it. The cut was not going to kill her and there was no point trying to wash it as water behaved entirely differently when she was moving at this speed. She jumped down off the wagon, a little tired and disheartened, and stuck her face right in front of the dreary couple.

'I'm looking for my friends – you wouldn't happen to know where Newgate Lane is, would you? No? I had a feeling you might not be able to help me.' Kate tugged at the woman's bonnet and managed to adjust it to a more flattering angle. Then she brushed some dust off the man's jacket. 'New in town, are you? I'm sure you'll both have a lovely time at Bartholomew's Fair – but if I were you I should avoid the fortune-teller's tent . . .'

I bet I'm walking in the wrong direction, Kate said to herself as she turned into the yawning darkness of yet another nameless street. Unlike the forest of giant shop signs all over London, she now realised that road signs were very few and far between. She could understand why Hannah always gave directions in terms of the shops that she knew. So instead of telling her, for instance, that she would find a good chop house on the corner of Shoe Lane and Fleet Street, she would say 'look for it between the Cheshire Cheese and the sign of the Leg of Mutton opposite the apothecary'. But Hannah was not here to help her and as she made her way through the dark, winding streets, Kate realised that she was fast losing her bearings. She was on the point of retracing her steps when she spotted, at some little distance, an athletic figure hurtling towards her. Her heart leaped. Frozen in time and yet evoking the very essence of speed, Gideon was running at full tilt. His hair had come loose from his ponytail and was flying behind him in blond ripples. He was looking over his shoulder at Peter who stood, some twenty paces behind, doubled up in pain, panting like a dog with sweat pouring off him. Her friend clearly could not keep up with Gideon.

'Gideon!' Kate exclaimed joyfully. 'Peter!'

She started to run towards them and, when she reached Gideon, she smiled up at him and gently touched his arm. As she suspected, nothing happened, so she continued running towards Peter. As she drew nearer, she saw that Peter's face was scrunched up in pain and that his fingers were clasped to his side. She could not help laughing. 'So much for *me* not being fit enough to keep up with Gideon!'

Kate looked around her at the eerie scene and slowly moved her hand towards Peter. She braced herself for that moment of violent rupture when the living universe broke back into her vacuum-like world.

'Do you know that you're my guardian angel?' she said to him. 'I don't understand why – but you're the only one who can bring me back.'

When the tips of her fingers were but a hair's breadth from Peter's arm, something made her draw her hand back. A thought burst inside her head like a bubble. I should have tied him up before I left! Kate pictured the Tar Man standing inside the fortune-teller's tent looking in amazement at the empty chair where, an instant before, she had been sitting. In another instant he would be out of the tent and would disappear into the heaving mass of people at the fair. What an idiot I am! He'll get away before Gideon can reach him! But then, without warning, another image crowded into her mind with such force that the rest of the world seemed to vanish.

Kate saw Peter at the top of a tall building, a tower perhaps, or a church, she could not tell. He was silhouetted against storm clouds and buffeted by a powerful wind. Below him modern London – although not a London she totally recognised – stretched out towards a misty horizon. Something was badly wrong. Peter was crying out in anguish and hitting his fists against a stone balustrade. Stop it! Kate shouted at him. You'll break your knuckles! But he could not hear her. The image faded slowly yet lurid echoes of the vision kept coming back at her. What had she seen? What could have made Peter so upset? She was left shaken and afraid. She stood for a while, not quite knowing what to do next. It was a waking dream, she told herself. It was nothing. But she instinctively knew that it wasn't a dream. If memories conjure up the past, these half-formed, will-o'-the-wisp apparitions brought the future momentarily to life. The night they arrived in the Marquis de Montfaron's chateau she had foreseen Peter being reunited with his mother at the farmhouse. That had come to pass. Would this, too? And was this a possible future, she wondered, or a definite one? Was the future as immoveable as the past, or were both now up for grabs?

Her hand still hovered above Peter's arm and she longed to grasp it and to return to the comfort of being with her friends. She stared at her friend's face and forced herself to think of the consequences of giving in to the impulse. If she did not stop the Tar Man from getting away they might not get another chance to catch him. It was up to her. No one would blame her if she bottled out – except herself. Kate lowered her arm and turned resignedly back towards Bartholomew's Fair.

As she walked along she found that her thoughts kept turning to what the Tar Man had said about Tom. She recalled his small, heart-shaped face and his troubled eyes as he stared down at her from the boughs of the great oak tree the day that the Carrick Gang had attacked them. Poor Tom. To have escaped the clutches of Joe Carrick only to be dragged off to a future century where his master had let him die – no doubt alone and with nobody to lay flowers on his grave. She wondered about the reckless girl of whom the Tar Man had spoken. Kate hoped that at least she had been a friend to Tom . . .

CHAPTER SEVEN

Anjali Does the Right Thing

In which Anjali has cause to be grateful
and a small domestic pet does its duty

The staff nurse walked through the ground-floor annexe wearing a waterproof apron over her dark blue uniform. A towel was draped over one plump and freckled arm and she carried a stainless steel kidney dish containing a hypodermic syringe. Her plastic apron squeaked with every step. The nurse stopped to dim the lights and then closed the glass door firmly behind her. Then she walked briskly up the corridor, all shiny linoleum and harsh fluorescent lighting, and disappeared around the corner. She waited for a moment, her cheek resting on the wall, out of sight, listening hard. Presently she heard the click of the door opening and shutting again. The nurse hurried to her office where she threw down what she was carrying and tore off her apron.

Now she retraced her steps, cautiously opened the door and crept noiselessly into the ward. She stood in the shadows, observing the slight figure leaning over the freshly made bed. The girl's short black hair had a blue sheen to it. She had a small rucksack strapped to her back that was decorated with badges and metallic beads. The fingers that held the boy's cool, unresponsive hands in hers were covered in silver rings. The nurse drew closer and reached out as if to tap the girl's shoulder. She changed her mind and her hand dropped back to her side.

'Is he a friend of yours?'

Anjali nearly jumped out of her skin and was already halfway to the door before the nurse called out: 'Don't go! This isn't the first time I've seen you . . .'

Anjali stopped in her tracks and turned around to face the nurse.

'I'll take a bet that your name is Anjali.'

Anjali's large, dark eyes took on the look of a cat who has seen a sudden movement in the long grass. She stared at the nurse, all attention. With her cropped, salt and pepper hair and her knowing face, the woman reminded her of the patient schoolteacher who'd eventually taught her to read. Anjali stayed hovering by the door but decided not to run – yet.

'Believe me, I'm happy you've come! It's been breaking my heart to think there's not a soul in the world who cares whether he lives or dies.'

'The law have been here—'

'The police haven't been round for a couple of days now. The boy's injuries are consistent with a fall. Only the boy knows if he was pushed or if he fell – and he's keeping that to himself at the moment . . . Of course they've asked us to keep them informed about his progress. That and if any visitors turn up . . .'

Anjali looked alarmed.

'But it's the boy I'm concerned about.'

'Is he gonna be all right?'

'Do you want me to see if there's a doctor on duty who can talk to you?'

'No! Can't *you* tell me?'

The nurse hesitated. 'Well, he's had a blood clot removed from his brain . . .'

Anjali's head dropped forward onto her chest. The nurse moved closer to her and put an arm around her shoulder.

'But there were no complications and, as you can see, he's already been transferred out of the High Dependency Unit . . .'

'He looks so white . . .'

'Give him time – he's doing fine . . .'

Anjali stared at Tom's bandaged head for a while and then asked: 'Did anyone identify him?'

'No.'

'So they don't know where he lives?'

'No. Do you?'

'No.'

There was a pause while the nurse and the girl weighed each other up.

'Was it you that hurt him?'

Anjali shook her head vigorously. 'He was trying to save me.'

'Well I'm glad he succeeded – though it was at a price . . .'

'Yeah.'

'*Are* you Anjali?'

The girl nodded.

'I heard him say your name yesterday while I was giving him a wash. Names are powerful things. You must be important to him. It'd be good to know *his* name. It'd be a start.'

'Tom. His name's Tom.'

The nurse broke into a huge smile, walked over to the bed and sat on the starched white sheets. She stroked the boy's smooth cheek and patted his hand affectionately. An intravenous drip was taped to his wrist.

'At last!' she whispered. 'Now we can introduce ourselves properly. I'm pleased to meet you, Tom. My name is Brenda. When you wake up you'll find you've got a visitor! And a pretty one at that.'

The nurse motioned for Anjali to come over. Anjali knelt on the floor so that her face was close to Tom's ear. 'Can he hear?'

'It's difficult to say. He's been drifting in and out for a while . . .'

'It's me, Tom. It's Anjali.'

Tom's left eyelid flickered and the nurse and Anjali exchanged hopeful glances. They waited in high anticipation for several minutes, staring at Tom's waxen face with its dark lashes and small, pointed nose and pale lips, but he remained motionless.

'Does he have any family?'

Anjali shook her head. 'He's an orphan. And the guy who was looking after him has—' She paused to sigh deeply. 'He's gone away.'

'Will he be back?'

'I doubt it.'

'So you're all he's got?'

Anjali looked pained. 'We're friends. That's all.'

The nurse nodded. 'I see.'

The following night the nurse arranged to be there when Anjali arrived. The nurse and the girl sat together on grey, hospital chairs, drinking mugs of hot chocolate that the nurse had made to help them through their evening vigil.

'I've brought something for him.'

The nurse watched as Anjali picked up her rucksack and undid the buckles. Anjali carefully removed a chocolate box fastened with two green elastic bands. Several small holes had been poked into the lid and sawdust escaped from the cracks. The nurse gripped the side of her chair as she heard a small but distinct scratching sound coming from within the box.

'I've been looking after his mouse. It gives me the creeps. I don't mind hamsters but mice *stink*.' Anjali turned to Tom. 'I wish you'd hurry up and get better so I don't have to look after your stinky little friend no more.'

'Please don't tell me that's his mouse!'

Anjali grinned. 'Tom always has it with him – in his pocket, climbing all over him. I reckon he prefers his mouse to people.'

The nurse put her hand to her mouth as she watched Anjali ping off the bands and raise the lid of the box a crack and then, with a shiver of distaste, pull out a wriggling white creature by the tip of its tail.

'Look who I've brought to see you,' said Anjali.

The mouse squeaked and squirmed as it was hoisted over the seemingly great divide between the chair and the bed. 'Put it back!' exclaimed the nurse as Anjali dropped the tiny creature onto Tom's chest. The startled animal landed with a barely perceptible thud and immediately started to burrow under Tom's short-sleeved hospital gown.

'We've got to get it out!'

'It's all right,' said Anjali. 'Tom likes it. You'll see.'

For a moment the nurse looked furious but Anjali flashed her such a winning smile that the nurse relented.

'If that mouse escapes my head's going to be on the chopping block . . .'

'It won't. Tom is its home.'

The nurse shuddered. 'How could he bear those scratchy little paws walking all over his bare skin . . .'

The nurse passed Anjali an antiseptic wipe and took one for herself even though she hadn't touched the animal.

'I knew you'd want to kill me for bringing a mouse into the hospital.'

'Well I should . . .'

Anjali turned to look at the nurse. 'Thanks. For being good to him, I mean.'

'Why wouldn't I be?'

'I don't think many people have in his life. Including me.'

'It wasn't easy coming back, was it? You did the right thing.'

Anjali's voice nearly cracked. 'I owed him.'

The minutes passed and then the hours. Once Anjali woke up to find her head in the nurse's lap. She murmured her apologies but the nurse only rubbed her back. The mouse emerged for a few seconds at ten o'clock but immediately disappeared again. Now it was nearly midnight and it was the nurse's turn to have fallen asleep. Her head hung over her knees, her mouth half-open. In the eerily silent ward Anjali stood guard over her friend and relived that awful moment. She recalled Tom's white and terrified face as he jumped onto the back of her attacker. The difference in size between the two youths was so marked it reminded her of the time she saw a hissing kitten jump onto the neck of a snarling Alsatian. And Tom, clinging on like the kitten, had been finally shaken off and hurled down those steep, hard stairs, rolling over and over and over, gathering momentum until, with a sickening crack, his head had hit the wall and he moved no more. She wondered if she would have the guts to risk her life for another as this skinny boy had for her. In real life, she thought, heroes come in all shapes and sizes.

Anjali scraped back her chair and stood up to stretch her legs. If she were dancing in a club the night would still feel young but in the twilight world of a quiet hospital ward it seemed late, so very late. Yawning silently, she got her things together, uncertain whether she should wake up the nurse to tell her that she'd had enough for one night. She decided it was best just to go. But as she zipped up her leather jacket Anjali realised that she was going to have to take the mouse back with her. Reluctantly she peeled back the sheet and the white cotton blanket and observed Tom's hospital gown. The mouse suddenly darted out of Tom's sleeve and ran over the tips of Anjali's fingers which made her cry out in surprise. The nurse awoke, groaning a little, and opened her eyes, and when they focussed she saw that a smile had appeared on Tom's dry lips. She grabbed hold of Anjali's arm.

'He's awake!' she exclaimed.

'And he's moving!' said Anjali.

Then, infinitely slowly, they observed Tom's right hand drag across the sheet and move, by degrees, towards his left shoulder. His wrist flexed and he cupped his fingers close to the opening of his sleeve. After a moment, white whiskers quivering, the mouse crept cautiously out of a fold in the pale blue cotton and sat on the palm of Tom's hand. It sniffed his skin and appeared to lick it. The smile on Tom's face grew wider and one eyelid flickered and opened. The mouse disappeared back into his sleeve.

'Tom!' cried Anjali, throwing herself at him. 'You're awake!'

The nurse had to dive over to save the stand that held the intravenous fluid from toppling to the floor.

'Anjali?' said Tom in a weak and croaky voice.

'I'm here! I think you're gonna be all right!'

The nurse put one hand on Anjali's head and the other on Tom's.

'I thought you was dead or I'd never have left you! It was only 'cos the bloke next to me on the bus was reading the local paper that I'm here now . . .'

Tom's eyes grew wide and moved about the room trying to take in his strange surroundings. Anjali and the nurse just looked at him. It was a little like witnessing a birth. Anjali fought hard to hold back the tears. The nurse looked over at her and stroked her cheek with the back of her hand.

'Let it out, love. It's allowed.'

'I don't do crying.'

Then Tom noticed the nurse. He looked wildly at this stranger in uniform and suddenly he panicked and tried to get up but could not. He clawed desperately at the intravenous drip.

'Ssssh! *Easy! Easy!*' said the nurse, gently pushing him back onto the pillow and smoothing back the tape over his wrist. 'There's no need to be scared . . . We're trying to make you better.'

Anjali grabbed hold of his mouse, who had surfaced in all the commotion, and gently put the creature back into his hands.

'Am I in prison?'

Anjali burst out laughing. 'If *this* is your idea of a prison, your century ain't as bad as you've made out! Can't you see that this is a *hospital*?'

Anjali met the nurse's confused stare. 'Just our little joke. Me and Tom go back a long way . . . Especially Tom!'

Tom was breathing more slowly but he continued to give side-long glances at the nurse. 'Where is Blueskin?' he asked abruptly.

Anjali was taken by surprise and since no plausible deception immediately sprang to mind she had to resort to the truth. 'I told him you were dead. I thought you were! It was right after it hap-pened. He didn't take it too well. He said he never wanted to clap eyes on me again . . . And now he's disappeared off the face of the planet.' Anjali hesitated for a moment and then said: 'There's no easy way to say this – but I think the Tar Man's gone back.'

'Blueskin's left me behind!' Tom looked stricken. 'But how can I survive here without him?'

He tried to sit up again and the nurse pushed him firmly back down.

Anjali frowned and then her expression cleared as if she had come to a decision. 'I'll sort something out, Tom. I don't know what yet. But something. Anyway, you ain't alone. You got your mouse.'

The nurse looked shocked. Anjali laughed her fruity laugh.

'And maybe, if you keep your stinky little friend away from me, you got me, too . . .'

CHAPTER EIGHT

Ring! Ring! Ring!

**In which Peter says sorry to Kate and
Bartholomew's Fair hosts a family quarrel**

Peter did not react to Kate's touch but let his head hang forward towards his knees. His legs had turned to jelly and the insides of his lungs were burning. He forced himself to stand upright and shouted at Gideon, sucking in a rasping breath after every few words.

'Don't wait . . . Don't let . . . the Tar Man . . . get Kate!'

But Gideon was staring in astonishment at something to Peter's left.

Peter followed his gaze and saw Kate standing next to him, hands on waist and head tipped to one side, a half-smile on her face. She had something tucked under one arm but Peter could not tell what it was in the semi-darkness. He stood up.

'I wondered when you were going to notice me.'

'Kate! How did you get here?'

'I'm a fast mover!' she said and suddenly started to giggle.

Peter shot a puzzled glance at Gideon as he started to jog back to join them. He was out of breath. 'The Lord be praised that you are safe!' he panted. 'Featherstone came after us and confessed that it was but a ruse. Alas, he has too many dependents to dare refuse Blueskin, though I do not think he is a wicked man. You are not hurt, Mistress Kate?'

'No – though my heart was beating so fast I thought I was going to die of fright!' Kate held out her hands and wriggled her fingers. She mimed bringing down the blade of a knife on them. 'The Tar Man said he'd chop them off if I didn't tell him the code. He must have believed me, otherwise he'd have done it. I know he would.'

Peter stared at his friend then gulped and looked down, consumed by guilt. But it was raw fury that blazed in Gideon's eyes. His nostrils flared.

'It's funny,' continued Kate, 'I was so scared I could have sworn I felt the blood trickling down my fingers.'

'Where is the brute now?' Gideon asked. 'Has he already skulked back to his lair?'

'If you hurry, you'll find him in the fortune-teller's tent. I tied him up – but I don't think I made a great of job of it.'

Gideon raised his eyebrows. '*You* tied up *Blueskin?*'

'I'd go after him right now if I were you,' she replied. 'Before he gets away.'

Gideon did not need to be told twice. He turned on his heels and charged up the street in the direction of Bartholomew's Fair, pale hair flying, swerving out of people's way. He stopped only to shout back: 'Peter! Be sure not to leave your friend's side.'

Peter turned to Kate. 'I shouldn't have left you like that. I'm sorry.'

'It's okay. You were worried about Gideon. Anyway, I can look after myself.'

Peter looked at her without blinking. 'But . . . how did you do it?'

Kate shrugged her shoulders.

'No. Tell me. How *did* you do it?'

Kate averted her gaze from Peter. While she kept this secret to herself she could pretend it was not happening. She could imagine what it would be like if everyone knew. She slipped her hand into Peter's. He let her. 'We'd better get moving. I'll tell you later.'

Kate set off but Peter pulled her back. She turned around to look at him and he scrutinised her face. 'What's up, Kate?'

She shook her head. 'Nothing.'

'I don't believe you.'

Kate shook her head again.

As they set off, the thing that Kate was carrying under her arm fell silently to the ground. Peter reached down to pick it up and held it, with distaste, between thumb and forefinger. 'Was this alive once?' Peter peered at it in the dark.

Kate laughed. 'Parson Ledbury is going to be well pleased when we see him.'

'Oh!' exclaimed Peter, laughing. 'It's his wig!'

Kate set off at a run, holding up her cumbersome skirts, already stained with dirt to a depth of six inches.

'What happened to your trainers?' called Peter after her.

'The Tar Man took them.'

'What! *Why?*'

'Just what I thought. Come on!' she said. 'I really, *really* want to see the Tar Man get what's coming to him!'

'Ring! Ring! Ring!' chanted a swelling crowd as they enclosed the two men in a tight circle. Hand in hand, Peter and Kate drove a path through the mass of onlookers as the news spread like wildfire that a fight was in the offing. They strained to hear the muffled sounds of combat over the babble of the spectators.

'Do you think it could be them?' asked Peter.

Kate nodded. 'Yeah, it's got to be.' Her eyes were narrow and shining. 'And I hope Gideon will beat him to a bloody pulp!'

Peter turned round to grin at Kate. 'That's not like you!'

'It is now.' Kate did not grin back.

Peter waited until he had turned round again before he let his smile melt off his face. Kate's ordeal with the Tar Man had been his fault. He wouldn't let it happen again.

Soon they hit a wall of backs which they could not breach. They jumped up as high as they could, using the shoulders of the protesting people in front to lever themselves up, but still they could see nothing above the rows of tricorn hats. Worse, a troupe of performers on stilts arrived, determined to find out the cause of all the excitement. They wore grotesque head masks, oversized and with bulbous noses and crude gashes of red paint for mouths. They loomed out of the darkness and pushed Peter and Kate unconcernedly to one side. To avoid being crushed the children were obliged to squeeze into the gaps between giant legs clothed with acres of flapping, striped silk. Peter craned his neck upwards at the towering figures that teetered about on their stilts for balance. He thought that he and Kate must look like baby giraffes cowering for protection under their parents.

'I hope they don't tread on us,' shouted Peter above the din.

'If they do we can always push them over,' Kate replied.

''Tis rare indeed to see Master Blueskin stoop to fist-fighting,' said a nasal voice ahead of them. 'He's a fellow who likes his reputation to speak for him . . .'

'And see how straight he holds himself,' exclaimed another. 'I do believe his neck has healed!'

'Ay, and look at the cut of his cloth – he's had rich pickings of late.'

'Who's the cove that has the bottom to challenge the Tar Man?' asked another. 'Faith, I don't fancy his chances.'

Peter nudged Kate. 'It *is* them!'

'Don't be so sure,' called out an older, croaky voice. 'We was at Tyburn when they tried to hang him. He's the cutpurse they say was rescued by angels. We was vastly entertained – why, we did not even take it amiss when no one got scragged that day. If memory serves his name is Seymour. I like his looks. He seems a likely lad . . .'

The voice tailed off as a great howl of pain rose up and the crowd at the front winced in sympathy.

'Ha!' cried the first voice. 'What say you now? Your Mr Seymour will be lucky if he can find his feet again.'

Peter and Kate exchanged desperate looks.

'It *is* him,' said Peter. 'We're going to have to push. Okay?'

Kate nodded and both took a step backwards before charging at the row of assorted jackets and greasy ponytails that separated them from the fight. They screwed up their eyes and heaved. Amidst a flurry of vociferous complaints the children broke through and emerged, blinking, at the edge of an open circle. The crowd was passing around flaming brands taken, under protest, from a fire-eater. The children peered into the flickering half-light and saw a figure rise unsteadily to his feet and stagger towards his opponent, swaying and shaking his head repeatedly much as a horse might try to rid itself of a cloud of troublesome flies. It was Gideon. Kate felt Peter lurch forward ready to spring to their friend's aid. She held him back.

'No! You mustn't! Gideon wouldn't want you to . . .'

Kate gripped Peter's hand and he could not help straining against her for he longed to throw himself at the man whose actions had caused them all such anguish. The Tar Man's poise and self-belief were written into every fluid movement as he prowled, cat-like, in a circle around his victim. Peter glimpsed the enjoyment in his eyes as he observed Gideon list drunkenly towards him. Peter's heart sank to his boots. Gideon was already hurt, how was he going to withstand any more punishment? The Tar Man was relishing playing to the crowd and he allowed an amused smile to play on his lips for good effect. Gideon threw a sudden punch at the Tar Man's jaw but it did not hit its mark. His opponent stepped to one side with a dramatic flourish, causing Gideon to lose his balance. He crashed to the ground and the crowd roared with laughter. The Tar Man shook his head and tutted.

'Now that you have seen fit to make a spectacle of our private disagreement, Mr Seymour, it is only seemly that we make a little more effort to divert these good people, do you not agree?'

Gideon tried to push himself up from the dirt but the Tar Man tripped him up with a well-judged kick to his ankles and proceeded to strut around the ring, adjusting his cream waistcoat and smoothing back his dark hair while he waited for his opponent to recover himself. People laughed even harder.

'Come on, Gideon!' shouted Peter, a lone voice in the crowd.

Kate joined in. 'You show him, Gideon!'

All of a sudden they were aware of another voice calling out Gideon's name.

There were a few *Huzzah!*s but even more *Boo!*s. The Tar Man was not a stranger to these people.

'Perhaps the others are here!' shouted Peter to Kate.

The Tar Man made a show of offering Gideon his hand to help him to his feet. Gideon spat at it. The Tar Man wiped his hand on his sleeve and shook his head in disappointment, then stood aside, gentleman-like, allowing Gideon to stand up. Some of the crowd booed and hissed as he found his footing. There was a large, muddy smear of dirt on Gideon's cheek and the Tar Man took pleasure in indicating as much. There was more laughter. A flower girl, carrying a large, flat basket full of posies, stepped forward into the ring, stood in front of Gideon and dabbed at his face with a handkerchief. The Tar Man looked on and smiled at Gideon as you would a wayward child.

'Please desist, madam, I beg of you,' said Gideon, embarrassed by the attention. He tried vainly to wave her aside but, ignoring the laughter, the girl would not be put off until she had removed the dirt.

'Oh, someone get her off him!' exclaimed Peter.

'At least it's giving him the chance to get his breath back,' said Kate.

Finally the girl withdrew, accepting the crowd's applause with a shallow curtsy. Then the Tar Man approached Gideon and said something in a voice too low for the crowd to hear. Whatever it was that he said, it had the same effect as a bucket of cold water to the face. Rage or hatred or both roused Gideon to the extent that he launched himself at the Tar Man in a wild fury.

'It is a lie!' he shouted.

The Tar Man was momentarily stunned as a succession of ferocious blows rained down on him and he took several hard punches before he recovered himself enough to deflect the majority of them. Enjoying the turn the fight had taken, the excited crowd started to roar its approval and the Tar Man's expression betrayed regret that he had goaded Gideon quite so successfully. He took advantage of the first brief pause in the onslaught to deliver not a punch but a high kick to his opponent's stomach. Taken by surprise, Gideon staggered backwards, badly winded and barely able to lift up his arms to defend himself from the blows that he knew were bound to follow. Everyone gasped as the Tar Man landed a devastating punch to Gideon's temple. Gideon staggered backwards, hardly managing to remain upright as he rocked first in one direction and then in the other. All eyes were now on the Tar Man as he started to circle once more, massaging his bruised knuckles and pushing up the sleeves of his shirt. Then he stood still, gathering his forces, preparing to deliver a final, knockout blow.

Peter and Kate clutched at each other, hardly daring to look.

'He's going to kill him!' exclaimed Kate.

Peter watched through the gaps in his fingers as the Tar Man drew back his right arm, ready to strike, but suddenly found himself cheering alongside Kate as Gideon fell, rather than dived, at the Tar Man's feet and instinctively grabbed hold of his ankles. Caught unawares, the Tar Man was floored. His skull cracked against the hard ground. He did not move.

'He's out cold!' screamed Peter, punching the air with his fist.

The ring of onlookers went silent. Disorientated though he was, Gideon's arms shot up in triumph. The crowd started to applaud, a little ungenerously at first, but Peter and Kate jumped up and down, whooping and cheering. Gideon looked down at the Tar Man's motionless body and shook his head in disbelief. How had he managed to win the fight? But suddenly there were shouts and Gideon recognised Peter's shrill voice. He turned to seek out his young friend's face in the crowd.

'No! Behind you!' shrieked Peter and Kate desperately.

But it was too late. The Tar Man had sprung up, unhurt and perfectly alert. As Gideon turned to face him he executed an impeccable drop kick to his jaw. Gideon's blond head flew backwards and the children watched him land, knocked finally senseless, in the putrid dirt of Smithfield Market.

The crowd roared their approval. 'Master Blueskin does not disappoint,' someone said as the children pushed forward to help

Gideon. 'It is a foolish man who thinks he can get the better of the Tar Man.'

As the children got closer Kate saw, with some satisfaction, the livid imprint of her teeth still on the Tar Man's hand. He acknowledged the children with a slight incline of his head, then leaned down over the unconscious Gideon and said, loud enough, for the children to hear: 'Let this teach you a lesson, little brother. *Never* turn your back on your opponent, even if you fancy that he is not long for this world . . .'

Kate and Peter exchanged horrified glances.

'It *is* true then!' murmured Kate. 'They *are* brothers!'

'I don't believe it!' said Peter hotly.

The Tar Man started to walk away.

'Stop that rogue!' came a cry.

Kate looked about her. 'Was that Sir Richard?'

'Stop that rogue, I say!' shouted Sir Richard from the back of the crowd.

Once the Tar Man had spotted Sir Richard he fixed him with a cool stare.

Sir Richard pointed at the Tar Man and addressed the crowd. 'This man is nought but a common thief!'

'You are not in the Court of St James' now, Sir Richard,' cried the Tar Man. 'Do not dare to stand in Bartholomew's Fair and blacken my name! A *common* thief I am not!' There were ripples of laughter. 'Look to yourself and your kind, Sir Richard. You say *I* am a thief but I say to you, when times are good, do you not steal our money in taxes but when times are bad do you not let us starve? *I* may have plucked the pearls from a duchess's neck. But *you* and your kind would take the bread from the plate of a hungry child. It will not be ever thus and I have cause to know . . .'

The crowd shouted their approval and nodded their heads and people stared angrily behind them at Sir Richard.

'You turn sense on its head, sir!' replied Sir Richard.

Now the crowd started to boo and hiss and there was a whiff of anarchy in the air. Bartholomew's Fair belonged to the people and no one was in a mood to bow to authority.

'You wouldn't catch Blueskin stealing the bread from a child's plate!' someone shouted out. 'He'd be sure to steal the plate, too!'

There was an eruption of raucous laughter. Sir Richard tried to push his way to the front but the crowd would not let him through.

'I have ten guineas in my hand for the man who brings me Master Blueskin!' shouted Sir Richard. 'Ten golden guineas!'

The Tar Man laughed but cast an eye over the crowd all the same. Ten guineas was a handsome sum, although no one, he was relieved to see, was tempted by the offer. Suddenly Gideon started to groan.

'He's coming round!' cried Kate.

The Tar Man looked down at Gideon. 'Have no fear, Mistress Dyer, he'll live.'

Then the Tar Man gestured that he desired to exit the ring and the crowd parted like the Red Sea for Moses.

'Stop him, I say!' cried Sir Richard in desperation.

But the Tar Man waved farewell to the crowd and vanished into the night, to the sound of hearty applause.

Now that the excitement was over the crowd quickly dispersed, although several men jostled Sir Richard, and two handsome women, who wore heart-shaped beauty spots on their faces and bosoms, spat at him. Soon Peter, Kate and Sir Richard were left alone tending the bruised and battered Gideon.

Sir Richard seemed shaken. 'He is a man of parts, our villainous rogue – and at all costs not to be underestimated. Though, by heaven, I swear he shall feel the full weight of my anger ere long.'

Gideon's eyes opened. 'I fear that there is a long list of men,' he croaked in a barely audible voice, 'who have the same thought, Sir Richard.'

Two figures loomed out of the darkness. Hannah and a bare-headed Parson Ledbury walked side by side. At first they did not notice their friends. The Parson was tearing the last morsels of flesh from a couple of ribs of pork. He wiped the grease from his mouth with the back of his hand. When he spotted the party he flung the bones to the ground where a couple of small dogs imme-diately pounced on them, yapping and snarling as they each pulled in opposite directions.

'Gadzooks, I am heartily glad to see you!' exclaimed Parson Ledbury. 'We have been waiting under the whirligig this past half-hour. Time enough for a monkey to make off with my wig, would you believe! A monkey! The little devil sat chattering to itself at the top of the whirligig and would not be persuaded down.'

'Yes! The creature even put the Parson's wig on its head! I do not recall laughing so much in my life!' Hannah giggled. 'Begging your pardon, sir.'

The Parson snorted. 'But what has detained you so long? Where is Mr Seymour? And has there been a sighting of Master Blueskin?'

Peter pointed without comment at Gideon who lay on the foul-smelling ground, bruised and bloodied. The flesh around one eye was so swollen that the eyelid was purplish and spongy and the skin stretched tight and shiny across the socket. Gideon peered up at Parson Ledbury with one bloodshot, watering eye. The Parson's face crumpled in consternation and he immediately knelt down next to Gideon.

'I see that the Tar Man lives up to his reputation. Indeed, if Master Schock speaks the truth, I can only say that this is a most disappointing way to express his brotherly affection—'

'He is *not* my brother!' exclaimed Gideon, trying to sit up.

Kate and Peter pushed Gideon back down and Sir Richard put an arm on the Parson's shoulder.

'As you say, my dear fellow,' said the Parson, hurriedly. 'But we cannot afford to tarry here. If we do not catch up with Blueskin tonight who knows when we might get another chance. Can you walk, Mr Seymour?'

'What are you thinking of, Parson?' exclaimed Sir Richard. 'Gideon is too hurt to do aught but rest!'

Gideon pushed himself up on his elbows, drawing in his breath slowly through his teeth. 'I can walk.'

'No, my friend, you have taken enough of a beating for one night,' said Sir Richard, laying a hand on Gideon's shoulder. 'I shall send for the carriage to take you back to Lincoln's Inn Fields.'

But Gideon rolled over onto his side, got onto all fours and tried to stand up, refusing all help. He swayed backwards and forwards, holding one hand to his temple, the other to his side, his features creased with the pain of it. The Parson and Sir Richard grabbed an arm each and propped Gideon up between them.

'Bless me, but you have spirit, Mr Seymour!' said Parson Ledbury, thumping Gideon on the back. 'It is to be regretted that you were pitted against your br— such a skilful adversary – but you are not a man to turn tail. And the game is far from over. Come, let us try a few steps—'

'No!' exclaimed Kate. 'Gideon has got to lie still! Look at his face. It's the colour of rice pudding!'

'You have no cause to be anxious on my account, Mistress Kate,' said Gideon in a voice that made it difficult to believe him. 'It is my own pride that pricks and stings me most. Twice he has overcome me. Once during Lord Luxon's race, when none but the birds and the trees bore witness to my humiliation, and now here at Bartholomew's Fair, with a baying crowd to compound my indignity. He will not lay me low again! I swear it. I swear it on my mother's grave . . .'

Kate looked at Gideon's poor, swollen eye, and at his waxen complexion, and she was not the only one to think that *if* what they had heard was true, thrashing the Tar Man – much as the idea might appeal to the assembled company – was unlikely to be what the siblings' late mother might have desired . . .

'Oh, Gideon,' said Kate, 'you don't have to prove yourself to *us*! No one could have done more than you have!'

'Anyway, the Tar Man cheated!' said Peter hotly. 'You don't have to feel bad about anything!'

Gideon did not look convinced. 'As Blueskin himself told me, I should have had more sense than to turn my back on him. It is not a mistake I shall repeat.'

Peter searched in vain for words of comfort.

'It is ever in my mind,' continued Gideon, 'that it was I who led you into the path of Blueskin on that very first day you arrived in this century. In consequence I cannot doubt that it is squarely my responsibility to put matters right.'

Sir Richard smiled. 'My dear fellow,' he said. 'How lightly you bear the world's weight on your young shoulders . . .'

Pulling Peter with her, Kate walked over to Gideon. Then, hesitating a little, she planted a swift kiss on his cheek. 'You don't owe us anything. I think it's the other way round . . .'

Gideon nodded by way of thanks and a twinkle came to his one good eye. 'Though 'tis true, on reflection, that were it not for you two wretched children, I should doubtless be supping ale in some pleasant inn . . . and in company that required cheerful conversation rather than a narrowly missed appointment at Tyburn and regular beatings.'

As Peter laughed the memory came to him of that moment in Derbyshire – it seemed so long ago now – when he had first admitted to Gideon that if this was 1763, everyone he knew and loved was centuries away in the future. Gideon, a total stranger, with no resources, and more than enough troubles of his own, had believed him and promised to help them get back home. Gideon had kept his word and had risked everything to help these strange children from another world while the Tar Man had done everything he could to thwart them. How could one family produce such different offspring?

'Alas, I cannot believe you, Mr Seymour,' observed the Parson. 'Having enjoyed your company for some goodly time, I believe I have the measure of you. There is a light which burns bright within you which a quiet life would swift extinguish.'

'I agree with you, Parson,' said Sir Richard. 'I fear Gideon will always have to search for some grindstone on which to sharpen the blade of his convictions.'

A quiet cough alerted the party to the presence of a woman who appeared at one side of this little scene, her jet-black hair glistening in the half-light. Her eyes kept finding Kate. The woman stepped forward, bracelets jangling, her flamboyant dress and confident air belying a deep unease. She clutched something in her hand. After a moment Kate realised that it was the fortune-teller. Sir Richard and the Parson were still propping up Gideon. The fortune-teller surveyed the three men uncertainly and suddenly stepped towards Sir Richard and, after executing a rather hasty curtsy, slipped a scrap of paper into his free hand. Kate noticed a tender blue bruise blossoming on her temple.

'What is it that you give me, madam?' asked Sir Richard. 'It is a picture of some kind but, alas, I can barely decipher it in this light.'

The woman replied in a low, hesitant voice, looking this way and that as she spoke. 'I have marked where you might find the lodgings of him whom you seek, your honour. I trust that you are gentleman enough to forget the identity of she who divulged the information.'

Sir Richard peered at the piece of paper and the Parson leaned over Gideon to see better. Smiles appeared on both men's faces and the Parson slapped Gideon on the back.

'Such timely information! Madam, we are your humble servants!' exclaimed the Parson gleefully. 'Please accept our most grateful thanks.' He shook the piece of paper in front of Gideon's nose. 'This is capital news,' he roared. 'Capital!'

The fortune-teller looked around her, anxious to avoid drawing any attention to herself, and Sir Richard gestured to the Parson to moderate his ebullient behaviour.

'Madam,' said Sir Richard, with a bow of his head, 'we are vastly indebted to you.'

Sir Richard drew out a guinea from his purse and held it out for her on the palm of his hand. She shook her head firmly, and made as if to push his hand away.

'But why is she telling us? How do we know that she is telling the truth?' asked Peter. 'She could have been sent by the Tar Man. It could be a trap!'

The fortune-teller glared at Peter and said: 'This young lady will vouch for me!'

Suddenly Kate let go of Peter to cover her face with her hands. Peter heard her sharp intake of breath.

'What's wrong, Kate?' asked Peter in alarm.

Kate quickly grabbed hold of Peter's hand again. 'Nothing . . . I'm fine.'

Peter raised his eyebrows in disbelief. Kate ignored him.

'We *can* trust this lady – she is a fortune-teller and it was the Tar Man who gave her that bruise.'

Kate looked over at the woman and was somehow certain that she, too, had suddenly smelled the stink of the river, had heard the lapping of water and had shared the selfsame vision of a high-ceilinged room, crammed with artefacts, its pale walls glistening with damp. Through a circular window the Thames had been visible, its greenish-brown waters swirling and heaving. She saw the billowing sails of cargo ships gliding by and the watermen plying their trade. Above all, she saw the unmistakeable and glowering profile of the Tar Man looking out over the city.

'Then why are you helping us?' demanded Peter.

'The Oracle has always been in my dreams. Her face has haunted me my whole life long.'

'The Oracle?'

The fortune-teller pointed at Kate. As she spoke her large eyes darted fitfully about as if she hardly dared even rest her gaze on this terrifying spectre of a girl. Her voice wavered. 'I was born with a gift to perceive echoes of what will come to pass but it is as nothing compared to the powers which will manifest themselves in you, my lady . . .'

'What do you mean?' asked Kate in alarm. 'What powers?'

'I'll wager you already have your suspicions . . . By rights I should pay you my respects as an apprentice would a master – save that in my dreams your arrival heralds destruction and despair. Tell me, I beg of you, my lady, is it the end of the world that I see?'

Kate looked at her companions in distress and shook her head.

'Stop calling me "My Lady"! I'm not your lady . . . I've no idea what you're talking about!'

'Then I can only pray that I have an imperfect understanding of my vision—'

The fortune-teller fell abruptly silent as a flamboyantly dressed group strolled by, talking loudly and passing around a basket filled with sweetmeats. One of the women wore her heavily powdered hair very high and it was dressed with tiny models of exotic birds, their blue and yellow plumage setting off the vivid hue of her silk dress, the colour of sunflowers. The wind had dropped a little since the party had arrived at Bartholomew Fair but now it was strengthening again and one of the little birds was blown off. The ladies and gentlemen paid scant attention to the party, even Gideon, whose face, as Hannah said, told an eloquent story. Soon the wind had blown the ladies and gentlemen on their way again and Kate, spying the little wooden bird lying in the mud, picked it up and held it tightly between the palms of her hands. When she stood up again she found the fortune-teller staring at her once more, seemingly mesmerised. 'I wish there were some greater service I could perform for you but the whereabouts of Master Blueskin will help you. Your fate is linked to his, although this is also, no doubt, already known to you.'

Peter did not try to hide his disbelief but let out a sharp cry as the woman grabbed hold of his wrist in her hot, dry hands. She was strong. She opened up his fingers and scrutinised his right palm, frowning in concentration. After a few seconds she let go of it as if what she saw was a disappointment to her. She turned her back on the party and they all saw her head suddenly droop.

'What is it, mistress?' It was Hannah who spoke. 'What did you see?'

The fortune-teller turned around slowly and faced Peter. 'You are her guardian but you will lose her. And yet you must hold on to her for as long as you can for all depends on it . . .'

Peter and Kate looked at each other in dismay, neither understanding, nor wanting to.

Finally the fortune-teller took Gideon's hand. 'Surely you do not need the word of a soothsayer to confirm the tie of blood. Your hand resembles Blueskin's.' Nodding towards Peter, she continued: 'Help the boy. He has need of you more than he knows.'

Through one bloodshot and horrified eye, Gideon returned the woman's searching stare. The woman's words caused ripples of distress to spread through the party, and before anyone spoke she vanished from sight, bowing her head to Kate as a mark of respect as she passed her.

After a prolonged pause Sir Richard roused himself. 'Ha! That woman is wasted in Bartholomew's Fair – she should be on the stage at Drury Lane at the very least . . .'

'Quite so, my dear fellow!' agreed the Parson as energetically as he could. 'She has a veritable talent for making the blood freeze! Besides, I fancy I caught a whiff of gin about her – doubtless she is intoxicated.'

'Come, my dear friends,' continued Sir Richard. 'Be not so downcast! Are we men of reason or do we jump at shadows in the dark? Come, let us return to Lincoln's Inn Fields. Supper and repose will quickly restore our spirits after such a night.'

'Ay,' said the Parson. 'Supper and repose. I shall make fine work tonight of Hannah's ox tongue, I promise you.'

Gideon unhooked his arms from his two companions and endeavoured to stand as tall as he could. 'Let Hannah return with the children, by all means, but how, my good sirs, can you think of abandoning our quest tonight? Blueskin holds every advantage! There is not a rogue in the city who would refuse him. Please, I beg of you, now that we know where he lives, and before the Tar Man disappears like woodsmoke into mist, let us pursue him while we may.'

'You're not leaving us behind!' cried Peter. 'And you can't go alone!'

'But if you are prepared to give credence to the woman on one point,' asked Sir Richard of Gideon, 'are you prepared to do so on another? Do you accept that you and the Tar Man might be brothers?'

Gideon looked at his hands. 'What say you, Mistress Kate? For this night you have had cause to observe the Tar Man at closer quarters than you should have liked.'

Kate cast a glance at Gideon's hands. She said nothing but Gideon read the expression on her face and she saw his agony as he contemplated the awful truth: the man he most despised and hated on this earth could also be his own flesh and blood.

Sir Richard looked over at the Parson. The latter nodded his head.

'Very well, if Mr Seymour insists on it, let us depart without delay.'

As the party began to walk slowly out of Bartholomew's Fair, scarcely noticing the wonders that had so struck them on their way in, Kate approached Parson Ledbury and pulled something from under her arm and handed it to him.

'Here's your wig, Parson. Everything else has gone wrong today but at least I found your wig.'

The Parson accepted her offering with quiet gratitude.

'My Mistress Dyer, you are ever full of surprises . . .'

CHAPTER NINE

The Splintering of Time

In which Anjali makes a decision, Sam wonders
if Kate is lost to him and the Marquis de
Montfaron watches ghosts on the internet

Vega Riaza, as Anjali still thought of the Tar Man, had secreted vast amounts of cash in the penthouse apartment in Docklands, more than enough for Tom's modest and Anjali's rather more exacting requirements. Tom had a talent for discovering these little stashes. He knew all the Tar Man's tricks. He found a fat roll of twenty-pound notes in the sugar, envelopes stuffed with tenners taped to the back of half of the kitchen drawers and, most satisfying of all, nearly seventy-five thousand pounds in six separate packets, slid up the back of the huge Italian sofa and the seam neatly re-sewn. Each time Tom found another secret store he would shout out, 'Pease Pudding! Pease Pudding!' – a habit which he had caught from the Carrick Gang because that's what they would eat after a good night's thieving. Then, with sparkling eyes, he would watch Anjali as she whooped with delight and threw armfuls of notes high into the air so that it rained down on her like giant confetti. But Anjali began to realise that what drove Tom to keep playing this game was not, in fact, the money but the excuse to spend a little time, in a manner of speaking, in his old master's company. It was plain, to Anjali at least, that Tom missed the Tar Man badly.

It therefore came as no surprise when, one fine summer night, while they were watching London's skyline blaze up into a violet sky, and Tom had regained his strength, he said: 'I do not belong here, Miss Anjali. I wish with all my heart that I could return to my own time.'

Anjali set fire to the corner of another ten-pound note and, leaning over the balcony so far that Tom got ready to grab her, she dropped it and watched the glowing fragments float down towards the dark river, leaving a brilliant, swirling trail until each tiny spark was extinguished.

Anjali closed her eyes and breathed in deeply. Her nostrils caught the acrid scent of burning. Then her eyelids flicked open and she turned to face Tom and asked: 'The girl you always go on about – the one with the machine who was good to you when she landed up in 1763. What was she called again?'

'Mistress Kate?'

'Yes. What was her surname?'

'Dyer.'

'I thought so. The helicopter pilot told me where he took Vega the day that he disappeared. *I* can't get you home, Tom, but I reckon I can take you to some people who might . . .'

Anjali spat out her chewing gum and threw it over the balcony.

'Ever been to Derbyshire?'

A kestrel hovered high above the stone farmhouse. Suddenly it made a vertiginous dive towards the lower pasture that bordered the stream where the Friesian cows were grazing. The valley was still green despite the dry summer. Sam, the second eldest of the six

Dyer children, sat at the kitchen table struggling over a maths worksheet. Through the open window his gaze followed the kestrel's trajectory. Its prey would be a field mouse, he guessed, or even a water vole. He wished he were with the others, gathering wood for the birthday bonfire. He wouldn't even have minded going to the airport with his dad to pick up Dr Pirretti. Sam hated being stuck inside. The distant baaing of lambs as they roamed the higher slopes beckoned him, as did the late-afternoon sunshine and the strong breeze gusting through the giant copper beech, a sound that always reminded him of breakers pounding the shore.

It was getting hotter. He hung over the windowsill above his mother's flower border, balancing on his belly, his feet leaving the floor and his arms stretched out in front of him. Bumblebees slipped drunkenly into snapdragons and emerged buzzing and sprinkled with yellow pollen. Presently his stomach began to hurt and he jumped back inside. Reluctantly he sat back down again at the table.

Sam was supposed to have loaded up the dishwasher but instead he had shoved everything up to one end of the long table. He helped himself to some cold chips and some more of the lemonade his mum had made for the barbecue. He took a gulp. It was so tart it made his mouth pucker and his eyes water. His brows knotted together as he tried and failed to remember how to do long division, and for the hundredth time his gaze left the worksheet and roved around the room instead. He looked at, without really seeing, the bright pictures stuck to the fridge with magnets and the jumble of birthday cards on the mantelpiece. There were so many Dyer children it always seemed to be someone's birthday. Even though Sam sometimes thought otherwise, birthdays weren't cancelled because something bad had happened to the family. And today happened to be Kate's birthday. Her thirteenth birthday.

Sam had been having extra lessons during the summer holidays because his grades had nosedived since his big sister's last disappearance. At first he had refused to go to school and then, when he did start classes again, he found that his concentration had been shot to pieces. If only Kate were here she would just give him the answers, he thought. She'd feel obliged to tell him he was stupid, too, of course, but that was okay.

A shard of sorrow stabbed at him. Despite everything his dad and Dr Pirretti and were doing to get the components to build another anti-gravity machine, Sam sometimes doubted that he would ever see his favourite sister again – although he would never give voice to his fears. It was an unspoken rule at the farm that you did not. But there were long, silent nights when his grief was so raw he would bury his head in his pillow, when the part of him that did not want to give up hope was overwhelmed by the part of him that needed to prepare for the worst. He was not sure whether that was somehow disloyal or cowardly or not the right way to think. But there it was – he could not help it. Who knew what the Tar Man had done to Kate and Peter once he had got them back to his lair in 1763 – and there was nothing anyone here could do about it.

To the rest of the world Kate was just another missing person – and since her disappearance the Dyer family had got to know just how many people do suddenly vanish, for all sorts of reasons, leaving their families in a state of perpetual limbo. All of which did not make this particular family's loss any easier to deal with. Perhaps in an effort to keep hold of her, Sam increasingly felt the urge to identify, as precisely as he could, that unique blend of qualities that made Kate Dyer who she was. Sam chose adjectives to describe her: brave, loyal, emotional, bright – in both senses of the word – impatient, determined . . . Absent she may have been, yet Kate's presence nevertheless roamed the corridors of his mind and would dart out unexpectedly: a swish of red hair, a shrill hoot of laughter, a wry look, her habit of pulling hats over faces, her undisputed ownership of the last spoonful of her favourite risotto. One bleak dawn Sam and Dr Dyer had emerged simultaneously, red-eyed, from their bedrooms, and in the instant that their gazes had crossed, each recognised what the other was feeling. Brother and father clung to each other briefly and had then returned to their respective rooms without exchanging a single word, for neither felt inclined to indulge in empty words of sympathy.

Sam jumped as someone rang the doorbell. As the only other person in the house was the Marquis de Montfaron – who was intent on catching up with two centuries of world knowledge in his father's study – Sam scraped his chair back over the red quarry tiles and got up to see who it was. But the Marquis had got to the entrance hall before him and, as he pulled open the door, Sam saw a girl's head appear, her blonde hair a luminous halo in the sunshine.

Kate's best friend Megan grinned at him. 'Hiya, Sam!' she called.

'Is it time for the bonfire already?' asked Sam. 'I've still got tons of maths to do! Mum'll kill me if I don't finish it.'

'No – the bonfire's not 'til six thirty. I wanted to come early. I'll give you a hand if you like . . .'

Sam's face lit up. 'Do you mean it?'

'I wouldn't have said if I didn't.' She looked up at Montfaron who towered above her, his hair scraping against the top of the door frame. 'Good afternoon, Monsieur le Mar-r-rquis de Montfar-r-ron!'

Megan rolled her r's just as Montfaron had taught her to do. Parisians, he said, would frown at such a pronunciation but his ancestors came from the sunny south and he was proud of his origins.

'*Tr-r-r-rès, tr-r-r-rès bien*, mademoiselle. Your pronunciation improves by the day. Br-r-ravo!' said Montfaron, taking hold of Megan's hand and kissing it because it amused him when she blushed. He bowed ostentatiously, knocking his head on the wall of the narrow hallway as he did so.

'This charming dwelling,' he said, rubbing the top of his head, 'would be greatly improved by a little judicious expansion . . .'

The Marquis made a show of placing the flat of his hands on each wall and pushing with all of his might until his face went red. When he heard a sound suspiciously like cracking plaster from beneath the old wallpaper, he stopped suddenly, and a guilty smile grew on his face.

'*Quelle horreur!* Demolishing the *salle d'entrée* of my most generous hosts is an unfortunate way to show my gratitude . . .'

'Don't worry,' said Sam. 'I'll tell Mum that Dad did it – she won't say anything then.'

The Marquis ruffled Sam's hair. 'An excellent stratagem, *mon cher ami*! Although, *hélas*, one untruth inevitably leads to another . . .'

Sam blinked as the hall light flashed on and off, on and off, on and off. Montfaron forced himself to remove his hand from the switch and sighed appreciatively. 'You, who take it for granted, like rain falling from the skies, cannot imagine how I *adore* electricity . . .'

'No need to panic,' laughed Megan, examining the wall. 'You can't see anything. The plaster's all lumpy anyway.'

When he had first appeared at the farmhouse with Kate and Peter's father, Megan had taken an instant liking to the charming Marquis de Montfaron. He had looked around him at the twenty-first-century kitchen with eyes that sparkled with wonder and excitement. Such vivid, intelligent eyes – large, and the precise shade that conkers have when they are freshly burst from their prickly shell and are still a waxy, mahogany brown. Not to mention his exquisite clothes! Even little Milly had been so fascinated by his embroidered waistcoat, buckled shoes and lace cuffs that she had clung to him like a limpet, refusing to climb off his knee and jealously fending off all rivals for his attention. But even now, in Dr Dyer's jumpers and some jeans loaned to him by Sergeant Chadwick, and with his black and silver hair tied back in a rubber band dropped by the postman, the six-foot-six Marquis still cut a striking figure. Sam and Megan both agreed that for a scientist-philosopher escaped from the French Revolution, the Marquis de Montfaron was the least boring grown-up they had ever come across.

'Have you learned any more amazing facts today, Monsieur le Mar-r-rquis?' asked Megan.

'Ha! I am *drowning* in an ocean of knowledge. My jaw *aches* from dropping in astonishment. I cannot sleep for I do not know how much time remains to me to acquire this mountain of wisdom. The one thing I *do* know is that I shall never come to the end of it.'

'Well, two centuries is a long time,' agreed Sam. 'It took me long enough to catch up after I had six weeks off school—'

'Is it such a long time? I am not far short of fifty years old – it is but four of my lifetimes. And yet, it seems to me that the *accumulation* and *acceleration* of knowledge in that time is *stupendous*! *Miraculous!* Man has stepped on the moon! Surgeons operate on patients without them feeling any pain! Aeroplanes carry people to the other side of the world in less than a day. Until I arrived in your century I fancied myself a scholar and a scientist. Now, I hardly dare open a book, so terrified am I that it will make a nonsense of things I have spent half a lifetime learning.'

'Why don't you give yourself a day off, then?' asked Sam.

Montfaron sucked his breath in and shook his head. 'Ah, *non*,' he said, 'I cannot rest. This effort is as nothing compared to its reward. For is there anything of greater value to mankind than *knowledge*? Even if Time will make fools of us all in the end.'

'When you return to your own century, will you keep this knowledge to yourself?' asked Megan. 'Because . . . well, you could cause a real mess if you didn't . . .'

'An excellent question, mademoiselle. If ever I manage to return to the past I shall consider that potential dilemma most carefully. Until then, *Je me livre en aveugle au destin qui m'entraîne* – I shall submit myself blindly to whatever fate has in store for me.'

'So what *did* you find out today, then?' asked Sam.

'For pity's sake,' exclaimed the Marquis, covering his face with his hands. 'Do not ask me to repeat it! My addled brain shall explode!'

Sam and Megan laughed.

'I *shall* tell you one thing, however. Your father, Sam, advised me – and with perfect logic – that I should become familiar with the discoveries of the nineteenth century before I proceed to the twentieth century and, thence, to the new millennium. So I have begun to study the work of a certain Charles Darwin and I confess that the gentleman's theory of natural selection has profoundly shaken me.'

Sam nudged Megan. 'Is Darwin the one who invented evolution?'

'I think so . . .'

'We've got a cow named after his granddad, or uncle, or something – Erasmus Darwin,' said Sam.

It was Montfaron's turn to laugh but Sam suddenly looked upset.

'Erasmus is Kate's favourite cow . . . She always says she's jealous of her eyelashes.'

The Marquis gave Sam a gentle pat on his back. 'I have witnessed your sister's strength of character,' he said. 'And have I not described to you what courage she showed in rescuing us from the chalk mines of Arras? Now I do not say that this is the best of all possible worlds, my dear Sam, but it is right to live in hope and something tells me that your sister's role in all of this is far from over.'

Sam nodded his head but still looked fixedly at the floor.

Megan took hold of his hand and squeezed it. 'You know Kate – she's a match for that stupid Tar Man. She'll be all right – don't you worry, Sam.'

Sam looked up at his two companions and forced a smile.

'Well, *mes chers enfants*, with your kind permission, I must take my leave of you and return, like Sisyphus, to my never-ending labours.'

Megan frowned. 'Sisyphus? Isn't that a disease?'

'Ah, *non*, mademoiselle! Sisyphus offended Zeus, the father of the gods. His punishment was to push a boulder up a steep hill. Each time the poor fellow was within reach of the top it would roll down and he would have to start all over again, and again, and again – for all eternity . . .'

The Marquis screwed up his face as he mimed pushing his own boulder towards Dr Dyer's study but Megan stopped him.

'Sir – before you go, I think there's something here that you might like to see. It's so . . . I don't know to explain it . . . it's amazing and weird!'

Sam and the Marquis looked on as Megan fished out her mobile phone from the pocket of her jeans and flipped it open.

'Look!' she exclaimed. 'My cousin sent it just now. I mean it wasn't even dark – it was in the middle of the day.'

Sam peered at it. 'Wow!'

The Marquis squinted but the moving image was a little too small for him to see without a magnifying glass.

'We can look at it on Dr Dyer's computer if you like,' said Megan. 'He said he's posted it on the internet, as well.'

Dr and Mrs Dyer had purposefully delayed showing the Marquis de Montfaron how to use a computer.

'One step at a time,' Dr Dyer had said to his enthusiastic, eighteenth-century guest. 'Not ten all at once.'

But now the Marquis stood behind Megan, looking over her shoulder in wonder as the screen came to life. His eyes darted from Megan's hand, sliding a perturbing object around on the table, to the screen and back again. Suddenly he got very excited.

'I see it! I understand!' He put his hand over Megan's. 'You will permit me?'

Megan nodded and the Marquis slid the mouse a little to the left.

'Ha! Look!' Montfaron shouted triumphantly. 'I can control the arrow!'

Megan and Sam, who was kneeling down next to her, looked at each other and smirked.

'I'll show you how to use it later, if you like,' said Megan. 'It's dead easy once you get used to it. But let me get onto the internet first. There's something you've got to see.'

Reluctantly, Montfaron removed his hand from the mouse but his pleading look made her relent.

'Oh, all right,' said Megan, 'I'll show you something else. I think this will be useful for you.'

Montfaron tried to follow what Megan was doing as she moved her hand in seemingly random circles, clicking the mouse as she went.

'This,' she said, pointing to a box on the screen, 'is a search engine.'

Montfaron looked at it sceptically and shrugged.

'You can find out pretty much anything you want to know in the whole world using this. Pictures, too. What can I ask? Mmm . . . Sam, help me out, here. Something that the Marquis would recognise . . .'

'Where did you live?'

'Brilliant! Yes! Where did you live, in France, Monsieur le Mar-r-rquis?'

The Marquis looked at Megan quizzically. 'Why, the Chateau de l'Humiaire, near Arras . . .'

'Okay. Type in the name here. You see the letters on the keyboard? Just press them one at a time until you've keyed in the name.'

The Marquis held down the first letter for too long and a whole string of c's appeared. Megan showed him the backspace key and, painfully slowly, the Marquis found all the letters and typed in the full name.

'Now,' ordered Megan, 'press the Enter key, look this big one here . . .'

The Marquis did as he was told and observed the screen as dozens of thumbnail images instantly appeared of a beautiful castle surrounded by a moat and an orchard of fruit trees. The photographs were all in black and white, but there was also an old oil painting and several tinted engravings. Megan clicked on one of the photographs and the image of Montfaron's old home filled the screen. In the middle distance, stooping over a beehive under the fruit trees, they saw a lady dressed in a long and very full dress that was cinched in tight at the waist. She wore a large, veiled hat. Megan looked up at the Marquis de Montfaron. He seemed dumbfounded, awestruck.

'But . . . How can this be? How did all these images of my house get into this com . . . com . . .'

'Computer,' prompted Sam as the Marquis peered under the desk and then leaned over the top of the PC, scrutinising the desk behind for evidence of piles of pictures.

'Oh,' said Megan, '*everything* gets put onto the internet now. Photographs and videos and books and music – it's all in there. Unbelievable amounts of information. I mean, I bet there's more information than a human being could sift through in a thousand lifetimes.'

'A million,' said Sam.

Megan shrugged. 'Maybe.'

The Marquis de Montfaron pointed in consternation at the computer. 'But all that information, it is *in there*?'

Sam and Megan both burst out laughing.

'No!' said Sam. 'It's on the internet!'

'Then where is the internet?'

Megan and Sam looked at each other, less sure of their ground.

'I think it's held on servers,' said Megan. 'All over the world . . .'

'*Servants* hold this information?'

'No! Ser-*vers*!'

The Marquis shook his head. 'I cannot understand . . .'

'Don't worry about it,' said Sam. 'I don't either. Most people don't. I'd just go with it if I were you. It's like cars. You don't have to understand how they work before you can ride in one . . .'

'Anyway,' said Megan, 'the important thing is that anyone can do a search on it to find stuff out. You just need a browser – like this one. Good, isn't it?'

But, to Megan and Sam's distress, they saw that the Marquis's warm brown eyes were brimful of tears. He felt obliged to turn away from the image of the Château de l'Humiaire.

'Oh, that was so stupid of me!' exclaimed Megan. 'I'm so sorry. You must miss your home and your family . . .'

'When we were not at Versailles, it was our home – at least before the troubles began . . . But for me, it was, above all, where I tried to understand the world.'

'It looks really nice,' offered Sam. 'Better than our farm!'

'Ah, *non*. This farm is a good place. A good home. Alas, my most recent memory of *my* home was of a bonfire, started by fools who knew no better. A bonfire that consumed a lifetime's corre-spondence. *Decades* of reflection and debate – with the great minds of Europe – destroyed, mindlessly, in moments.'

'I'm sorry,' said Megan. 'Kate told me. Those letters must have been really important to you.'

'They were irreplaceable; they were my children, as surely as Louis-Philippe is my son. I guarded the ideas that they contained for posterity. I slept with them under my pillow . . . And now? Ashes, nothing but ashes. I have not yet had time to grieve for such a bitter loss. I regret, mademoiselle, that sometimes the heart reacts more quickly than the mind.'

'I'm so sorry,' murmured Megan.

'No. No. In point of fact, your example demonstrated *perfectly* this astonishing tool. I should very much desire to investigate it further.' The Marquis forced himself to smile. 'And I wonder if this attractive lady in the hat belongs to my bloodline . . . You say that you can find out *anything*? *Anyone* can find out *anything*?'

'Well, most things. I think so,' said Megan, looking up anx-iously at Montfaron. 'Do you want to see some other stuff, to give you more of an idea?'

Montfaron nodded. 'By all means.'

For the next few minutes the computer screen burned bright with images: galaxies at the other side of the universe; trailers for Hollywood films; white sandy beaches on the Isle of Mull; an ice cream maker's blog from Naples; train times for the T.G.V.

between Marseilles and Paris; a jerky film of a band playing at last year's Glastonbury Festival; a tug of war between lions and crocodiles for a baby buffalo; slot machines in Las Vegas; the structure of the atom; recipes for clam chowder; a webcam pointed at an office's coffee machine in Sydney; weather forecasts for the Arctic and Mombasa; Sam's horoscope; CNN; an Oxford college's reading list for students studying quantum physics. Montfaron stood stooped over the desk, shaking his head.

'Enough! I grow dizzy!'

Megan's fingers returned obediently to her lap.

'If only Diderot, and all those men of reason who put their faith in knowledge, and who battled so hard against ignorance and superstition, could see what I am privileged now to see. If only they could have seen where their efforts would lead. A society that gives to *all* men, no matter how humble, access to such knowledge is surely a society that has learned the true nature of Equality. What name did you give to this tool?'

'The internet.'

'Then this *internet* is surely the eighth wonder of the world!' Montfaron exclaimed.

The children were unused to seeing the Marquis so emotional. Sam felt he should say something. 'The internet *is* useful,' he said. 'Mum orders the weekly shopping on it and I know I shouldn't but I'm always pasting bits from it into my homework. Instant messaging's good, too . . . And there's some great games . . .'

Montfaron and Sam looked at each other but neither had anything but the haziest notion of what was passing through the other's mind. There was such a long pause that Megan only just stopped herself commenting that the lack of colour photographs of the Château de l'Humiaire suggested that it was no longer standing.

'Anyway,' said Megan after a long silence. 'I was going to show you the video that my cousin has taken . . .'

The grainy moving image was of poor quality, particularly when viewed on full-screen. The sound, too, left much to be desired. This did not detract, however, from the astounding subject matter. They watched it five times and were still looking at it when Mrs Dyer, along with Sam's youngest sister, Milly, came back to collect the food for the bonfire.

'Where have you got to, Sam?' his mum shouted. 'I thought you were supposed to be doing your maths! And why haven't you cleared the kitchen table like I asked you?'

'Mum! Mum!' he shouted back. 'We're in Dad's study. Come and look at this! You've never seen anything like it!'

Mrs Dyer watched the video in rapt attention. Then she asked Megan to go to the BBC homepage where they found links to many other images and videos revealing the same compelling, inexplicable and terrifying event, all of which had been posted in the last couple of hours.

Moments later they heard the Land Rover pull up in the drive. Dr Dyer had arrived back from Manchester Airport with Dr Pirretti. Currently suspended from her post at NASA, it was Dr Pirretti who had led the anti-gravity research project which Kate's dad had worked on, the project which, unwittingly, had sent Kate and Peter hurtling back through the centuries. Normally courteous to a fault, on this occasion Dr Pirretti barely uttered a word of greeting but planted herself instantly in front of the computer screen and all but snatched the mouse from Megan's grasp.

'What in the world is happening?' exclaimed Dr Dyer. 'They even interrupted "The Afternoon Play" on the radio with a news-flash. Not that the reporter was making a whole lot of sense . . .'

'We heard there'd been no reports of injuries,' interrupted Dr Pirretti. 'Is that right? No buildings collapsing, gas mains exploding . . .?'

'No. Nothing like that,' said Mrs Dyer. 'They said there'd been a few road accidents. Nothing serious. I mean, who could concentrate on their driving with all that happening?'

Dr Dyer looked over Dr Pirretti's shoulder and shook his head in disbelief. 'What *is* it?'

The clearest image had been taken from a helicopter hovering over the city of London, close to Tower Bridge. The aerial view displayed London in all her sprawling glory, square mile after square mile of urban proliferation, a maze of streets with a few arterial roads cutting through the city. There were the familiar, winding curves of the Thames, snaking her way across the capital towards the sea. There were the Houses of Parliament and, just visible in the east, the Docklands. Waterloo Bridge, the South Bank complex and the Gherkin were also easily discernible. However, at first sight at least, one portion of the city did not appear to be in focus. It was as if someone had wiped a cloth over a wet painting and the image had become smeared and a fraction lighter in tone. The segment measured roughly a mile by perhaps three hundred metres and it included the Millennium Bridge that spans that particular stretch of the Thames. Neither St Paul's Cathedral nor Tate Modern were any longer visible under this gigantic, elongated, smeary mass. As the cameraman zoomed in it became increasingly difficult to interpret the images, in part because the lens was shaking so much. What started off looking like billowing clouds was not. Rather, it was an accumulation or gathering together of perpetually moving, indistinct shapes that swirled and dispersed and came together again like high tide in a rock pool. Over and above the alarmed exclamations of the cameraman and the *wup, wup, wup* of the helicopter, a great roaring could be heard, a roar like the ocean, or the first grumblings of a giant storm.

As the cameraman succeeded in drawing closer to the phenomenon, it became clear that a line bisected this strange mass. The line appeared as a kind of ravine, or a giant crack in the city, and at first sight it seemed to reach deep into the earth's crust save that buildings and red double-decker buses and black cabs were visible. These familiar London vehicles were not, however, distinct. It was a little like looking at objects which have been submerged in a fair depth of water – their forms ebbed and flowed in reaction to some gigantic, unseen force.

'I've spent time in the Sahara Desert,' said Dr Pirretti. 'And if I didn't know better, I'd say that I was looking at a mirage . . . Except that's impossible . . .'

At first, the circle of people gathered around the computer screen had watched in fascination but soon a creeping horror overtook them. The most terrifying moving images had been sent to the BBC's website from an office worker's mobile phone. The undulating, echoing, unworldly sounds that he had recorded cast terror into everyone's hearts. Figures appeared and disappeared, vivid one moment and hazy the next, like ghosts in mist, figures not only from our century but from *all* centuries. There was an old gentleman in a three-cornered hat, his mouth gaping open in horror, clutching to his chest a small white dog with a black spot over one eye. Then, running as if death itself was upon him, a Roman soldier, breastplate gleaming, stared through the centuries with terrified eyes. Two horses, pulling an ornate carriage, reared up, their hooves pawing the air. A woman in a lavender crinoline stood stock-still, her pale face betraying no emotion while a young child in knickerbockers buried his face in her skirts.

'Could it be some kind of mass hallucination?' asked Mrs Dyer. 'I mean, it only lasted two or three minutes . . .'

Dr Dyer scratched his head. 'A mass hallucination? How would that work? But if it's not a mirage and we're not hallucinating, what could it be? What's your take on this, Anita?'

Dr Pirretti merely looked straight ahead, deep in thought.

'We're seeing ghosts, aren't we?' said Megan. 'What else *could* it be? It's a massive sighting of ghosts!'

Mrs Dyer shut down the computer. Milly, who was gripping her father's desk with her plump fingers, suddenly started to cry, her chest heaving in sudden, juddering sobs. Her father scooped her up and bounced her gently up and down until she returned his smile. The room went suddenly quiet. The floral print curtain flapped in the warm breeze and the sounds of summer drifted through the window: birdsong and crickets and the buzzing of insects. Megan looked over at Sam and saw that he was clenching his fists tight together. He seemed to be holding in his breath. A deep crease had formed between his eyebrows and he was trembling. Megan touched Sam's arm.

'Are you okay?' she whispered.

But he did not reply. His eyes burned into his father and Dr Pirretti. 'You started all this!' he suddenly exploded. 'Why did you have to mess with stuff even you don't understand? You're supposed to be experts but you're not! Now there's . . . weird earthquakes . . . and ghosts! The whole world's been damaged! And you don't even know how to get Kate back, do you?'

Sam didn't wait for a reply but ran out of his father's study slamming the door behind him. They heard him thunder up the rickety wooden staircase to his bedroom and then there was a second, muffled slam and the squeal of bedsprings as he threw himself onto his bed. His mother and father stared blankly at each other.

'I'll go to him,' murmured Mrs Dyer in a flat voice.

'No. Best let him calm down first.'

Dr Pirretti let out a deep sigh. 'Sam's right, of course. We couldn't be certain that producing anti-gravity was risk-free. But still we went ahead . . .'

'Madame,' said the Marquis de Montfaron. 'Surely it is the pursuit of knowledge that makes us human? What has ever been achieved without taking risks?'

'Thank you, sir, although right now that is of little comfort. You talk about the pursuit of knowledge which puts me in mind of a phrase in the Declaration of Independence – a document, written at the birth of my country, which talks about a person's rights to—'

'I know of it, madame. Benjamin Franklin spoke of it to me in Paris.'

'My, my! You are full of surprises, Monsieur le Marquis! You actually *knew* Ben Franklin?'

'I did. After all, we French emptied our coffers helping the American Patriots win their independence – although I admit that our rivalry with the British might have had something to do with it.' The Marquis gave a small bow in the direction of Dr and Mrs Dyer. 'It goes without saying that I, personally, have always found the British a *charming* nation.'

Dr Pirretti smiled. 'Then you'll know that the Declaration upholds all men's unalienable right to *Life, Liberty and the Pursuit of Happiness*.'

Montfaron nodded. 'A most memorable turn of phrase – and with much wisdom therein . . .'

'I agree. But isn't it the case that the pursuit of knowledge, *our* pursuit of knowledge, our *appetite* for pushing scientific knowledge to its limits, our discovery of time travel, in particular, just tramples all over everyone else's basic human rights?'

'Oh, *please*!' snapped Dr Dyer. 'This is hardly the moment for a philosophical discussion!'

'On the contrary, my friend,' said the Marquis, 'a crisis of this magnitude surely demands that we listen both to our minds and our hearts . . . Science is not immune from the laws of ethics.'

'Well, *my* heart and *my* mind,' exclaimed Dr Dyer, 'say the same thing – that we've got to find a way to get Kate and Peter back as soon as possible before who knows what else happens! Right now, debating the rights and wrongs of all this falls so far back down the line of *my* list of priorities, it's out of sight.'

The Marquis de Montfaron took hold of Dr Dyer's shoulder. 'Courage, my friend. Courage. Do not lose hope, all yet may be well.'

Mrs Dyer, if not her husband, smiled at him.

'Sam is right about something else, too,' said Dr Pirretti. 'Or at least he wasn't so very far off. I've been warned that this would happen . . .'

'You've been warned?' said Dr Dyer. 'Ah, this would be your *other* self, speaking to you from a parallel universe . . .'

Mrs Dyer gave her husband a sharp look. 'Andrew—'

'It's okay,' said Dr Pirretti to Mrs Dyer. 'It's a scientist's duty to be sceptical. But, as it happens, yes, I *have* been warned that the proliferation of parallel worlds caused by time travel is beginning to damage the time mantle. I believe we have just witnessed a time quake . . .'

'A *time quake*!' repeated Megan.

'Yes, though I suspect this wasn't the first and it won't be the last . . .'

CHAPTER TEN

A Curious Duet

In which Peter vows to do his best for his friends
and the party makes the acquaintance of a singing dog

Leaving St Bartholomew's Fair was a frustrating process, for the surrounding roads were still, even at this hour, jammed with carriages and sedan chairs. Yet at least the flaming torches carried by the revellers allowed them to see where they were going. Once they drew closer to St Paul's Cathedral even the bright moon, three-quarters full, did little to lighten the darkness of the narrow medieval streets. Here, Sir Richard took the reins while his driver walked ahead, the rumble of the carriage announcing their arrival as clear as any bugle call to the army of throat-slitting rogues that, in the wretched driver's mind, lurked in every shadow ready to run him through with a dagger – or worse. He held up his lantern and peered anxiously into the darkness, starting at every shop sign swinging and creaking in the strong wind and at every rat that scuttled across the cobbles into the foul-smelling gutters. From time to time a noise would make the driver stop in his tracks and he would grab hold of the bridle of the leader horse until the sweating animals drew to a standstill, their eyes rolling and their ears pricked, probing the stillness of the night-bound city. At such moments it seemed that animals and men were holding their breath, straining to hear whispers drifting from an alleyway or the sound of footfall. Once they heard sudden, raucous laughter that reverberated through the maze of streets and echoed like a pistol shot across St Paul's churchyard.

Peter sat between Hannah and a sleeping Kate and both held on to him. Hannah's hand was warm and solid but Kate's fingers scarcely left any impression. They felt cool and insubstantial, as if the laws of gravity no longer acted on her in the same way. What would happen if Kate kept on fading? And even if they managed to get her home, *could* she get better? What if she were permanently *damaged*?

'You must be chilled, Master Peter!' exclaimed Hannah as she felt him shudder. 'Here, let me wrap my shawl around you.'

Peter thanked Hannah as she struggled to cover him, for it was so dark inside the carriage that she could not see her hand in front of her face. Peter felt coarse wool brush against his skin. They lapsed into silence once more. Peter suspected that if what was happening to Kate were happening to him instead, he would not have coped as well as she had. She was brave, much braver than he was. He wondered how he would have reacted if the Tar Man had threatened to cut *his* fingers off.

Invisible in the inky blackness, Gideon moaned in his sleep. It would be better for Gideon, he thought, if the Tar Man *did* manage to elude them once more, for he was in no shape for another encounter with his elder brother. Gideon had done so much for them and yet he had never asked for anything in return. As the horses trotted on through the empty streets, the weight of responsibility slowly settled on Peter's shoulders. He sensed Kate's ephemeral touch on his arm and listened to Gideon's laboured breathing. Peter made his friends a silent promise in the dark. *I won't let you down.*

It was almost midnight when, to the driver's amazement, they emerged unscathed from the maze of streets below St Paul's and came to a halt on the moonlit waterfront. Now they would continue their search on foot.

'The Thames, the Thames!' called out Parson Ledbury. 'Never was I better pleased to smell its stink. I hope from my soul that the fortune-teller has not sent us on a fool's errand! Come, Mr Seymour, rouse yourself! We cannot idle here!'

Gideon groaned and Peter started to disentangle himself from Hannah and the still-sleeping Kate whose fingers he gently unpeeled, one by one. When Peter had extricated himself from her grasp she rolled over to one side, tangling her legs in her long skirts. A shaft of moonlight cut through the darkness of the carriage and the state of Kate's, dirty, swollen and bleeding feet was suddenly revealed. Why hadn't she said something?

'Hannah, look.'

'What is it, Master Peter?'

He pointed to Kate's feet.

Hannah gasped. 'What has happened to her shoes?'

'It was the Tar Man – he stole them.'

'He is a *wicked* man,' said Hannah with feeling, 'to take the shoes of a sick young girl.' She peered at the soles of Kate's feet. 'I shall need to bathe and bind them – not that there's anything to be done until we return to Lincoln's Inn Fields.'

Hannah propped Kate up in the corner of the carriage and covered her with the shawl. She rested her hand tenderly on Kate's head. 'She is in a deep sleep. I think it is best we do not waken the poor soul. I shall stay with her.'

Gideon was now awake; he sucked his breath in through his teeth as he tried to find the least painful way to manoeuvre himself out of the carriage. He looked over at Kate as, wincing with every movement, he finally managed to get down. 'Let her sleep while she can,' he whispered to Hannah. 'She has been through enough for one night.'

'And she is not alone in that!' said Hannah softly as she caught sight of Gideon's eye. The flesh around it was now so swollen the lid had completely closed.

Peter glanced at Kate's pale face as he followed Gideon out of the carriage. I know she prefers being with me at the moment, he reasoned, but I'm not leaving her on her own: Hannah will be with her . . . and I've got to look out for Gideon, too. Besides, he thought, while she's asleep Kate won't know whether I'm here or not.

It was good to be out of the stuffy carriage and, as rivers draw the eye and soothe the soul, Peter stood for a time watching the moonlight dance on the water. Fast-moving currents and swirling eddies corrugated its surface while, directly below him, gentle waves lapped against the quayside where a line of barges was moored. The wind drove them incessantly one against the other so that a succession of hollow, percussive sounds rang out towards the opposite bank like irregular drumbeats. He watched a handful of small ferry-boats, their lanterns reflected in the black water, picking their way precariously through the currents from Bankside. They bobbed up and down on the waves, dwarfed by two sailing ships, anchored for the night, whose masts creaked and groaned in the wind.

Parson Ledbury cleared his throat noisily and stretched. 'And now to find that slippery brother of yours, Mr Seymour—'

'I have already told you that he is no brother of mine!'

'All families have their black sheep, Mr Seymour. You must not permit the existence of a freshly acquired relative to trouble your peace of mind, unsavoury though he is. Besides, what is the purpose of a sibling if not to vex us?'

'And the same could be said of parsons!' quipped Sir Richard. 'The relationship is not yet proven.'

Gideon looked so put out that Peter felt he should say something. 'Even if the Tar Man is your brother – and I'm not saying he is – but even if he is, it doesn't change anything. You're still the same person. You're still Gideon Seymour.'

Gideon met Peter's gaze but did not trust himself to reply.

'I mean,' said Peter, 'no one's going to make you go round to the Tar Man's house for tea every Sunday or anything.'

Even over Parson Ledbury's laughter Peter could hear Gideon's sharp intake of breath.

'I didn't mean to—'

'Best not to say any more,' whispered Sir Richard into Peter's ear.

Peter walked over to look at the boats while Gideon, Sir Richard and the Parson pored over the fortune-teller's map trying to work out the whereabouts of the Tar Man's lodgings. He looked down at the river flowing quickly past him. Sometimes this century really got to him. Mostly he avoided thinking in that way because it was pointless, but everything was so *primitive*. Everything took so *long*. How difficult could it be to find the Tar Man, for crying out loud? For a boy born into an age when information travels at the speed of light, it was cruelly hard at times to accept that in this century news could only travel as fast as the fleetest horse. Scotland could have sunk into the sea and all its inhabitants been consumed by dinosaurs yet it would still be three or four days before anyone in London even heard a whisper of it. Even if someone spotted the Tar Man in the next street, by the time news got back to them he'd be far away. A niggling doubt crept, uninvited, into the back of his mind, as it occasionally did. A persistent, negative voice taunted him: *you're going to be stuck here for ever just like your alternative self and there's nothing that you or Kate or Gideon or anyone back home can do about it.*

A random memory of home – the soft glow of street lamps on Richmond Green, shining through thin, striped curtains – reminded him how badly he missed *electricity*. He closed his eyes and pictured that other, illuminated London, *his* London, ablaze with a million lights, like a gigantic flare sent up from an ocean of darkness, announcing our presence to the universe. Whenever his dad took him into the city they would never take the tube from Waterloo station but would always catch a black cab so they could see his favourite view of the city from the bridge. He could hear his father saying to him – Look, Peter, look around you! Where else in the world would you rather be? Then Peter opened his eyes again. How dark it was in comparison. And yet he knew that this younger, smaller city was the parent of the London that was to come.

Suddenly he became aware of raised voices.

'Hold the lantern still,' cried Sir Richard to the driver, trying to marry up the fortune-teller's map with the rows of neat terraced houses, some whitewashed and some red-brick, that jutted onto the cobbled quayside. He screwed up his eyes. 'I cannot make it out. What say you, Parson? Has the fortune-teller deceived us?'

'I pictured some hideous hovel, dripping with slime and damp,' said Parson Ledbury. 'These are respectable dwellings . . . I fear that the wretched woman is in the pay of the Tar Man.'

'What's to be done?' exclaimed Sir Richard angrily. 'Even if the woman did not set out to deceive us her map is useless. The Tar Man could be hiding in any one of these houses!'

'Ssssshhh!'

Gideon put a finger to his lips. He looked around as if he were listening for something. The Parson took out his pistol and started to tiptoe away from the river and towards the impenetrable black shadows behind them. Gideon, Peter and Sir Richard followed.

It was Peter who spotted it first. 'There's nothing to be scared of – it's a dog! It's just a little dog!'

'Peter! Wait!' shouted Gideon in alarm.

But Peter had already plunged into an alleyway between the rows of houses. A moment later he reappeared carrying a small white dog with a black patch over one eye which he deposited gently onto the cobblestones. The animal stood wagging its stumpy tail and observed the party expectantly. The Parson leaned over, picked up the dog by the scruff of its neck and lifted it up to eye level. The creature let out a strangulated growl while its short legs kicked back and forth in mid-air like a clockwork toy running down.

'I'll thank you, gentlemen, to unhand my dog!' cried a croaky voice from within the shadows.

The Parson dropped the dog like a hot coal and all eyes followed the indistinct white shape as it scampered, whimpering, back into the shadows.

'Show yourself, sir!' roared the Parson. 'I do not care to be addressed by a fellow that cowers up an alley!'

Presently an old gentleman, thin and bent, shuffled into view. He held a cane in one hand and clamped the dog protectively to his chest with the other.

'You do not have the look of robbers,' the old man said, peering out at them.

'Indeed, we are *not* robbers,' said Sir Richard stepping forward. 'And we are gratified to discover that nor are you a member of that profession! May we wish you a good evening, sir.'

Sir Richard went on to introduce himself and the other members of the party, and once the old gentleman had satisfied himself that he had nothing to fear from them, his countenance relaxed. 'I am your humble servant, my good sirs,' he said, inclining his head in a small bow. 'Robbers cause me no anxiety, I assure you. See, I have a fearsome array of weapons with which to defend myself!'

He deposited the dog on the floor in order to open his frayed brocade jacket, revealing two pistols, a piece of rope and a dagger which he pulled out of their respective pockets and replaced one by one.

'Upon my word,' said Sir Richard. 'I pity the villain that attempts to deprive you of your purse. Are you then in the habit of taking the air at this late hour?'

'I am, good sir, indeed I am. Toby prefers the night to the day and as he is such a remarkable animal I like to humour him.'

The old man scooped up the dog from the ground. 'I have children and grandchildren aplenty – and a wife besides – but Toby is better company than any of them.'

'If only we could all be blessed with such an animal,' said Parson Ledbury, 'we should be spared the inconvenience of finding human company.'

'You mock me, sir, I know,' said the old man good-humouredly, 'and yet I am not about to deprive myself of diversion and affection because my companion happens to have four legs. He is an admirable singer, don't you know.'

'Your dog sings?!' exclaimed Peter.

'Faith, Toby sings like an angel in heaven,' said the old man. 'I assure you he needs naught but a little encouragement to set him off. Come, Toby, let us give these gentleman a tune:

The heavy hours are almost past, that part my love and me;

My longing eyes may hope at last their only wish to see.'

The old gentleman's voice was dry as dust, but he could hold a tune. As the old gentleman repeated the refrain, the dog, cradled in its owner's arms, obligingly started to sing. Peter laughed out loud for the voice that came from its white and clean-angled jaws was at once melodious as well as uncannily human.

'Watch out!' Peter screamed all at once.

Instinctively Gideon ducked and only just in time. Out of nowhere a tin bucket filled with slops crashed and splattered onto the cobbles at their feet. The impact echoed over the river and caused the dog to bark wildly. All looked up and flickering candlelight appeared in several windows. A dark figure leaned out of a window a couple of houses away.

'God's teeth,' the figure bellowed, his face obscured by the night. 'Can a man not find repose in his own home without having to listen to such caterwauling? Get you gone before I come down to knock your brains from your heads!'

The window slammed shut and Peter, Gideon, the Parson and Sir Richard exchanged incredulous looks. Large smiles spread over all their faces.

'Why so cheerful, my good sirs, after such a rude outburst?' asked the old gentleman.

'Let us just say,' said Sir Richard, 'that your dog appears to have a talent for ferreting out rats. Toby has rendered us a most valuable service: he has found him whom we seek.'

CHAPTER ELEVEN

These Are the Times that Try Men's Souls

In which Lord Luxon encounters
George Washington and marvels
at the power of the written word

Lord Luxon contemplated the tall, quiet figure who stood some fifty yards downstream. General Washington wrapped his cloak about him against the savage winter storm, all his energy and all his will focussed on transporting the remnants of his army across the ice-choked river. Unaccustomed to physical discomfort of any kind – other than the consequences of drinking too much wine – Lord Luxon nevertheless willingly endured this icy vigil. His mind and body were on full alert; every nerve tingled with excitement; never had he felt more *alive*, for tonight he would decide the manner in which he would leave his mark on the world.

Can it really be true, he thought, that here, in this place, the future of America is balanced on a knife-edge? All at once Lord Luxon questioned Alice's counterfactual advice, for how could the fate of such a powerful nation hinge on the outcome of one reckless attempt to cross a river? What unique circumstances had contrived to bring history to its tipping point on the banks of the Delaware on

Christmas night, 1776? Looking out at the desperate scene playing out before him, Lord Luxon was struck by the yawning gap between Alice's bare description of the event and the urgent, chaotic reality. He even felt a twinge of compassion for the ragged American Patriots who swarmed over the riverbanks, battling with frightened horses, heavy artillery and rampaging nature. But how could he be *certain* that a military failure would ensure that Britain retained control of America? And, just supposing that Alice's hypothesis *were* true, did the Commander-in-Chief of this struggling army have any notion of the significance of this night? Could Washington feel the weight of history on his shoulders, as he did? There was something about the General's demeanour that made Lord Luxon suspect that he did. Besides, to cross the Delaware on a night such as this was nothing if not an act of desperation, a last-ditch attempt to snatch at least one victory from the British redcoats and their mercenaries.

Lord Luxon brushed away the ice that was forming on his greatcoat as he contemplated how best to make a well-placed incision in the fabric of time. Nothing was certain in life but this game was surely worth the candle. In his mind's eye, he saw his prize: a glorious vision of New York rose into a blue sky from the harbour, and he recalled Alice's story of how the people of that city had melted down the statue of George III for bullets. Let General Washington beware, thought Lord Luxon, for he has a new enemy, whose very presence, here on this battlefield, he cannot begin to comprehend, and whose most dangerous weapon is undoubtedly history itself.

And so, from his vantage point, wedged halfway up the largest tree on the riverbank, Lord Luxon observed General Washington and his troops brave the ice floes, and the snow, and the biting north-easterly wind, in order to cross the Delaware River from

Pennsylvania to New Jersey. He watched a flotilla of assorted civilian boats that had been commandeered into service. He counted more than twenty of them. Some were small but others, like the Durham barges, were very long. Indeed, the largest must have been close to sixty feet in length. The river was alive with the sound of ice – it creaked and groaned and rumbled as giant slabs of it were carried downstream.

The open boats were quickly awash with icy water so that the passengers mostly stood for the duration of the crossing. The tortuous process had started at nightfall. Now it was past one o'clock and there was still much work to be done. Through his night-vision binoculars Lord Luxon watched one boat, crammed with a dozen soldiers, crash into a block of ice big enough to pitch a tent on. The boat would have capsized but for the efforts of two of the men, who dug into the riverbed with their long poles and blindly, inch by painful inch, forced the boat to the bank. What a pity, thought Lord Luxon with a smile, that the Americans are so poorly equipped. How much better they would fare with a twenty-first-century spyglass which allowed one to see in the dark – though he wasn't about to lend them his own.

Gradually the determined Patriots began to make some headway. The patience of vast crowds of soldiers waiting for passage was rewarded as they disembarked gratefully at Johnson's Ferry. The number of bonfires, twinkling like stars, on the far Pennsylvania side began to diminish, while the number of bonfires blazing on the New Jersey bank began to increase. Sentries were sent out to guard the landing place and hundreds of men stood in front of the bonfires while they waited for the rest of the horses and the artillery to be brought over. They all turned like meat on spits, for no sooner had they warmed one side than the other was already frozen again.

Lord Luxon had never experienced such cold, although his earliest memory was of clinging on to his mother's hand during a frost fair when, unusually, the Thames had completely frozen over. Whilst they had stood marvelling at the sight of a whole ox roasting on a large fire built on the thick ice, a thief had stolen his mother's purse. He remembered watching gleefully as all their servants gave chase, slipping and falling and crashing into stalls as they did so. To his disappointment the Thames had not frozen since, but if one had to endure cold like this in order to have a frost fair, he would rather do without.

In any case, one could hardly compare the Thames with the Delaware. If the former ran through one of Europe's great cities, the latter appeared to flow through the middle of a windswept and inhospitable wilderness. The powerful, glacial winds made it feel even colder, slicing through his greatcoat and making his hands numb and his feet throb painfully despite the layers of warm clothing that William had provided for him and Sergeant Thomas.

The sergeant had taken up position a few feet below Lord Luxon, on the same tree. His legs were straddled over a stout branch and his back was pressed into the trunk. All night they had listened to an officer barking instructions to his army on the move, his stentorian voice carrying even over the howling storm.

'My throat aches just listening to the fellow,' commented Lord Luxon to Sergeant Thomas.

'Ay, sir, they are lucky to count him among their number. It would be difficult to imagine how the task could have been accomplished without him. I freely admit that I could not have done what he has this night.'

'Then he deserves our first shot, what say you?'

'He would make an easy target – he is the size of a house!' But even as Sergeant Thomas spoke, he felt a pang of sadness. The anonymous officer with the booming voice had earned his respect that night. In the heat of battle there was never time for reflection or pity. It was a case of kill or be killed. But there was something unpalatable about hiding in a tree with an aristocrat with hands as soft as a girl, and plotting the death of a man in this way.

'But you have not answered my question. Should he die first?'

'If that is what you wish, sir.'

'Pshaw! It is not a case of what I wish. I brought you here, Sergeant Thomas, in order that *you* could advise *me*. I'd wager you've seen more action in your time than Washington himself—'

'I've been in the army man and boy, sir – almost thirty years.'

'I cannot imagine such a thing! Do you not dream of taking your ease in some cottage by a stream? Of taking a wife, perhaps?'

'The army is my wife, sir.'

'Ha! I believe you! And so, Sergeant Thomas, at what point should we strike? How many men do you suppose I need to transport here to sabotage Mr Washington's stratagem?'

'I should prefer to see how the night unfolds before expressing an opinion.'

'Very well, Sergeant. Even though I can scarcely feel any of my limbs, if these men can brave this howling north-easterly I suppose that we can do likewise. Although I must say that I can think of more cheerful ways to spend Christmas night.'

Sergeant Thomas put his binoculars to his eyes and watched the American Patriots struggle to disembark through rows of blocks of ice that were collecting close to the bank like sets of jagged teeth. He pitied them, for rarely in his long career had he seen more trying conditions.

'If I had not witnessed it myself,' said Lord Luxon, 'I should have said that this crossing was an act of utter folly.'

'But is that not the beauty of General Washington's plan, sir?

The Hessian mercenaries at Trenton will be warm in their beds on Christmas night, believing the Americans to be on the other side of a broad river without a hope of getting across in such weather. Washington has made an ally of the storm.'

Night-vision binoculars pressed to their eyes, like two unblinking owls, Lord Luxon and Sergeant Thomas continued to survey the scene from their high and windswept perch.

'What a ragged-looking bunch they are!' commented Lord Luxon.

'They are battle weary, and poorly supplied, without a doubt,' returned Sergeant Thomas. 'But then, if you say that our redcoats and the mercenaries have driven them out of New York and chased them across New Jersey, it is not surprising that their uniform does not pass muster.'

'If uniform is a measure of an army, the American Patriots do little to inspire confidence.'

'The lack of a handsome jacket will not trouble a fighting man, sir, but the lack of shoes will. I have observed many men with nothing more than rags tied around their feet. Have you not noticed the trails of bloody footprints in the snow? This night will bring forth a fair crop of frostbitten toes. Cannon and musket fire do not scare me but I have a horror of the gangrene. Gangrene has the stink of hell about it.'

'Why so? Have you ever been afflicted with it?'

'No, thank God, but many is the time I've held a gag for my comrades to bite on while the surgeon got to work with his saw . . .'

Lord Luxon gulped. 'Upon my word, Sergeant, what vastly disagreeable images you conjure up.'

'War is not for the faint-hearted.'

'Have a care, Sergeant Thomas – you are impertinent. My father was a fighting man as were all my uncles. He who pays the piper calls the tune, and you and your little band do not come cheap. Like it or not, men of action will not survive long without men of ideas.'

'My apologies, sir, I did not mean to imply . . .'

'Yes, yes, I did not employ you for your silver tongue.'

There was a lull in the conversation during which the wind howled and the branches creaked all around them. It was Lord Luxon who spoke first.

'You know, Sergeant Thomas, I am a betting man. But were the outcome of this night not already known to me, I should not bet so much as a bean on this lamentable, rag-tag army of amateurs. Lady Fortune is nothing if not surprising. To think that they will defeat the Hessians within a few hours – why, it beggars belief!'

'No one can predict the fortunes of war, sir. It seems to me that courage is indispensable but it is not enough; nor is skill; nor is heart – no matter how much one would like to think it is. I have seen astonishing victories and unforeseen defeats. Nothing is ever certain until the final shot has been fired.'

'Ha! And not even then . . . Tell me, Sergeant, if Trenton is eight or nine miles distant, how long do you suppose it will take them to march there in these conditions?'

'Two hours would suffice for the men – but they must carry heavy artillery over winter roads. I should guess three hours if all goes well.'

'In which case Washington will be lucky to reach Trenton by dawn.'

Suddenly Sergeant Thomas made a shushing sound. Lord Luxon swept the ground beneath them with his night-vision binoculars and spotted one of the sentries walking in their direction. He watched as Sergeant Thomas waited until he was directly below, jumped on him and wrestled him to the ground. There was a brief altercation, inaudible to Lord Luxon, during which Sergeant Thomas disarmed the man and held the blade of a knife to his throat. Presently he tore off the sentry's jacket, his tricorn hat and the grimy scarf which he had used to tie it around his head, and then proceeded to bind and gag him.

He called up to Lord Luxon: 'With your permission, sir, I should like to stand with the infantry awhile – it will give me a better idea of where to mount the attack.'

'But what of the sentries? Your life is your own but I had rather you not risk it while you are in *my* service.'

'I have persuaded this fine fellow to divulge the password.'

'Then, by all means, Sergeant Thomas.'

'He should not cause you any trouble – I have bound him tightly.'

'I am astonished that you spared him—'

'The password bought him his life.'

'And you are a man of your word?'

'What would I be if I were not?'

'Like the rest of the world, Sergeant Thomas. And what, out of curiosity, *is* General Washington's password?'

'Victory or Death!'

Lord Luxon flexed his fingers in the fur-lined leather gloves he had bought in Saks on Fifth Avenue – how he loved twenty-first-century shopping – and wrapped his heavy coat tight around him against the wind. Even so, he still felt in danger of freezing to death if he let himself drift into sleep which somehow the cold beckoned him to do, like a siren willing a sailing ship to crash and falter on her rock. He longed for his vigil to end. Images from his past haunted him – of the balls his mother would arrange at Tempest House and of the men of his family, strutting about like

138

peacocks in shiny black boots, erect and proud in their immaculate uniforms, making the young ladies blush and giggle. How frightened he had been of these good-looking, arrogant men. He would cower behind the pillars of the ballroom and peep out, marvelling at these glamorous creatures who looked as if they had ridden out after breakfast and conquered the world. They had probably, Lord Luxon now realised, spent most of the day losing small fortunes at cards but a dashing uniform still aroused in him feelings of envy and admiration. All of them were dead now, yet they continued to look disapprovingly down at him from their portraits hung in the Long Gallery.

Half an hour later Lord Luxon heard Sergeant Thomas clambering back up the tree. He reached up to him, a fluttering piece of paper in his hand.

'What is this that you give me?'

'Read it, sir. It is a pamphlet written by a certain Thomas Paine, an Englishman, it seems, but no friend to the crown. It has been read or heard by every man in the American army. It has given them hope and purpose.'

Turning towards the tree trunk to obscure the tiny pool of light, Lord Luxon took out a small torch and read out loud.

'*These are the times that try men's souls. The summer soldier and the sunshine patriot will, in this crisis, shrink from the service of their country; but he that stands it now, deserves the love and thanks of man and woman. Tyranny, like hell, is not easily conquered; yet we have this consolation with us, that the harder the conflict, the more glorious the triumph . . .*'

'Ha! Tyranny! It is a *British* colony! Their relatives still live out their lives in Surrey and Norfolk and the Yorkshire Dales! It is but a small matter of paying tax to the Crown . . . In any case, the Americans will invent their own taxes soon enough and doubtless they shall prove as painful to pay as any of those levied by King George. But I agree that this Mr Paine knows how to pen a sentence. "These are the times that try men's souls . . ." It sounds like a drumbeat.'

'Those words are on every man's lips. Their morale is high – they have a purpose. They are fighting for their own freedom.'

'Did I not say to you, Sergeant Thomas, that every man of action needs a man of ideas?'

'Some men need to be inspired before battle.'

'But not you?'

'No, sir, I am a war horse. Put my blinkers on and I shall fight until death takes me or I am told to stop. It is what the army has taught me.'

'Then, Master War Horse, tell me what information you have learned on your reconnoitre.'

'I saw General Washington sitting on an old beehive—'

'A beehive! Does the Patriot Army not run to chairs?'

'I cannot comment, sir. The General was deep in thought while his men struggled with the cannon and the horses around him. I fancy he was wondering if he should give up the task – and perhaps he was thinking, too, that it would be just as foolhardy to turn back. I liked the look of him – he is in a tight spot yet he is resolute and there is a calmness about him—'

'Yes, yes. General Washington impressed you. What else?'

'It seems that most of the men are signed up until the new year – in a week they will be free to return to their homes but they know General Washington will ask them to stay until the job is done.'

'Which is a worry for him but hardly for me. What else?'

'The officer in command of the crossing – with a voice so powerful it carries over the roar of the wind – he is Colonel Henry Knox. I pity the horse that has to carry him for he is a mighty figure of a man. From what I have seen tonight, he is a man with the instincts of a soldier – which is rarer than you might suppose. I also learned of something else which has given me some cause for concern.'

'And what is that?' asked Lord Luxon sharply.

'It is not Washington alone who attempts to cross the Delaware this night. There are two other forces – one at Trenton and another further downstream. If Washington fails this night it may be that other forces will arrive to take his place.'

'Damn your eyes, Sergeant Thomas! Why did you not tell me at once! That is bad news, indeed!'

'Perhaps they fail, sir – in this storm—'

'And perhaps they succeed,' snapped Lord Luxon. He sighed. 'No matter. I shall consult Alice on my return – if she has not been frightened to death by your wretched hound!'

They watched the last cannon being unloaded and saw the men assembling into a snaking column, ready for their long march to the Hessian mercenaries' encampment at Trenton. It would be a march not only to Trenton, but, if Lord Luxon's plan failed, also to a glorious victory that would revive the Patriot cause and save it from military disaster. Lord Luxon felt a pang of doubt for the first time that night. How could he stop Washington and the Patriots wrenching the colonies from Britain's grasp?

'And so, Sergeant Thomas, what should be our strategy? Have you formed an opinion?'

'I have, sir. My first thought was that we could make do with fifty or sixty men if our attack was timely enough – but I am now of the firm opinion that if we strike early in the evening, when the storm raged fiercely and morale was at its lowest ebb, we need only a party of four. The death of two men should seal the Americans' fate.'

'Four! I fancied you were going to ask for two hundred! As for the two men, you refer, I imagine, to General Washington and Colonel Knox.'

'I do, sir.'

'Then, so be it! With your words you have signed their death warrant, Sergeant Thomas. Rather than passing into the golden annals of history, the crossing of the Delaware shall be held up as a failure; it shall be viewed as an ill-judged attack in which a rarely remembered general called George Washington met his death. Above all, this night shall be remembered as the beginning of the end of a short-lived adolescent rebellion against Mother England!'

Sergeant Thomas could not reply. The emotions that quickened his heartbeat were conflicting ones and Lord Luxon's words rang in his ears. He found he was trembling, but not on account of the cold.

CHAPTER TWELVE

Brothers in Blood

In which the Tar Man confronts Gideon
with a truth he is reluctant to accept
and Gideon recalls an early memory

'By the laws!' the old gentleman exclaimed when he heard the Tar Man's name. 'Do you speak of the impudent hound with the scar down his cheek who has every villain in London under his thumb or in his sights?'

When Sir Richard verified that the party was, indeed, in hot pursuit of this very individual, the old gentleman grew agitated.

'Why, then, he is the same rogue who swindled my brother out of two brood mares and took so much off him at the card table he had to sell his cutlery!'

When the old gentleman would not be dissuaded from coming to their assistance, Sir Richard grew finally tired of arguing with him. He asked him to stay with Peter. They could both, he said, be on guard duty at the entrance to the alleyway leading to the Tar Man's house.

Following Sir Richard and Parson Ledbury into the alley, Gideon shot one last look at Peter and mimed lobbing a stone.

Peter held up the cobblestone he had managed to prise up from the path and gave Gideon the thumbs-up sign. Gideon nodded and disappeared into the alley.

Tucked under his master's arm, Toby's ears lay flat against his head and, as its owner had promised, the animal did not make a sound. Peter let out a long sigh of frustration. The old gentleman turned and put his mouth to his ear. Peter could smell his warm, brandy-laden breath.

'Though 'tis done with the best of intentions,' he whispered, 'the old and the young are oft protected from dangers they would be happier to face. It can be vexatious in the extreme, can it not, Master Schock?'

Peter nodded. 'It's true. Grown-ups think they're looking after you when half the time it's them that need looking after . . .'

Peter became aware of the old man scrutinising him so long and so hard he became uncomfortable. He looked away. The sound of distant thunder rumbled across the city like a succession of explosions. The atmosphere felt heavy and oppressive as if it were about to pour with rain, yet the skies were clear.

'Who are you, child? Your speech is strange and your circumstances the more so.'

Peter could not help sighing again. He wished Sir Richard had not left him with the old gentleman to deal with. 'No, I don't come from here. But I can't return home until we get our hands on something the Tar Man has stolen. We've absolutely got to get it back – and it's not going to be easy.'

'An unhappy predicament . . .'

'You can say that again – and the Tar Man is a seriously nasty piece of work, I can tell you. And he's clever.'

'Well, may success attend you, my boy! We shall not let the brute pass, shall we, Toby? We shall tear him to shreds before we let him get away. What say you, young sir, that we display a little more spirit than perhaps your companions would ask of us? I feel my juices stirring!'

'What do you mean? Gideon said he needed me for a lookout – I don't want to let him down . . .'

'Lookout? 'Tis naught but a ruse to keep you out of harm's way. Where is your bottom, young sir?'

'It's not a question of bottom!' Peter protested. 'I've got plenty of bottom! But please try to keep your voice down! We could ruin everything if—'

The old gentleman ignored him and started to hobble energetically towards the Tar Man's house, his cane clicking against the cobblestones. He paused, however, to turn around to face Peter and hold up a knife. Its short blade glinted in the moonlight.

'If this villain is as dangerous as you say, your companions will welcome reinforcements – and see, I am armed!'

Then he pulled out a length of cord from an inside pocket which he tossed over to Peter.

'And now so are you!'

Peter caught the cord in one hand. 'Please come back!' he begged as loudly as he dared. 'Please!'

But it was too late, for the gentleman had already disappeared out of sight, Toby tucked under his arm. *I've got enough people to worry about*, thought Peter furiously, *without having to mind an old man and his dog!* But perhaps the old gentleman was right. Gideon *could* do with his help – even if he didn't know it yet. Peter had realised something about Gideon while witnessing his fight with the Tar Man. It was just not in Gideon's nature *ever* to give in or go back on his word. Even when no one else would think of blaming him. This time, Peter thought – if it comes to it – I'll be there to save Gideon from himself. Clutching the heavy cobblestone to his chest, Peter followed in the old man's footsteps. As he disappeared into the alley he glanced over at the moonlit carriage where, he hoped, Kate slept peacefully on, oblivious to all.

Sir Richard took the Parson's gunpowder horn and began to charge and prime the pistols. Gideon, meanwhile, crouched down next to the Tar Man's back door to examine the keyhole. He took a small penknife from his pocket and probed and rattled the mechanism. In less than a minute he had picked the lock and, with the blade of his knife, had lifted the inside latch. He rose to his feet and, with the tip of his index finger, pushed the door very gently. It creaked open a thumb's width.

'Bravo, Gideon!' whispered Sir Richard.

The Parson was even more impressed. 'Upon my word, Mr Seymour! You are a man of parts! I can see how your guilty conscience has cost Lord Luxon dear! Indeed, I begin to perceive why he was angry enough to wish to see you hang!'

'I am not proud of possessing such a skill,' replied Gideon sharply. 'I do this solely because Master Peter and Mistress Kate are in dire need . . .'

'Come, come, Gideon!' whispered Parson Ledbury. 'Would even a saint object to breaking into a thief's house in such circumstances? You are too scrupulous!'

'And *you* are too loud, my friend,' hissed Sir Richard. 'The Tar Man is within and I doubt not that he has sharp ears . . . Come, let us do the deed.'

Holding the door with both hands, Gideon swung it wide open in one rapid movement in case the hinges should squeak. They peered inside the yawning entrance. The air that escaped from the house was cool and smelled of damp. On the ground floor all was in darkness, but on the floor above, straight ahead of them, they saw a stripe of yellow light pouring out from a gap at the bottom of an ill-fitting door. This scrap of candlelight was sufficient to reveal a bare and narrow stairwell whose steep steps led down to the whitewashed hall where the three men now stood huddled together.

Sir Richard handed one of the pistols to Gideon. He took it and weighed it in his hand, taking a moment to get used to the feel of this untried weapon. It was a handsome pistol with an engraved brass barrel. Gideon ran his thumb over the flintlock and cast an eye over the primed flash-pan, taking care to blow away the dusting of powder Sir Richard had left on the barrel of the pistol. Then, pointing it at the floor, he slowly squeezed the trigger to test its resistance. Sir Richard smiled. Finally satisfied, Gideon grasped the pistol and held it in front of him.

'Will it pass muster, Colonel Seymour?'

'Ay, it will do.' Gideon's good eye twinkled. Then he added: 'I once saw a man's hand blown off on account of a poorly primed pistol.'

Sir Richard raised an eyebrow at Parson Ledbury but made no comment. Gideon started to move slowly and carefully towards the staircase. He motioned to his companions to stay put.

'If it came to it,' whispered Parson Ledbury into Sir Richard's ear, 'do you suppose either of them would be capable of killing his own brother?'

Sir Richard put his mouth close to the Parson's ear in his turn. '*If* they are brothers I doubt not that the Tar Man would have few scruples about the matter. But in the fever of combat I believe that a man is capable of anything – even Gideon. And knowing him as we do, I fear his keen conscience would plague him ever afterwards.'

'I shall endeavour to put myself between them if I can,' said Parson Ledbury.

'Well said, my friend, I shall attempt to do the same. But I hope that no blood will be shed. Blueskin is nothing if not shrewd – provided we make it worth his while to return the device he may yet be tempted to give it up. I shall put my faith in diplomacy.'

They watched Gideon climb the narrow flight of stairs, with steps as light and sure as a cat's. When he reached the top, he held his pistol at the height of a man's heart and aimed it at the door. The Parson and Sir Richard saw him cock his head to one side as if he were listening to something and presently they, too, became aware of a regular, rasping sound coming from the other side of the door. Gideon turned towards them and mimed the forwards and backwards motion of someone sharpening a knife on a grindstone. Sir Richard felt the Parson's hand on his sleeve.

'God go with you, my friend,' whispered the Parson.

'God go with us all,' Sir Richard replied.

The gathering storm was still threatening to break. Gideon signalled for Sir Richard and the Parson to join him under cover of a distant thunderclap that rumbled over the city towards them. They climbed up the stairs on tiptoe, treading as delicately as they were able which, in the Parson's case, was not easy. A floorboard creaked underfoot and the sound of the Tar Man sharpening his knife abruptly halted. They all stared, unblinking, at the door, not daring to breathe, fear pricking at them, listening to the sound of blood thumping in their temples. After a few seconds the swish of a knife blade against well-oiled stone started up again and all three men slowly let out their pent-up breath.

'Ready, gentlemen?' mouthed Gideon to his two companions.

They nodded.

Gideon swallowed, hesitated for an instant, then hurled himself at the door. The adrenaline rush of fear sharpened his senses to that extent that time itself seemed to slow down and nothing seemed quite real. He was aware of a circular window to his left and of the door slamming hard against the wall behind him to his right and, in front of him, flickering red flames and a sudden blast of heat. His eyes darted about the well-lit room in search of the Tar Man but he saw only a pair of boots warming by the hearth and a long black coat draped over the back of a chair next to them. Then he felt Sir Richard and Parson Ledbury push roughly past him. He barely had time to ask himself why they were doing this when he heard a dull thud somewhere to his right. A flurry of panic rose in his chest, like a dying bird. Gideon swung around but even before he had turned ninety degrees, a pistol went off inches away from his face and the sheer force of the detonation knocked him off his feet. He crashed to the floor, the pistol shot booming in his ears and the pungent odour of gunpowder stinging his nostrils. Gideon was too dazed to know if he were wounded or unhurt, and then, as bits of the lath and plaster ceiling, damaged by the grapeshot, started to fall down on him, he had the happy sensation that he was lying on his back in a heavy snowstorm. Was that his pistol flying across the room? Something skidded across the bare wooden floor. Gideon's fingers closed over his empty palm and, through his confusion, all he knew was that he had to get up and retrieve that pistol at all cost. Gideon blinked, conscious of a terrible ringing in his ears, and tried to focus his one good eye. If only he could move; if only he could *see* . . . Gradually the swirl of shapes in front of him stopped spinning and solidified in the form of two figures looming over him. One of the heads leaned over at an unnatural angle while the other seemed to have a vertical line drawn down one cheek, rather like a scar . . . *Blueskin!* Gideon shot up, crying out with the pain of it, but relieved, at least, to realise that the electric pains that streaked down every nerve in his jaw and back and arms were not caused by any new wound but were simply those inflicted earlier in the evening.

The Tar Man observed him coolly over Sir Richard's shoulder. Something was not right. Sir Richard was standing awkwardly. His face was grey and contorted with pain while his watery eyes seemed to look straight through Gideon without seeing him. Then Gideon noticed the knife pressing into Sir Richard's neck and saw how the Tar Man was pinning his right arm behind his back. Gideon had seen this manoeuvre before. He prayed that Blueskin would not continue with it.

'Tis a little premature, would you not say, Gideon, for a second beating? You should have a care for your good looks – if I did not know better I should have said that Featherstone's wagon had rolled over you.'

Gideon struggled to take in the situation. His eyes slid sideways towards Parson Ledbury who lay slumped over a table strewn with clutter. Blood oozed from a cut on the Parson's forehead. It was forming a small red pool on the tabletop and was then trickling, drop by drop, onto the bare wood floor. The Parson was semi-conscious and groaned loudly as if he were in the middle of a nightmare.

Gideon looked back at the Tar Man. Though his lips were moving, Gideon's ears were ringing too much for him to catch most of what the Tar Man said. He shook his head violently. When he looked up again, Sir Richard's desperate and terrified gaze now met his own, pleading silently for help. The point of the Tar Man's knife pressed into Sir Richard's throat, his skin white and barely resisting the pressure of the blade.

Murder, Gideon knew, was something the Tar Man tried to avoid – on account of the complications in one form or another that would always ensue – but he would not shy away from the deed if circumstances demanded it. Everyone who knew Blueskin had some gruesome tale to tell. This was, of course, only what the Tar

Man would have encouraged for, as Lord Luxon's henchman, terror was his currency. Gideon himself had once witnessed an attack on the Tar Man as he had stood drinking beer one afternoon in Covent Garden Piazza. The assassin had made the fatal error of attacking with the sun behind him so that his shadow gave him away. Gideon recalled how dispassionately the Tar Man had turned and slit the wretch's throat from ear to ear before walking away, brushing down his jacket as he did so, even remembering to toss a coin to the landlord in payment for his ale. The grotesque fountain of blood, spurting forth in the warm sunshine before ebbing gradually away, had cowed the bustling crowd into a deep and eerie silence. Yet a few minutes later porters had removed the corpse, the landlord had sluiced down the cobblestones with buckets of cold water and the robust Covent Garden crowd, who had seen everything, continued about their business.

Gideon's heart sank. How could this possibly have happened? There had been three of them, all armed! How had Blueskin contrived to turn the tables so effortlessly?

'Sir Richard's pistol,' said the Tar Man, 'was pointing at your head when he started to squeeze the trigger. Were my reflexes not so fast, your brains would now be spattered over my floorboards. To survive long in this world, brother, you either travel alone or you are fastidious in your choice of companions.'

'You, who ride with Joe Carrick, dare to lecture *me* on my companions!' Gideon croaked. 'And as for any connection between us – I am no brother of yours, as well you know!'

'No? Unless I am better informed than you suppose. But pray do not trouble yourself to disguise your joy at the news . . .'

'You must allow me to know how many brothers I may or may not have.'

'And you must allow me to think that you are mistaken! Faith, a younger brother is the last thing I desire or need. It seems to me that relations are good for little aside from causing grief – as your present visit demonstrates.'

'Why do you persist in such a lie when you know full well that the fever took my mother and stepfather and all my brothers and sisters. All saving Joshua—'

'Joshua is your *half-brother*,' interrupted the Tar Man. 'Whereas *we* share the same mother and father.'

Gideon exhaled loudly in frustration. 'What game do you and Lord Luxon play?'

The Tar Man held his tongue, continuing all the while to hold his victim in check and to study Gideon's face as if searching for the answer to some unspoken question.

'As you wish . . . Let us agree that I am *not* your brother. Let us agree that our mother did not abandon her firstborn during his hour of need. Let us agree that our mother did not uproot herself and the rest of her brood in order to escape the shame of admitting that I was her son . . .'

'*Our* mother!' Gideon cried. 'Do not dare—'

'She was my mother before she was yours and I know of what I speak!' barked the Tar Man. He sounded angry for the first time. His grip slackened for a moment and Sir Richard took advantage of his lapse in concentration by trying to break away. The Tar Man shouted at him to keep still and yanked back his arm so violently that Sir Richard let out an agonised scream.

'You will hang for this!' cried Sir Richard.

'I suggest you persuade your friend to hold his tongue,' said the Tar Man coldly, frowning with the effort of holding on to his struggling victim. 'He does not know me as you do . . .'

Gideon did not reply but staggered backwards to steady himself. A lock of blond hair fell over his eye and he pushed it back feverishly, transfixed as he was by that most ephemeral of things, the Tar Man's frown. He focussed on it, with his one good blue eye, with such intensity that for a moment he was aware of nothing else in the room but the deep, vertical crease between the Tar Man's thick, black eyebrows. Suddenly Gideon found that he was no longer looking at Blueskin but, as the years rolled back, at a man wearing that self-same frown. A man who had stepped back for a moment from the chair leg he was carving in order to examine his handiwork. Was this a waking dream or a memory? Yet the image did not fade; rather it intensified, and Gideon watched the man's frown dissolve as he looked up from the chair and met his gaze. He was a still a youngish man with dark hair, and he had the quiet hands of a craftsman. His eyes were full of pride and delight in his small son. The man laid down his tools and opened his arms wide in greeting. Gideon had no doubt that it was his own father who looked at him across the arc of the years. When Sir Richard let out another cry it jolted Gideon out of his trance and he found that he could not contain the anguish that coursed suddenly through his veins.

'No!' he exclaimed in despair. 'No!'

'I did not think you so squeamish, Gideon! Sir Richard is not made of porcelain. He shall not break so easily.'

For a moment the room seemed to swim before Gideon's eyes. His conscious mind would resist to the end the notion that Lord Luxon's henchman was his own brother, but Blueskin's frown had dredged up a memory that he did not even realise he possessed. His father had been so young when he died. Gideon covered his face with his hands. *Could* it be true? Could this monster be his own flesh and blood? When Gideon took his hands away the Tar Man observed the loathing and anger that he read, as plain as day, in his younger brother's eyes. When the Tar Man spoke, his voice was flat.

'My arm begins to tire. You had best tell me the purpose of your visit before I find a more permanent way of restraining your friend. Although I can guess easily enough . . .'

Refusing to accept a truth so repugnant to him, Gideon clenched and unclenched his hands, anger and distress pulsing alternately inside him like a series of electric shocks. He would not accept it! How could he? When everything he had strived to combat in his own life was made flesh in this odious villain. He did not want to be stained with the same brush; he did not want to belong to a family that bred such monsters . . . The possibility tugged at the very root of his hard-earned self-respect. Even Sir Richard seemed to forget his discomfort temporarily as he watched the hurricane of emotions play out on his young friend's face.

'We have come to take what rightfully belongs to the children,' gasped Sir Richard.

'But you do not possess the code—'

'Perhaps we do,' said Gideon.

'*Do* you?'

Gideon opened his mouth and shut it again. The Tar Man laughed although he did not look amused.

'You could not lie if your life depended upon it! Besides, I know that you do not have the code. Mistress Dyer is as poor a liar as you.'

Gideon glared at him. 'What kind of man does not balk at torturing children?'

'The kind of man who does what needs must. No more and no less. And you, Gideon, did you come to my home hoping to get the device by engaging me in idle conversation? No! You came, three against one, in the dead of night, armed with pistols – though it would have been better for you had you chosen companions with a morsel of talent between them.'

'You ripped these children from the bosom of their families!' cried Gideon.

'Pshaw! The streets of London are awash with tragic stories and with ragged children who deserve my pity a thousand times more than your young charges! Did anyone, even my own family, come to *my* aid with words of comfort as the noose tightened around my neck and I bade life farewell to the ugly taunts of a jeering crowd? The worst I was guilty of was to steal our neighbour's chicken. I was scarcely more than a child, Gideon! Our own mother believed the word of strangers over those of her own son—'

'I am not your brother . . .'

'As you like.'

'And if the world has sinned against you, you have more than made up for it since . . .'

'Have a care, Gideon. Even my patience – and, believe me, I have learned to be patient – has its limits.'

'But if you remember the agony of being abandoned by a parent,' cried Gideon, 'and as you lack the knowledge to profit from the machine, can you not find it in your heart to return it to Master Schock and Mistress Dyer?'

'Heart? As I know that you do not credit me to have one, I am amazed you waste my time and yours with such a question. What care I if Master Schock and Mistress Dyer return to their family or rot in hell? They are nothing to me! Whereas I would go back to the hour of my birth and be my own guardian angel as Fortune has not seen fit to provide me with one . . . Besides, if they do not know the secret code, nor will it be of any use to them!'

'But it will allow them to live in hope, whereas at present they are doomed to perpetual exile in a foreign century. Where is the device, Blueskin? Is it in this house?'

'Ha! Do you think me a fool?!'

Gideon thought he detected the subtlest of changes in the Tar Man's tone of voice. *Could* the anti-gravity machine be hidden within these very walls? Suddenly Gideon felt able to push his tumultuous feelings to one side and he resolved to concentrate on the job at hand. His eyes swept slowly around the room searching for clues. A large, rusting key lay at the foot of brass candlestick on the mantelpiece. His eyes flicked back to the Tar Man to test his reaction. Whether Blueskin had noticed where his gaze had landed he could not tell for certain, but there was an unfathomable expression in his eyes that led Gideon to believe that he was disguising his agitation.

Parson Ledbury let out a loud groan and with his eyes still firmly closed he tried to push himself up from the table. The Tar Man cast a swift glance in the Parson's direction. As he did so Gideon dived to the corner of the room, grabbed hold of his pistol, swung around, and aimed it at square at the Tar Man's face. Then, facing his opponent he stepped carefully backwards towards the mantelpiece and felt with his left hand for the key. The Tar Man watched him slip it into the pocket of his blue jacket.

'Where is the machine, Blueskin?' cried Gideon.

'I advise you to drop your pistol,' replied the Tar Man, 'if you wish Sir Richard to see the dawn!'

'Harm Sir Richard, Blueskin, and, by all the gods, I swear that I shall shoot you!'

'Ha! *You*, shoot *me*! You, whose conscience is too *delicate* to continue as a cutpurse, threaten to turn assassin! Shoot me if you dare, Gideon! Rid yourself of a troublesome brother!'

Gideon stood, the pistol aimed at the Tar Man's face, barely in control of himself. His hatred for this man was written on every pore of his face. Sir Richard closed his eyes, suddenly limp in his captor's grasp, unable to look. 'No, Gideon!' he mouthed.

A few seconds passed and then, holding his breath, the Tar Man watched Gideon's finger slowly squeeze the trigger. Gideon stared deep into his brother's eyes and, unflinching, the Tar Man returned his gaze. Sweat pearled on Gideon's brow.

'What are you waiting for? Take your chance while you can. In your shoes I should not hesitate. Damn your eyes, Gideon, I did not take you for a lily-livered coward! Kill me if you dare!'

Gideon let out a desperate cry and pulled the trigger. The explosive crack caused the room to shake. The air filled with white smoke. The Parson leaped to his feet, holding his injured head in his hands. As plaster rained down on their heads everyone slowly opened their eyes. There was a gaping hole in the ceiling above the Tar Man.

'As I thought!' said the Tar Man, laughing, although he looked shaken.

'I shall not fail a second time!' cried Gideon, white-faced and trembling, as he cast about for the Parson's pistol, the only one yet to be discharged. 'I should as soon cut off my right hand than admit to the world that we are brothers.'

Unable to locate the third pistol, Gideon launched himself at the Tar Man who warned him off with a tremendous shout and jabbed the dagger deeper into Sir Richard's neck so that it drew blood.

'So, brother mine, my very existence offends you, like the rest of the world! Yet still I live on, Gideon, if only to spite you and our dead mother!'

Without ever taking his eyes off Gideon the Tar Man suddenly twisted Sir Richard's arm with such violence that he pulled it clean out of its socket. Gideon and the Parson looked on, helpless and horror-struck, as Sir Richard let out an excruciating scream that seemed to go on for ever. Then, as Sir Richard fell into a faint, the Tar Man pushed the dead weight of his body at Gideon in such a way that both he and the Parson, who stood unsteadily behind him, were toppled like skittles at a fairground. As the two men groaned and writhed to slide out from beneath Sir Richard, the Tar Man flew out of the room and down the stairs, slamming the door behind him.

CHAPTER THIRTEEN

In the Wake of the Tar Man

In which Peter, Parson Ledbury, the Old Gentleman and his dog tackle the Tar Man, Hannah nurses Sir Richard, and Kate tries to understand the corridor of Time

Inside the carriage, Kate awoke with a start at the sound of a pistol shot. She sat bolt upright and reached out blindly in the dark.

'Peter!' she cried. 'Where are you?'

Her hands found Hannah.

'Calm yourself, Mistress Kate. He'll be back soon, no doubt. You've been asleep and Lord knows you need the rest . . .'

'What's happened? Where are we?'

'We are close to the Tar Man's house. If you look through the window, you can see the Thames.'

Kate pushed her head through the window into the moonlight. The air was cool and she could smell the river. She could hear it, too, flowing fast towards London Bridge. She stood up to get a better view. There was the Thames, its surface scoured by the wind into glittering ripples. Watermen mooring their wherries downstream called goodnight to each other under a star-studded sky. Towards the south a menacing flash of green lightning flickered on the horizon and a thunderclap rolled slowly towards them.

'Where are the others, Hannah?'

Hannah hesitated. 'Sir Richard told me to wait with you. They found the Tar Man's house . . . Peter is with Gideon – and Sir Richard and the Parson, of course.'

'Peter went without me!'

'You were so sound asleep, Mistress Kate, and with you being so poorly! And then we saw the state of your feet – I've never seen the like! When we return to Lincoln's Inn Fields I shall prepare a paste of comfrey and camomile which is most soothing—'

'I'm fine, Hannah!' interrupted Kate. 'And I'm not poorly. Being tired isn't the same thing as being poorly.' She hoisted up one foot onto the opposite knee and examined her injured sole as well as she could by the light of the moon. 'My feet aren't *so* bad. They don't hurt. I could still walk on them.'

'But, Mistress Kate, they are swollen and bleeding!'

But Kate scarcely heard Hannah's reply. All at once the image of Peter's face had filled her mind. He was thrashing about in the water, coming up for air and crying out for help until he started to go under again and his mouth was filled with river water once more. Peter was drowning, she was sure of it, and her own lungs burned as she sensed Peter struggle to breathe. Moonlight shone on dark water as Peter's head slowly sank under the surface, his hair streaming behind him like weed in the strong current.

Kate did not for an instant doubt the truth of her vision. In the perpetually flowing stream of time, looking forwards had felt no stranger than looking backwards. Glimpses into the future were, like memories, vivid and fleeting – and unpredictable. The fortune-teller's words rang in her ears: 'The Oracle has always been in my dreams . . .'

'Are you not feeling well, Mistress Kate?'

'No – I'm fine . . . Really. Was that a shot I just heard? Or was it thunder?'

'I was asking myself the same question. I *hope* it was Master Blueskin getting a taste of his own medicine.'

All at once the carriage was filled with the sound of tearing material.

'What are you doing?' exclaimed Hannah. 'Tell me that is not your dress!'

'My petticoat. Don't worry, I'll still be decent. Will you help me bind my feet? You don't have to come with me, but I *am* going after them.'

Peter and the old gentleman stretched the cord taut across the second step from the bottom. Toby looked on from the doorstep, as silent as his owner had promised. Even by moonlight, the black patch over the dog's eye gave him a cheerful air. The animal yawned, and scratched behind his ear with his back leg and settled down to wait. But a second later, when Peter had barely finished tying the cord to the wooden banister, the piercing crack of a pistol shot catapulted the little dog into the air. It scampered to its master and hurled itself into his arms.

After an exchange of alarmed glances Peter and the old gentleman both retreated into the shadows to wait, Peter passing the heavy cobblestone nervously from one hand to the other whilst his companion grasped his knife at shoulder height, ready to strike. Twice Peter heard a terrible cry, uttered, he thought, by Sir Richard but he could not be sure. The hairs bristled at the back of his neck and a cold sweat pricked at him. Peter was in an agony of indecision. Should they burst in? Or was it better to keep the advantage of surprise and stay put? He strained to make out what the voices that carried from upstairs were saying but all he distinguished was an anguished 'No!' When the second shot sounded the tension was almost too much to bear – Peter let out a strangulated cry, as did Toby, though his master quickly clamped the dog's jaws together in his hand. Peter's breathing was so rapid and shallow he was starting to feel dizzy. Then an anonymous cry reached them that was so appalling it turned Peter's blood to ice. He did not even dare imagine what terrible thing had just happened. He stared, unblinking, at the strip of flickering light that escaped from the upstairs room. Seconds later the Tar Man burst through the door and slammed it behind him so violently it sounded like another pistol shot.

Peter jumped in shock. Now that the moment had come to act, he could not. He felt stunned, disorientated. What was he supposed to do? He stood with his mouth open, gawping at the athletic figure who hurtled down the stairs two steps at a time. The stone! Peter hurled the cobblestone at his moving target before it was too late. It grazed the Tar Man's shoulder, smashed into the opposite wall with an explosion of plaster and ricocheted back at Peter who had to dive to one side to avoid being hit. A speck of plaster lodged behind Peter's eyelid so that it was through a veil of tears that he saw the Tar Man trip over the cord. He landed on his knees, one elbow buckling under his weight as he stretched out his hands to stop his face smashing into the stone floor. The Tar Man cursed roundly. As he pushed himself up he saw a glinting dagger come at him. He swiped at it with his fist and sent it spinning across the floor until it hit the far wall with a bright, metallic clang. Surprised to note the age of his assailant, the Tar Man still grabbed hold of the old gentleman's wrist in one hand and his opposite shoulder in the other, using him as a lever to hoist himself up. Without pausing for breath, he proceeded to lift the old gentleman into the air. He did this with such ease he could have been picking up a child. The expression on his victim's creased face was closer to surprise than terror, and Peter noticed in that instant how painfully thin the old man's legs were as they kicked in mid-air, encased in their wrinkly white stockings and worn, buckled shoes. The Tar Man flung him across the hall. The old gentleman's frail body smashed against a wooden door that led to an inner room. The door opened under the impact, breaking the old gentleman's fall before he slid to the ground. Peter half expected him to crack into a thousand fragments like a china vase and disintegrate piece by piece in front of him. As it was he collapsed in a heap and came to rest on the cold flagstones. The attack elicited an eruption of distressed barking from Toby who now leaped fearlessly at his master's aggressor, his blackcurrant eyes flashing in fury. He growled and bared his teeth.

'Pshaw! Have half the waifs and strays of London found their way to my door? Am I to be licked to within an inch of my life by confounded lapdogs?'

Toby closed his jaws on the Tar Man's ankle.

'Aargh!'

A second later Peter saw the little white dog fly through the air and land with a thud in the corner of the hall where it lay as still as the grave. It was then Peter's turn to become the object of the Tar Man's attention. He sprang towards him. Through streaming eyes Peter knelt down and fumbled for the cobblestone. He was shaking with fear. A creature caught in the hypnotic gaze of a striking snake. No sooner had Peter's fingertips closed, too late, around the cobblestone than the Tar Man was upon him. Peter felt himself swung, in his turn, across the hall. He flew through the air. His head hit the wall and for a moment all he could see was a shower of stars. He wondered if he might be unconscious or in the middle of a dream and lay quietly, calm and detached from everything. Presently, however, he became aware of footsteps. He opened his stinging eyelids and squinted into the darkness. Wiping the tears away with the back of his hand, he tried to focus on a dark shape that crossed his angle of vision. The Tar Man was re-entering the hall from one of the rooms that led off it, stepping over the old gentleman who still lay groaning on the threshold. He was carrying something in both hands and now stood, head bowed in concentration as if he were praying. After a minute or so, the Tar Man seemed to grow exasperated and he flung the two objects he was holding into the far corner of the hall, walked a few paces, bent over, pulled something up and proceeded to disappear into the floor! Peter struggled to understand what he was seeing. He blinked and rubbed his eyes. A trapdoor! There must be a cellar, or even a secret passageway, beneath the house! A stink of mould and stagnant water wafted towards him in waves. The contour of the Tar Man's head was now all that Peter could make out as he pulled the trapdoor down after him. It closed with a clang that echoed within the unseen space into which the Tar Man had vanished.

Peter looked up at the door at the top of the stairs. His heart began to race. What terrible sight awaited him up there? Peter tried to heave himself up but found he was too shocked and winded to move, so he lay still, helpless as a baby. His ribs hurt and his mouth was so dry his tongue stuck to the roof of his mouth. He felt a terrible longing for an ice-cold glass of Coca-Cola. He licked his lips; he could almost taste it. Fat chance of him getting his wish, he thought. Perhaps he'd never taste his favourite drink ever again . . . Or perhaps somewhere, in one of those parallel worlds Kate's dad had told them about, there was a house on Richmond Green, with a mum and a dad and a boy called Peter, who would come home from school and raid the giant fridge for salami and Coca-Cola.

Suddenly the existence of such a world seemed highly improbable. Home. He hadn't thought about home for so long. He rubbed at his watering eyes, trying to get rid of the speck of plaster.

Like a ceasefire, all was eerily silent in the Tar Man's house while the trail of victims left in his wake tried to recover from their encounter with Lord Luxon's henchman. The calm was of short duration. The door burst open again and this time Peter saw Gideon hurry down the staircase.

'Gideon!' cried Peter in delight. 'You're alive!' And then: 'Stop! Cord! Bottom of stairs!'

The golden candlelight that now poured down from the Tar Man's sitting room illuminated the cord that was stretched taut across the stairwell. In the nick of time Gideon spotted it and leaped high into the air, landing heavily on the stone flags next to Peter.

Gideon looked about him. He saw the old gentleman hauling himself slowly up by the door handle; he saw the little white dog lying still and silent at the far end of the hall and he saw Peter, slumped up against the wall, legs stretched out in front of him like a drunk recovering in a gutter.

'We were trying to stop the Tar Man . . .' said Peter.

'I do not need to ask how you fared . . .'

'There's a trapdoor,' said Peter quickly, rolling on to his side but failing to push himself up from the floor. 'Over there – he opened it and disappeared down the hole.'

'Then there's no time to lose. Come, Peter, if you are not too badly hurt, I need you to fetch Hannah.'

Gideon offered Peter his hand and, with some grunting on both their parts on account of their respective injuries, he heaved him to his feet.

'Sir Richard needs a doctor,' panted Gideon. 'As does the Parson.'

'I'll have no doctor prodding at me! I've lost enough blood. A glass or two of port is all I need to steady my nerves.'

It was Parson Ledbury who spoke, his bulky form swaying to and fro, black against the flickering light. He clung unsteadily to the door handle.

'May I suggest, Parson, that you take the precaution of sitting down before you break your neck.'

The Parson slithered obediently down the door frame, and sat with a loud thump on the top step. He rested his elbows on his knees and held his bloodied face in his hands. 'I fear for my cousin, Gideon. Can such an injury be mended? It is his right arm. Please God, Richard will not lose the use of it.'

Meanwhile the old gentleman had started to crawl towards Toby.

'I'll get him for you,' said Peter hurriedly. His head was spinning as he walked down the hallway and he had to steady himself by leaning against the wall. He looked down at the motionless dog and picked it up as you would a baby and cradled it in his arms so that its short legs stuck up in the air. Its dense, bristly fur felt coarse against Peter's fingers and its head drooped backwards, its jaws slightly apart, revealing black and pink gums.

The old gentleman had stopped crawling but remained on all fours, his eyes fixed on his canine friend. 'Tell me the truth, young sir, have I room for hope? Is he warm or cold?'

'He is warm, sir,' said Peter.

The old gentleman let his forehead sink to the floor and his back heaved.

Gideon knelt down next to the old gentleman and put his hand on his back.

'May I help you to your feet, sir?' he asked.

The old gentleman shook his head and remained in this semi-recumbent pose.

Gideon stood up, full of rage. 'The devil take Blueskin! Is his sole purpose on this earth to dispense an unending stream of misery and fear? Peter, run and get Hannah. I have to bring the Tar Man back to mend Sir Richard's arm.'

'What?!' exclaimed Peter.

'There is no time to explain,' said Gideon, pulling up the trap-door. 'Sir Richard will be in an agony of pain when he begins to stir. He will need a nurse.'

As Hannah helped Kate wrap strips of her petticoat around her feet, a set of fingers suddenly appeared and gripped the bottom edge of the carriage window. A head rose up out of the darkness with open mouth and wild hair. Hannah screamed.

'Don't *do* that!' exclaimed Kate. 'You made me jump!'

'The Lord preserve us! I took you for a highwayman, Master Peter!'

'Kate! Hannah!' he panted, in such a rush to get his words out they were almost incoherent. 'Sir Richard is badly injured and needs help. And the Parson's been hit on the head and the old gentleman is hurt. Even the dog's unconscious . . .'

'Whoa! Slow down!' said Kate. 'You're gabbling! *What* happened to Sir Richard and the Parson? And what old gentleman? What *dog?*'

'Has the Tar Man shot Sir Richard?' asked Hannah in alarm. 'Should we call for a surgeon?'

'No and yes. I haven't seen Sir Richard but he's bad . . . The Parson thinks he might lose his arm.'

'What happened?' cried Kate.

Hannah crossed herself.

'No time to explain,' said Peter, backing away from the carriage. 'Gotta go. Gideon's gone after the Tar Man alone.'

Peter's face vanished as suddenly as it had appeared. Kate thrust her head through the open window.

'Peter!' she shouted after him. 'If you wait for me to bind my other foot I'll come with you . . . *Peter!*'

Peter stopped and looked at her. 'You'll have to catch up with me, Kate. You haven't seen what the Tar Man's done. I can't wait – everyone else is injured and Gideon needs some back-up *now*. You and Hannah come as fast as you can – the Parson and Sir Richard need you.'

Peter turned and ran.

'And I need *you*,' she mouthed into the dark.

Hannah instructed the driver to find a surgeon and hurried after Kate, her blonde hair coming loose as she ran. Despite her assertions to the contrary, Kate's feet were causing her problems. The uneven cobblestones hurt her even through the layers of petticoat. She prayed that she would not fast-forward again before she reached Peter.

'You poor soul,' said Hannah sympathetically. 'You're hobbling along like an old woman.'

'Thanks a lot, Hannah!'

They stopped at the Tar Man's half-open door and instinctively held hands, unwilling to cross the threshold.

'Just in case,' said Kate, bending over and scraping off some dry dirt from between the cobblestones. 'Gideon taught us this trick. If anyone comes at you, just throw a load of dust right into their eyes and then run like there's no tomorrow.'

'With your feet like they are,' whispered Hannah, 'let's hope you don't need to . . .'

They pushed open the door with great care and crept silently into the house. They heard voices. In the middle of the hall floor, a single candle cast a circle of weak light. A strong river smell hung in the air. Until she recognised one of them, Kate's heart missed a beat when she spotted two figures in the shadows. Parson Ledbury and the old gentleman were sat on the stone flags, legs outstretched, backs to the wall and shoulders propped up against each other. Kate breathed a sigh of relief. They reminded her of two ancient tomcats at the farm, favourites of hers, both strays with torn ears and a good crop of fleas, who would swagger up and down the farmyard bumping shoulders as they went. The old gentleman had tipped back his head and was gulping something down from a small flask, wiping his mouth with a large handkerchief and letting out a deep sigh of appreciation. He offered the flask to Parson Ledbury who took it gratefully and downed a generous mouthful.

'Nectar, my dear fellow!' he said.

In return he offered the old gentleman some snuff from a silver box.

'Finest snuff in London. Recommended to me by Sir Richard. I'll send some over if it finds favour with you.'

The old gentleman put a pinch on the back of his hand, covered up one nostril and sniffed.

'Upon my word, Parson, it's very fine. Very fine indeed. I often think it is the small pleasures of Life that are the sweetest of all. When you are recovered I hope you will do me the honour of dining with me at a most agreeable chop house I know in Red Lion Square . . .'

'The Parson seems to have made a friend,' whispered Hannah to Kate.

'With the greatest of pleasure, my dear fellow,' said the Parson.

Hannah coughed to announce their presence and when the two men looked up Hannah bobbed a curtsy.

'Kate! Hannah!' exclaimed the Parson. 'Ah, but you are a sight for sore eyes. The Tar Man has run through us like a fox in a hen house but at least none of us is dead – although Sir Richard is bad, very bad. As for this courageous gentleman and his dog, they have both been ill rewarded for coming to our aid.'

Hannah immediately took out a handkerchief and a water bottle and started to dab at the cut on the Parson's head. Toby was laid out motionless over his master's knees. The old gentleman looked up at Kate, his pale features suddenly animated. He bowed his head.

'You are a friend of the young gentleman?'

Kate smiled and made an attempt at a curtsy.

'I am, sir. My name is Kate.'

'Come nearer, child.'

Kate knelt down next to him.

'It is an honour to meet any friend of Master Schock – we are comrades in arms. Do you, too, come from foreign parts?'

'I do, sir.'

The old gentleman scrutinised Kate's face. 'Your complexion has a delicacy about it which is very rare, indeed one might almost call it *transparent* . . . Tell me, my dear, can you sing? It might revive my dog who loves nothing better in the world than a good tune.'

Kate's eyebrows crept upwards of their own accord. She got to her feet. 'Perhaps later once we've attended to Sir Richard . . . Where *is* Sir Richard?'

The Parson pointed to the door at the top of the stairs.

'And the Tar Man?' asked Hannah. 'Where is he?'

'Would that I knew,' said the Parson. 'All I can only tell you is that he disappeared down the trapdoor which you see before you. Gideon is in hot pursuit although I do not hold out much hope of success. I cannot deny that Blueskin is a formidable adversary. Master Peter joined in the chase but a few minutes ago.'

Kate picked up the candle and peered down the gaping black hole in the floor. She could see nothing beyond the first few steps but the strong draught of air that rose up from the darkness made the candle gutter.

'I fancy it leads to the river,' said the old gentleman. 'Most useful if your business is of the sort that demands secrecy.'

Kate nodded and the vision of her friend floundering in dark waters flashed into her mind. She was tempted to dive down the trapdoor there and then. Hannah, meanwhile, had satisfied herself that Parson Ledbury and the old gentleman had suffered cuts and bruises but, as far as she could tell, nothing worse. The dog, however, did give her cause for concern for it did not respond to her touch and when she rested her head on its ribs its heartbeat was barely perceptible.

'How could anyone bring themselves to hurt such a pretty little creature?'

'If Toby dies,' said the old gentleman, 'I shall consider it a point of honour to bring his assassin to justice.'

'It is too early to give up hope,' said Parson Ledbury. 'He is a game little fellow, and I have observed that in both man and beast, stature and spirit may often be found in inverse proportion.'

Upstairs, they found Sir Richard flat on his belly, one hand formed in a fist and held to his ear, while his pale, blotchy face was squashed into what Kate recognised as being Gideon's jacket, folded up into an improvised pillow. His legs were spreadeagled over the bare floorboards. It was hard to witness Sir Richard, a man of such dignity and bearing, being brought so low. Suddenly Kate put her hands to her mouth. She felt sick to her stomach.

'Oh, Hannah, look how his arm is lying! It looks like . . . it's not joined on properly!'

Hannah crouched down beside him. 'Can you hear me, sir?'

Sir Richard groaned a little but did not open his eyes.

Hannah spoke softly into Sir Richard's ear: 'It is Hannah. Mistress Kate is here with me. I've sent the driver to fetch a surgeon.'

'Do you think he can hear you?' asked Kate.

Hannah nodded her head and started to slip the sleeve off Sir Richard's good arm.

'We're going to take your jacket off and roll you onto your back, sir.'

Then she turned her attention to his injured arm. Hannah hesitated, both hands hovering above the second sleeve. She and Kate exchanged apprehensive glances. The arm stuck out from the shoulder socket at an impossible angle.

'Go on,' said Kate. 'You're doing so well – anyone would think you were a nurse . . .'

Hannah sat back on her heels and put her hands firmly back in her lap. Suddenly she looked tearful. Unwilling to let Sir Richard hear what she said, Hannah leaned over and whispered into Kate's ear.

'I've had to nurse more folk in my time than I care to remember on account of one thing and another – my brothers back from the war, and all the fevers that have laid low Mrs Byng's brood – not to mention Master Jack's scrofula. It's often fallen to me. But I don't know as I dare touch Sir Richard. He is Mrs Byng's brother – what if I damage his arm further?

'I think Sir Richard is lucky to be looked after by someone who knows what they're doing,' said Kate.

'But I don't! They say that the body can heal itself but from what I've seen of life, it often doesn't . . . I've never seen an injury like this. I don't know how to treat it, Mistress Kate, save try and make him comfortable – but how can I do that without hurting him?'

Kate sighed. 'If we were in my century, all we would have to do is telephone 999 and within minutes an ambulance would come and take Sir Richard to hospital. And they'd give him a pain-killing injection and sort him out in no time. Sorry. This isn't helpful. You must think I'm talking rubbish . . .'

Hannah looked blankly back at her.

'Perhaps we should just leave him be,' said Kate. 'At least until the driver comes back with a doctor.'

Hannah nodded uncertainly and started to stroke Sir Richard's head, her gaze studiously avoiding his arm. His breath came out in short, hard bursts. If it were not for being reluctant to leave Hannah in the lurch, Kate would have gone down that trapdoor by now . . .

Kate stared blankly at the heavy folds of Sir Richard's jacket which lay half on and half off his gently heaving back. The log fire glowed bright, hissing and crackling from time to time, and the heat began to redden her cheeks. In the stillness and the quiet, Kate gradually became aware of another vision forming at the back of her mind, like a wall of thunderclouds blowing in from the horizon. It crept up on her stealthily, growing, demanding her attention. A bat squeak of fear sounded in her head. What was it? What did it mean? It unnerved, even angered her. She resisted confronting the darkness that loomed over the landscape of her mind. She also resisted admitting that she could detect a figure in that darkness. Instinctively she wanted to fight it, crowd it out. So, instead of looking at the vision, Kate forced herself to think of her valley in Derbyshire and how a sudden break in the clouds would allow a ray of sunshine, dazzling against the grey, to pierce the valley as if heaven itself had decided to break through the gloom. She pictured the sunlight, skittering and dancing over the patchwork of yellow and green fields as the clouds moved across the sky.

'Is anything the matter, Mistress Kate?'

Hannah's words dragged her back.

'I . . . No. I'm fine.'

Hannah reached out to hold Kate's hand.

'How cold you are!'

'I was just thinking about what you said — about people not always getting better. That's all.'

'Oh, forgive me, Mistress Kate. I didn't mean to worry you. Sir Richard *will* get better, I am sure of it . . . at least, I hope so.'

Hannah warmed Kate's hands in her own. Kate smiled at her and realised how young and pretty she was. Having spent so much time with Hannah when she was approaching fifty, Kate knew every last wrinkle of the plumper face she would have in her middle years, and was still not quite used to seeing her like this, with fresh young skin and shining hair and teeth that looked like they could have been bleached.

'You know,' Kate said, 'you were really good to me when Peter's father and I ended up in 1792. You looked after me when I didn't feel well. It meant a lot . . .'

'Oh, please don't talk to me about the future, Mistress Kate! I'd rather not know if it's all the same to you — although I'm glad that I was of service to you . . .'

'Don't worry, Hannah, if my dad and Dr Pirretti are right, we're overwriting that particular future, anyway!'

Hannah shook her head in bewilderment and resumed stroking Sir Richard's brow.

Time, Kate decided, was not as straightforward as she had once thought. It was not as if the past, present and future were obliged to keep in their correct order like good children standing in a queue, and in the same way that stories are supposed to have a beginning, a middle and an end. With everything that had happened to her, she had started to see time through a different lens. The Marquis de Montfaron had likened time to a corridor with many doors leading off it and she was beginning – finally – to grasp what he had meant. He had suggested that, in one sense, all times happen at once, and it was primarily a question of choosing which door to go through – and, of course, how to open that door. To travel through time, it was not necessary to live through each moment in sequential order – it was perfectly possible to leapfrog from one time to another.

Perhaps it wasn't such a difficult concept. Memory, she thought, means that we're all used to juggling the past and the present. After all, she did not have a problem with reconciling the young Hannah whom she saw in front of her with her memory of Hannah on the very first day they'd met in Derbyshire, or with the middle-aged version of Hannah who had accompanied her and Peter's father to France. Similarly, she only had to bend her mind a little and she could see Hannah in the future. There she was with a baby in her arms sitting in the spring sunshine . . . Kate's train of thought suddenly screeched to a halt. She screwed up her eyes and clenched her teeth together so hard it hurt. Had she just invented an image of a potential future for Hannah, or had she just foreseen the future with no more difficulty or effort than if she had tried to remember where she had gone on holiday last summer? The fortune-teller's words rang in her ears, and not for the last time that day. I'm no oracle, she told herself. I'm not!

'Would you hold Sir Richard's hand, Mistress Kate? I shan't mean to but I'm sure to hurt him.'

Kate looked up with a start. 'Yes – of course.'

'Well,' Hannah said. 'I don't suppose there's any point delaying. I reckon I'll be more careful than most of the doctors I've seen. Though, to be fair, Dr Darwin in Lichfield *was* gentle. And best do it now, while he's half-asleep.'

Kate nodded and Hannah, with her face settled in a firm resolve, started to pull the sleeve softly. Disconnected from the shoulder socket, Sir Richard's injured arm behaved more like a joint of meat than a human limb. It made Kate want to heave.

Sir Richard was clearly in shock. Kate took his hand in hers. It was cold and clammy to the touch, and he was already groaning and pursing his lips together trying to hold in his pain. Kate watched apprehensively as Hannah gave a little tug to get the sleeve over his elbow. Sir Richard instantly responded by squeezing Kate's fingers violently enough to make her knuckles crack. At the same time he raised his head from the floor, opened his jaws and bellowed. It was the cry of an animal, a cry of pure agony.

The sound was unbearable. Kate tried to cover her ears but Sir Richard would not release her hand. The terrible cry went on and on, getting louder and deeper, until she felt it more than she heard it, his pain throbbing in her heart.

'Oh, Hannah,' she cried. 'What can we do to make him stop? Hannah? *Hannah!*'

Hannah's face was flushed with anxiety and the effort of taking off Sir Richard's jacket. A row of small white teeth bit into her lower lip; a bubble was forming in the corner of her mouth. Although her back arched precariously backwards after the sleeve had suddenly come away, Hannah remained absolutely still. As was Sir Richard, his mouth fixed open in a scream; as was the candle; as were the orange flames that licked around the logs in the hearth.

'No!' wailed Kate. 'Not again! Not with Peter gone!'

CHAPTER FOURTEEN

A Bonfire in Derbyshire

In which the Marquis de Montfaron comforts Sam and the farmhouse receives some unexpected visitors

The Marquis de Montfaron found Sam buried in a ball under the bedclothes. When Sam refused to come out he perched elegantly on the end of the bed with a very straight back, and studied the duvet cover printed with skyrockets and stars. He noted that its depiction of the night sky was wholly inaccurate. Presently Montfaron noticed a page, torn out of a newspaper and stuck to the back of Sam's bedroom door with strips of yellowing sticky-tape. He scanned the articles but found nothing which he thought would interest a ten-year-old boy. He looked at the date. December 15th.

Montfaron waited patiently and started to hum the piano sonata which he was currently learning and which he found particularly uplifting. The composer was new to him. He had noticed the sheet music open on the upright piano that Mrs Dyer sometimes played in the dining room. After idly picking out a few notes with one finger, he had been so taken with the melody that he had rolled up his sleeves and played it until he had a proper grasp of the piece. He wondered if this fellow Beethoven had achieved any fame – he would not be at all surprised.

'Ssshh!' hissed Sam from under the duvet. 'Please leave me alone. I'm not a baby. Humming me a tune isn't going to do anything.'

Montfaron was tempted to argue the case for music in life's more difficult moments but instead paced around the tiny room, stooping as he approached the open window on account of the pitched roof. Swallows were diving after the clouds of midges that hovered in the sunny farmyard. Beyond the mud-caked yard, cattle grazed on sun-bleached grass and, moving between the docile beasts towards the far end of the field, Montfaron could make out a line of people, of assorted heights, all carrying baskets. Mrs Dyer brought up the rear. She was holding Milly's hand as she skipped along. Montfaron smiled.

'I'm not going,' said Sam. 'What's the point of having a birthday picnic for Kate when we she's not even here? And when the world is probably going to self-destruct. For all we know Kate might even be—'

Before Sam could finish his sentence, Montfaron, whose head was now halfway out of the window, let out a loud peal of laughter.

'What?' asked Sam, put out that Montfaron should come into his room and then not even bother to listen to him.

'Oh, it is nothing of any consequence, nothing at all,' the Marquis chuckled.

There was a pause and then Montfaron started to laugh again.

'What is it? What are you looking at?'

'I do not wish to disturb your contemplations. It is but a trivial thing, I assure you.'

Sam peeped out from under the duvet. Montfaron's shoulders

were shaking. Sam stared at him with round, tear-stained eyes. Slowly, he rolled off the mattress onto the floor and crawled towards the window on his hands and knees. Montfaron glanced down at the boy and held out his hand. Sam took it and Montfaron pulled him up. Sam looked out at the farmyard and at the patchwork of fields beyond but saw nothing out of the ordinary except a shiny black car snaking down the steep road that led to the farmhouse.

'I can't see anything funny.'

Montfaron pointed upwards and made a noise that sounded like *oink*. The puzzlement on Sam's pale face melted away as his mouth cracked into a grin.

'That is so random!'

The bright blue sky was clear apart from one huge, billowing cloud. It was the precise shape of a pig – ears, snout and four legs. As it sailed over Derbyshire there was even a wispy bit of water vapour at the end for its curly tail.

Montfaron turned around to look at the scrap of newsprint stuck to the door. He fixed Sam with his intense brown eyes.

'On what day did Kate disappear?'

'Saturday, December 16th.'

'Ah, now I understand. The past is safe; the future never certain, is that not so, Sam? Yet there is wisdom in this that one grows to understand . . . I am sorry you are so angry.'

'I'm not angry! . . . I just want things to go back to normal. I'm fed up of feeling frightened all the time!'

Montfaron saw the tears welling up again in Sam's eyes and he had to blink away his own. The tall man put an arm around the boy's shoulder and squeezed it. They both stared in silence at the cloud floating over the valley.

'We are men, my dear friend,' said Montfaron finally. 'We are creatures of reason and will, and are therefore able to look our fear in the face. All things pass, Sam, in the end. Happiness *will* return.'

'I don't mean to get like this. Everyone says I am too sensitive. I wish I were like the others.'

'Do not wish to be rid of a quality which may serve you well . . . You remind me a little of Kate. Your sister is a remarkable person and I think you share some of her qualities.'

Sam's face lit up. 'Do I?'

'Yes.'

'I'm still not going on the picnic, though . . .'

Suddenly the sound reached them of car tyres crunching on gravel.

'It appears that we have visitors!' said Montfaron.

'Mum said Inspector Wheeler might come today.'

Sam ran onto the landing and looked down from the window onto the front drive. 'Who the heck are they?' he exclaimed.

Montfaron peered over his shoulder. 'You do not know them?'

Sam's eyes widened. 'We don't know anyone who looks like *that*! And we definitely don't know anyone who has a chauffeur-driven Mercedes!'

The chauffeur opened the door for his passenger. Dressed all in white, accessorised with heavy chain jewellery and with her nails painted black, Anjali climbed out of the car and squinted at the Derbyshire landscape. Her shining black hair was streaked with electric blue. She slid her giant sunglasses down onto her nose, and turned in a circle, surveying the sunny, stone farmhouse, the rippling brook, the towering beech, its coppery leaves fluttering in the breeze, the swooping swallows. She halted when her gaze encountered the black and white cattle in the adjoining field.

'Wow! *Real* cows!'

The chauffeur opened the door for Tom who hesitated before stepping out of the safety of the Mercedes and stood, shoulders hunched anxiously and brow furrowed.

'Come on, city boy!' Anjali cried, 'take a deep breath of all that fresh air and manure and stuff.'

On cue, Tom sneezed violently. Anjali cackled with laughter. 'Don't tell me you're allergic to the countryside!'

Anjali eyed the stone farmhouse with its small-framed windows and hollyhocks and ragweed growing from cracks between the paving stones. A lace curtain at an upstairs window dropped abruptly as she looked at it. Anjali gave a little wave.

'Canary Wharf, it ain't,' she said.

Anjali rooted about in her Prada handbag and drew out a couple of ten-pound notes. She offered them to the chauffeur who was standing to attention in his peaked cap, awaiting orders.

'Here – go and buy yourself a Bakewell tart or feed the ducks or something. Wait in town and leave your phone on. I'll give you a bell when we need you.'

'Would you like me to unload the gentleman's luggage, miss?'

'I told you – the name's Anjali. No. Thank you very much. We don't know if he's staying yet.'

As the Mercedes disappeared up the drive, the front door opened and Sam and the Marquis de Montfaron appeared. Tom flinched at the sight of such a tall, upright man.

'C'mon, Tom,' said Anjali encouragingly, 'let's say hello.'

She walked confidently up to the front door, dragging Tom by the hand.

'Hi! This *is* the Dyer farm?'

'Yes, it is,' said Sam.

'That's a relief! It'd be a long hike back to town in these . . .' She indicated her boots. 'I'm Anjali – and this is Tom.'

She shook Sam's hand and then held out her hand to Montfaron. He took it and kissed it. 'I am delighted to make your acquaintance. I am . . . Mr Montfaron.'

Anjali looked at him quizzically and noted the erect stance and the shoulder-length hair tied up in a ponytail.

'So you're not Dr Dyer, then?'

Sam tried not to stare too hard at Anjali or at the boy in jeans and T-shirt who could not look them in the eye. 'My dad's down in the valley. I could get him if it's important. Is it him you want to speak to?'

'Yeah. We could walk down . . .'

Sam looked at Anjali's suede ankle boots with their pointed heels which would be ruined before she reached the first gate. 'I could lend you a pair of Kate's wellingtons, if you liked . . . they'd probably fit.'

At the sound of Kate's name, Tom looked up sharply.

Anjali accepted Montfaron's offer of refreshments and they all trooped into the kitchen. Sam became suddenly contrite on account of all the mess.

'Sorry, I was doing an assignment for school—'

'You're kidding me!' said Anjali. 'It's the holidays! That's harsh. What is it?'

'Maths . . .'

Anjali pulled a face. 'Rather you than me, mate.'

Too much of a gentleman to enquire what business the guests had with their host, Montfaron nevertheless eyed Anjali with great curiosity. The feeling was mutual.

'This might sound mental,' said Anjali to Montfaron. 'But I reckon you come from the eighteenth century? Am I right? 'Cos

I'm becoming a bit of an expert as it happens.' She cocked her head at Tom. 'This one is 'n'all. And I want to get him home.'

Montfaron's large chestnut eyes grew round and Sam started like he'd received an electric shock.

'Tom?' Sam exclaimed, wheeling around to look at him. 'Tom who was in the Carrick Gang that attacked Kate and Peter?'

Tom returned his stare anxiously. 'I'll wager you are Mistress Dyer's brother.'

Sam flew at him, grabbed him around the neck and pushed him against a kitchen cupboard. 'What have you done with her?' he yelled in Tom's face. 'Where's the Tar Man?'

'Oi!' shouted Anjali. 'Put him down right now or we're out of here.'

Montfaron peeled away Sam. He was pale and trembling. Tom remained flattened against the cupboard. He was panting and looking desperately at Anjali for guidance.

'These people aren't about to help us! Please, Miss Anjali, let us leave while we can!'

'You're all right,' Anjali said to him, motioning at him to calm down. 'No harm done. He's only a kid.' She turned to Sam who was still staring, glassy-eyed, at Tom. 'I ain't seen the Tar Man in months. He disappeared – right after he'd hired a helicopter to come to this place. I was hoping you was going to tell *us* where he was.'

'I think it best,' said Montfaron, 'that I take you to see Kate's parents and Dr Pirretti without delay.'

'You *are* from the eighteenth century, ain't you?'

'Yes,' said Montfaron. 'As you have been so open with us, I shall not deny it.'

Anjali nodded, satisfied. 'Thought as much. So, do you know Vega Riaza, then? You know, the Tar Man?'

Montfaron raised his eyebrows. 'The Tar Man and I shared neither the same decade, nor the same country, nor, I am relieved to say, the same acquaintances . . .'

'Only asking,' Anjali grinned. 'Vega's all right once you get to know him . . .'

While the children played hide and seek and gathered more dry kindling for the bonfire, the grown-ups talked in earnest. Mrs Dyer was listening with one ear but kept looking anxiously back towards the farmhouse, hoping to see that Montfaron had persuaded Sam to come and join them.

'Has Tim admitted leaking the story to the US press?' asked Dr Dyer.

'No,' Dr Pirretti replied, 'and I'm still hoping it might blow over. Even if Tim *has* approached journalists directly, the serious papers aren't going to be fool enough to print the story without proof and confirmation from NASA. All we've got to do is to continue to deny everything.'

Mrs Dyer pulled a face. 'Anita! What newspaper editor would show restraint if there's even a remote possibility that someone's discovered time travel? And after what the whole world has just witnessed, how long do you think it'll be before people start putting two and two together? Sooner or later all hell is going to break loose, you know it will.'

Dr Dyer and Dr Pirretti exchanged glances. Dr Pirretti tore up a handful of grass and scattered it in front of her. 'In which case we'd better get moving while we still can.'

'How long do you think it will take you both to build another anti-gravity machine?' asked Mrs Dyer.

'Two weeks?' said Dr Pirretti. 'Maybe.'

'At least,' said Dr Dyer. 'But with both of us suspended from duties, the biggest problem will be getting hold of the materials. I might have to resort to breaking into my own lab.'

'Ah. *That*, at least, we don't have to worry about,' said Dr Pirretti.

'What do you mean?'

'I mean that Inspector Wheeler is going to lend us a hand.'

'Inspector Wheeler! You've been in contact with him?'

'Yes. He's been looking into something for me. I got an email, the same day that the *New York Post* published a piece entitled *Is time travel possible?* The writer preferred to remain anonymous. They had contacted the journalist who wrote the piece. He told them, in turn, that it was *our* anti-gravity project that was implicated in the rumours . . .'

'You mean Tim actually told them it was *us?*' exclaimed Dr Dyer.

'How else would the journalist have known?'

'But what was the email about, Anita?' asked Mrs Dyer.

'They suspect that a man they've recently got to know actually comes from the past. They've even attached a couple of photographs of some guy in New York.'

'How strange!' said Mrs Dyer.

'It's bound to turn out to be a hoax – but in the circumstances I asked Dan Wheeler if it would be possible for him to check the identity of the sender.'

'Dan?' said Dr Dyer. 'So you're on first name terms now!'

Dr Pirretti laughed. 'He's kind of sweet – in a gruff, Scottish, don't-mess-with-me sort of way. But the point is, while I was talking to him about the email, I told him about our decision to build a second replica of Tim's machine. I also mentioned how tough it was going to be to getting hold of the materials. And straight away he offered us his support.'

'That's excellent news!' exclaimed Dr Dyer. 'It makes a change to have a policeman on our side!'

'I know. He even said that if necessary he'd go to the NCRDM management and confiscate laboratory equipment "for analysis".'

Mrs Dyer smiled at Dr Pirretti. 'Well done, Anita!'

As the summer afternoon wore on, long fingers of violet shadow started to creep down one side of the valley. Crickets chirruped, feathery grasses rippled in waves across the fields, whilst, overhead, larks called anxiously as the children strayed too near their nests, picking blue harebells and scarlet poppies. Unseen as yet by the three adults sitting in a circle around the growing pile of logs and twigs, four figures were approaching them from the farmhouse and an unmarked police car had just drawn to a halt in the drive.

Mrs Dyer stared absently at the beauty that surrounded her. But she saw none of it. Her shoulders hunched and her eyebrows were knotted together in a little frown.

Dr Dyer leaned towards her. 'Penny for them,' he whispered.

Suddenly Mrs Dyer sat up straight and looked up at her two companions. She looked as if she had finally come to some kind of decision. 'There's something I've been meaning to tell you ever since Kate came back the first time – but there's been so much else to worry about that I haven't wanted to add to it. And in any case, I'm still not sure whether it was my imagination or not . . .'

Dr Dyer looked sharply at his wife. 'What is it? Is it to do with Kate?'

Mrs Dyer described how she thought she had seen Kate moving faster than a human being could possibly move and how Kate had been entirely unaware of what was happening to her.

'We'd just done the milking. It was beginning to snow – you know how much Kate loves snow. One minute she was behaving perfectly normally and the next she was flitting about as fast as a

186

bat. No faster than that, a humming bird . . . Far faster, at any rate, than is normal.'

'Now that *is* weird,' said Dr Pirretti. 'Are you sure it couldn't have been a trick of the light – something flickering perhaps?'

'Well, exactly, it's what I've been trying to tell myself. I wondered if I was just imagining things – after all we'd been under so much stress. But you see, Kate then asked me why I'd been staying still for so long – but I *hadn't*. I realised that relative to the speed at which *she* was travelling, it must have seemed like *I* was standing still. Of course, I didn't tell Kate what I was thinking.'

'But why didn't you tell me, for goodness' sake?' cried her husband.

'What could you have done about it? Look, I suppose I doubted the evidence of my own eyes. It was like she'd been . . . disconnected from normal time. She was moving so quickly she was blurred – any faster and I think she would have disappeared altogether.'

'And she didn't notice anything?'

'No, nothing. And am I the only one who noticed a change in Kate before the Tar Man carried them both off? There was something about her appearance that reminded me of a colour photograph that is beginning to fade – even the red of her hair seemed less intense. Oh, I don't know . . . it was all very subtle, nothing dramatic.'

'I didn't notice anything,' said Dr Dyer.

Mrs Dyer looked relieved. 'Oh, I hope you're right. The imagination can play such strange tricks.'

'I noticed it, too,' said Dr Pirretti.

Dr Dyer looked crestfallen.

'What could be happening to her to cause such a thing?' cried Mrs Dyer.

'I suspect it means that time travel is having a physical effect on her . . .' replied her husband.

'My – alternative self – has a theory,' said Dr Pirretti.

Dr Dyer gave her a sharp look which made Dr Pirretti hesitate.

'A theory about Kate? How does she know about Kate if she's in a parallel world?' asked Mrs Dyer.

'In the same way that she can sense me, she can sense Kate. If you accept the possibility that parallel worlds exist, it doesn't require a great leap of faith to believe that there might be some kind of link between them. She believes that Kate is *pivotal* to finding a solution to all this. The first time event happened in our world. Change things here and the rest follows.'

'And because Kate belongs to the original world, she has the power to change things?' asked Mrs Dyer.

'That's my *alter ego's* theory . . .'

'And can she talk with Kate?'

'She tells me she is trying to.'

'So she's definitely alive?' cried Mrs Dyer joyfully.

Dr Dyer opened and closed his mouth, torn between conflicting emotions.

'I know, I know,' said Dr Pirretti. 'Beware of false hopes. But for what it's worth, Andrew, I am a hundred per cent certain that – no matter how ludicrous it seems -I *am* able to communicate with an alternative me in a parallel world which would not have existed were it not for our little fiasco with an anti-gravity machine. And this other Anita Pirretti is equally convinced that she is on the verge of being able to communicate with Kate.'

'All right, I agree to suspend my disbelief for a minute,' said Dr Dyer. 'Tell us about her/your theory about what is happening to Kate.'

'She compares what is happening to the universe to what is happening to the atoms in Kate's body . . .'

Mrs Dyer's face creased into anxious lines. 'Kate's *atoms?*'

Dr Dyer took hold of her hand. 'Remember that this is to be taken with a large pinch of salt . . .'

Mrs Dyer withdrew her hand. 'I'm fine! Go on, Anita! I'm listening.'

'Okay. We know that left to its own devices gravity would slow and then reverse the expansion of the universe, ultimately squeezing everything down to a single point where even time itself would stop. But this isn't happening. It seems that something is countering it. And that something is pushing the stars and galaxies apart so that rather than the expansion of the universe slowing down, in fact the expansion is *accelerating*, with the distances between galaxies becoming greater and greater . . .'

'And although we don't yet understand what that something is, we're calling it dark energy,' said Dr Dyer.

'Exactly. And dark energy appears to be acting as a counter-force to gravity. This battle of the forces seems to be shaping the way the Universe expands, the way galaxies and stars move – *and*, according my alternative self, how the atoms in our bodies behave.'

Suddenly Dr Dyer stood up and started to pace around. 'Of course!' He turned to his wife. 'You know how I always said that what puzzled me in all of this was why the anti-gravity machine chose the precise moment that Kate and Peter bumped into it to become a time machine? And I said that it must be something akin to oxygen making a flame burn more brightly?'

Dr Pirretti started to nod her head. 'Go on,' she said.

'Could it be possible that there are circumstances in which *people* can act as a kind of conduit – a kind of *conductor* – for dark energy . . .'

189

'Precisely the conclusion my alter ego came to,' said Dr Pirretti. 'It makes sense, doesn't it?'

'And if that *is* the case,' continued Dr Dyer, 'it would be more accurate to say that people are powering the anti-gravity machine than it would be to say that the anti-gravity machine is transporting passengers across time . . .'

Squeals of laughter suddenly carried over to them on the warm breeze and they all turned to watch the children chasing each other in the meadow.

'My alternative self has another theory,' said Dr Pirretti. 'She believes that some people are better conductors of dark energy than others. Using her logic, Kate, for instance, is a particularly good conductor. She likens it to copper being a better conductor of electricity than rubber. Kate is copper – and my instincts tell me that the Tar Man is, too. Peter, on the other hand, seems to be less sensitive to the side effects of time travel which makes me think he could be a much poorer conductor.'

'I can see her reasoning,' said Dr Dyer. 'She would argue that in Kate, the balance between gravity and dark energy has become unstable – dark energy is getting the upper hand. And it's the excess of dark energy in Kate that makes her susceptible to slipping out of the normal flow of time.'

Dr Pirretti spread out her hands in agreement. 'Exactly – although we can't yet prove any of this, of course. And I am beginning to suspect that the reason I am able to communicate with a parallel world is that I, too, am a good conductor of dark energy. Perhaps we all have the capacity to do this.'

'You're seriously suggesting that we can all communicate with our alternative selves in parallel worlds!'

'Perhaps. I don't know! But think of it this way – and there's been a lot of speculation about this: imagine parallel worlds as a series of ponds. While we are stuck in our own pond we are convinced that there is nothing else – until, one day, we stick our heads above the surface and we realise that our pond is just one of many. And what if all these ponds are linked in so far as they sit in the same earth? Would it be such a crazy idea to think that communication between ponds ought to be possible?'

Dr Dyer ran his hands through red hair. 'Anita, this is a step too far for me – I honestly don't know what I think any more . . .'

'All right . . . but, in any case, if we take the idea that Kate has been conducting dark energy to its logical conclusion, do you see what effect this might have on the human body?'

Mrs Dyer's eyes darted from one to another and caught her husband's expression change from one of excitement to dismay in half a second.

'What is it?' she cried.

'I've just understood your reference to the link between the galaxies in the universe and the atoms in Kate's body . . . If dark energy fills the spaces in atoms in the same way that it fills the empty spaces in the universe, then Kate's atoms could, quite literally, like the universe itself, be drifting apart . . .'

Mrs Dyer's eyes opened wide with horror. 'Which would explain why Kate looks like she's fading! Oh, Andrew, we've got to get her back! We've got to get her back and reverse it!'

Dr Dyer held his wife in his arms but over her shoulder his eyes met those of Dr Pirretti. Both knew what the other was thinking. Suddenly Mrs Dyer pushed her husband away and turned to Dr Pirretti.

'Anita, you've got to tell your alter ego to hurry. Tell her to keep trying to contact her. If she can give Kate the security code for the machine they might stand a chance. What *is* the code, Andrew?'

'One that she won't have any problem remembering – it's her date of birth.'

'Tell her, Anita! Tell her that we're doing everything we can to get her back!'

'I will. Of course, I will.'

CHAPTER FIFTEEN

The Law of Temporal Osmosis

In which Kate makes a scientific
discovery and keeps company with
The Tar Man on his boat

It took Kate an unbearably long time to extricate her hand from Sir Richard's grasp. He felt like a corpse: cold, stiff and unresponsive. She had to tear back his fingers with every last scrap of her strength until she went red in the face and her forehead became drenched in sweat. Finally she managed to slide her hand out. It seemed to her that her ability to interact with the physical world was diminishing with each new episode of fast-forwarding. Relative to her own mass, everything she touched now seemed so much denser. It was as if she were losing her strength in this dimension – a butterfly beating its wings against a windowpane. Just how fast must she now be hurtling through time?

Kate was anxious to get out of the room. In the same way as London pavements bear witness to the passage of an underground train tens of feet below, the air that she breathed transmitted Sir Richard's pulsing cry even though it was no longer audible. Glancing around the Tar Man's sitting room, she tried to avoid letting her gaze settle on Sir Richard's arm or the expression on his face, or the pool of someone's blood under the table. The room was furnished with taste and care, which both surprised and intrigued Kate. The surface of the table was strewn with ancient-looking objects. Kate wondered if the Tar Man liked to collect beautiful things, or whether this was merely where he stashed his stolen goods. Most of the items would have looked at home in the British Museum – amulets and urns, small statues of athletes and wood nymphs and the like. There was a tinderbox, too, similar to the one she had often seen Gideon use to light fires.

Stepping over Sir Richard's sprawling legs, Kate hurried out of the door, down the stairs, past the old gentleman and the Parson, and stood looking down into the mouth of the trapdoor. The yawning hole was pitch-black and smelled bad. The candle was still burning in the centre of the hall and Kate decided that she would have to requisition it. After all, the old gentleman and the Parson would not miss it – it would be back again within a blink of one of their eyes. But when she crouched down, expecting to pick it up in one hand, she found that she needed two. It was a peculiar sensation: it was not that it felt enormously heavy, it was more a case of her own flesh seeming insubstantial compared with the density of the candlestick. After a short while she felt as if her arms might tear like tissue paper if she didn't put the candlestick down. Kate placed it back on the floor. Trying to convince herself that her flesh did not look as fragile as it felt, Kate held out her hands in front of her, reassuring herself that their waxen translucence was merely an effect of the candlelight. At length she decided to go outside to look for Gideon and Peter rather than descending into that black hole by herself and without a light.

She looked over at the old gentleman who was now passing his flask over to the Parson. The latter was looking very pleased at the prospect of another mouthful of brandy.

'See you later, you poor little thing,' she said to Toby the dog, and planted a loud kiss on its head. 'Bye, Parson Ledbury and your new friend! Don't drink too much bingo while I'm away!'

Kate stole out into the night and walked painfully over the cobblestones towards the river. At the quayside she stopped and turned a full three hundred and sixty degrees, searching the darkness for any sign of Gideon or Peter. Time had turned the Thames into a great slab of black glass. Silhouettes of houses and church steeples rose up all around, dwarfed by the towering dome of St Paul's which glowed in the moonlight like a gigantic beacon over the city. The night was exceptionally clear. The longer Kate gazed at the sky, the more layers of stars she could see; an infinity of stars shining down on her from the farthest stretches of the universe. Kate sighed and looked out at this still and silent world where she was its only fully-functioning inhabitant. It was like having her own desert island or, which was nearer the mark, like being the only inmate of a vast prison whose sole key holder, to the best of her knowledge, was Peter Schock, who was currently nowhere to be seen.

Suddenly Kate noticed a dark shape above her that made her heart thump in her chest. It blotted out a tiny pocket of stars and she could not account for it. But when she walked a few paces to one side she realised what it was. A bat hung in the air only a few feet above her head, as if suspended by elastic from an invisible ceiling. Kate jumped up to take a swipe at it, an action she regretted when she landed back on the cobblestones.

She walked to the edge of the quayside and looked down, half-expecting to see the Tar Man or Gideon and Peter. But there was no one in sight, just a line of rowing boats and, beyond them, a few larger vessels anchored in deeper water. She leaned over and peered first to one side and then the other. Where could they have got to? Kate felt certain that the trapdoor must lead to a secret passage, so surely its purpose must be to link the Tar Man's house to the river? Unless, of course, they had never got out of the cellar . . . She became uneasy. There was nothing for it, she was going to have to go back.

Back in the Tar Man's house, the gaping hole did not look any more inviting. Even if I can't carry the candlestick very easily, she said to herself, at least I can move it closer to the trapdoor. The flame did not even flicker as she pushed it across the floor but it cast too weak a light to illuminate more than the stairs. Kate stared down into the darkness and imagined damp, slimy walls and scuttling creatures. After a lengthy hesitation Kate worked up enough courage to climb down the rough wooden steps. The odour of rottenness and stagnant water intensified. She walked straight ahead, her arms outstretched, but soon, as total, suffocating darkness swallowed her up, she found herself scrambling back up the steps in a panic and collapsed on the floor, face to face with Parson Ledbury, still as cheerful as ever at the prospect of a nip of brandy.

She sat there, recovering her breath, until her gaze happened to rest on two objects, barely visible in the gloom, that lay in the corner of the Tar Man's hall. Kate hurried over to investigate and heaved the objects off the floor and held them in front of her.

'My trainers!' she cried.

Unpeeling the soiled strips of petticoat from her red and blistered feet, she struggled to put on the well-loved blue and white trainers with their spongy soles and soft lining. But once she had finally managed to get into them, her feet trailed as if she were wearing blocks of wood. Rather than allowing her to walk better, she feared that they would actually prevent her from walking at all. She cried out in exasperation and, if the action had not required so much strength, would have pulled them off and flung them across the hall in disgust. She trudged from one end of the house to the other, furious with her trainers for behaving in this way when the rest of her clothes had the decency to cooperate. Soon, though, she began to notice that the soles started to yield a little to the pressure of her foot. She persevered. Yes, there was no doubt about it, with each step the trainers grew more pliable. Curious and encouraged, she shuffled up and down the hall like a toddler wearing her mother's high heels. Was this process, she wondered, like defrosting a chicken in the pantry overnight? Just as the heat would transfer from the air into the meat until both reached the same temperature, the rates at which she and her trainers travelled through time needed to equalise.

Kate felt so pleased with herself for this feat of scientific deduction that she had to share it. She sat at the feet of Parson Ledbury and the old gentleman and, as she stroked Toby's white belly, she told all three of them about her idea. Travelling forwards and backwards in time was amazing enough, but being able to affect the speed at which adjacent objects move through time was incredible! She told them that if her dad were here he would probably make her hold different objects and sit in baths of water – and who knew what else – to test her theory. He might even name a scientific law after her: *Kate Dyer's Law of Temporal Osmosis* . . . She looked at her unresponsive audience and suddenly her head sank down onto her knees. 'Oh, Dad,' she whispered into her skirts. 'When are you coming to get me?'

Kate woke up with a start. The first thing that came into her head was that she had to find Peter. She had not meant to fall asleep.

When she lifted her head up the Parson's expression was subtly altered. One of Toby's ears was turned half inside out and she wondered how it had happened. Had she done it? She stared down into the black hole once more and without understanding how she could be so certain, decided that she could not detect Peter's presence – it was to the river that she must return. Kate waited until she was able to run on the spot in her trainers, then set off at a jog.

Kate loved to run: to feel the wind in her hair and see her feet pounding the earth, eating up the ground in front of her. Here, there was no wind and she was obliged to lift her heavy skirts to avoid tripping up, but running was still a pleasure. She headed westwards, past Blackfriars, and then, when there was no sign of anyone save a young couple stealing a kiss by the water's edge, she turned back on herself. Kate continued for some way in the direction of London Bridge but after a while her lungs began to burn with the effort of it. She stopped and bent over, resting her hands on her knees, trying to get her breath back. Some of the pins fell loose from her hair and long red tresses hung down, swaying from side to side, brushing the cobblestones. While she waited for her heart to stop hammering, she looked through strands of hair at the river below her. She could see five or six small boats sailing over this stretch of the Thames. The waterman nearest to her had just pushed off and his boat – which was nearer in size to a rowing boat than a wherry – was still only six or seven feet from dry land. The waterman stood balanced at the centre of the boat's floor, one arm outstretched to steady himself. His stance caught Kate's attention. Watermen spent their whole lives bobbing about on the river in these precarious little vessels so that keeping their balance under all conditions was second nature to them. It was all in the legs according to Sir Richard – so it was surprising to see one who had to resort to using his arms for balance. Perhaps he wasn't a waterman. The man had his back to her but his stance reminded her of a javelin thrower, and he held one of the oars provocatively as if rowing with it was the last thing on his mind. Kate stood up and strained to see what he was doing. Then she ran over and walked right up to the edge of the quayside to take a closer look. He was aiming at something in the water, his lean and athletic body a perfect expression of coiled-up energy about to strike. She was familiar with the watermen's uniform. They wore distinctive red jackets and, more often than not, a particular kind of hat. It was too dark to differentiate between colours but she felt sure that this man's jacket did not belong to a waterman, nor was he wearing a hat. His longish hair, black from what she could tell, was tied back in a ponytail. A shiver of recognition ran down Kate's spine.

Estimating the distance between the boat and the quayside, she walked twenty or thirty paces away – enough for a good run-up – and charged towards the river at full pelt. Holding up her cumbersome skirts to the level of her knees, she leaped high into the air and landed heavily in the bottom of the wooden boat, narrowly missing the man and toppling forwards onto her hands and knees. Although she was expecting the flimsy vessel to rock violently in the water, it behaved instead as if it were on dry land and did not shift even a fraction of a millimetre. Just how fast must she be travelling through time for her not to feel even that? Kate crawled past the man and slowly turned her head upwards. She hardly dared look.

Kate lay at the feet of the Tar Man. He was angry, that much was obvious. His eyes smouldered and his mouth was open in a ferocious shout. Kate felt uncomfortable. To be at such close quarters with him went counter to all her instincts, even though common sense told her she was perfectly safe. She stood up and confronted him.

'You're at my mercy now!' she said in as fierce a voice as she could manage. 'I could chop all *your* fingers off if I felt like it . . .'

He continued to stare furiously back at her, defiant, fearless, indomitable. His presence was so powerful Kate took a step backwards. The brutal scar was clearly visible, even by moonlight, a vivid white through his burgeoning stubble. Seeing it so close, the scar provoked a pang of pity. What a terrible fight it must have been to have left him so disfigured.

Stillness had conferred on the Tar Man an air of unreality. He was a study in ferocity, rendered harmless by Time. He brought to mind a wax figure at Madame Tussaud's, or a snarling, stuffed tiger in a natural history museum. When she followed his gaze, she saw a hand clinging to the edge of the boat, knuckles white and fingernails biting into the wood of the boat. Kate stood up with a start.

'Gideon!' she breathed.

She had misread the Tar Man's stance. He was not about to strike with his oar; on the contrary, he had just struck. Gideon was splayed out in the water, totally submerged apart from his face and one arm. His loose hair floated about him and by the light of the moon it seemed white against the black water. He was clutching at his chest whilst trying not to lose his grip on the boat. Like his brother, Gideon was crying out, only his was a cry of pain.

All at once Kate's heart leaped into her mouth. Where was Peter? She looked all about her, at the quayside, at the other boats, at the Thames's glassy surface. Her gaze scoured the darkness but she could not find him. She felt the blood pulsing in her neck. What if he were already dead, drowned as in her vision?

'Peter!' she screamed out loud. 'Don't leave me! Don't leave me here by myself!'

Kate, who had been trying for so long to keep her spirits up, felt despair wash over her. She covered Gideon's fingers with hers. His hand was as cold and white as alabaster and made her think of graveyard angels. A single teardrop rolled down her cheek, dropped off her chin and fell, sparkling in the moonlight, onto the surface of the Thames. But even her tear was rejected, for it merely rolled away, like a bead of mercury, refusing to be assimilated, like a rebuke. As she pushed herself up something pale caught her eye in the water behind Gideon, only ten or perhaps fifteen feet away. Instantly she understood what she saw. Her vision of the future had been accurate to a fault.

'Peter!'

His white face had already sunk below the surface. Kate screamed again with the shock of it. Her friend was dying before her eyes. She looked up at the heavens.

'I'm *not* an oracle!' she cried. 'I'm not!'

Kate had been lying stretched out on the bottom of the boat for a very long time. Who could express, in this world where seconds and minutes had no meaning, how long she had lain there? Had she slept? She could not have said.

She saw no solution to her predicament. Kate had quickly given up trying to jump back to the quayside, for the boat was too small to allow a sufficient run-up. But neither could she risk immersing herself in the river – her arms and legs were not strong enough to cut through the water and if she tried to swim she might well drown. Kate now accepted that Peter alone, for reasons she did not understand, was able to ground her. But Peter was out of reach and drowning. If she tried to rescue him then she, too, would perish in the process. And so it was checkmate: she was trapped indefinitely on this tiny boat in the unwelcome company of the Tar Man.

Kate wondered how long she could survive in this condition. Food and water had barely crossed her mind and, although she would gladly have drunk something, she was surprised not to be thirstier. Kate had considered putting some solid river water in her mouth to see if it would melt like an ice cube, but when she remembered some of the things she had seen floating in the Thames she decided to put off trying this until she was really desperate.

And so Kate sat at the bottom of the boat trying to pretend that the Tar Man was somewhere else. Searching for a meaning to it all, her mind roved over all the circumstances that had led to her sharing this boat, perhaps for eternity, with a villain who had threatened to cut her fingers off. She also thought about the fortune-teller's assertion that she was an oracle, and she tried to see her own future, but only ever discerned a massive wall of impenetrable darkness. Only one thing came out of her prolonged meditation, and that was the intermittent sensation, which she felt as a prickle at the back of her neck, that she was being *watched*.

CHAPTER SIXTEEN

On the Steps of New York Public Library

In which Lord Luxon poses some
questions, Alice draws some conclusions
and Tom proves to be invaluable

Two figures emerged from the New York Public Library on Fifth Avenue, blinking in the sunlight. They began to pick their way through the crowd that milled about on the stone staircase that led to the sidewalk. Alice looked about her for somewhere to sit, and found a couple of metal chairs adjacent to one of the marble lions that stood guard over the majestic edifice. Yellow cabs honked and heat radiated from the sidewalk baking in the midday sun. Alice dropped her heavy bag of books and sat down, wafting herself energetically with a card folder.

'Do you even *own* a pair of shorts?'

Lord Luxon raised one eyebrow by way of a reply. Alice smiled. Her companion's affirmative replies about military re-enactments and his interest in the *What If?*'s of history had calmed her fears about the redcoats in Prince Street. What, precisely, *had* she imagined was going on? Was it more likely that this good-looking English milord was a visitor from another century or that he and his friends were into military history? She thanked her lucky stars that he had not spotted her grappling with that scary dog on the emergency stairs – now *that* would have been a difficult one to explain . . .

Lord Luxon stood on the sidewalk to admire the library's architecture.

'I told you it was worth seeing,' Alice called down to him.

Lord Luxon raised his hands in the air and shouted back. 'It is a veritable temple to reading! I feel devilishly clever merely walking past such a prodigious quantity of books! Though I confess that scholars tend to bore me – and I should sooner have a tooth pulled than be forced to read a book.'

The library steps were crowded with people hunched over paperbacks and eating their lunch. Several people stopped chewing their sandwiches to give Lord Luxon hostile looks.

Alice laughed. 'I wouldn't have put you down as an academic underachiever!'

'It is the truth, I assure you. For some fellows, books are as meat and drink to them, but for me, making sense of words and letters on a page is a sorry business . . .'

'If you say so! And what do you think of Patience and Fortitude?'

Lord Luxon looked at her askance. 'I cannot say they are my favourite virtues – though doubtless they are attractive in a maiden aunt. No, on balance, give me rather *Pleasure* and *Appetite*.'

'I can never be sure when you're being serious!' said Alice. 'Patience and Fortitude are the names of the *lions*!'

'Ah. The lions. Then, yes, I like the lions *inordinately*.' Lord Luxon walked over to the nearest beast and took off his straw Panama hat. 'Is this Patience or Fortitude?'

'Fortitude – I think.'

A lady in a sari seated above Alice leaned over and said softly into her ear, 'I think you'll find it's Patience, dear.'

'Thanks,' replied Alice. 'Make that Patience,' she called.

Lord Luxon stroked Patience's mane and growled at her. Alice reached for her mobile and took a picture.

'You're in a good mood! Being in America must suit you.'

'It does. Indeed, you might say that it both gives me pleasure and stimulates my appetite.'

Lord Luxon laughed, a little louder and a little longer than Alice thought his comment deserved.

'Well, I'm delighted that you approve of this side of the pond! How do Patience and Fortitude measure up to the lions at the bottom of Nelson's Column that I love so much? Only they're made of metal not stone, aren't they?'

Lord Luxon shrugged his shoulders.

'No, I can't remember for sure, either,' Alice continued. 'You get an awesome view of them from the National Gallery. You must be able to walk to Trafalgar Square in ten minutes from your house – do you go there much? Are you an art lover?'

Alice paused, for Lord Luxon suddenly looked very uncomfortable – as if he had no idea what she was talking about and was trying to conceal the fact. Yet he'd *said* that he lived in the heart of London, in Bird Cage Walk.

Lord Luxon spoke without choosing to acknowledge her question.

'Come, Alice, my stomach tells me it is time to eat. And I am hoping that you may be able to shed some light on a subject which has been preoccupying me.'

Lord Luxon stepped towards the street and hailed a taxi. As Alice got into the yellow cab next to her companion a cold feeling of dread passed over her. She gave an involuntary shiver which prompted Lord Luxon to ask if anything was the matter.

'No, I'm fine. Someone just walked over my grave, that's all.'

Could he be a con man who had smelled the scent of money and had made up his identity and his address and this stilted manner of speaking? Or had Lord Luxon just not heard her question over the traffic noise? Get a grip, Alice, she told herself as she pulled herself together.

'It was good of you to pick me up from the library,' she said. 'After all that studying I could eat a horse – well, a club sandwich at any rate. Where are we going for lunch?'

The inviting table for two overlooking the lake in Central Park revived Alice's spirits. They both leaned back in wicker chairs on the wooden deck and surveyed the view. Ducks quacked. Sunshine glowed on the white linen tablecloth and sparkled on the water. Were it not for the skyscrapers towering over the trees in the distance, it would have been difficult to believe that they were lunching in the heart of Manhattan. Lord Luxon was studying the menu. Alice sipped her glass of chilled wine and watched ducks and swans gliding lazily on the water and the antics of two girls in a rowing boat.

'This is lovely,' Alice sighed. She stretched her arms above her head and rubbed her neck, stiff from poring over piles of books in the reading room. She looked up at the light streaming through the red and white striped awning above them. The wine and the hum of conversations and hunger were all making her feel a little light-headed. Suddenly she was aware of Lord Luxon's keen blue gaze cutting into her. She came to with a jerk and sat up straight.

'Thank you for bringing me here. It's been so long since I've been to the Boathouse,' she said. 'I've always loved eating in the park.'

'I know. Your aunt told me . . .'

Alice raised her glass. 'Well, thank you, good sir.'

Lord Luxon raised his own glass. 'The pleasure is all mine, Alice . . .'

Alice took another picture of her companion against a sunny Central Park.

'I confess that something has been troubling me since our last meeting. It regards your advice about how best to sabotage the Revolutionary War . . .'

A tiny frown appeared on Alice's forehead. 'Go on – what's been troubling you?'

Lord Luxon opened his mouth to speak but before he could get a word out a waiter appeared at their table.

'What can I get for you folks today?' he asked with a warm smile.

'I'll have the Grilled Chicken Caesar Salad,' said Alice.

'And for you, sir?'

Lord Luxon glared at him, furious at the interruption.

'Chef's specials today are Sesame Crusted Salmon Fillet served on a bed of shiitake fried rice, with poached scallion and a reduced ginger soy glaze, or sirloin steak gently braised with organic root vegetables from Vermont, black pepper sauce and—'

'Sir, I have come here to *eat*. I desire neither a list of ingredients nor instructions on how to prepare the dish.'

The smile withered on the waiter's face. Alice's shocked expression prompted Lord Luxon to soften his tone.

'Be so good as to fetch me some meat and some bread – and some vegetables if you must – the precise combination is all the same to me.'

The waiter started to ask if he could be a little more specific but Lord Luxon waved him away. 'The name of the dish, the provenance of the ingredients and the method of preparation are, I assure you, all matters of *utter* indifference to me.'

'Anything you say. Sir.'

Alice smiled weakly at the disgruntled waiter who turned on his heels and walked away down the wooden deck.

'Are you always this rude to waiters?'

Lord Luxon sighed. 'You disapprove. But, I am unrepentant. Servants should cultivate a soothing presence. It is vexing in the extreme to be lectured on what your palate might presently discover for itself.'

'He'll spit in your soup . . .'

'Pish pash! Enough of waiters. You told me that if you had a mind to sabotage the Revolutionary War, your first choice would be to act on Christmas night, 1776, when Washington succeeded in crossing the Delaware River . . .'

'You were listening! Absolutely. Things were looking pretty shaky for the Patriots. But Washington managed to win a surprise victory at Trenton, and that, alongside another victory at Princeton a few days later, totally revived the Patriot cause. It was a pivotal moment, a real turning point in the war. If Washington had not succeeded in crossing the Delaware that night, who knows if there would have been the will, the opportunity, or that precise mix of circumstances on another occasion which would have guaranteed America's independence from Britain . . .'

Lord Luxon had been listening, nodding his head vigorously. How this pretty historian should have liked to have seen what his own eyes had witnessed. 'But, correct me if I am wrong, is it not true that if Washington had failed, other generals would have succeeded in crossing the river on that same night?'

'You really *have* been looking into this, haven't you? Yes, there *were* two other attempts – both downstream of Washington. Two of his commanders, General Ewing and Colonel Cadwalader, attempted to get men and guns across the Delaware but the ice floes and the terrible weather defeated them. It was only Washington who succeeded in the end.'

'Yes!' Lord Luxon's face lit up in triumph and he sprang up from the table, just as their food arrived. The waiter hurriedly set it down and fled without a word. Alice watched Lord Luxon as, hands gripping the wooden railing at the edge of the deck, he stared out across the lake with burning eyes. She admired his profile set against a backdrop of greenery and the Manhattan skyline and took a picture.

'You certainly take your re-enactments seriously!' said Alice. 'Though I don't know how you do your research if you can't abide reading.'

'Reading hurts my eyes,' said Lord Luxon, returning to the table.

'I don't believe you! Go on, who are your favourite authors? You can tell so much about a person from what they like to read . . . Let me guess. Do you like thrillers? John Le Carré perhaps?'

'I beg your pardon?'

'Clearly not. Then perhaps I can see you appreciating Jane Austen . . .'

Lord Luxon's utterly blank expression caused the feeling of dread she had experienced in the taxi to flood over her again. Suddenly Alice recalled his joke about refusing to admit to being more than two hundred and seventy years old. When was Jane Austen writing? The 1790s and early 1800s? For a moment she grappled madly with dates and arithmetic, leaving her salad untouched.

'Or how about Charles Dickens? The boy who asked for more – *Oliver Smith*.'

Alice waited for a reaction. None came. *Oliver Twist* – when was that written? 1840s?

Lord Luxon shook his head, his mouth full.

'Fielding, then, Henry Fielding – I'm sure you like *him*.'

'Ah, yes, I shall make an exception in the case of Fielding. I am particularly fond of Fielding. *Tom Jones* is vastly entertaining . . .'

Lord Luxon calmly returned Alice's questioning gaze.

Alice looked away and stared fixedly at the view of the park. This man, whose favourite author was writing in the first half of the eighteenth century – at a time when a British monarch still ruled over his American colonies – had not even *heard* of Jane Austen or Charles Dickens! And this same man had repeatedly asked her for advice on how to sabotage the Revolutionary War . . .

'Yes,' she managed to say. 'I admire *Tom Jones*, too.'

Lord Luxon started to look bored with the direction their conversation was taking. 'I have told you, Alice, that reading holds little appeal for me. I should rather hunt or play cards or fight – or even dine with an historian . . .'

'All right, you've convinced me,' said Alice, finally. 'You don't like reading. Either that, or Austen and Dickens are just too darned contemporary for your tastes . . .'

Lord Luxon scrutinised his companion's face for he sensed a change in her mood. Alice looked into his blue eyes and reasoned: So he's not a big reader – and what he *does* read is from his favourite period in history. That's still no reason to think two and two make five . . .

Anxious to clear her head, Alice thanked Lord Luxon for her unfinished lunch but told him that she still had work to do. She remembered, however, to pass on Mrs Stacey's invitation to a small party she was throwing at the weekend. Perhaps they could meet up beforehand so that they could go together? Lord Luxon took

Alice's hand and kissed it. He would look forward keenly, he said, to their next liaison.

Alice sat for a long time on a park bench in the company of office workers taking their lunch break. Her rendezvous with Lord Luxon had unsettled her, and a deep sense of foreboding refused to go away. How could she admit her unsubstantiated suspicions to anyone, particularly to her colleagues at Princeton? What could she say? I think I've just had lunch with a time traveller who has designs on the United States of America? She would be a laughing stock. Alice tried to think about something else, and when an office worker left his copy of the *New York Post*, she picked it up and idly flicked through the pages. She spotted a small article on page three that made her heart skip a beat. It was entitled: *Is Time Travel Possible?* When she had finished reading the article she reached into her bag and took out her mobile phone.

The children clustered around the small, skinny teenager who kept his expressive eyes lowered to the floor and who was so attached to his white mouse. The Dyer family plied their unexpected visitors with food and drink and tried not to ask too many questions all at once. However, the excitement at being introduced to this boy from the eighteenth century was quickly tempered by the realisation that Anjali and Tom were also the sidekicks of the villain who had abducted Kate and Peter. Not only that, but they were also associates of the man who had single-handedly thwarted all the scientists' attempts to undo the harm time travel had inflicted on the universe.

Dr Dyer and Dr Pirretti tried to explain to Anjali and Tom what had happened.

'This is doing my head in,' Anjali exclaimed as Sam and Megan put in their own words what the grown-ups had been saying about dark energy and parallel worlds and the time quake.

'But it should be Vega you're telling this to,' said Anjali. 'I can't do nothing. And you got to see it from his point of view. I'm sorry about your daughter and her friend, but Vega was only doing his job – he's a thief. It's what thieves do. When you see an opportunity you get straight in there or it's gone. You can't hang about. How was he supposed to know how much trouble you could cause with an anti-gravity machine? If you don't mind me saying, it doesn't seem right you scientists going about inventing stuff that's so dangerous even *you* can't control it . . .'

Inspector Wheeler opened his mouth to speak but changed his mind. The girl had a point.

Tom pulled on Anjali's arm and whispered something into her ear. She pulled away.

'Tom thinks I should keep my big mouth shut. But I think we've got a right to tell it how it is. The plain truth is that Tom wouldn't be in the mess he's in if it weren't for you people. You got to get him back home. *I* can't. Vega's scarpered back off to the good old days and by the look of it he's not coming back. That's why I've brought him here. *You* gotta help him.'

'Believe me, Anjali, we'll do our best,' said Dr Dyer. 'We're building another anti-gravity machine and – if we succeed – I undertake to return the Marquis *and* Tom – to their own century. And then—'

'There you go!' said Anjali, taking hold of Tom's shoulders. 'I told you they'd help you!'

'And then,' continued Dr Dyer, 'we'll search for Kate and Peter and bring them home—'

'And,' interrupted Sam, 'get the other two anti-gravity machines and destroy them so no one else can go back in time and change anything . . .'

'And then everyone will live happily ever after?' Anjali looked at Dr Dyer. A smile flickered on her face. 'I hope you've got a plan B, mate . . .'

'Well, what do you suggest we do?' exclaimed Mrs Dyer.

Anjali looked contrite. 'Sorry – I didn't mean—'

'No, I'm sorry,' said Mrs Dyer quickly. 'Don't think we don't realise we're clutching at straws . . .'

'I hate to tell you, but there's something else you ought to know about,' said Anjali. 'You say that whenever anyone goes back in time, a parallel world pops up – 'cos you reckon you can't destroy what's already happened. Am I right?'

'We don't *know* but, yes, we're working on that assumption,' said Dr Dyer.

'And that's why you want to destroy the machines – to stop any more parallel worlds or universes or whatever popping up because you think they caused the time quake?'

'Yes.'

'And you're worried what time quakes could be doing to us?'

'What are you getting at, Anjali?'

'Well, I can see your logic in destroying the machines, but I just thought you ought to know that Vega can travel through time without the machine . . .'

Dr Pirretti and Dr Dyer looked at each other in alarm.

'He can do *what*? . . . You must be talking about *blurring*, Anjali. That happened to Kate and Peter, too. It seems that if you find yourself transported to a different time there's a tendency to re-materialise in your own time until you settle into it. A strange phenomenon . . .'

'No,' said Anjali. 'He could do that, too. But Vega used objects to go back in time. He lifted something from the Museum of London, didn't he, Tom? What was it? I forget . . .'

'A helmet,' said Tom shyly. 'And some coins . . .'

'That's right! A Roman helmet and some old coins.'

'And he took Tom with him once. He offered to take me with him but after I'd seen the state of Tom when he got back I said no, thank you very much, I'm not going to risk getting stuck in the past where they'd probably burn me as a witch or something – they brought back some good stuff, though.'

Dr Dyer stared at her speechless.

'I'm sorry, but that's the way it is . . . Vega doesn't need the machine.'

'Let me get this straight, Anjali,' said Inspector Wheeler. 'When you said that the Tar Man – Vega – uses objects, what did you mean?'

'Vega couldn't always do it . . . he had to kind of . . . tune in, if you know what I mean. He said that the simpler the object the easier it was . . .'

'When Blueskin held the helmet,' said Tom, 'he could not do it. But the coins worked like charms. It was when using a coin that he took me with him.'

'And he was always complaining how unreliable it was,' said Anjali. 'Sometimes it worked and sometimes it didn't. He wanted to get his hands on your machine.'

'What time in history did he take you to, Tom?' asked Inspector Wheeler.

'I do not know, sir. I saw soldiers wearing helmets like the one Blueskin had stolen from the museum. They spoke a language I did not understand . . . Everyone looked at us. Blueskin took pleasure in such journeys but I was afraid. He did not offer to take me again.'

'But how did that work?' asked Dr Pirretti. 'Did you have to hold on to him, or what?'

'Yes. Blueskin kept his arm around my shoulder.'

The two scientists and Mrs Dyer looked so crestfallen Anjali felt she had to say something. 'I'm sorry – but no point crying over spilt milk, though, eh?'

While the Dyer children, encouraged by their father, started a game of rounders, explaining the rules as they went along to Montfaron – who proved to be an exceptional bowler – Inspector Wheeler sat next to Anjali. He could not help but admire the Tar Man's judgement in choosing this streetwise girl as his guide in a new century. He knew that she was not about to grass on the Tar Man to a Scotland Yard detective but he was burning to know some of the villain's secrets. Inspector Wheeler therefore persisted in throwing enough oblique questions her way so that even though Anjali managed to field most of them, she still let enough slip about Vega to satisfy his curiosity. To Anjali's relief, Inspector Wheeler finally changed places in order to have a word with Dr Pirretti.

'You've got to hand it to him,' Anjali overheard Inspector Wheeler say to Dr Pirretti. 'The Tar Man's no fool. Who could have predicted that an eighteenth-century villain could have achieved so much?'

Dr Pirretti leaned over to whisper something in Inspector Wheeler's ear. 'You're not going to arrest her?'

Inspector Wheeler thought for a moment. 'No. But in her line of work it's only a matter of time.'

'Being this close to a policeman is bringing me out in hives,' said Anjali to Tom. She shooed away a cloud of midges. 'And I'm not sure how much more fresh air I can stand neither . . . Look, Tom, no point in prolonging the agony – I'm gonna head back to London now.'

Anjali ignored Tom's forlorn expression and took out her mobile.

'They'll get you back! Don't get cold feet about it now – it's what you wanted. And if they foul up . . . Well, I'll come and get you. Okay?'

Tom nodded miserably.

'Meet me up at the Dyers' farm in ten minutes,' Anjali told the chauffeur.

She got up and said an abrupt goodbye to one and all, refusing all offers to accompany her back to the farm.

Before she went, Inspector Wheeler asked her for a contact number. Anjali wrote down the number of her local Chinese takeaway. She would not let Tom walk with her because she hated goodbyes. But he followed at her heels halfway up the field anyway.

'I'm not going to see you again, am I?' asked Tom.

''Course you are,' said Anjali.

'What are you going to do?'

'The usual. I can live off what Vega's left behind for years . . . decades . . .'

'You could be a nurse like the lady who looked after me at the hospital.'

Anjali looked at him incredulously.

'Don't stay a thief, Anjali – please . . .'

'Don't you worry about me – it's yourself you should be worried about!'

Tom looked at the floor.

'You got the mobile I gave you?'

Tom put his hand in the pocket of his jeans to check. He nodded.

Anjali punched his shoulder.

'See you then, Tom.'

She carried on up the field while Tom stared after her, tears rolling down his cheeks. He thought she was not going to look back. But at the last moment, just before she vanished from view, Anjali turned around, her dark hair gleaming in the sunshine, and she blew him a kiss.

'Farewell, Mistress Anjali,' called Tom.

By the time Tom had summoned up the courage to rejoin Mistress Kate's family, two photographs were being passed around. The Marquis de Montfaron looked at them and shook his head. '*Non*.' He passed them to Megan.

She grinned in approval. 'Not bad!'

Dr Dyer was still scratching his head. 'I'm sure I recognise him from somewhere but I can't for the life of me think where.'

'Maybe he's a celebrity,' said Sam.

'Well, he's in New York, at any rate,' said Dr Pirretti. 'That lion he's patting is in front of the New York Public Library on Fifth Avenue, and the other photo was taken in Central Park.'

Mrs Dyer spotted Tom and made room for him. She saw his red-rimmed eyes. She patted the grass next to her. 'Come and join us. Anjali will be back to visit us, I'm sure she will.'

Tom sat down.

'Someone in America has sent Dr Pirretti these photographs of someone that they think could be a visitor from the past.'

'Is it the Tar Man?' asked Tom eagerly.

'No, it's definitely not him,' replied Mrs Dyer. 'Dr Pirretti and Inspector Wheeler have both had close encounters with the Tar Man! No, it's bound to be a hoax. Sam, pass it over. Let Tom have a look.'

Mrs Dyer watched Tom's eyes widen as she placed the picture on his lap.

'What is it?' she cried. 'Don't tell me you know who it is!'

Tom nodded energetically. 'I do, madam, it is Lord Luxon! I was his footman for a short time. The Tar Man was his henchman!'

'Of course it is!' exclaimed Dr Dyer. 'I didn't recognise him in modern clothes! I saw Lord Luxon at Tyburn – when we rescued Gideon from the gallows and the Tar Man had to be physically restrained from killing his former master! Lord Luxon was a real peacock. Clever, too – and nasty with it from what Gideon said. If he has got hold of an anti-gravity machine . . .'

'If he's still here, we'll find it!' said Inspector Wheeler. 'If he's in the States, it'll have to be done unofficially, but we'll get him.'

'Andrew, our priority must still be building a third machine,' said Dr Pirretti. 'You can't go, and neither can I.'

'Don't you worry about that,' said Inspector Wheeler. 'I'll go. Why, I might even try and cajole young Tom into coming with me. He'll be able to pick out this Lord Luxon for me in a crowd . . .'

Tom looked terrified.

'You don't have to go if you don't want to,' said Mrs Dyer quickly to Tom.

'The Tar Man was in the habit of fading back to 1763 to ask Lord Luxon's advice,' said Tom. 'He told him how he loved the future and about the fortune he had made. Lord Luxon knows all about the twenty-first century . . .'

'That's all we need,' exclaimed Dr Pirretti angrily. 'A time tourist loose in America.'

'It might yet be nothing to worry about,' said Mrs Dyer. 'Lord Luxon will probably be just into seeing the sights like anyone else. It looks like he's having a good time! What harm can one foppish aristocrat do to a continent as big as America? Anyway, he can't be worse than the Tar Man.'

'The Tar Man is wary of Lord Luxon,' said Tom. 'He says he is like a cat who purrs and then scratches you for the pleasure of it.'

Mrs Dyer looked at Tom and didn't know how to reply. 'Don't worry, Tom, we'll keep you away from Lord Luxon's claws . . . Anyway, despite all the excitement, there was a reason for us all being here today – and it would be good if we did not forget it. This gathering is about *Kate*.'

'If it will help Mistress Kate,' Tom whispered to her mother, 'I shall go to America with the policeman.'

As the sun began to set on that summer afternoon, casting a red glow behind the valley that was now in deep shadow, Sam and Megan helped Dr Dyer to light the bonfire while Mrs Dyer and the other children laid out the food on a large tablecloth. Before they began to eat, Mrs Dyer asked everyone to raise their glasses. She held her own glass high and said in a firm voice: 'This is for you, Kate, to celebrate your thirteenth birthday. Wherever you are, know that we miss you and that we love you and that everything that *can* be done *will* be done to bring you and Peter home.'

The mood became thoughtful and for a while people were reluctant to eat or talk. Presently, though, the children started to play again and Molly made a nuisance of herself, begging for leftovers. Then Inspector Wheeler and Montfaron started to argue the pros and cons of living in a time when everyone was ignorant of world events, as opposed to living in the twenty-first century, when news travels around the planet at the speed of light.

The large bonfire glowed orange in the dark meadow, infusing everyone's clothes and hair with the smell of woodsmoke. Dr Dyer encouraged everyone to lie flat on their backs and look up at the heavens as a meteor shower had been forecast. Only Tom was left sitting up and he stayed close to the fire, poking it every so often with a stick so that the logs glowed fiercely. By the flickering light Sam watched Tom's white mouse scampering about on his master's shoulders before darting back down into his collar.

Dr Dyer and his wife lay side by side, holding hands.

'Do you remember,' said Mrs Dyer suddenly, 'when Kate was still really little, and I told her to eat all her dinner up or she'd get no pudding—'

'Yes,' Dr Dyer interrupted. 'And *she* said, "If I ate all my dinner up there'd be no room for pudding!" I do remember. Like it was yesterday. Our Kate's smart. She was smart right from being a tiny baby . . . She's going to get through this.'

'It's so hard . . . the hope and despair that you feel. Hoping that she'll pull through, fearing that it's too late. Knowing the difference between keeping your spirits up and being in denial.'

'I'm so sorry,' said Dr Dyer softly to his wife. 'If I could go back in time, right now, to that Saturday, last December, I'd go straight into Tim Williamson's laboratory and smash this machine into smithereens and put a restraining order on anyone who even expressed an interest in anti-gravity—'

'Look!' shouted Sam, jumping up and pointing. 'Meteors!'

Suddenly everyone was on their feet and fighting for the binoculars. Intense streaks of light shot across one corner of the sky and for a moment everything was forgotten as it seemed that stars were raining onto the earth.

'*Magnifique!*' exclaimed the Marquis de Montfaron when it was finally over.

'It was worth getting out of the city lights just for that,' said Inspector Wheeler. 'I've never seen anything like it.'

Everyone settled down again and soon Milly and the other

younger children and even Sam were all dozing near their parents, lulled by the crackle of the burning logs and the comforting heat.

'We really should get these children to bed,' said Mrs Dyer.

But no one moved. It was so peaceful. The air was still and fresh. Far away, on the other side of the valley, a barn owl screeched.

As Dr Pirretti lay on the hard Derbyshire earth, she listened to herself speaking from a parallel world. She listened to a description of the universe duplicating itself at an exponential rate like a deadly virus. 'With each time event,' she heard, 'another parallel world appears, each one containing the seeds of time travel. We fear that the universe is fast reaching saturation point, like a dead sea unable to absorb a single extra grain of salt. If we do nothing to stop it, this will be the end of all things. Nothing can survive. Not even Time itself.' Dr Pirretti listened but did not speak. Let Kate's parents enjoy the peace of the night and their thoughts of a beloved daughter.

It was late. Arm in arm, or hand in hand, everyone made their way across the fields through a fragrant night. The younger children led the way with their mother; the Marquis de Montfaron carried a sleeping Milly, draped over one shoulder; Dr Pirretti and Inspector Wheeler were still deep in conversation; Sam and Megan escorted Tom.

Only Dr Dyer walked by himself. He was the last to return to the farmhouse and had lagged behind so that he could be alone. 'Happy thirteenth birthday, my dear Kate,' whispered her father to the stars. 'Whatever is it that you're going through, I've got to accept that there's little I can do to help. You're on your own with this, Kate. Just know that I *love* you and that I *believe* in you. There's not a day goes by that I don't think how lucky I am to have you as my daughter.'

CHAPTER SEVENTEEN

Ghosts on the Waterfront

In which Kate witnesses a shocking apparition,
has an important conversation
and discovers an interesting property of water

All Kate wanted to do was to lose herself in sleep. She managed to escape the agonising present only in brief snatches, for although her mind longed for oblivion her body did not. Each time she awoke she would roll over onto her back at the bottom of the boat and would let her eyelids slide slowly open onto this permanent night. The constellations of stars stared down at her accusingly. How could she lie there when Peter was drowning not ten feet away?

And yet, sleep she did and it helped for a while. Kate closed a door against the present and the future and buried herself in the safety of her dreams and memories. She found herself in the kitchen at the farmhouse, her back hot against the Aga and her arms and knees wrapped around Molly's barrel chest and with her chin resting on her dog's golden head. She tickled Molly's soft ears and listened to the dog making a contented sound that alternated between a high-pitched whine and a growl of pleasure. Then she recalled Molly as a puppy, placed in a pale blue blanket on her pillow on her ninth birthday, the most exquisite creature she had ever seen, who, from that day on, only ever had eyes for her. As Kate drifted into sleep, her hands resting on her stomach, she half believed that it was Molly's breath which she could feel gently rising and falling.

Much later, the vision of the grown-up Peter Schock came to her. She was observing his profile as he looked out to sea, standing on the prow of the Dover packet, the white cliffs of the Opal Coast looming on the horizon. She could feel the wind whip her face and smell the salt tang of the English Channel. Kate understood now why he had wanted to conceal his true identity, but how furious she had still been with him then. She missed him: his thoughtfulness and his intelligence. She remembered how angry he had been when she had gone off with Louis-Philippe and what he had said to her when they exchanged their final goodbyes. He had made her cry. It was clear to her now how very much he had cared for her – and how much he had *always* cared for her.

I've got to save Peter! thought Kate. If I don't find a way of saving his younger self, this world will miss out on having an adult Peter Schock in it and that will be a tragedy.

A faint noise prompted Kate to sit up with a start. She had only very gradually become aware of it, like being awoken by someone stroking a feather across your cheek. She held her breath as she listened to the rhythmic noise growing closer. It was like footsteps, only too slow. The sound rang into the night. Kate crawled to the stern of the little boat and peeped over the edge, her eyes searching the darkness. Oh, for some street lamps! All she could see with any clarity was St Paul's and the moonlit rooftops, and the glittering river. The slow footstep sounds drew closer. How could this be? She was this world's sole inhabitant. Fear quickened her heartbeat and made her flesh crawl. She put her knuckles in her mouth. As long as she made no sound and did not move she would remain invisible.

Then she saw it: a pale shape floating along the quayside, from London Bridge. Kate wanted to scream. How could this figure be gliding so smoothly over the cobblestones? Could it be a ghost? The figure continued to head in her direction. It was a girl. Every instinct told Kate to run but she forced herself to remain, rigid with terror, crouched at the bottom of the boat. Kate felt a shudder of recognition which she could not yet acknowledge. The figure hugged the edge of the quayside, stopping every few steps, to look this way and that, but at only half the speed you would expect. She had long hair, like her own. She wore a long dress, like her own. Now the figure moved directly towards her, so slowly it seemed that she had rolling castors instead of feet, and that an invisible person was pushing her along. Kate ducked below the edge of the boat, her head bowed towards her chest, her ears straining. All she could hear was her own breathing. Could ghosts walk over water? After what seemed an age Kate slowly lifted her head. There, bathed in bright moonlight, a replica of herself stood before her in a light-coloured dress whose hem was spattered with mud. Long strands of pale red hair had come loose and tumbled over white cheeks. Two frightened eyes peered directly at her. Kate shot to her feet and opened her mouth in a scream of pure terror that echoed over the sleeping city. After a few seconds delay her mirror image echoed her scream, only it was at once a slower and a deeper cry, the sound waves pulsing out towards her like the roar of an animal. The hairs stood up on the back of Kate's neck. She covered her ears and screwed her eyes tight shut. When she dared to open them again the pale figure was retreating back into the darkness, skating over the cobblestones, sending back long, slow looks over one shoulder at her alternative self. Suddenly the spectre vanished from sight and Kate stood in the middle of the Tar Man's boat, nauseous, and with her limbs shaking violently with the shock of what she had just seen.

For a long time Kate crouched on her heels, too bewildered to think, too horror-struck to do anything save rock backwards and forwards. Was this strange place where parallel worlds met? Time passed. The stars still shone down. From time to time she would glance over at Gideon, spreadeagled in the water; at Peter, fully submerged, his dark hair floating about his white face; at the Tar Man who still looked as if he would tear his younger brother apart given the chance. She tried again to look at her own future but could not push her way past a solid wall of darkness. And so, cradled in the Tar Man's little boat, Kate drifted, lost in time, unhooked from all certainties.

'Can you hear me?' asked the voice inside her head. 'I can hear you sometimes. Kate? It *is* you, isn't it? I've sensed you for a while. I can talk to my parallel self in your world but I don't know for sure that you even exist in mine . . . But that's not important. It's *your* world that is the important one. *Your* world can make things right again. Mine can't.'

Kate groaned in her sleep and her forehead wrinkled.

'I can sense how lost you feel, how brave you've had to be. I am going to ask you to suspend your disbelief. You *must* talk to me for all our sakes. You see, Time is beginning to splinter. The number of parallel worlds has increased exponentially. We don't believe that the universe can contain them all. Massive disturbances are being triggered in the time mantle. We're calling them time quakes but we've no idea how destructive they are. We need your help, Kate. If you can hear me, try to talk to me. Reach out with your mind . . .'

Kate opened her eyes and blinked, unsure whether or not she had been dreaming. She scanned the darkness looking for signs of another Kate Dyer. There had been a voice, a woman's voice, with an American accent. She had wanted to speak with her. All at once Kate remembered the amazing celebration at the farmhouse after she and Peter had both managed to make it home. Everyone was there: Peter and his family, Inspector Wheeler, the Marquis de Montfaron, Megan, her brothers and sisters . . . and *Dr Pirretti*. It was her last memory of home. The celebration was short-lived – within a few hours the Tar Man had abducted them and brought them back to 1763. But she had a vivid memory of Dr Pirretti going into a kind of trance during the dinner. Suddenly Dr Pirretti had started to speak in a voice which was her own and yet not her own at the same time. That *alternative* Dr Pirretti had spoken of the parallel worlds formed as a consequence of time travel. Her father had seemed highly sceptical. But if the existence of parallel selves in parallel worlds seemed far-fetched, Kate herself had just seen proof of it with her own eyes . . . And, no, she hadn't dreamed that voice – a Dr Pirretti from another world really had just spoken to her! Kate sat up abruptly, now wide awake. She *must* remember everything that she had said. Dr Pirretti had talked of the splintering of time. She had talked about needing *her* help! But what could she, Kate Dyer, possibly do for anyone? I can't help Peter, she thought, I can't even help myself.

'What can I do?' she cried into the night. 'Is anybody else out there?'

But all she could hear was a deafening silence.

Kate sat looking out over the city, and after a while she felt a surge of anger rise up inside her, anger at the injustice of her dilemma, anger at her father and Dr Pirretti and Tim Williamson for their part in the accidental discovery of time travel, anger at the whole string of events that had led to a situation that was now spiralling out of control. Suddenly she rounded on the Tar Man.

'This is *your* fault!' she shouted in his face. 'You walked off with the anti-gravity machine in the first place. And then you couldn't resist stealing it back again. But Lord Luxon ran off with it, didn't he? And who knows what he's been doing with it . . . Don't you realise what you've done? It sounds like the universe is about to explode because of your greed! What makes people like you think they've got a right to spoil everything for the rest of us? You're a grown-up! My baby sister has got more sense. How can you have lived so long and still be so stupid? Do you hear what I'm saying, Tar Man? I *hate* you!'

As the word *hate* fell from her lips she drew back her hand and struck his scarred cheek with a stinging slap. But at the instant Kate's flesh came into contact with the Tar Man, a tremendous jolt flung her backwards and electricity crackled all about them. The two of them were bound together at the eye of a sudden and violent storm that crashed through the dead calm of her world like a witch's spell. A strange wind sprang up and swirled around them in powerful eddies, catching at her dress and causing strands of hair to whip wildly in front of her so that she could see nothing. Kate tugged her hair away from her face and looked up at the Tar Man. His eyelids snapped wide open and his eyeballs swivelled in their sockets so that he was looking directly at her. The rest of him remained statue-still. The effect on Kate could not have been more shocking if she had seen a dead man walk. Kate was petrified. She leaped to the far end of the boat and, without thinking of the consequences, launched herself off the stern hoping to reach dry land. Her cries were lost in the roar of the wind. But even the powerful rush of adrenaline which put renewed strength into her limbs did not provide sufficient momentum to reach the quayside. Kate fell through the air, stomach lurching, the skin on her hands and arms grazed by the coarse stone of the supporting wall, then landed on the surface of the water.

She braced herself for the icy immersion but felt – nothing at all! When Kate looked down, she realised that she was *sitting* on the Thames. She shifted to one side and the water yielded a little but still she did not penetrate its surface. Now she threw a wary glance over in the direction of the Tar Man's back; he had not moved, or at least as far as she could tell. She relaxed a little and, once her heart stopped fluttering in her chest, the novelty of her new-found skill brought a smile to her face. And so she bounced up and down, gently at first, and then with more confidence. It was as if she were sitting on a hard mattress. She patted the ripples of water with the flat of her hands and marvelled at their cool softness. There was nothing in her old world that she could compare it to and she delighted in the unique texture that soothed the palms of her hands.

She looked over again at the Tar Man. He was as motionless as ever. What had happened when she touched him? It reminded her of an experiment the Marquis de Montfaron had described, in which he had passed an electric current into the thigh muscle of a dead frog. The resulting twitch had caused his assistant to run, screaming from the room. But what force had *she* transmitted into the Tar Man? Was she a conductor of some unknown force – did it merely flow through her? Or was she the source of it? She sighed. She suspected that even her father and Dr Pirretti would-n't know the answer to those questions. At least it was only the Tar Man's eyeballs that had moved. How awful if she had brought the whole of him to life, a cross between Frankenstein's monster and Man Friday to share her desert island. Except, of course, it wasn't exclusively hers, not any more – Kate's gaze swept the riverside anxiously, looking for any further sign of movement.

Thankfully the unearthly wind had eased, the ferocious gusts having reduced to a gentle breeze. Slowly and cautiously she got to her feet, arms outstretched for balance. Kate walked on water. It was slippery, and she kept falling over, landing painlessly on the cushioned surface. As she pushed herself up once more she noticed, a little way away, the small blob of white just below the surface that she knew to be Peter's face.

'Peter!' she exclaimed. It suddenly dawned on her that she could now reach him. Kate started to shuffle over the slippery ripples towards her friend but soon decided that it would be easier to crawl on all fours. A feeling of dread came over her. What if she were too late? But something flickered in the far reaches of her mind: Peter's future. She could sense it. He was not dead. He had a long life in front of him. She crawled on.

Covered by perhaps a finger's width of water, Kate observed his face. Peter's eyes were wide open and a stream of air bubbles that escaped from his mouth confirmed that he was alive. Kate let her forehead sink with relief onto the soothing surface of the river. She stretched out her hand towards him. All she had to do was touch him and it would be over. But just as she was about to touch the tip of his index finger, the only part of him that which not submerged, she stopped herself. The Thames was a fast-flowing river and she could not be sure that Peter was capable of swimming.

Crawling back to the quayside as fast as she could, Kate jumped up to catch hold of a metal mooring ring and hauled herself up, pushing with her feet against the roughly hewn stones until she had heaved herself onto street level. She ran off into the darkness.

Presently the river echoed to her footsteps once more and she appeared, out of breath and clutching a pile of soiled strips of petticoat that she had used to bind her sore feet, along with a shirt she had found drying in the Tar Man's scullery. Kate dropped onto the spongy surface of the Thames, checked the Tar Man's face for further signs of movement and, satisfied that he was not suddenly going to come to life like a zombie in a horror film, made herself comfortable on the water, crossing her legs and pulling out her skirts around her like a picnic blanket. More cheerful than she had felt in an age, she sorted through the pieces of cotton and struggled to tear the shirt into strips. Then she started to knot them together. The pieces of petticoat had already lost much of their pliability. This was doubtless, she deduced, on account of the law of temporal osmosis – oh, how she longed to tell her father about this – but she still managed to work the material without too much difficulty. The shirt was a different matter. However, once she had finished, Kate clambered back on board the boat and, being extremely careful not to touch him, tied one end of the rag rope around the Tar Man's wrist, using a triple knot. Then she walked back over to Peter and sat down next to him. She formed a loop, large enough for her and for Peter, which she dropped over her head and under her arms. Then she looked around at the silent, dark, no-man's land of a world and shouted, 'Goodbye, Limbo Land!'

Kate sat poised to touch the tip of Peter's finger with hers, knowing that all hell would break loose the moment she did so. For a moment she clung to the peace and silence of this static world.

'Dr Pirretti, I don't know if you can hear me—'

'Kate!' Dr Pirretti's urgent voice came straight back at her.

Kate gasped at the clarity of it. She could have been wearing headphones.

'Dr Pirretti! How are you doing this?'

'That's not important. The important thing is that you can hear me.'

'I'm with Peter again – I'd lost him for a while. Can you tell everyone we're okay?'

'Yes, of course, but listen to me, Kate, listen while you can. I need to tell you the code for the duplicate anti-gravity machine. It's a six-digit code and it's the same as your birthdate . . . Did you hear me?'

Kate's face broke into a grin. 'I heard you!'

One hand clutching the loop around her chest, Kate's finger hovered over Peter's. She looked down at the pale moon of his face, and at the life escaping from his lungs, trapped under this layer of water. She wondered if he were still conscious. Her finger was now so close to his it was pulsing in anticipation and felt almost hot. It was like balancing on the edge of a diving board, confronted with the heart-stopping leap into the void. She wanted to do it, she *had* to do it, but now it came to it her nerve failed her. 'Now!' she ordered. But she faltered again. What if she got swept away? What if she couldn't save him? 'Do it!' she shouted, channelling all her fear into her cry. '*Now!*'

Two fingers touched, two worlds united, two bodies thrashed around in swirling currents. Spitting out the foul water, her head burst through the surface of the water like a rebirth. Coughing and spluttering she passed the loop over Peter's shoulders. Kate Dyer was back in the real world.

CHAPTER EIGHTEEN

Time Quake

In which many centuries collide, two brothers make a pact and Kate tells Peter her secret

Peter shook the hair from his face and coughed up the water that was making him choke. He felt himself being dragged through the strong current. What was happening to him? Out of the darkness he saw the Tar Man in his boat looming towards him. The water was choppy and the boat bobbed up and down. The Tar Man appeared to be leaning backwards, legs set wide apart for balance, and he was digging his heels into the floor of the boat. He was pulling on something, too. In fact, it occurred to Peter that the Tar Man looked exactly as if he were taking part in a tug o' war contest. Peter glanced down at the taut rag rope in front of him and felt it cut into his back as he surged through the water. The Tar Man, he realised all at once, was hauling him in like a big fish! But why, having tossed him into the river in the first place, had he now decided to rescue him?

Within the space of half a second Peter noticed several things. Firstly – and inexplicably – he became aware of Kate right next to him, clutching at the rope and gasping for air. Then he grasped what the Tar Man was trying to do – he was struggling to free his hand from the rope that was tied so tightly around his wrist. Next he spotted Gideon, shirt clinging to his chest, clambering back into the boat from which he had been pushed by the Tar Man's oar only a moment before Peter himself had been tossed overboard.

A thought flashed through Peter's mind as he was propelled through the water. If the Tar Man *was* trying to untie the rope, surely that implied that he *didn't want* to pull them in. On the other hand, if the Tar Man did not resist the pull of the rope, then he, too, would be dragged into the Thames by the same tidal current that was sweeping Kate and Peter towards London Bridge. But who had worked out that little scenario? And, for that matter, who had tied the rope? Gideon was in the water so it couldn't have been him. And, come to that, how had Kate managed to fall into the river, unnoticed, at exactly the same spot? What on earth was going on?

Now they were less than a man's length from the boat. Then Peter saw Gideon stagger over to the Tar Man and grab hold of the twisted cotton rope. Together the two of them hauled Peter and Kate over the side, grasping at their elbows and knees and at their sodden clothes. For a few seconds all four of them sat panting at the bottom of the boat. Kate, alone, did not seem bewildered.

Without warning Gideon leaped up, made his hand into a fist, and thumped the Tar Man hard enough on the jaw that he lost his balance and fell backwards, cracking his head on the edge of the wooden boat. Like a farmer getting ready to shear a sheep, Gideon turned the Tar Man over in one swift movement, knelt on his back, extracted his knife from its scabbard and threw it into the black water. Peter heard the splash as it hit the river.

'Sit on his legs!' Gideon cried to Peter and Kate. 'This time he shall not escape us!'

Peter and Kate did as they were told and shuffled along the

bottom of the boat in their wet clothes, manoeuvring themselves onto the Tar Man's white-stockinged calves.

'Sir Richard is in an agony of pain,' said Gideon between teeth clenched with the strain of pinning the Tar Man down. ''Tis not the first time I have seen you use that heartless trick and I know you have the secret to mend what you have broken. As you value your life, you will come back with me and attend to his arm.'

The Tar Man's face was pressed into the bottom of the boat but he managed to raise his face sufficiently to produce an indulgent laugh.

'Ha! A single evening's combat with me has taught you to raise your game. I admit I did not even feel you tie the rope around my hand. Just think what a week in my company would achieve. Why, Joe Carrick could use an extra footpad – I fancy you could make a tolerably good one—'

Peter flashed Kate a look of surprise as Gideon smashed the Tar Man's head against the boat's floor. 'I did not tie the rope around your hand. Agree to attend Sir Richard and I'll agree not to throw you to the fishes, which is less than you deserve!'

'I am not minded to tend your good Sir Richard. I fancy he can afford the services of a doctor, and I do not like to steal business from that honourable profession . . .'

Gideon ground his knee into the Tar Man's back causing him to expel his breath in a barely controlled cry. 'And *I* am not minded to let you go before you do . . . It is your stock in trade. I'll warrant the doctor who attends Sir Richard has never performed such a procedure in his life, whereas barely a month goes by without you putting some cove's arm back in its socket – leastways, once he's agreed to squeak on his fellows or has handed over the pickings. Sir Richard has shown me too much kindness for me to stand by while a doctor ruins his arm. No, *you* must do it. I ask you in the name of our dead mother who would be ashamed—'

The Tar Man interrupted him with a growl and began to push the flat of his hands against the bottom of the boat, raising up his own mass, as well as that of Gideon and the children, off the damp wooden planks. Gideon bore frantically down on him but the Tar Man had slipped out from under the dead weight of three bodies and was already scrambling to his feet. Gideon followed suit and the two men stood, grappling with each other, causing the boat to list violently to one side and then the other. Peter and Kate exchanged desperate glances, pressing their bodies into the sides of the boat to avoid being trampled.

'Stop! Both of you!' screamed Kate in a sudden, shrill cry that echoed over the river. 'There's something you should both know!'

Her tone was so urgent and convincing that the two brothers paused, still grasping each other's biceps. The Tar Man turned his head and looked hard at Kate and, whatever it was that he saw in her eyes, he appeared all at once unnerved. She watched him put a hand to his cheek.

'I know the secret code,' she said.

Peter turned to her. 'How?'

Kate glared at him. 'I just know. Okay?'

Peter nodded, furious with himself for opening his mouth.

'You know the secret code that will allow me to return to the future?' asked the Tar Man.

'Yes.'

'Is this the truth?'

'Do not judge her by your own standards. Mistress Kate is not a liar!' exclaimed Gideon.

'It's not a lie,' said Kate gently. 'I *swear*. I know the secret code.'

A shadow of a smile appeared on the Tar Man's lips. 'And so, Mistress Dyer, you have come to bargain with me?'

Kate nodded. Peter looked at her in astonishment. His friend was full of surprises.

'Let me guess the nature of your bargain. You will furnish me with the code if I will take you home?'

'Yes,' said Kate.

'Agreed,' replied the Tar Man.

Kate turned to Gideon and Peter. 'That was easy! Do *you* agree?'

'Well . . . I . . . *Yes!*' said Peter.

Gideon slowly released the Tar Man's arms and frowned. 'I do not trust him. I agree to the terms if first he sets right Sir Richard's arm.'

The Tar Man looked up to heaven. 'Agreed. I shall, however, keep possession of the machine on our arrival in the future.'

Kate looked at the others.

'I just want to get home,' she said.

'Me too,' said Peter.

Gideon nodded.

'In which case,' said the Tar Man to Gideon, 'you had better return the key which you took from my mantelpiece . . .'

Gideon put his hand to his side as if to take the key from his pocket but his face fell. 'My jacket was too heavy in the water. Your key is at the bottom of the Thames.'

Peter turned to Kate and whispered in her ear: 'Did *you* tie the rope around the Tar Man's hand?'

Kate smiled at him innocently and shrugged her shoulders.

They all agreed to meet at Sir Richard's house in Lincoln's Inn Fields at noon to discuss how they were to proceed. Grudgingly, the Tar Man returned to his house with Gideon, Peter and Kate. The driver was waiting at the door and, looking warily at the Tar Man, informed the party that a gentleman at St Paul's coffee-house had recommended his own doctor whom he had delivered here but a moment ago. In the hall they passed the old gentleman and Parson Ledbury, both of them sound asleep on each other's shoulders, the bottle of brandy still clasped in the Parson's hand.

'I am pleased to see your friends have made themselves comfortable in my house during my absence,' commented the Tar Man.

Gideon opened his mouth to comment on his brother's notion of hospitality but thought the better of it. Peter looked over at Toby, still unconscious on his owner's legs.

A doctor, thin and stooped, and wearing a dusty black jacket, was at Sir Richard's side. He was instructing Hannah to hold a bowl to catch the blood from the incision he had just made in his patient's good arm. The Tar Man pulled the doctor to his feet and practically kicked him down the stairs, throwing a couple of gold coins after him to quell his complaints.

'Get him to his feet,' barked the Tar Man. 'That way I can get sufficient purchase for the twist.'

The Tar Man opened a cupboard in the corner of the room and brought out a bottle of brandy. Then he stooped over a basket of kindling by the fire and picked out a stout twig. He gave both to Hannah.

'Let him have a swig of bingo then give him the gag to bite on. I can't abide screaming.'

So, wooden gag in mouth, brandy dripping down his chin, the trembling Sir Richard was heaved to his feet in the arms of his friends. The Tar Man grabbed hold of his arm, raised it to shoulder height, and started to manipulate it, getting a feeling for the precise position when he should turn and push. Satisfied at last, and ignoring the muffled cries of Sir Richard and the streams of cold sweat that ran down his face, the Tar Man took a deep breath and, with an explosive cry and a deft twist, forced the arm back into the shoulder socket. The resounding click announced that the arm was finally back in place. Sir Richard slumped to the floor. No one spoke for a long moment and the only sounds to be heard were the hiss of the fire and Sir Richard's laboured breathing. The Tar Man went to his table, covered with jumbled artefacts, and stained with the Parson's blood, and came back with an earthenware jar plugged with a cork, which he gave to Kate.

'This will revive him. I shall take a turn to London Bridge. On my return I expect my house to be clear of all visitors.' The Tar Man turned to Gideon. 'I have done as you asked.'

'I hope you do not expect my thanks.'

'No, but I expect you to keep your side of the bargain.'

'Do you doubt me?'

The Tar Man made no reply but disappeared into the dark stairwell, leaving Sir Richard in the tender care of his friends. They heard a door shut downstairs. Peter walked over to the circular window and watched the Tar Man stroll down the street towards the river. Kate joined him at the window, holding the jar. Another peal of thunder rumbled over the city although the sky was still clear.

'This is weird weather,' she said, rubbing her arms through the wet sleeves of her dress and shivering. 'I'm a bit worried that I might have set it off.'

'What are you talking about?' asked Peter incredulously.

He looked at her with such intensity that Kate had to look away.

'Just what is going on, Kate? When are you going to tell me what's up? I know I'm not a genius like your dad, but I'm not stupid either. I thought we were supposed to be in this together.'

'We are!'

'Well, you could have fooled me . . .'

Kate tried to remove the cork from the jar and when she couldn't Peter helped her. Inside was a spherical pomander. Kate opened it to reveal a small compartment covered with a fine metal mesh. A sharp, vinegary odour met their nostrils. Kate bent her head and sniffed it.

'Oh! that is *disgusting*!' she said, holding the pomander away from her with watering eyes. 'The Tar Man is right – that will definitely bring Sir Richard round!'

Peter grabbed hold of the pomander, sniffed it and thrust it right back into Kate's hands.

'Phwoah! That's supposed to make him feel better? It's lethal! It's worse than hot chilli ice cream!'

Kate laughed and pointed to his dripping nose. She offered him a damp handkerchief that smelled of the river. Peter used the back of his hand instead.

'When are you going to tell me?'

'I'll tell you in the morning – it's not simple. And I'm tired . . .'

'Yeah, yeah.'

'I *promise*.'

'You know, you don't look so good, Kate.'

She held out her hand and looked at it. 'Thanks.'

'Maybe it's the light . . .'

She shrugged. 'I think Sir Richard's been through enough already without having to smell this, too. I might try it on the dog, though.'

'You've seen Toby? After he bit the Tar Man's ankle he kicked him clear across the room. He sang a duet with the old gentleman – you should have heard them!'

'Molly joins in when I sing, too, it always makes me laugh.' Kate was trying to close the pomander. The hinge suddenly felt stiff. 'That's weird. I can't close it. Can you have a go?'

Kate held it out towards him but no hand came forward to take it. She turned to look up at him but it was a statue that Kate saw staring back at her. A sinking feeling that began in the pit of her stomach spread right through her. Kate returned Peter's stare with blank, expressionless eyes and fought back the tears. It's like I no longer belong in my own time any more. Through the window she saw the Tar Man, caught in mid-step on his way to the river. She spun around to look at Hannah and Gideon tending Sir Richard. Gideon was moistening his lips with a drop more brandy and Hannah was cleaning the cut inflicted on him by a doctor determined to bleed him, no matter what his complaint. The scene reminded her of a museum display with particularly life-like dummies enacting a typical domestic scene from the 1760s. She imagined the explanatory notes: Tended by a maid and a reformed cutpurse, an aristocrat recovers from a dislocated shoulder inflicted on him by a time-travelling henchman.

But at least she knew where Peter was this time around. He was a mere arm's length away. A question occurred to her. Why had she not touched him straight away? She looked out again at the Tar Man, his unmistakeable contour black against the glittering river, the memory of the explosive consequences of her slapping him still vivid in her mind. And it was precisely that slap, she realised, which accounted for her not touching Peter. She was curious. She wanted to know why it had happened and if it might happen again. She wanted to know what she was becoming. The loneliness of fast-forwarding filled her with dread, and Kate worried about what it might be doing to her. Yet, at the same time, there was the undeniable lure of the unknown. In truth, a part of her must enjoy being the first human to experience existence at such high speeds. It was like being the first person to climb Everest or to reach the North Pole. And, as with any scientific experiment, an initial observation was not sufficient – there had to be proof. An expression of her mother's popped into her head which she chose to ignore as, she told herself, curiosity doesn't *always* kill the cat. In any case there was only one way to reproduce this experiment.

On her way to catching up with the Tar Man, Kate systematically touched everyone in the house – excluding Peter but including Toby. It failed to provoke even the tiniest tremor. Kate decided to leave the pomander on the old gentleman's lap, next to Toby's nose. Half-formed theories ran through her head. When she was fast-forwarding, the only two people who seemed to interact with her were the Tar Man and Peter. Both had travelled through time, though, from what she had gathered, the Tar Man was better at blurring than Peter. Did this mean that he was a better 'conductor' of whatever energy was causing all of this? Or did it mean that he was more sensitive to it? And then, Peter had an effect on *her*, whereas *she* had an effect on the Tar Man. Almost as if they were from opposite poles, like magnets, or something like that . . . Anyway, she and Peter came from the same century; The Tar Man came from another . . . Oh, enough! she thought. My brain is going to explode.

Kate hurried outside and ran down the cobbled street to the river. The Tar Man was striding cheerfully out. The prospect of returning to the twenty-first century must appeal to him, she thought. Kate positioned herself right in front of him and scruti-nised his face. He really was not as old as she had imagined him to be. In fact, he looked a lot younger than her mum and dad. She decided it was his scar and black stubble that created the illusion of age; that and his fearsome reputation which, she now realised, he both deserved and encouraged. The Tar Man's dark eyes shone and a smile played on his lips, which made Kate want to smile, too.

As she stood looking up at him she became aware of something flitting about in her peripheral vision. She looked around, thinking it must be another bat, until it occurred to her that if it were a bat it would be motionless. Each time she tried to focus on the movement, it seemed to vanish, but if she looked straight ahead the movement was visible once more. Kate could not make it out and, in the end, put it down to exhaustion and an overactive imagination.

She stood on tiptoe and reached out her hands to touch the Tar Man's face, gradually bringing the palms of her hands closer and closer towards his cheeks. They tingled and grew hot but she did not altogether trust the sensation. She resolved not to touch him fleetingly like the last time, but to press her flesh into his, determined to observe the consequences of keeping in contact with him for a prolonged period of time. Kate reassured herself that it would be no worse than touching the dome of the Van der Graaf generator in her dad's laboratory. Perhaps there would be some static electricity produced. That would be enough to account for the Tar Man's eyes flipping open, wouldn't it? After all, what was the worst that could happen? Perhaps her hair would stand up on end . . .

All at once Kate shied away from touching his face, so she lowered her heels, counted down from ten and then grabbed tight hold of the Tar Man's arms just below the elbow. The frozen calm of her world was instantly shattered; her touch akin to a spark igniting clouds of escaping gas. It set off an immense detonation, which reverberated all around them, sending out shooting, luminous fingers of energy far into the night sky. Kate gasped with the shock of it but dug her fingers deep into the Tar Man's arms. She became conscious of an alarming, crackling sound reminiscent of treading on dry twigs in an echoing wood. A sheath of flickering energy encased them and she was aware of a dazzling light. Her skin crawled with an intense prickling sensation that came close to pain;

she felt that every hair must be standing on end; the very air seemed saturated with an unknown, potent force.

When the Tar Man's body suddenly jerked back to life in a violent spasm Kate screamed. His eyes flicked open and he strained against her grip. In her confusion, she hung on even more tightly, her hands stuck to him like limpets to a rock, even when she found herself lifted fully off the ground. The Tar Man's face was shining with reflected light and all at once she understood that *she* was the source of it. Glancing down, she saw that her hands were *glowing*. Waves of greenish light rippled over them. With a shuddering jolt the Tar Man took a step forward. His face was creased with pain.

'Witch!' he screamed. 'Be gone from me!'

The Tar Man threw Kate off and she fell backwards onto the cobblestones. Instantly the Tar Man was a statue again, only instead of smiling, his face was contorted into a mask of pain and terror. She looked at her hands – the light was almost gone, like a fading electric element when the current has been switched off.

'What have I done!' she cried, for she sensed that she had torn away a curtain that up until now had protected her. She had looked at the sun. Not only that, she had been on the verge of making the Tar Man fast-forward with her. And she also knew, in her heart of hearts, that she should *not* have done it. She was already damaged; she did not have the right to inflict such damage on another person – not even the Tar Man. Kate ran through what seemed like a howling hurricane back to the house, back to Peter. He called me a *witch*! Is that what I've turned into? Is that who I am, now – a witch and an oracle? She hurtled up the stairs and grabbed hold of Peter's hand. Nothing happened. Kate squeezed Peter's fingers.

'Oh please!' Her heart started to race. 'It must work! It must! I promise I won't do it again.'

'Well, give it to me then,' said Peter.

Hot tears of relief welled up in her eyes.

'That stuff stings! You should see your eyes!' he said.

'Yes,' Kate replied, sniffing, and smiling a lopsided smile.

The sound of distressed barking came from below.

'Oh,' exclaimed Hannah. 'Praise be! The dog lives!'

'Toby!' cried Peter. 'Come on!'

Peter grabbed Kate's hand and pulled her downstairs. Gideon followed them.

Kate stood there panting and trembling while a small group of people gathered round the small dog. Peter tried to take his hand away from hers but she would not let him. The old gentleman was giving Toby another good sniff of the Tar Man's pomander for good measure and laughed in delight when the dog started to smack its jaws open and shut as if it had eaten something unutterably disgusting.

Peter turned to Kate, a big frown on his face.

'But how did the pomander get down here?'

Kate pretended not to hear. The dog sneezed violently over and over again. How comical the bemused animal looked with his black patch over one eye. The old gentleman kissed his head and lifted him to his cheek.

'Ah, Toby, my dear soul! How should I have lived without you?'

Gideon leaned forward and tickled Toby behind his ear.

'Ay, I should like to hear you sing again – and perhaps I shall join you.'

The driver had brought Sir Richard's coach and six directly to the Tar Man's front door. Another thunderclap sounded as Gideon and Hannah helped Sir Richard down the stairs and out onto the street. The pain and the brandy and the loss of blood had all made him groggy, but he could walk, and he managed to exchange a few warm words with the old gentleman. Hannah, together with her three patients, sat inside the carriage while Kate and Peter sat on top. Gideon tried to persuade Kate to ride inside for her teeth were chattering but she refused, insisting that she wanted to stay with Peter. Now they sat, propped up one against the other, Kate resting her head on Peter's shoulder and holding his hand tightly in hers.

'What in Heaven's name ails the horses?' asked Parson Ledbury, observing how they pawed the earth and whinnied. 'I can see the whites of their eyes, and the leader has built up a fine sweat.'

'I cannot tell you, sir,' replied the driver. 'They've been fretting since we arrived. I fancy 'tis the storm – though it is a queer kind of storm with no rain clouds in sight. They shall be happy once they are back in their stables at Lincoln's Inn Fields.'

'As shall we all,' said Parson Ledbury with feeling.

Their first destination was to be the old gentleman's residence off Ludgate Hill. Gideon took the reins while the driver stood balanced at the back of the carriage. They rumbled over the cobblestones, heading for the Thames, but had barely reached the quayside when the leader horse abruptly refused to go a step further. The black mare reared up, eyes bulging and whinnying in fear. The driver jumped down from the back of the carriage and tried to get her to walk alongside him but she would have none of it and continued to rear up, until she upset the rest of the horses. The driver threw up his hands in exasperation. Now Gideon climbed down and started to stroke the leader's nose and to whisper gently into her ear. Gradually the animal quietened and Gideon asked the driver to try walking by her side again. Soon the six horses were stepping out in unison and Gideon clicked his tongue and talked to them in a soothing voice until they were settled and moving again. The driver ran back to take up his position at the rear once more and Gideon quickened the pace to a trot.

Peter was glad to be going away from this place at long last; he felt sick with tiredness. All he wanted now was to go to sleep. Kate was warm, if a little too bony to make a comfortable pillow, but within half a minute he was already drowsing. Despite this, he soon became conscious that Kate was trembling and he shifted around to check on her through half-opened eyes. Her pale skin seemed transparent in the moonlight.

'There's nothing wrong, Kate. Something's just spooked the horses. And even the Carrick Gang would think twice before attacking us lot . . .'

Kate shook her head and put her lips to his ear. 'Can't you feel it? It's coming. Just like the last time. At Hawthorn Cottage with Gideon.'

Just the mention of that day conjured up terrible images in Peter's head. He vividly recalled how Kate had sensed something was about to happen long before he had. At the time he'd seriously wondered if Kate was going mad – until he saw it for himself. The following morning they had tried to explain what they had seen to Parson Ledbury, but on a calm, sunny day in Derbyshire, with the larks singing overhead, all talk of ghosts and of the apocalypse had seemed suddenly absurd and they'd ended up making lighter of it than it deserved. Then, as the days went by and they did not come across a single other person who had witnessed the phenomenon, they slowly began to doubt the evidence of their own eyes.

'Are you sure?' he asked. Peter was wide awake now. He did not want to believe her.

Kate nodded 'I'm sure . . . And there's something else.'
'What?'
'I'm beginning to think I'm causing them.'

Peter stared at her. 'You need to get some sleep, Kate. You're talking rubbish.'

Kate barely registered his comment. 'Please can you do something for me? It's really important . . .'

'What?'

'Whatever happens, don't let go of me . . .'

'Okay,' Peter replied a little doubtfully.

'Promise?'

'I don't get why but I promise . . .'

Suddenly Kate put her head to her knees and covered it with her free hand while she rocked to and fro, biting her lips to stop from crying out. There was a part of Peter who wanted to tell her to stop making such a fuss but he held his tongue.

'What ails Mistress Kate?' asked Gideon in alarm.

Before Peter could reply, all the horses started whinnying and rising up, but instead of refusing to move, this time the leader quickened her pace. Gideon was forced to stand up and pull hard on the reins.

'Whoa!' he cried.

But it was to no avail for the horses were already thundering up the narrow thoroughfare towards the dome of St Paul's. As the carriage hurtled up St Andrew's Hill, the driver, who had been clinging on for dear life, was thrown off, unnoticed by the party, rolling over and over until he came to a halt in the doorway of the Cockpit Tavern. Then the horses careered into Thames Street, parallel to the river, and galloped eastwards. All the while the carriage listed violently, first to one side and then to the other, and with each juddering encounter with a pothole the passengers braced themselves for fear of overturning. Gideon stood up, his stance reminiscent of a charioteer, pulling hard on the reins, ducking to avoid being hit by oversized shop signs, leaning into the bends whilst grabbing hold of Peter's arm to prevent him and Kate sliding off the narrow wooden seat. Cries and screams and the occasional alarmed bark emanated from the inside of the carriage as the passengers were thrown violently about. Parson Ledbury contrived to poke his head through the window, bellowing at Gideon to pacify the horses before they all broke their necks.

'I cannot hold them!' shouted Gideon over his shoulder. 'I do not understand what makes them so afraid!'

Peter held on to the edge of the seat, hampered by Kate's refusal to let go of him. The dark city street sped past and Peter looked up at Gideon and down at Kate and wondered how much more of this he could take. The creaking of wooden axles and the thunder of the iron-rimmed wheels on stone was deafening and yet, over and above this he gradually became aware of an ominous noise. Kate, like the horses, was becoming increasingly distressed. Like a never-ending and inconceivably powerful thunderclap, the sound was so deep you could feel it in your bones. Peter looked up at the sky and saw that the stars had become blurred, as if they were dissolving into a liquid night.

Suddenly, out of nowhere, a rider, borne on a magnificent white horse, appeared, rearing up in front of them. The image was clear, yet it undulated in waves like a billowing curtain. In the split second Peter had to take in his appearance, he made a vivid impression. Dawn was hours away, yet the sun – a sun – poured down onto the fair-haired figure so that he shone out like a beacon in the darkness. The rider wore chain mail and the cross of Saint George was emblazoned across his chest, red on white, and he carried a metal helmet under one arm. A thin white cape flapped about him in the strong wind. Too shocked to move, a peasant girl, barefoot and dressed in a simple shift, stood on tiptoe offering a basket of apples to the knight. The russet fruit glistened in the sunshine and for a short moment the tang of warm, ripe apples laced the air. Peter's mind reeled. He was looking at a different century!

Nostrils flaring, the soldier's stallion neighed, and rose up on its hind legs, and pawed the air whilst its rider stared at the fast-approaching carriage with pale, incredulous eyes. The basket of apples tipped up and the fruit tumbled down in a scarlet shower and rolled into the night and vanished. Sir Richard's horses were beyond fear. For the first time in his life Peter heard a horse scream and it made his blood freeze. The leader stopped in her tracks causing the horses behind to plough into her. The carriage lurched and teetered for a moment on two wheels.

'Hold tight!'

Gideon's urgent cry was the last thing Peter heard as the carriage overturned, pulling down the six horses with it. Kate's knee knocked into Peter's forehead with a resounding crack as she, along with Gideon, grappled to catch hold of the roof of the carriage. Peter slid down Kate's legs, the crook of his arm catching on her trainers, and landed in a heap on the cobblestones. Winded and temporarily blinded by the blow to his head, it was a few moments before Peter could open his eyes. When he did, he saw Kate kneeling at his side and leaning over him, alternately looking down at him and shooting apprehensive glances at something he could not see. Peter pushed himself up on his elbows and saw Gideon straining to release the horses from their harnesses. They were in a terrible tangle, struggling and kicking and making shrill whinnying noises.

Kate put her lips to Peter's ear and shouted to make herself heard above the deafening roar that enveloped them and caused the earth to vibrate as if the earth's heart were beating.

'Are you all right?'

Peter nodded uncertainly.

Wincing, for the cobblestones had bruised his ribs, Peter turned around to follow Kate's gaze. She put her arm around him and helped him to heave himself up.

'Do you suppose this is the end of the world?' she asked.

Peter did not reply. If this were the end, he could believe it. But how could anyone make sense of any of this? He certainly couldn't. The tall, narrow buildings, all the taverns and shops and private houses that lined Thames Street, had all simply melted away into the darkness. *This* world, if that was the right word, ebbed and flowed like the sea and everywhere – below them, above them, all around – were spectres from different centuries. And if these figures terrified him, Peter could see his fear echoed in their eyes. A sunset, last seen when the Romans controlled this ancient city, glinted on the gleaming breastplate and helmet of a soldier. The deep-chested man shielded his eyes with one hand and brandished a short sword with the other. He peered at them through the darkness as if he were looking into a deep, dark cave. A few yards away, a woman, young and pretty, carrying a parasol and wearing a wide crinoline dress the colour of lilac, stood immobile, pressing the head of a small child into her skirts. A wilting daisy chain hung from the child's plump fingers. The woman, in her turn, was staring at the old gentleman in his battered tricorn hat. He held Toby in his arms, the black patch over his eye making him look cheerful even as he trembled and whined.

But while the boundaries of the centuries bled one into another, became confused, and converged on this segment of London, Gideon busied himself unfastening the last of the horses. For an instant Gideon and Peter exchanged glances and Peter tried to work out what his friend was calling out to him. Then he realised.

'Courage! All will be well!'

Peter closed his eyes tight shut against a reality that he could not comprehend and felt Kate's cold hand in his, gripping it tight, clammy with fear. He allowed the thunderous roaring to wash over him. But, very gradually, Peter realised that the roaring sound was beginning to diminish so that, louder with every minute, he could hear . . . a *melody*! Gideon was singing! Peter slowly opened his eyes. The pools of light that surrounded the figures from other sunlit centuries now flickered, like guttering candles. Peter wondered what he must look like to them: would their light penetrate his darkness? Is night visible by day? And now, out of sight on the other side of the carriage, Peter heard Parson Ledbury and Hannah singing hymns alongside Gideon. Presently the vertical forms of houses and swaying street signs began to materialise and he knew that it was over. He squeezed Kate's hand to catch her attention and pointed at Gideon who had picked up Toby and had tucked him under his arm. Both had opened wide their jaws and both were singing to the moon.

'For a moment there I didn't think we were going to make it!' said Peter to Kate.

'Nor did I,' Kate replied. 'Maybe we won't the next time . . .'

'Kate!'

'What? We've damaged Time. It's not going to stop. Can you tell me who knows how to mend it?'

Gideon's elder brother had been caught on the edge of the time quake. It appeared to him like a great wall of swirling, luminous cloud that loomed out of the darkness. It teemed with ghostly figures that stared out at him and it set every hair on end. He fled, racing through the empty streets, until he could run no more. He bent over while he got his breath back. His forearms stung as if he had been scalded and he could not shake from his head a bizarre waking dream in which Mistress Dyer had taken on the appearance of a witch and had clutched at him with hands that burned like hot coals. The Tar Man was badly shaken: he who was afraid of nothing felt his courage ebb away. Had she wanted to pull him down into hell itself? 'Tis nought but a nightmare, he told himself. Brought on, no doubt, by this citadel of ghosts . . .

He looked behind him at the unearthly, billowing wall that blotted out even the dome of St Paul's and made every sense and instinct bristle with a primeval fear. All the same, he felt compelled to face this unknown horror and discover what it was. What I need, he said to himself, is a high place. He looked around him and realised that he was a stone's throw away from the Monument where, many years before, he had fed meat to an eagle that was kept in a cage on the viewing platform. He decided to break in. The vertiginous stone column rose into the sky like a giant mast. Its height was equal to the distance between its base and Pudding Lane where, a century before, a fire had broken out that had all but destroyed the City of London. It was this calamitous event, he knew, that had inspired the Monument's construction but, more importantly, it would provide him with a bird's eye view of London – not as tall as St Paul's, but then, nothing was. He ran up the narrow spiral staircase, stopping occasionally for breath, until he reached the viewing platform. The eagle had gone. The Tar Man was glad for he could not abide prisons of any kind. He leaned over the railing of the balcony and scrutinised the horror that had struck London. He had been right to come here for he now had a clear view of the disease that threatened his city.

He saw an amorphous, living mass whose dark contours merged with the night. It stretched over the river from Bankside to beyond St Paul's. It was as tall as the great cathedral itself – the gilded tip of the dome was only just visible. Luminous patches glowed within it and there was a motion to it, almost as if it breathed. He could not see as clearly as he would have liked, but it seemed to him that this mass was billowing up from either side of a line, as if the earth had cracked and this ominous accumulation was bleeding into the air. His eyes were drawn to a small area well lit by moonlight. At first he did not believe his eyes and strained to see better, but after a few moments he was certain that he could see a line of traffic consisting of two red double-decker buses and several black cabs. 'Has all order departed from the world?' exclaimed the Tar Man. 'Has Nature herself grown sick?'

CHAPTER NINETEEN

An Appointment in Manhattan

In which the Marquis de Montfaron acquires a taste for flying and Alice makes a guilty confession to Inspector Wheeler

It was less than forty-eight hours after the bonfire on the Dyers' farm, and a policeman, an Enlightenment philosopher and a henchman's apprentice had an appointment to keep in Manhattan.

Tom had merely screwed up his eyes and dug his nails hard into the seat when the plane left the ground at Heathrow. The Marquis de Montfaron, on the other hand, emitted a piercing cry which competed with the scream of the engine and grew louder and stronger until it reached a crescendo when it suddenly stopped in order for him to make urgent use of the brown paper bag handed to him by Inspector Wheeler. Once Montfaron had calmed down a little, everything fascinated him, from the tiny screens that informed him of the stupendous altitude and speed at which he was currently travelling, to the white plastic utensils, wrapped in plastic, with which, he supposed, he was meant to eat some rather curious food which an attendant had delivered to him on a miniature tray. Tom caused the policeman fewer problems as his approach to the transatlantic flight was to pretend it was not happening.

The curiosity of the Enlightenment philosopher and scientist, of whom the policeman had grown so fond, knew no bounds and, on their arrival at JFK, Inspector Wheeler felt obliged to urge Montfaron not to spin around quite so much, with his eyes wide in astonishment, for he was in danger of looking like someone who had forgotten to take his medication. The Marquis succeeded in assuming a less feverish attitude but his bright chestnut eyes missed nothing. However, when their cab approached Manhattan from the Brooklyn Bridge, even though he had seen photographs of the city, Montfaron's eighteenth-century sensibilities made his heart pound in his chest and his head shake from side to side in disbelief.

'*Quelle merveille!*' said Montfaron, his voice cracking with emotion. 'Tom, can you truly desire to return to 1763, knowing that . . . all *this* awaits the world? Truly, if I were to die tomorrow, I should feel satisfied with what these eyes have seen.'

'Don't forget to breathe, my friend,' said Inspector Wheeler. 'I'm going to need you to talk some eighteenth-century sense into Lord Luxon if any of us are to have a good chance of surviving beyond tomorrow . . .'

Montfaron replied without taking his eyes off the view. 'Forgive me, *cher ami*. But you must remember that when Mistress Kate first demonstrated her torch to me in my chateau in Amiens, I was struck dumb. It was the most miraculous thing I had ever seen. Can you begin to imagine, then, what passion this astonishing sight kindles in my heart?'

'Ay,' said the Scottish policeman, 'I suppose New York's not bad. Though give me the Isle of Mull any day with just my fishing rod for company . . .'

Montfaron laughed. 'Very well, Inspector Wheeler, I see you wish me to keep my feet on the ground in this city of dreams. Do not fear, I understand why you have permitted me to come. Lord Luxon is of high social rank. He will be an educated man and doubtless a man of reason. He will listen to me, I am certain of it. Once he understands what damage time travel is inflicting on the world, it will be easy to persuade him to return the machine.'

'Ever the optimist!' said Inspector Wheeler. 'What do you think, Tom? If we ask ever so politely, do you think Lord Luxon is the sort of fellow to help the police with their enquiries?'

Tom, too, was mesmerised by the view. 'When my Lord Luxon sees this prospect, sir, I do not think he will wish to listen to reason.'

'But how did you know it was *me* who sent the email?' Alice had asked when she and Inspector Wheeler had first spoken on the telephone.

'Let's just say that if you're serious about wanting to remain anonymous, Miss Stacey, I would advise you to stay clear of computers. My colleagues at Scotland Yard managed to obtain your personal details in less time than it took me to fetch a cup of tea. Oh, and I'll give you another tip for nothing – when you're taking a photograph, try not to catch your own reflection in the ice bucket in front of you.'

Alice groaned. 'So I may as well as have sent NASA a picture with my name taped to my forehead . . .'

Inspector Wheeler tried not to laugh. 'I take it that your reason for wishing to remain anonymous was professional?'

'Yes.'

'Well, I can understand that . . .'

Inspector Wheeler was reluctant to divulge any information to

Alice over the telephone until he had satisfied himself that her mystery friend was, indeed, the same Lord Luxon about whom he had received certain information.

'*About whom you have received certain information!* Give me a break, Inspector! You can't keep me in the dark over something like this!' exclaimed Alice. 'You'd hardly be willing to drop everything and fly over from London for a parking violation or for late payment of taxes! What are we dealing with here? Is he dangerous? Is he mad? Is he a wanted criminal? Is there a connection between Lord Luxon and the rumour that NASA has invented time travel?'

Inspector Wheeler steadfastly refused to be drawn.

Alice had already arranged to meet Lord Luxon at seven o'clock on Saturday evening on the roof garden of the Metropolitan Museum of Art. They were due at her aunt's party at eight. Inspector Wheeler undertook to be there, together with two colleagues, at six p.m. Hopefully they would be able to identify her acquaintance there and then and, if he did, indeed, turn out to be one and the same Lord Luxon, then they would take it from there.

'Just one last thing, Miss Stacey. I am puzzled why this gentleman sought you out if, as you say, you were total strangers until recently. What is the connection? Can you think of anything that can have drawn him to you in particular?'

Alice thought for a moment. Now it was her turn to be guarded. 'He's into American history. And I'm an historian . . . That's it.'

'There's nothing else that you can think of?'

'No . . . but, Inspector Wheeler . . .'

'Yes?'

'At the risk of sounding foolish, I'd be grateful if *you* could answer one question for *me*.

'What question might that be, Miss Stacey?'

'Can you tell me, categorically, that this is not a man from the eighteenth century who has come to the future with a particular purpose in mind?'

There was a pause on the other end of the line just long enough to make Alice's heart miss a beat.

'I will do my best to answer all your questions on Saturday afternoon. In the meantime, I think it might be best if you avoided speaking or meeting with him.'

Alice replaced the receiver with a click and clutched her face with her hands. He had not laughed at her suggestion! He had not dismissed the idea as the most ludicrous thing he had ever heard. She staggered to the window of her aunt's Upper West Side apartment as if she had received a blow to the stomach.

The roof garden of the Met was bathed in the golden sunshine of a summer afternoon. Couples were draped over the rails looking out at the stunning views of Central Park against its backdrop of midtown skyscrapers. There was the hum of conversation and laughter as people milled around the deck edged with green hedges. Alice sat at a small table drinking tea with her three new acquaintances. While Detective Inspector Wheeler fitted Alice's preconception of an aging Scottish policeman, she was surprised when she was introduced to his so-called colleagues. The boy, she felt, could have been cast as one of Fagin's boys in *Oliver Twist*, and she did not yet know what to make of the tall Frenchman with the impressive title.

Inspector Wheeler sensed the young woman's anxiety straight away. She looked as if she had not slept and she could not keep still, crossing and uncrossing her legs and running her hands repeatedly through her hair.

'Inspector, are you able to tell me who Lord Luxon is?'

'All in good time, Miss Stacey. I'd prefer it if you would first tell me what made you contact NASA? What aroused your suspicions?'

Alice slid a pair of large-framed sunglasses onto her nose. 'Lord Luxon asked me for an opinion – on an historical event – and I gave it. Why wouldn't I? I'm an historian – it's what I do for a living. But afterwards certain things that I observed about him prompted me to make . . . some assumptions. And although I had no firm evidence to go on, those – admittedly far-fetched – assumptions made me wish that I had been less free with my advice.'

'Could you be a little clearer, Miss Stacey – what advice are we talking about here? What assumptions have you made?'

Alice opened her mouth to speak but the words would not come out. Whether this was due to guilt or to a fear of ridicule she was not quite sure.

'*Courage, chère mademoiselle*,' Montfaron said to Alice. 'Upon my word, whatever you might have told the fellow, we have come here to help you – and to reason with Lord Luxon.'

'*Upon my word!*' Alice repeated. She looked at the Marquis de Montfaron and her eyes widened. She stared at his ponytail and then at Tom's less than perfect teeth. Suddenly she leaned over towards Tom, and practically spat out a question.

'I've forgotten the name of King George III's wife. What is it?'

Tom looked startled. 'Qu . . . Queen Charlotte, madam.'

'And their son, their eldest son, how old is he now?'

'George is but a babe in arms . . .'

Alice shot up in horror. Inspector Wheeler raised his eyes to heaven.

'What year are you from?' she said to Tom. '1762? 1763?'

'Can I please ask you to stay calm, Miss Stacey . . .'

Alice was pointing her finger at Montfaron and Tom. 'They . . . they . . .'

'Yes,' replied Inspector Wheeler quickly. 'They are, but let's not shout it from the rooftops.'

'But if *they* are, then Lord Luxon is, too!' cried Alice, looking around her at the crowds on the roof terrace. 'Just how many visitors *are* there from another century?'

'To the best of my knowledge, three. And very shortly all three of them should be congregated here, on the roof garden of the Metropolitan Museum.'

'So the streets aren't teeming with them, then?'

'No, Miss Stacey, and they never will be if we have anything to do with it. Now will you please tell us what he wanted to know.'

Alice took a deep breath. 'Lord Luxon wanted to know how to sabotage the Revolutionary War – so that Britain would emerge victorious and America would never win her independence.'

Inspector Wheeler raised his bushy eyebrows. 'You're not serious! The man wants to win back America for Britain? He's vain and foolish enough to have ambitions to overturn – *all this*?' Inspector Wheeler gestured to Manhattan rising up all around them. 'He's mad!' Inspector Wheeler observed Alice's face, creased with foreboding. 'Isn't he?'

'Does Lord Luxon have the means to travel back to 1776?' asked Alice.

'It's a possibility – yes.'

'Oh no . . .'

The colour drained from Alice's cheeks as the significance of Inspector Wheeler's response sank in. Her three companions watched her in silence as she took some deep breaths to calm herself.

'Let's not lose our sense of perspective, eh, Miss Stacey?' said Inspector Wheeler. 'After all, how could one man change all of this? It defies belief, surely?'

Alice looked at the policeman. 'Do you know what he said the very first time I met him? He said that he would have ordered the British redcoats to trample our sainted General Washington into the dirt – and I thought he was joking! How was I to know he'd escaped from his own century? But Lord Luxon means to reclaim America for King George III. And the really terrifying thing is that – if he does what I suggested – I reckon he stands a pretty good chance of succeeding.'

Alice's speech wiped the smile off Inspector Wheeler's face. He exchanged glances with Montfaron.

'You see,' continued Alice, 'from the questions he's been asking me, I believe that he plans to prevent Washington crossing the Delaware River on Christmas night 1776. It was a pivotal moment in the Revolutionary War. It is perfectly possible that a British victory at that point could have changed *everything* . . .' Imitating Inspector Wheeler, she gestured to Manhattan rising up around them. 'Would all of *this* still be here if Washington had failed? I don't know the answer but I'd rather not find out.'

Inspector Wheeler reflected for a moment. 'Jumping to hasty conclusions isn't going to help matters. We don't yet know if the man we're interested in and your friend are one and the same person. If he's *not*, we'll all feel very foolish . . .'

'Or very relieved,' said Alice.

'Ay, well, that is why I've brought along young Tom here. He's my witness. In 1763, Tom was Lord Luxon's footman.'

Alice looked in wonder at the scrawny, shy teenager. 'And this gentleman?'

'This, Miss Stacey, is the Marquis de Montfaron, formerly of Arras, who was in frequent attendance at the Court of Versailles on the eve of the French Revolution. He came to us from 1792. I'm no scholar, but even I have heard of many of his acquaintances – Rousseau, Diderot, Benjamin Franklin, Marie-Antoinette . . .'

Alice's eyes grew very round and shivers ran up and down her spine. She had no idea what to say. 'Wow!' was the only response that came to the young Princeton historian. 'And I'm guessing I'm not allowed to write this up or talk to anyone about this encounter . . .'

'No,' said Inspector Wheeler bluntly. 'But rest assured you wouldn't do your career any good if you did.'

Inspector Wheeler and Tom took up position close to the entrance of the roof terrace, on the lookout for Lord Luxon. Alice, meanwhile, begged for the opportunity to talk for as long as she could with the Marquis de Montfaron. She knew that in her career as a historian, no conversation in her life had or would come anywhere close to this one. She couldn't even record it. Alice tried to clear her mind – she would soak up everything he said like a sponge. She would remember every precious word. The two of them stood in the mellow, evening light, silhouetted against the green of Central Park. Alice, her eyes alight, peered up at this tall progeny of the Enlightenment and question after question poured out of her, making her forget, at least for a few minutes, the trying circumstances of their meeting. And Montfaron, who had, all his life, put his faith in reason and knowledge in the hope that, one day, ignorance and evil would be erased from the earth, was more than happy to answer each one of them – and more. Soon Alice realised that, irrespective of which century he came from, she was in the presence of a remarkable man: one whose intellect was tempered with great heart, and whose bright, chestnut eyes displayed the depth of his curiosity about the universe as well as an unquenchable optimism. They were so wrapped up in their discussion, that neither noticed the cluster of redcoats gathering under a clump of trees below them, not a hundred yards from the walls of the Metropolitan Museum of Art.

CHAPTER TWENTY

A Moving Target

In which the Marquis de Montfaron tries to make Lord Luxon see reason and the Metropolitan Museum of Art witnesses a death

As Alice listened to the Marquis de Montfaron speaking about the life that he had left, Central Park, the hum of distant traffic and the New York skyline all seemed to ebb away. Instead, Alice found herself in another century, on another continent – and she had no need of a time machine. Their all too brief conversation touched on the excesses of the Court of Versailles, Montfaron's correspondence with the great minds of the Enlightenment and Benjamin Franklin's odd taste in hats. When the Marquis mentioned that he happened to be travelling through Paris on 14th July, 1789, the same day that an angry mob stormed a prison called the Bastille, Alice's excitement knew no bounds. The Marquis had witnessed the beginning of the French Revolution! She begged him to give her a flavour of that fateful day. The Marquis described the terrible clamour of the crowds, his own fear, and his wish that Rousseau or Diderot could have been there to help him understand what he saw, for he felt more at ease with the certainties of science than with the unpredictable nature of society. He was in the middle of describing the release of a handful of prisoners from the Bastille and how the people were intoxicated with the idea of liberty, when Inspector Wheeler grabbed hold of his arm.

'He's on his way, Miss Stacey,' said Inspector Wheeler to Alice as he pulled the Marquis firmly away. 'Tom has just confirmed that your Lord Luxon and his former employer are one and the same man. Proceed with caution: we're counting on him to lead us to what we need to know.'

Alice nodded. 'I'm ready.'

'We'll be watching you closely,' said Inspector Wheeler. 'Signal if you need help . . .'

Alice was back in the twenty-first century with a jolt. She watched the heads turn, as they always did, as Lord Luxon strolled slowly towards her with an effortless elegance acquired from a lifetime's practice. She followed his blond head as he snaked through groups of people spread out on the terrace. They all seemed so happy: raising their glasses, laughing, enjoying their weekend. Alice's rising panic caused her heart to thump in her chest. It occurred to her that if Lord Luxon had his way, this meeting on the roof garden of the Met could prove to be as pivotal a moment in the history of America as the storming of the Bastille had been a pivotal moment in the history of France. She had become a historian because she believed that it is only by understanding the past that we can understand the present. But how could she deal with a man who intended to change the past in order to create a present which was more to his liking? Oh, how she regretted helping Lord Luxon understand the significance of a tipping point. But it was too late for regrets. What she had to do now was to keep a clear head.

Alice tried to compose her face into an agreeable expression. To stop her hands from trembling, she gripped the handrail of the viewing terrace, assumed as relaxed a posture as she could muster, and feigned taking in the superb view. As she turned to face him, a ray of sun blinded her so that, for an instant, Lord Luxon looked like the negative of a photograph, not human at all, and Alice went cold, as if a jagged fingernail had been drawn down her back.

'Hi! How have you been?' she asked.

The breeze blew strands of gold hair across Lord Luxon's forehead; he was wearing his shoulder-length locks loose today, and, as had become his habit in New York, he was dressed in shades of cream and ivory. A blood-red handkerchief had been artfully arranged in the chest pocket of his linen jacket. 'Good evening, Alice,' said the man who would snatch back America from its citizens. 'A new T-shirt, I see.'

'Oh . . . yes,' said Alice, looking down at her T-shirt with its large, asymmetric spirals, white on black. 'It's one of Marcel Duchamp's "Rotoreliefs".' She turned around. 'Look, I've got one on my back, too.'

'It makes you look like a moving target . . .'

'Oh. That wasn't actually my intention.' Alice failed to disguise the tremble in her voice.

Lord Luxon searched Alice's face and she could not help turning away from his piercing stare. He reached into his pocket and drew out a postcard. 'I was particularly happy to encounter this painting downstairs. See, I have purchased a memento of my visit.'

Alice glanced at it and her grip tightened on the handrail.

'Do you know it?'

'"Washington Crossing the Delaware". Of course. Every American child knows this painting.'

'A stirring image – yet clearly painted by someone who had not witnessed the event . . . But then, our heroes owe as much to those who represent them as to the heroic acts themselves. Would you agree?'

'You should have more faith in people. The world has produced some genuine heroes . . .'

'You think me cynical?'

'To put it mildly.'

Lord Luxon laughed. Alice took some deep breaths and tried not to let her eyes wander towards Montfaron and Inspector Wheeler. She feared that she had given herself away for Lord Luxon directed his gaze more than once over to the incongruous pair who stood close to one of the large metallic sculptures that adorned the roof garden of the Met.

'The view from here is sublime, although I am at a loss to understand why these objects have found a home here. Do *you* admire them, Alice?'

'Yes, I like them – but, if it's all the same to you, I'm not in the mood for a discussion on modern art.'

Lord Luxon laughed. 'Very well. If that topic of conversation holds no interest for Miss Stacey we shall move on to another. For example . . . I have lately been preoccupied with preparations for a short trip.'

Alice felt her muscles tense. 'Oh? Where are you headed?'

Lord Luxon smiled benignly at her. 'Trenton, New Jersey . . .'

A police siren heading towards mid-town echoed over Central Park. Alice suddenly became intensely aware of the blood beating in her temples and for a moment she thought she was about to faint. *Trenton!* She found herself seeking out the reassuring figure of the Marquis de Montfaron and when he saw the fear in her eyes he immediately started towards her, motioning to Inspector

Wheeler to let him go alone. No! she wanted to shout, I didn't mean for you to . . . But it was too late. Lord Luxon had already spotted the Marquis.

'Good evening, Miss Stacey,' said the Marquis, kissing her hand.

'May I present . . . Mr Montfaron,' said Alice hesitantly and then, being at a loss to know what else to say, added: 'He's from France.'

Lord Luxon inclined his head and eyed the tall man a little suspiciously. He seemed annoyed at the intrusion.

'Can there be a finer prospect than this in all of America?' said the Marquis de Montfaron to Lord Luxon with a sweeping bow. 'Does not Central Park please you, sir? It is as if Nature herself has been *imprisoned* by artifice.'

'It is a fine prospect, *monsieur*, although I prefer to see Manhattan from afar, rising up out of the ocean.'

'Ah, yes,' Montfaron replied. 'It is always wise to put some distance between oneself and the object of one's desire.' Lord Luxon looked sharply at Montfaron who merely smiled back pleasantly. He continued: 'A Manhattan sunset is a wonder to behold, is it not? Who would wish to change a single detail of it?'

'Life is change, monsieur, change and movement – it is in the nature of things.'

'Change is one thing,' replied Montfaron. '*Destruction* is quite another . . . I suppose that you are aware of the phenomenon which recently took place in London?'

'I heard tell of some curious occurrence . . .'

'There were reports of ghosts and phantoms and a great roaring sound was heard all over the city as if the end of the world had come. Those with greater knowledge than I have called it a *time quake*. Nor was it the first. Rather these time quakes might be

267

viewed as the first symptoms of a fatal disease. Who knows how long Time itself will be able to sustain the damage *you* are inflicting on it.'

'I? Damage which *I* have been inflicting on the fabric of *time?*' exclaimed Lord Luxon incredulously. He looked at the Frenchman. 'Who the devil are you, sir?'

'The same century witnessed our births and the same device transported us to the future,' replied Montfaron. 'I know of what I speak.'

Alice was trying to take in what the Marquis had said. She put her hand to her mouth. 'A *time quake* . . . ?' she breathed. 'And it was caused by Lord Luxon?'

Lord Luxon made as if to leave but the Marquis grabbed hold of his arm.

'Who would not wish to travel to different centuries if he could? But you must know that with each use of the device more parallel worlds are formed and the closer we all move to *oblivion.*'

'What device?' asked Alice.

Lord Luxon shook Montfaron's hand off his arm. 'You talk in riddles, sir!'

Montfaron pressed on: 'Existence cannot be undone. To go back in time is to *change* time. Yet the universe will duplicate itself rather than permit a single second of existence to be destroyed. You, sir, have unwittingly created parallel worlds whose number defies belief—'

'Parallel worlds!' exclaimed Alice. 'What are you talking about?'

Lord Luxon drew out his handkerchief and waved it at Montfaron as if he were shooing away a fly.

'Madam, this is not to be borne . . . I no longer care to listen to the ravings of this . . . *Frenchman.*'

'But you *must* listen,' said Montfaron. 'For all depends on it!

Understand that you are like a fox running through the forest with a burning torch tied to your tail. Soon everything will be burning, soon everything will be destroyed . . .'

'Your affection for metaphor, sir, is tedious.'

Montfaron paused for a moment and tried a different tack. 'I beg of you, Lord Luxon, to see beyond this vainglorious ambition of winning back America . . .'

Lord Luxon glared accusingly at Alice.

'I am a man of reason as, I hope, are you,' said Montfaron. 'A man born into privilege as, I believe, were you. I ask you, as one gentleman to another, to surrender the anti-gravity machine – while you still have the opportunity to do so . . .'

'Do not *dare* to threaten me, monsieur!'

It was at that moment that Lord Luxon noticed a movement out of the corner of his eye and he turned to see Inspector Wheeler signalling to the Marquis de Montfaron. He looked back at Alice.

'Oh, Alice,' he said. 'You disappoint me.'

There was only one exit. Lord Luxon sprang forward through the crowds, heading for the elevators. As he drew level with Inspector Wheeler he shoved a large and bulky man at the policeman. They collided heavily and both men were floored.

Momentarily taken aback, Alice now tore after Lord Luxon herself, keeping his blond mane in her sights and pushing through the good-humoured crowds, calling out apologies as she did so. But Lord Luxon's head abruptly disappeared from view, and when she drew closer she saw that Tom – whom the Carrick brothers had at least taught how to disappear into a crowd – had put out his leg to trip his former employer. This time it was Lord Luxon's turn to find himself sprawled out on the floor. In a flash of recognition Lord Luxon snarled some unheard threat in Tom's direction. Alice saw the look of fear on the boy's face.

Montfaron was tall enough to have seen what happened, too. 'Bravo, Tom!' he called over the heads of the crowd.

Lord Luxon lay only feet away from one of the elevators whose doors were slowly closing. Alice put on a spurt, praying that Lord Luxon would not have time to get in. She lost sight of him for an instant and by the time she had reached the elevator the doors were barely a finger's width apart. The gap was just wide enough for her eyes to meet those of Lord Luxon. He stared at her in cold fury and mouthed something at her which she did not understand. The doors clanged shut.

Alice banged the flat of her hand repeatedly on the elevator button and searched the faces in the crowd for her companions. Tom had vanished once more but she glimpsed Montfaron helping Inspector Wheeler to his feet. He was holding his head and seemed dazed or winded or both. They'll just have to follow when they can, she thought desperately. I *mustn't* lose him. She pushed the button again and put her ear to the doors of the second elevator. Please, *please*, she thought, hurry up . . . A second later she heard the cranking of cables and a few seconds after that it arrived. The doors opened agonisingly slowly . . . Alice hurtled in and begged the lift attendant to wait for no one else. If he loved his country he should go *immediately*. She looked so desperate the attendant gave her the benefit of the doubt. 'Yes, ma'am!' he said. 'Going down!'

Had a large party of elderly art lovers from Oslo not chosen that precise moment to rise from their tables and leave the roof terrace *en bloc*, Alice would have had assistance sooner. As it was, the Norwegian seniors spilled out over the deck and clustered in a dense mass in front of the elevators. Tom, Montfaron and Inspector Wheeler were caught up in the cheerful morass of white-haired tourists likes seagulls in an oil slick.

'Let us through!' barked Inspector Wheeler as the three of them pushed past frail shoulders in cardigans.

When, at last, they emerged out of the elevator onto the first floor, Lord Luxon and Alice were nowhere to be seen. Inspector Wheeler could not disguise his exasperation. What he had envisaged as an initial meeting to identify a potential suspect had suddenly escalated – quite literally – into a race against time. The stakes were now so high it was dizzying. And he had blown it – there was no question of that. He contemplated ringing 911 for back-up. But then he conjectured that in the time it would take to get through to the right person, and to convince them that they should mobilise half the city's police force, if necessary, to hunt down Lord Luxon, it would already be too late. And what could he tell them? The truth? No. It was not an option.

'If he's out of the building already, which I suspect he is,' he said to Montfaron through gritted teeth, 'then we've already lost him.'

The three of them hurried towards the Great Hall, scanning the crowds for a glimpse of Lord Luxon's blond hair or the target of Alice's T-shirt. Pink-cheeked, and with sweat beading on his brow, Inspector Wheeler strode towards the main entrance like a bloodhound straining at the leash. He saw every plinth, every archway, every balustrade, every cluster of museum attendants, as a potential place of concealment in this desperate game of hide and seek. Finally they stood in the vast, galleried hall, the grand staircase on their left and the main entrance, leading to Fifth Avenue, on their right. Inspector Wheeler looked up at the balconies of the upper floor, at the lofty arches above, and at the rows of stone columns on all sides; he observed the people milling about around them and listened to footfall reverberating around the museum and to the muted babble of conversation. *Had* he left the building? Was Miss Stacey with him? Perhaps she was already dodging between the traffic, hailing a yellow cab in hot pursuit of Lord Luxon. He hoped so. She couldn't do any worse than he had.

'You and Tom stand guard here, I'm going to take a look in the street,' the Inspector said to Montfaron as he walked outside past a gaggle of security guards.

Tom and the Marquis de Montfaron circled the enquiry desk and then walked at a breathless pace through some of the nearby galleries, Tom often having to trot to keep up with the Marquis's long legs. They were blind to the exquisite marble forms that graced the Greek sculpture court, to the armoured knights on horses and to the four-poster bed that Montfaron would have felt at home sleeping in. They returned after only a few minutes, somewhat disconsolately, to the Great Hall. It was then that Tom saw her. Tom put his hand on Montfaron's arm and pointed up to the balcony. Alice was leaning over the broad balustrade on the left of the hall, somewhere above the Greek and Roman galleries, still searching the labyrinthine museum for any sign of Lord Luxon.

'Wait here for Inspector Wheeler while I fetch Miss Stacey,' Montfaron told Tom. 'If he comes back, tell the Inspector where I have gone.'

Tom watched Montfaron hurry towards the grand staircase and then looked to see if there was any sign of Inspector Wheeler. There was not. Tom stood self-consciously in one corner of the Grand Hall, a small and lonely figure, and he put his hand in his pocket, wishing that his mouse was here with him and not in a farmhouse in Derbyshire. But when he looked back up at Alice, he started with shock for he saw someone standing behind her, hands poised above her shoulders . . . Tom immediately bolted towards the stairs.

*

Lord Luxon stood so close that she could feel his warm breath on the nape of her neck. Alice spun around and Lord Luxon gripped her shoulders. She stared into his blue eyes. He shook his head disapprovingly. Alice's legs refused to move.

'Now, Alice, you are going to atone for what you have done by escorting me through your guards at the door,' he said.

Alice tried not to show her confusion. Then all at once she understood. He must mean the security guards at the entrance! He thinks they are ours! Alice's hopes rose a little. 'I'll help you if you tell me what you're planning to do at Trenton . . .'

'Surely I do not need to tell *you*! Your advice has been invaluable – it grieves me that I cannot repay my debt . . .'

'You cannot seriously be tempted to sabotage the Revolutionary War . . . you're an intelligent man – this is *absurd* . . .'

'You disappoint me,' he said in a flat voice. 'Does not the rewriting of history fuel your scholar's ardour? I had hoped you possessed more imagination.'

'Please – you *mustn't* do this! How can you think of destroying a single second of history, let alone a couple of centuries?'

'Is it not what all historians would desire to do – to lay out the past on the floor, see the patterns, move the pieces, rearrange it in a manner more pleasing to them?'

'*No!* How can you even contemplate playing God like this? It's . . . it's *obscene!*'

'It seems that you wish to study life, Alice, whilst *I* wish to *live* it.'

'You tricked me into betraying my country!'

Lord Luxon put a single finger to Alice's lips. 'The time is past for remorse. I am about to rescue America from itself. Soon I—'

But then Lord Luxon let out a strangulated cry and Alice watched, bewildered, as he fell backwards. The Marquis de Montfaron's elbow tightened around his neck. Crying out with the effort of it, Montfaron managed to heave Lord Luxon away from Alice and forced him backwards until he was pinned down across the wide stone balustrade. Montfaron pressed all his weight against Luxon's chest.

'Aaaagh! Call off your Frenchman, Alice! He is breaking my back!'

Lord Luxon struck Montfaron's back repeatedly with his one free hand and kicked furiously with his legs.

'What can I do to help?' cried Alice.

Lord Luxon strained against Montfaron. 'Do you have something to tie his wrists?' panted the Marquis.

'My belt!' exclaimed Alice, already unbuckling it.

People on the opposite balcony started to point and shout. One of the security guards downstairs began to run towards the stairs. Montfaron pushed hard against Lord Luxon's shoulders. 'If you behave well, monsieur,' he panted, 'you *may* be permitted to return to your own century. But know that you have failed in your quest.'

Alice held out her belt for Montfaron. But the moment he relaxed his pressure Lord Luxon managed to bring up his knees and thrust the Marquis to one side so that he lost his balance and toppled forwards onto the balustrade. For once his height was against him: in one swift movement, Lord Luxon dived at his legs and swung them, too, over the balustrade. The Marquis de Montfaron dropped the twenty-five feet to the ground like a stone, without uttering a single sound. When his body crashed onto the marble floor, far below, there was a dull and sickening *thud* that resounded around the museum. Alice and Tom stared, dumbstruck, from the balcony. For the briefest of moments a profound silence descended on the cavernous space as if it were in the eye of a storm. Then, all at once, the museum was filled with screams and it seemed that everyone was running across the Great Hall.

Along with dozens of others, Lord Luxon hurried down the stairs, asking everyone he encountered what could possibly have happened. What was the commotion about? With all attention elsewhere, Lord Luxon managed to walk calmly out of the main doors, unnoticed even by Inspector Wheeler who, on re-entering the museum, had been attracted by the screams. Once on the street Lord Luxon smoothed down his hair and walked smartly up Fifth Avenue and into Central Park where, a hundred yards away, he spied the red jackets of Sergeant Thomas and his men. When Lord Luxon reached them they formed a tight circle into which he stepped.

'We leave immediately for Trenton,' said Lord Luxon. 'My historian has disturbed a hornet's nest of those who would stop us.'

Inspector Wheeler ran to the circle of onlookers. Some people had hands over their mouths, some were crying, others just stood, staring at the floor in shock. He heard a security guard call for the emergency services. As Inspector Wheeler edged forwards he was overcome by a terrible foreboding. He looked over someone's shoulder to see who it was.

The Marquis de Montfaron's eyes stared blankly ahead and a trickle of blood dripped from the corner of his mouth onto the marble floor. His elegant fingers twitched for a moment and then lay still.

Inspector Wheeler uttered a terrible cry. 'Montfaron! . . . Oh no . . .'

People stood to one side to let the Inspector through. He knelt down next to Montfaron's lifeless body. The policeman reached down and closed his friend's bright, chestnut eyes for the last time. Then he took off his jacket and placed it over his head and shoulders. How could this gentle soul, this man of reason, who believed in the ultimate goodness of man, be *dead*? What had happened? Inspector Wheeler buried his face in his hands. When he looked up he found that Tom and Alice were kneeling next to him. Tears flooded down Alice's face.

'Was this Lord Luxon's doing?' asked Inspector Wheeler.

Alice nodded.

'Where is he?'

Both Alice and Tom shook their heads.

'This is all my fault . . .' said Alice.

Inspector Wheeler put his hand over hers. 'You were a pawn in his game. How were you to know? If anyone's to blame it's me. I underestimated him . . .'

Sirens in the street announced the arrival of the police and an ambulance.

'Who can stop Lord Luxon now?' asked Tom.

Inspector Wheeler could only shake his head in despair as he wept for the loss of his extraordinary friend.

Inspector Wheeler telephoned the Dyer farmhouse with the tragic news. Still numb with shock after hearing of the Marquis de Montfaron's death, Dr Pirretti and Dr Dyer went straight back to work on the anti-gravity machine.

'But how can you concentrate at a time like this?' asked Mrs Dyer.

'Easy – it's the only way to stop me thinking about the consequences of failing . . .' her husband replied.

Meanwhile, Tom left a message on Anjali's answering machine in Canary Wharf. An hour later a text came through from her: C U @ Heathrow. Sorry about your news. Was in Harrods yesterday. Saw cute mouse cage. Let's U & me go buy it. Ax

CHAPTER TWENTY-ONE

The Tipping Point

In which George Washington prepares to cross
the Delaware on Christmas night and
encounters an unexpected enemy

Sergeant Thomas did not relish the role of spy. He relished even less the role of assassin. Nevertheless, he wore the uniform of the enemy and joined in the fighting talk of the men and the ribald insults aimed at King George and the British army, although he tugged repeatedly at the collar of his jacket as if his lies would choke him. In order to avoid arousing suspicion, Sergeant Thomas and one of his lads, Corporal Starling, who was almost as reliable a marksman as he was himself, had separated. They now found themselves at opposite ends of the columns of men. The corporal was under instructions to target Colonel Henry Knox, whose powerful voice Sergeant Thomas had heard rising above the coming storm. The plan was a simple one: Washington and Knox were to be shot simultaneously when the boat transporting the General was a third of the way across the river – near enough for Sergeant Thomas to get a good shot, yet deep enough into the icy waters to prevent an easy escape should the first shot not find its mark.

Sergeant Thomas's stolen uniform was as ripped and muddy as those of his battle-soiled comrades. Many of the men who surrounded him were poorly shod, including the determinedly cheerful blacksmith on his left, who was forever stopping to fasten the rags he had tied around his swollen and bleeding feet. Sergeant Thomas, however, was not prepared to do without shoes, for he knew what conditions lay ahead. This settled weather would not last for long.

It had been around four o' clock in the afternoon that General Washington, two thousand four hundred men and a couple of hundred horse set off from New Town. Now, as they marched along snowy roads towards the Delaware River and McKonkey's Ferry, the setting sun tinged the wintry landscape red and for a while the rim of the horizon glowed as if it were on fire. The American Patriots had fear in their hearts, as well they might, embarking on a secret mission and facing an army that was larger, better equipped and better disciplined than their own. Yet Sergeant Thomas envied them more than a little, for they did not trudge through this snow because they had been forced to, nor because, like him, they were career soldiers or mercenaries. Rather, they were here because they had *chosen* to be here. They were here to fight for their rights and their freedoms and a cause they believed in. Sergeant Thomas did not understand the politics of it all, nor did he seek to, for in his experience of life there were always several sides to any argument. But he recognised that they fought with a purpose and with a passion that had not been laid on them by their superiors. They had seen defeat after defeat; the superior British forces had chased them across New Jersey; they had seen their numbers drastically depleted. The Patriot cause was on the brink of failure. Nevertheless, this night each one of them was prepared to follow their general whose watchword was *Victory or Death!*

All around him, men kept up their morale by reciting Thomas Paine's words. How ironic it was, thought Sergeant Thomas, that it was an Englishman who incited the colonists to rise up against his own monarch, against his own country. But now that he had seen with his own eyes how powerful a nation America would become on the world's stage, he could understand why Lord Luxon wished to tip the scales in Britain's favour. The stakes were of the highest order.

The foot soldiers who surrounded him had committed Paine's stirring lines to memory, and repeated them so often in the darkening gloom that they rang ceaselessly in Sergeant Thomas's ears like a refrain:

These are the times that try men's souls . . . Tyranny, like hell, is not easily conquered; yet we have this consolation with us, that the harder the conflict, the more glorious the triumph . . .

Sergeant Thomas distrusted peddlers of words. Before every battle, every campaign, the officers would practise their rhetoric on the men. Like the Pied Piper, those with mastery over words could inflame passions and incite violence and make men follow them, irrespective of the truth of what they said. Give me the plain honest talk of an inarticulate man, he thought, over any number of Thomas Paines. Words are deadlier than any weapon.

As dusk fell, Sergeant Thomas caught sight of George Washington riding ahead of them on his chestnut horse, an erect figure in a billowing cape, his resplendent uniform contrasting starkly with the tattered rags that covered his men. The General brought his mount to a halt and turned around to look at the columns of soldiers marching towards the Delaware. There was resolve and determination on the face of the colonial rebel. It suddenly seemed to Sergeant Thomas that Washington's stare hovered over him, as if he had pierced his disguise, and he turned away, unsettled. When the time comes I shall look the General square in the face, Sergeant Thomas told himself. He shall not doubt who has fired the shot. But I shall not look on him now, not until I have to.

The column came to a halt, as happened very frequently, though he could rarely see the cause of it. The men fell to talking quietly between themselves. Thick clouds had gathered overhead and it was beginning to spit with rain. The blacksmith turned to look at Sergeant Thomas with what little light remained of Christmas Day.

'Will you sign up to fight beyond the New Year, as General Washington would have us do?'

'I am committed to following General Washington until he draws his final breath,' Sergeant Thomas replied.

'Then let us hope your service will be a long one! As for me, I am torn. My wife and children have already endured more than a man can ask of them. Without my labours to provide for them, how can they eat? How can they tolerate this bitter cold?'

The large-framed man patted his chest pocket, pulled out a folded letter and immediately pushed back the precious document to protect it from the rain.

'My wife begs me to return. Our youngest is sick. Yet how can I refuse General Washington's call? Do you have a family? Must you also choose between your loved ones and your country?'

Sergeant Thomas had fought on two continents for more years than he cared to remember and, to him, all soldiers from any country were alike, pawns in their masters' game. If he encountered this blacksmith on the battlefield he would skewer him with his bayonet without hesitation. It was the way things were.

He patted the man's back. 'I am truly sorry to hear about your child. No. I have no family. My life is my own to lose . . .'

'A man should have children,' said the other. 'I have eight. Five boys and three girls. When I first came to Virginia, twenty years ago and more, I vowed I should give my family a better life than my parents had been able to give me. It has not always been easy but I've reaped the rewards of my labours. This country has been good to us. I fear what will happen if we lose this war.'

The blacksmith put Sergeant Thomas in mind of the Irishman, Michael, in his air-conditioned SoHo bar, who was forever showing him photos of his family and urging him to settle in America where if you worked hard anything was possible. Two and half centuries later it would be a different world but in that way, at least, things had not changed.

'Why do you smile?'

''Tis nothing,' replied Sergeant Thomas. 'A memory, that is all . . .'

Sergeant Thomas fell silent and the blacksmith did not interrupt his thoughts. Presently the columns of men started to move off again and Sergeant Thomas looked up at the sky and the mass of ominous black clouds moving towards them from the north-east.

By eleven o'clock the wind was whipping into a hurricane and driving sleet stung the cheeks of Lord Luxon and William. The two men were disguised as farmers, with scarves tied around their heads to prevent their hats blowing away. It was an attire that appealed little to Lord Luxon. But even he was too preoccupied to think much about appearances that night. The wind roared through the branches overhead, and blew so hard they struggled at times to keep upright.

They had not intended to bring with them Sally, Sergeant Thomas's faithful, if hideous, hound. As they embarked on their fateful journey to the past, she had leaped onto her master at the very moment the anti-gravity machine left one century for another. As there was no way to send her back without disrupting their plans, Sergeant Thomas had entrusted her to William while he did his duty for King and country. Powerful scents met the dog's sensitive nostrils: of horses and gunpowder, and wounded, unwashed men. And she sniffed the air, alert and fearful. There were unfamiliar sounds, too, that sent her off kilter: the incessant trudge of thousands of feet through snow, the murmur of a great crowd echoing over the empty distances, the whinnying and snorting of horses, reluctant to step onto icy ferries, the crunch of cannon wheels over frozen ground . . . For a city dog, more used to the honking of horns and the smell of pizzas and gutters, this overload of her senses was too much to bear. She lifted her large head and barked repeatedly. The wind carried her cries away from the river and into the starless night. Lord Luxon kicked the animal mercilessly in the ribs, pushing her onto her side. She struggled to get back up again, whimpering pitifully, her coat covered in snow. When William approached her she snarled at him.

'Shhh!' whispered William into her ear. 'We are within a hundred yards of the enemy. Would you have us all killed?!'

William crouched down in the snow and tied his handkerchief around the animal's muzzle to muffle her cries before Lord Luxon carried out his repeated threat to silence her himself. When he had finished, William grabbed her by the collar, pushed down her rear so that she sat, whining through her gag, on the frozen earth. He stroked her head and caressed her floppy ears to comfort her.

Lord Luxon, meanwhile, peered out at the army massing on the Pennsylvania side of the Delaware River. The night was very dark but long tongues of flames from the bonfires, dancing and spluttering in the gusts of air, cast enough light over the scene for Lord Luxon's purposes.

He watched ranks of men stamping their feet and blowing on

their fingers and rotating close to the fires. Behind them, a ghostly flotilla of ferries and boats waited on the black river.

'One would think we were gathered on the banks of the River Styx!' exclaimed Lord Luxon. 'But where is the ferryman to transport these wretched sinners to hell?'

William said nothing, assuming, rightly, that no response was required. But, he thought to himself, they had their own Cerberus, watchdog of Hades, in Sally. She might not have three heads but she was, without doubt, the ugliest dog he had ever clapped eyes on . . .

Presently, above the howling wind, they heard the deep bass voice of Colonel Henry Knox ordering parties of men to shift the great slabs of ice that were gathering at the river's edge making embarkation impossible. Lord Luxon caught a flash of steel as the big man waved his sabre in the air, directing the men.

'There is our man, at last!' exclaimed Lord Luxon, steam coming from his mouth with every breath. 'But where the devil are Sergeant Thomas and Corporal Starling?'

He took out his night-vision binoculars and scanned the faces of the soldiers. After several minutes he gave up looking for his own men and concentrated on looking for the whereabouts of the commander-in-chief of the American army. The sound of men hacking at the ice and levering it away from the bank with poles punctuated Lord Luxon's feverish thoughts. Adrenaline raced through his veins and made him forget the cold and the wind. He thought of glory, and of his father's disapproval of him, and of his dead uncles, and of sweeping aside once and for all the mistakes of his youth. This, he thought, would be his legacy to England, and England would forever be in his debt.

Suddenly, Lord Luxon saw what he had been waiting for and his heart missed a beat. The time had come! General Washington was climbing into a boat manned by perhaps a dozen men.

Through sheets of snowflakes Lord Luxon could distinguish his hat and cape and sabre, and saw the mariners holding up their oars and poles to attention whilst blocks of ice smacked against the side of the boat. The rim of the boat had been painted yellow and Lord Luxon watched this thin stripe bob up and down in the water as General Washington climbed in, causing the vessel to list from side to side. General Washington seemed to be about to sit down but then changed his mind on account of the freezing water sloshing about at the bottom of the boat. He remained standing, legs wide apart for balance.

'William, do you see Sergeant Thomas?'

'I do not, sir.'

'Damn his eyes! Where *is* the fellow?'

Lord Luxon was becoming agitated. He reached up and tore off a bare branch from the tree that swayed above them. Sally, who had not taken her eyes off Lord Luxon, flinched, fearing another beating. She whimpered despite William's handkerchief. Lord Luxon glared at her.

'And confound his wretched hound!'

He took a swipe at her and William cried out as the animal yanked her head from his grasp and bounded away from her tormentor and towards her beloved master. Sally knew he was near. She could detect his scent even amidst thousands of others. Lord Luxon and William both ran after her but even with her clumsy, lolloping gait, she could outrun them with ease. They stopped under cover of trees some fifty yards from the bank. Lord Luxon stood white-faced and grim-jawed. He surveyed General Washington standing proud in his boat and Colonel Knox cupping his hands to his mouth and bellowing orders to the watermen from high on the bank. He could see the ripple of movement as men moved out of the way of the rampaging canine.

'Shoot, damn you, shoot!' hissed Lord Luxon. 'Before all is lost . . .'

Astride in the boat amidst the seated mariners, General Washington made an easy target. Sergeant Thomas stood in the dark willing him to turn around for he had no desire to shoot the man in the back. The wind was very strong now. His ears were full of the howling wind and Colonel Knox's incessant commands bellowing out across the river. Flurries of snow swirled in front of his eyes, sometimes making his victim disappear completely. Twenty yards and two bonfires separated Sergeant Thomas from Corporal Starling and each had managed to catch the other's eye. Now that the General's boat was ten or fifteen yards from the bank, the moment had come. This was it. They had arrived at the tipping point of history. Sergeant Thomas's stomach lurched. His mouth had gone dry. He gave the prearranged signal, a double nod of the head, which Corporal Starling repeated back to him. Sergeant Thomas started to count to thirty which he knew his accomplice would be doing at the same time. Then Sergeant Thomas knelt down, placed his musket on the ground and took out the small twenty-first-century revolver from his pocket. He screwed on the silencer as they had practised a hundred times. Under cover of the snow and the wind and the dark, and in the midst of all this frantic activity, not a soul noticed him taking aim.

'Twenty-one, twenty-two, twenty-three, twenty-four—'

Sally's forelegs landed square in the middle of his back, pushing him forward onto the hard ground. His forehead hit something hard and for several moments he saw stars and was unable to move. After hours in the freezing wind he suddenly felt warm. Sally lay on top of him. As he tried to get up, the dog nuzzled his neck and William's handkerchief, now soaked with slobber, wet his ear. Sergeant Thomas pushed himself up, aghast, and thrust Sally roughly away from him. A terrible panic came over Sergeant Thomas as he heard shouting and the sound of running feet. He stood up. Hundreds of men were rushing in the direction of Colonel Knox. Confusion reigned. Soldiers raced around the bank as if someone had kicked over an ants' nest. He glanced at the river. General Washington was shouting at the oarsmen to return to shore. The gun! The gun! Sergeant Thomas dropped to the ground and felt blindly for the weapon. His fingers closed over the barrel of the gun and he leaped to his feet, feeling for the trigger as he took aim. Sally bumped up against him.

'Heel!' he cried.

The gagged animal sat down obediently and looked up at her master as he pointed his gun at George Washington's heart. She whimpered. Sergeant Thomas glanced down at her and the thought scorched through his mind like a fork of lightning that the animal was Washington's guardian angel. Was she telling him that he was not meant to assassinate the first President of the United States? The faces of the blacksmith and Michael in his bar in SoHo appeared to him. He thought of the people going about their business in Prince Street, and then of all the people who must have come to America from every corner of the globe to start a new life. And then he thought of the corrupt aristocrat who had hired him, whose wish it was that General Washington should die so that Britain should retain its colony. And for what purpose? Who would benefit? Ever so slowly, as if his arm had a mind of its own, Sergeant Thomas lowered the gun . . .

Neither man nor beast saw the slight figure pushing his way through crowds of running men, hurtling towards them through the wind and snow. Sally was as slow to react as her master when Lord Luxon tore the gun from his hand.

'No!' shouted Sergeant Thomas into the wind.

The cry reached General Washington who turned instinctively towards it, even in the midst of all the commotion on shore, his keen eyes searching the darkness. By the flickering light of a bonfire, he saw first the shape of a man and then the shape of a great dog collapse to the ground. As he opened his mouth to raise the alarm he glimpsed the glint of metal and a hand wielding a strange weapon that pointed directly at him. Lord Luxon squeezed the trigger. It weighed so little, the bullet that sped across the stormy night to lodge in a human heart, and yet it had gathered enough momentum to topple a nation. Without a sound, the commander-in-chief of the Patriot forces fell into the Delaware River, his blood staining the blocks of ice that knocked against the boat. Four brave mariners jumped into the freezing waters to rescue their leader. By the time General Washington's lifeless body was heaved onto dry land, Lord Luxon had disappeared into the night and the Patriot cause was already lost.

CHAPTER TWENTY-TWO

The Veil

In which Peter finally learns of the problems that
have beset his friend, and the consequences
of time travel become impossible to ignore

In the middle of the night, when all was silent and she could not
even see her hand in front of her face, Kate would sit up in bed and
stare all around her, searching for signs that she had slipped into a
world where time flowed faster. She would reach out to Peter, and
listen to his even, easy breath and know that for now, at least, she
was not alone. Reassured, Kate slept fitfully on.

It was past midday when a pale and bleary-eyed Hannah knocked
on Peter's bedroom door bearing a bowl of steaming hot water. She
deposited it on the dressing table by the casement window. The
blackbirds sang and the sun shone down on Sir Richard's house in
Lincoln's Inn Fields as if all were right with the world. She found
not only Peter but also Kate. They had dragged the mattress from
the bed, turned it sideways and had taken half each, so that their
top halves were cushioned whilst their legs lay sprawled out over
bare floorboards. Both wore long white nightshirts. Peter slept on

his back, with his mouth open, whilst Kate lay on her stomach. A lace *fichu*, that had decorated the neckline of Kate's dress, now bound the children's wrists together. Hannah wondered which of them thought the other was going to get away in the night. She sighed. But in a topsy-turvy world such as this, what did it matter? She knelt down next to them.

'It grieves me to wake you after such a night, but the Tar Man is waiting on you and Master Gideon in the drawing room. Though it does not seem right to see a rogue like him sitting in Sir Richard's armchair and sipping tea from a china cup . . .'

Peter pushed himself up a fraction and muttered: 'Could you tell him we'll be down in a minute?'

Kate kept her head buried in the mattress. All she could manage was a groan. Hannah was, herself, too tired to cajole. 'Very well,' she said, closing the door, 'I shall tell the Tar Man you will join him presently.'

When Peter tried to get up he discovered that he was tied to Kate. All of this was really getting to her. He untied the *fichu* and got up as quietly as he could. He splashed his face with the hot water. He looked down at the sleeping Kate and then dried his face with the linen cloth. When he took the towel away from his eyes, a second or two later, he was shocked to see Kate standing next to him, touching his hand.

'I didn't see you—'

But Peter stopped mid-sentence and stared at Kate open-mouthed. His hand flew to his mouth. Suddenly Kate vanished and reappeared simultaneously on his other side. Peter cried out in shock.

'*Don't* let go of me,' she said. 'Every time you do I fast-forward.'

'Fast-forward?' Peter just stared at her. 'What are you talking about?'

'Why are you looking at me like that?'

'You . . . I . . . I think you'd better look in the mirror . . .'

There was a small, oval mirror in a gold frame above the dressing table. Kate looked into it for a long moment. Her contours were hazy, and the colour of her skin, and even that of her hair, was as diluted and delicate as the finest silk chiffon. A single ray of afternoon sunshine penetrated the room through a high window and passed right through her shoulder. Kate showed no expression but hot tears started to flow down Peter's cheeks. His friend could no longer be said to be solid.

'I'm sorry,' he said, wiping his nose with the back of his hand. 'I can't help it. You look . . . like a ghost.'

Kate merely nodded in agreement.

'What's happening to you, Kate? I don't understand!'

And so the conversation that Kate had been dreading for so long took place. Things had gone too far for it not to. She could no longer pretend that nothing was wrong – either to herself or anyone else. Something was very wrong indeed. They sat down side by side on the mattress and Kate told Peter about fast-forwarding and seeing the future and what had happened when she touched the Tar Man and about being able to talk with Dr Pirretti – or at least an alternative Dr Pirretti in a parallel world. At first Peter just listened but soon the questions started.

'You mean you were fast-forwarding and seeing the future when you were with my dad and the grown-up version of me?'

'Yes.'

'Did *I* know what was happening to you?'

'A little . . . not everything.'

'Well, why couldn't you tell me? It was obvious something was wrong, that you were beginning to fade. Did you think I was too stupid to understand?'

'I'm telling you now . . .'

'I might have been able to help!'

'This isn't about *you*! I didn't *want* to talk about it! I thought I might stop doing it, acclimatise, or something. Like getting used to the heat on holiday . . . We stopped blurring after a while, didn't we?'

Peter nodded miserably.

'And anyway, you're the only one who *can* help.'

'What do you mean?'

'You're my lightning conductor. You ground me.'

'Is that why you won't let go of me?'

'Yes. Why do you think I tied our wrists together? Without you I just spin off at a million miles an hour. It might seem like one night to you. For me these past twenty-four hours feel like a year. I lost count of the number of times I fast-forwarded before I tied us up. I was talking to Dr Pirretti during the night and—'

'Can you hear her now?'

'I only hear her while I'm fast-forwarding.'

'But why?'

'She's got a theory – which I couldn't follow. Something to do with parallel worlds and dark energy. I can see the future much more easily when I'm fast-forwarding, too.'

'Can you see my future?'

Kate nodded. 'I've seen something. I didn't understand it – you were upset. You were standing on a tall building with a city in the distance that looked a bit like London but I'm not sure.'

'Eighteenth or twenty-first century?'

'Definitely not eighteenth . . .'

'But that's fantastic! It means we get back! Can you see your future?'

'No . . . I've tried.'

'Maybe no one's supposed to see their own future.'

Kate shrugged. 'Maybe I don't *have* a future.'

'Don't talk like that!'

Kate shrugged again and turned to look at the fluffy clouds through the high window. Peter heard the call of swallows and observed the light penetrating through Kate's skull. He could scarcely feel her hand. Her touch was feather-light. Peter squeezed Kate's hand very gently. Kate turned around and shot a look at him. She knew what he was doing. She squeezed back. Peter looked down and saw how she was straining – Kate was gripping him as hard as she could and yet he could barely feel it.

'Maybe another Kate Dyer has a future—'

'Stop it!'

'No, no I mean it! I saw myself. I guess I saw a version of me from one of Dr Pirretti's parallel worlds.'

'Are you serious?'

'I was terrified.'

'What did you do?'

'I hid. She – I – was moving at a slower rate than me. It was funny, I looked like I was gliding on ice skates or something. If I hadn't been so scared I would have laughed. But seeing yourself like that, like others see you, but being on the outside looking in, not being able to know what's going on in your head . . . it's weird. Horrible weird. The other me had an expression on her face like Sam when I told him I'd put his name down for a bungee jump from the church steeple on April Fool's Day . . .'

'If there's an alternative Kate Dyer out there . . .'

'Not just one, loads of them if Dr Pirretti's right.'

292

'All right, if there are loads of Kate Dyers out there, does that mean there are loads of Peter Schocks, too?'

'Of course! But she says that the important thing to get clear in your head is that all the other Peters and Kates are in parallel worlds – the duplicate worlds created at the precise moment a time event happens. But *this* is the original world. It is in only in *this* world that it is possible to put things right . . .'

'So your Dr Pirretti in her parallel world can't do anything to help?'

'No. Do you remember what the Marquis de Montfaron said? If you want to cut down ivy from a house, you don't snip it off a leaf at a time, you just cut through the trunk at the base. We're the trunk of that tree . . .'

Peter got up, inadvertently dragging Kate along with him, with no more effort than pulling a balloon on a string.

'Oh, I'm sorry,' he said. 'I forgot. I wanted to pace up and down a bit.'

'That's okay.'

Peter looked down at Kate's gossamer hand holding on to his. 'I guess it's going to be like this from now on.'

'You do understand? I *need* to hold on to you. Each time I fast-forward I think I'm accelerating through time. I see shapes in the air now. I don't know what they are but I think they're alive. At first they moved about so fast I thought my eyes were playing tricks on me. Then it was like seeing insects flitting past. Now they float and drift around like thistledown or something.'

Peter nodded and remembered the thistledown floating in the valley in Derbyshire the first day they were catapulted back in time. How could it possibly have all come to this?

'Now, each time I stop fast-forwarding,' said Kate, 'I look at my hands . . . and each time it looks like there's a little bit less of me.'

Peter looked away.

'I'm sorry,' said Kate.

'It's not your fault!'

'Touching you is the only way I can stop it . . . I feel so alone when I'm fast-forwarding . . .'

Peter squeezed Kate's hand. 'Have you asked Dr Pirretti why you're . . . fading?'

'She reckons it's to do with dark energy.'

'A guess or is she sure?'

'A guess, I think. You know how some materials conduct electricity better than others? Like copper's brilliant but rubber's useless?'

Peter nodded. 'I think so.'

'Well, when it comes to conducting dark energy, I'm copper. She thinks the Tar Man is a good conductor, too. But you . . .'

'I'm rubber?'

'Yes. And my dad. Dr Pirretti reckons that it is the way dark energy and time react with each other that caused us to shoot off to 1763 in the first place. She thinks the accidental discovery of time travel is partly my fault for being such a good conductor of dark energy . . .'

'I don't get it. Is that what's making you fade?'

'You know how gravity attracts one thing to another, holds us down to earth and stops us floating off into space?'

'Yes.'

'Well dark energy does the opposite. And you know how too much gravity is not good. Like with black holes. Everything being sucked in until even time itself stops . . .'

'Time stops in a black hole?'

'Apparently. But dark energy does the opposite – it pushes things apart. Dr Pirretti says it's gravity that keeps things together and dark energy that keeps things apart. And as the universe is expanding it looks like dark energy is winning out . . . So it's the *balance* between gravity and dark matter that makes the universe the way it is. Do you see what I'm saying?'

Peter pulled a face. 'Don't ask. But you still haven't said why you look like you do.'

'Do you want me to explain again?'

'No!'

'Well, anyway . . . She says that what is happening to the galaxies in space is happening to the atoms in my body.'

'What?!'

'It does make sense if you think about it. You know how there's a nucleus at the centre of every atom with loads of electrons spinning round it and empty space in between?'

'Not really.'

'Imagine some planets revolving around a sun.'

'Okay.'

'Well, it's the same sort of thing, only instead of space and massive distances, we're talking atoms and tiny distances.'

'So what does Dr Pirretti say is happening to your tiny suns and planets?'

Kate opened her mouth to answer but stopped. They heard footsteps approaching up the hallway and there was a knock on the door.

'I'll tell you in a minute . . .'

Hannah opened the door.

'Master Blueskin is growing impatient, he asked me to—'

It was then that Hannah caught sight of Kate, standing next to Peter in front of the window. She screamed and ran out of the room. Peter and Kate looked at each other.

'I'll tell you about my planets later,' she whispered to Peter. 'I think we'd better get dressed and go and frighten the Tar Man next . . .'

'I can guess what's happening to your planets,' said Peter quietly. 'You've got too much dark energy in you – your atoms are drifting apart . . . Aren't they?'

Kate held up her hand to the light. 'And having your atoms drift apart is definitely not good.'

'Have you asked her how you can get better?'

Kate looked at him. 'Don't you think she would have told me if she knew?'

They got dressed back to back and somehow managed never to lose contact, even if it was just their heels touching. And even in such dire circumstances they could not help laughing. Hannah found a veil and a pair of gloves to disguise Kate's increasing transparency but if she had been brave tending Sir Richard, Kate's condition terrified her. She was still trembling half an hour later when she opened the door to Sir Richard's drawing room. They were expecting to find the Tar Man but it was empty save for Parson Ledbury who stood up and bade them all a good afternoon.

'Ah, Mistress Kate,' he said, approaching her and taking her gloved hand. 'Hannah has told me of your condition. Do not feel you have to hide yourself behind a veil. We are friends, are we not?'

Kate slowly pulled off her veil and Parson Ledbury's expression did not change except to smile at her. 'That is better. Now I can see your pretty face.'

Hannah drew out her handkerchief and wiped her nose and damp cheeks.

'The Tar Man was anxious to depart for Tempest House and would wait no longer. He was anxious to arrive before nightfall.

Gideon has accompanied him. They have taken the cart in order to transport the device—'

'But do you think we can trust him?' interrupted Peter. 'You remember what happened the last time Gideon and the Tar Man rode off together to Tempest House—'

'True, Master Schock, Gideon was lucky to come out of it alive. But as *we* have something he needs, and *he* has something we need, what alternative do any of us have? Mistress Kate, forgive me for putting the question to you – but tell me that it was not a ruse. You do possess the code, do you not?'

Kate tapped the side of her nose. 'That would be telling.'

Peter and Parson Ledbury looked so crestfallen, she relented. 'Yes, yes, I do. I promise.'

'I am most gratified to hear it!' said Parson Ledbury.

He turned to Hannah. 'Hannah, Sir Richard cannot spare you, so I will accompany Mistress Kate and Master Peter in his carriage and six myself.'

'Oh, I had forgotten about Sir Richard!' Kate exclaimed. 'How is he?'

'He is much improved,' Hannah replied. 'I do not doubt that he will soon be up and out of his bed for all his doctor tells him to rest.'

'If all goes well, pray tell Sir Richard that we shall return with the device on the morrow.'

'Yes, Parson, I will. And I shall buy the biggest goose in High Holborn to celebrate your homecoming. Should I set a place for the Tar Man, do you think?'

'Pish pash, Hannah, has last night's excitement stripped you of your common sense? Do you see Sir Richard agreeing to entertain the Tar Man at his table?'

'Even though he *is* Gideon's brother?' asked Peter.

'Enough unto the day are the troubles thereof,' said Parson Ledbury. 'Let us first hope that the rogue will not lead us astray . . .'

As the clock struck three, Hannah placed the veil on Kate's head and accompanied the children to Sir Richard's carriage. She handed Peter a basket piled high with bread and cheese and apples and, ever so delicately, put her arms around Kate as if she feared she might break.

'God bless you, Mistress Kate. Bring back the machine as fast as you can so that we might send you home to your family.'

She leaned over and kissed Peter, too. 'Look after her, Master Peter.'

'Don't worry, Hannah, I will. I shan't let go of her, no matter what. I'll bring her safely home, I promise.'

Kate smiled up at Peter and squeezed his hand in gratitude, but he did not notice her gesture for he could not feel her fingers gripping his.

'Goodbye, Hannah!' called Kate as the carriage pulled away. 'Thank you!'

As the six horses turned in unison to leave Lincoln's Inn Fields, Peter stuck his head out of the window and looked back at Sir Richard's house. Hannah was still standing wistfully on the doorstep, but he also saw Sir Richard standing looking down at them from an open upstairs window, one arm in a sling. Peter shot his hand up in greeting, and gave him the thumbs-up sign, and hoped that Sir Richard had seen them as they left behind the green oasis of Lincoln's Inn Fields and entered the never-ending stream of city traffic.

CHAPTER TWENTY-THREE

Tempest House

In which the two brothers co-operate, Gideon
resumes his career as a cutpurse and
Tempest House plays host to some unexpected visitors

And so it was that for the first time in over two decades, Gideon and his elder brother set off on a journey together. Neither wanted the other to drive the cart as both preferred to be in control of the horses. In the end, and to Gideon's relief, the Tar Man decided to take his own horse and rode sometimes behind and sometimes in front, as the fancy took him. Each time the Tar Man overtook the cart, or waited while Gideon drove past, he would taunt him with some barbed comment, for the pleasure of provoking a reaction from his younger brother. Gideon barely managed to keep his temper and the Tar Man could see him brace himself each time he drew near. At this point the Tar Man would change tactics, opening his mouth to say something and closing it again as soon as he saw Gideon glance up at him, jaw clenched in irritation. Then the Tar Man would smile good-humouredly, or even whistle, which would exasperate Gideon to the point of fury. It was in this way that Blueskin kept himself amused while they followed the path of the

Thames, past Westminster and St James's and then, when city started to turn into country, past the pretty village of Chelsea with all its fine, large houses, before proceeding to Putney and Mortlake. By the time they reached Richmond, early in the afternoon, Gideon felt exhausted, but was too proud to ask the Tar Man if they might stop awhile. By the time they reached the riverside at Twickenham, Gideon could go on no longer and pulled on the reins so that cart and horses drew to a halt outside the Swan Inn, opposite Eel Pie Island. The Tar Man rode back to the cart.

"Tis a fine prospect, Gideon, but we have not come on a grand tour, we have business to settle at Tempest House . . . Or do I detect fatigue in my brother's features?"

'The horses need water,' retorted Gideon quickly, stroking the black nose of the Tar Man's horse whose hot breath tickled his ear. 'And there is no need to remind me that we are brothers with every sentence – I have grasped the truth of it, I assure you!'

The Tar Man smiled. 'Ay, grasped it like a nettle! I shall fetch us some vittles. I know the innkeeper here of old and his wife is a tolerable cook.' The Tar Man leaned close to Gideon and scrutinised the purple and yellow bruise that covered half of his face. His eye was still very swollen and had the look of raw meat. The Tar Man reached out to pat it gently, making Gideon flinch. 'You'll live! But I shall have the landlord bring table and chairs to the bank, else your face might drive away custom.'

Gideon did not respond. In fact, it was his face that was causing him least trouble. His ribs and his back were a different matter, however. With every jolt and pothole in the road he winced with pain. The fight had only taken place the previous evening yet, to Gideon, it seemed half a lifetime ago.

While the Tar Man went to the inn in search of refreshment, Gideon unharnessed the horses and led them to the banks of the

Thames. It was a different river here, pretty and fringed with tall trees. In the city the river was thronged with watermen and sailing boats but here it was a quiet stretch of water inhabited by ducks as much as men. The horses waded in amongst the weeds and drank. A pair of swans and their cygnets, almost full grown, swam nearby on the ribbon of bright water that separated the inn from Eel Pie Island. Gideon looked over in the direction of Ham House on the other side of the river, and saw the old ferryman tugging at the oars of his boat. A heron flew past and landed at the foot of a great willow on the island.

Presently the Tar Man reappeared, followed by a boy carrying a table, the landlord carrying two chairs, and a serving wench carrying a large tray. The furniture was arranged, the dishes were piled on the table, and the Tar Man gestured to Gideon to join him. The landlord had provided good bread and a ham baked in hay, and roast parsnips. They both ate greedily, having had little else that day. Once they had taken their fill, the two men stretched out their legs and, with a tankard of ale in their hands, listened to the water lapping on the bank. The mellow sun shone down and the air was warm and balmy. They did not talk, and the significance of this shared meal that brought them together after so many years apart did not escape either of them. Gideon looked at his brother's profile as he gazed out over the Thames. He thought of some of the terrible things he had seen him do, of his reputation as Lord Luxon's henchman, of the beating he had given him the previous day. And then, despite everything, Gideon detected a flicker of comfort in a corner of his soul. He was not, after all, the last remaining child to share the same mother and father. He was not alone. When the Tar Man turned, at last, to look at him, Gideon thanked him for the meal and the Tar Man saw that he meant it.

*

The Tar Man must have grown tired of taunting his brother, for he mostly rode on ahead now. For mile after mile, through Esher and Cobham, and into the rolling Surrey hills, Gideon listened to the rumble of the cartwheels and found that questions were bubbling up in his mind. The sun was low in the sky and they were nearing their destination before he resolved to put them to his brother. They had stopped at a shallow brook and Gideon stood next to the rippling water watching the horses tear up fresh green grass.

'Were you guilty of the crime that they hanged you for?'

The Tar Man wheeled around, startled and outraged at the question.

'What does that matter now? And would you believe my reply?'

'Yes,' said Gideon. 'I would believe you.'

'Our mother did not.'

'Is that why she did not go to Tyburn?'

'Why do you ask me? I cannot pretend to know her mind! All I know is that when the noose was placed around my neck, I was alone, and I had received no word from her.'

'You were barely more than a child. Her silence must have been hard to bear.'

The Tar Man mounted his horse. 'Did our mother ever talk of me?'

'All she would say was that the eldest had been lost to her in an accident. The memory was so painful to her that we were never to speak of it.'

'She hated the sight of the scar that you gave me.'

'*I* gave you?!'

'You were playing in the hayloft. I walked into the barn an instant after a scythe had escaped your grip – you were too young to understand what you did. Our mother did not believe me then, either . . . Yet I have had cause to be grateful. That scar has served me well.' The Tar Man lifted his hand to his cheek. 'Though in the twenty-first century I was tempted to have it removed . . .'

The Tar Man picked up the reins and clicked his tongue. The black horse started to trot down the road.

'I thought you had got the scar in some fearsome fight!'

'Like the rest of the world . . .'

With a shrug of his shoulders the Tar Man moved on.

'Nathaniel! Wait!'

Of all the names he had gone by over the years – the Tar Man, Blueskin, Vega Riaza, and worse – none had pricked him like the name he had been given at his christening. Nathaniel. It came to him that the last person to address him by his own name was the hangman as he placed the noose around his neck when he was fourteen years old. In most ways Nathaniel had died that day. The Tar Man found himself overwhelmed and, although he stopped, he did not turn to face Gideon but, instead, inclined his head a little.

'Nathaniel! Do you truly intend to help the children?'

'If Mistress Dyer provides the code, I shall return them to their own time.'

'Will you remain in the future?'

'I may. I may return and pause while the scythe strikes the barn door before I open it. I may return and prove my innocence. But I shall not count my chickens before they are hatched. It remains to be seen if Mistress Dyer has mastery over the device. We shall soon find out . . .'

All at once the Tar Man slid down off his horse and walked towards Gideon. His mood had changed like quicksilver.

'Yet I am minded to tell you a secret. I have shared it with Tom, why should I not share it with you? Come here. Put your arm around my shoulders.'

Gideon looked at him suspiciously.

'Come! Trust me – you will be astonished! I have learned to navigate time even without the device.'

Gideon approached the Tar Man and tentatively did what he was told. He stood side by side with his brother and curved his arm around his shoulders. He felt the rough cloth of his brother's black jacket under his fingers and smelled the beer on his breath.

The Tar Man took a coin out of his pocket. 'See – this is the head of a Roman Emperor . . .'

'What—?'

'Do not speak! Wait and be amazed . . .'

The Tar Man held the coin between the palms of his hands as if he were praying. Gideon became aware of the horses snorting and pawing the ground nervously as if they sensed something was amiss. Then he began to feel giddy. Gideon gripped the Tar Man's shoulders more tightly and looked at his brother whose eyes were screwed tight shut in concentration. He listened to his long, slow breaths and saw his chest rising and falling. Then luminous spirals formed in Gideon's mind and all at once he was aware that the light had changed and that the temperature had dropped steeply. Sheets of freezing rain splattered them. Both men opened their eyes.

'By the devil, that wind cuts straight through you!' said the Tar Man, then added quickly: 'Do not let go of me. Keep hold of my arm.'

Gideon did as he was told. A wintry dawn met his eyes. They stood on a straight road that crossed uncultivated land. There were fewer trees and the shallow brook had disappeared. The sky was the colour of lead, with sickly yellow streaks towards the horizon.

'So how do you like my little trick?'

But Gideon remained speechless and continued to stare at this different Surrey with round eyes. The road ran very straight across the undulating landscape and in the near distance Gideon saw a lone figure on horseback. He pointed and the Tar Man turned to look.

'Excellent,' exclaimed the Tar Man. 'We have company. Now you shall see something to interest you. Come, let us not alarm the fellow.'

The Tar Man pulled Gideon backwards and both peered out from behind a large gorse bush.

'Where am I?' asked Gideon.

'We have not moved. We are close to Tempest House – or rather, where Tempest House will be. It is not a question of where, it is a question of *when*.'

Soon they could hear horse hooves strike the muddy road. The light on this dismal winter morning was poor, and Gideon wiped the rain from his eyes as he tried to focus on the approaching figure through the prickly branches of gorse. Then despite himself, Gideon let out a small gasp as he caught sight of a Roman helmet. It was enough to alert the soldier to their presence and he immediately rode towards them, shouting something which neither man crouching in the bushes could make out, and pulling out a short, flat sword. Gideon prepared to flee, and let go of the Tar Man. Instantly he found himself fading back into a different landscape where the sun shone and it was warm and he could hear the babble of a brook. A moment later and his brother reappeared, very entertained by the look of alarm on his face.

'But if you can do this at will, what need have you of the device?' exclaimed Gideon.

The Tar Man held up the coin. 'With the device I can select a time at will. With this cruder manner I am at the mercy of the objects I use. You have not told me what you think of my secret, Gideon.'

305

'But how do you do it? Is it magic?'

'Do you understand how you touch your nose? Well? Touch your nose!'

Gideon did as he was told and moved his index finger to the tip of his nose.

'How did you do it?'

'I do not know – I willed my finger to move and it obeyed . . .'

'It is the same thing. I sense something in an object, like a hound following a scent, and I will myself to move towards it. Where is the point in questioning how I do it? I *can* do it – that is all I need to know. So, how do you like my new-found skill?'

'I do not know how to answer you,' said Gideon. 'But, upon my word, Nathaniel, you are full of surprises.'

The other half of the party travelling to Tempest House that day had hoped to reach their destination in daylight. Alas they realised that this would prove impossible when they found themselves only in Cobham at sunset. Lulled by the creak and rattle of Sir Richard's carriage, Peter had fallen asleep. Kate held on fast to his hand, the fear of fast-forwarding and the toll it took on her fading flesh always on her mind. Soon she felt a damp chill in the air and a bright moon rose in a clear sky. Kate could just make out Parson Ledbury's silhouette, black against the moonlit landscape. He had pulled off his wig and was slowly stroking the dome of his bristly head with both hands. A sixth sense made him aware that he was being watched.

'I see that sleep evades you as much as it does me, Mistress Kate,' he said.

'Can I tell you something, Parson Ledbury?' said Kate.

'By all means, Mistress Kate. I am all ears.'

'The woman, at Bartholomew's Fair, what she was saying about me – she was right, in a way. I *have* become a kind of oracle. Since I started to fast-forward, I can see the future. It's even beginning to feel like normal . . . seeing the future doesn't seem any stranger than being able to remember the past.'

'Then I pity you with all my heart for that is a burden unfit for young shoulders. What is it that you see, Kate?'

'Lots of things. But most of all I see Peter at the top of a tall building. He's tired, and shouting, and very upset, but somehow I know he's going to be all right. I know he's going to work out what to do . . . But when I think of me . . .'

Parson Ledbury tried to find Kate's hand in the dark. 'Go on . . .'

Kate tried to speak but could not. Parson Ledbury waited patiently. 'Every time I think about me, what will happen to me, all I sense is a burden. It feels like I've got to do something but I don't know what it is . . . And beyond that . . . I see nothing – nothing at all . . .'

Parson Ledbury heard Kate's shuddering breath.

'And I'm frightened.'

Peter had been awake for a while. He lay in the darkness, feeling that he was intruding on a private conversation but was unable to do anything about it. He tried to keep still.

'You have shown great courage, Kate,' said Parson Ledbury. 'We are not meant to know the future . . . I dearly wish I could take the burden away from you.'

All three passengers listened to the thunder of hooves and the creaking axle as Sir Richard's carriage took them ever nearer to Tempest House and the anti-gravity machine. Each was lost in their own thoughts. Presently Parson Ledbury broke the silence.

'Will you pray with me, Kate? I hope it may bring us both comfort.'

'Yes,' said Kate. 'Thank you. I should like that.'

Parson Ledbury knelt down at Kate's feet as best as he could on the bumpy carriage floor. He took her hand in his and prayed that Kate might be given the strength and the courage and the wisdom to play her part in whatever it was that awaited her. Then he rested his hands gently on her head and prayed that both children might be restored to their families.

Peter listened in the dark and hoped that Kate was wrong to be so fearful. After all, they were going to fetch the anti-gravity machine! Kate knew the code! They might be back home in a few hours!

The Parson finished his prayer and as he and Kate said 'Amen', Peter fervently hoped that someone up there was listening to them.

The Tar Man's attention was taken by a magpie perched on the marble head of Aphrodite. The goddess stood over a splashing fountain that formed the centrepiece of the herb garden on the south side of Tempest House. Gideon and the Tar Man both sat astride the high brick wall under cover of a spreading oak. Heat radiated from the russet-coloured bricks after an afternoon of baking sunshine. Dusk was not far away, but the pale stone of Lord Luxon's residence still glowed with the golden light of a fine sunset. The magpie flapped down and perched on the rim of the stone pond at the base of the fountain, its head cocked to one side. A long table and two benches had been placed between the beds of sage and thyme and the bird had its beady black eyes on some bread left unnoticed on the grass. The bird walked underneath the table and emerged with a chunk of it. It flew back onto the marble plinth and leaned forward, dunking the crust into the gushing water before swallowing it down. A smile came to the Tar Man's face.

'That bird,' he said to Gideon, 'has got more sense than the Carrick Gang put together!'

Gideon put his finger to his lips. 'Hush . . . we do not wish to announce our presence!'

'There is no one about – with the master away, the servants will play. See – my Lord Luxon never permits anyone to eat in his gardens excepting himself. I'll wager they are in the kitchens helping themselves to their master's claret.'

'We do not know that for certain. And we need the key.'

'Yes,' said the Tar Man. 'And, as it was you who lost it in the first place, I am happy for you to risk your neck breaking into William's key cabinet.'

Gideon scanned the horizon and pointed to a plume of white smoke rising up into sky from the other side of the house.

'The gardener is burning leaves. There is always a bonfire burning at Tempest House. It is nothing.'

'I am astonished that you thought to hide the device in Lord Luxon's crypt when you no longer have access to his house.'

'When did our old master ever visit the crypt excepting the day of our race? Never! No, Lord Luxon has more pressing matters to concern him than to visit his long-dead relations . . .'

Gideon took a deep breath before he started to manoeuvre himself off the high wall. The air smelled of lavender and bonfires. The Tar Man held his weight until he was ready to drop. Gideon landed lightly but it hurt his bruised ribs and he winced. While he recovered, his brother tutted unsympathetically above him.

'You do not do justice to your reputation as a cutpurse. Parson Ledbury would make less noise!'

The Tar Man watched Gideon run silently across green turf and crouch beneath the diamond-paned windows of one of the small parlours Lord Luxon used for card games in the evening.

He saw him worrying at the edge of a window with the blade of his knife and, after half a minute, he saw the rays of the setting sun glinting on glass as Gideon levered it open. The Tar Man nodded in appreciation and leaned back against the tree to wait. He had a steady nerve and knew better than to move from his post on top of the wall, for he knew he would be needed the instant Gideon reappeared. However, as darkness fell, and the hooting of owls echoed across the valley, the Tar Man began to fear the worst. Gideon was taking too long. There was something else, too. He regretted positioning himself so close to the fountain. The steady splashing of water onto the pond tended to mask other noises, and he was aware of something, some subtle and indistinct sound, that he could not distinguish. He resisted the temptation to investigate. From his vantage point, he could see the side of Tempest House and, if he leaned sideways a little, he could also see the elegant frontage, with its stone columns and the sweeping gravel drive that led through parkland to the road. He could see nothing to alarm him. The Tar Man had sat still for so long he was growing cold. Now the sun had sunk below the horizon the temperature had dropped sharply. He rubbed his arms and noticed that they still felt sore. Had it been a dream that Mistress Dyer had grabbed hold of him?

Candlelight had now appeared in several of the downstairs rooms but then he caught sight of a flickering light in an upstairs window on the front corner of the house. It opened – he heard the creak of the hinges even over the sound of the fountain – and then he saw something white being lowered slowly from it. Quickly he realised that it was two sheets, twisted and knotted together. The Tar Man froze in concentration.

But what, he thought to himself, is Gideon doing upstairs? William's key cabinet is next to the pantry! He watched his brother climbing out of the window, pressing his heels into the wall of the house and leaning outwards as he held onto the sheet. Then, to the Tar Man's astonishment, he saw Gideon reach up towards a hand that came from the window and take something from it. The Tar Man had a very bad feeling about all this and watched in trepidation as Gideon began his descent. He kicked himself. For all his brother was a talented thief he should have gone himself.

The Tar Man decided to move further up the wall to get a better view. He was stiff and numb from sitting so long and did not trust himself to walk across the wall without losing his balance. So he shifted himself sideways until he had moved perhaps three or four yards. His jaw dropped in disbelief.

'Numbskull!' he cried. 'Why did I not follow my instincts and check the grounds first?'

Pitched in the apple orchard on the other side of Tempest House were rows of white tents. He saw a large bonfire with figures seated around it. There must have been at least two dozen soldiers.

'Redcoats!' exclaimed the Tar Man out loud. 'What the devil does Lord Luxon plan to do with redcoats?'

It was at that moment that he heard the pounding of hooves and crunching of gravel on the drive. Now, to complicate matters further a carriage was approaching! The Tar Man's heart leaped into his mouth – could it possibly be Lord Luxon arriving back from his adventures? Clearly he was not the only one who thought so – the Tar Man looked helplessly on at the commotion in the house. Servants appeared at the front door with lanterns and torches; uniformed officers joined them, pulling on their jackets as they went; several dogs ran, barking, into the night. Meanwhile the Tar Man watched his brother climb halfway down the sheet only to change his mind and start to climb back up again.

'Don't be a fool!' cried the Tar Man. 'Don't go back into the house now!'

One of the dogs, a black and white sheepdog, spotted Gideon struggling to get back through the window and he stood at the foot of the wall and started to growl. The Tar Man contemplated priming his pistol and shooting the beast but decided that it would take too long and make matters worse besides. Before anyone paid too much attention to the overexcited sheepdog, the carriage and six crunched to a halt in front of Tempest House. Parson Ledbury got out, taken aback by all the attention. His powerful voice boomed out over the garden so that even the Tar Man on his high perch could hear every word.

'Good evening, gentleman! I did not expect a welcoming committee! I would not impose on your hospitality, but we are a good five miles from the nearest coaching inn and night has fallen. Would you be so kind as to let me have water for my horses?'

While Parson Ledbury remained the focus of attention, Gideon slid down the sheet, dropped to the ground and started to run across the herb garden. The sheepdog started to bark excitedly, distracting the Parson's attention and causing him to glance in Gideon's direction. Catching sight of his friend's blond pigtail he immediately looked away again but by then it was too late. The white sheet hanging from the window and the escaping figure were all too visible.

'Stop thief!' someone cried.

'After him!' cried another.

The herb garden was instantly swarming with redcoats and servants bearing flaming torches. The Tar Man undid his belt and returned to his original position under the oak tree. Gideon was running as fast as his legs would carry him towards his brother, pursued by a growing crowd of shouting men.

'Take hold of my belt, I will lift you,' he shouted down to him.

Gideon was so close now the Tar Man could hear him panting.

As soon as he felt the tug on his belt he started to heave, locking one leg around a bough of the tree as leverage. He pulled with all his might but at this angle Gideon was too heavy for him. The crowd was hot on his brother's heels. The Tar Man tried again, straining with the terrible effort, but this time he was helped by Gideon who pressed his toes in the shallow cracks between the bricks and pushed himself up. A charging redcoat in full cry aimed his bayonet at Gideon's back. The Tar Man let out a great shout and suddenly Gideon found himself flying through the air. He caught hold of the top of the wall and then balanced precariously on one foot while he steadied himself on the tree trunk and on his brother's shoulder.

'Thank you,' Gideon croaked as they climbed down the tree on the other side of the wall. 'They'll not be able to climb it from that side – they must fetch a ladder or go by way of the road. If we make haste we can lose them.'

The two men dropped to the ground and began to run in the direction of the crypt and their horses. When they reached a small copse, the Tar Man slowed down a little and turned to Gideon.

'Tell me you found the key, at least!'

'Ay, I have the key – even though Martha, the scullery maid, came upon me skulking in the pantry. The lass took pity on me. She fetched the key and helped me to escape besides.'

'Ha! You and your pretty face!'

They ran on through masses of bracken, tripping over stones and the roots of trees. After five minutes of this, Gideon, whose injuries were slowing him down, had to stop. The Tar Man stood with his hands on his waist and waited.

'Were the children in the carriage with the Parson?'

Gideon was stooped over, hands on his knees, trying to catch his breath. 'I do not think so.'

Presently Gideon stood up and turned full circle and listened. Hearing nothing, he knelt down and put his ear to the ground. He stood up again and shook his head.

'No one has been murdered in their bed. They will have given up the chase by now,' said the Tar Man. 'And if they have not, I doubt they will guess our direction – why should a thief make for a graveyard?'

'I hope you are right.'

'We shall soon find out. Give me the key while I think on it.'

Gideon reached into his pocket and pulled out a large, ornate key. The Tar Man took it.

'Good. But why the devil have a gang of redcoats set up camp at Tempest House?'

'Now, *that* I do know,' said Gideon. 'The kitchens and servants' hall were full of officers playing cards. It is why I could not get to William's key cabinet. Martha told me that Lord Luxon may take them to the colonies where he is acquiring land. It seems that while he decides what to do with them, they grow impatient of waiting for their marching orders . . .'

Gideon and the Tar Man ran on through moonlit fields, stumbling and stopping for breath, straining to hear if they were pursued. A cloud passed over the moon and it was so dark that, tired of having their faces slashed by unseen branches, they were forced to walk with their arms bent in front of them. It was the sound of one of the horses whinnying that told them they had arrived at the crypt. There was a thick carpet of dry leaves under the giant beeches that sheltered the Luxon crypt from the elements and as Gideon and the Tar Man made their way blindly forward there was a great rustling and a cracking of twigs.

'Who's there?' asked a small and nervous voice.

'Master Peter?' cried Gideon. 'It is I, Gideon, and the Tar Man.'

314

'I'm so glad you've come at last!' exclaimed Peter. 'It's so spooky here.'

The moon came out again from behind a cloud and shafts of bluish light penetrated the tree cover.

'But why did the Parson leave you here by yourselves?' asked Gideon.

'We knew you'd arrived because we found the cart and horses. But we waited and waited for you. We were beginning to get anxious. Parson Ledbury and the driver went off to Tempest House to see if there was any sign of you. He was going to ask for some water and see what he could find out. We wanted to go with him but he refused because . . . because . . .'

Kate finished off his sentence. 'Because I look like a ghost.'

Kate stepped out of shadow into the moonlight. The Tar Man backed away from her.

'I am truly sorry we gave you cause to worry,' said Gideon, trying to conceal his own reaction to Kate's appearance, 'but, as you can see, here we are, safe and sound. And we have the key to the crypt.'

The Tar Man snorted. 'Ay, Gideon filched the key, and alerted a band of redcoats to our presence into the bargain.'

'Redcoats?' asked Kate.

'Soldiers,' Gideon explained. 'They have not followed us.'

'Is Parson Ledbury all right?' asked Peter. 'Where is he?'

'He is doubtless on his way back as we speak,' Gideon replied. 'Let us move the device onto the cart while we wait—'

'No,' said the Tar Man sharply. 'I shall not hand over the device yet. First I need some assurance that Mistress Dyer has told us the truth. Let her prove to me that she knows the secret code.'

'If you like,' said Kate, hoping that what Dr Pirretti had told her had not been some terrible hallucination.

315

'There is no need for that,' said Gideon fiercely, 'Mistress Kate is no liar. And the hour is late and it is dark. Let us wait until morning.'

'Yes,' said Peter, who was half-convinced that Kate was bluffing. 'Let's wait until daylight for that.'

'It's all right,' said Kate, turning to the Tar Man. 'If *you* unlock the crypt and show us that the anti-gravity machine really is in there, *I* will key in the code.'

The Tar Man fetched a candle and his tinderbox from the wagon and presently a small flame illuminated the darkness. The Tar Man inserted the heavy key into the lock. He tried to turn it but it would not. Kate and Peter exchanged glances. The candle-light illuminated the heavy grain of the wooden door and the elaborate wrought iron lock.

'Damn your eyes, Gideon!' exclaimed the Tar Man. 'You've got the wrong key!'

'No! It is the key, I am sure of it!'

Gideon took the key from his brother's hand and inserted it again. They all held their breath as he turned it. There was a satisfying click.

'Phew!' said Peter.

The Tar Man said nothing. A smell of damp and musty air hit them as the door of the crypt creaked open. Gideon disappeared into the impenetrable darkness followed by the Tar Man. They found a fat candle on a sconce close to the door and they lit that, too. Soon they could all see the anti-gravity machine by its guttering light. Kate could also see many thick cobwebs and at least two big spiders. She hated spiders. She pointed to the biggest one and saw by Peter's face that he was not too keen on them either.

'Very well, Mistress Dyer,' said the Tar Man. 'To work.'

Peter and Kate walked over to the incongruous object in the

corner of the crypt. The anti-gravity machine was as tall and wide as a big man and it had a transparent dome. Kate examined it as best she could in the weak light. It looked the same as Tim Williamson's machine – her dad and Dr Pirretti must have made an exact replica. Kate flicked the on/off switch and they heard a familiar humming sound.

'Yes!' cried Peter, holding up the palm of his hand for Kate to strike in a high five.

She struck it, though he could barely feel anything. But for the first time both of them started to believe that they might actually get home! The machine was here and in working order. The Tar Man had not tricked them! The Tar Man pointed to a luminous display without comment. It read: *Please enter six-digit code*. Kate nodded. Peter looked at her and she could tell by the fear in his eyes that he was not convinced that she knew it.

Kate knelt down and tried to key in the first number. But nothing appeared on the display. She did it again and again. Still nothing. Kate started to panic and looked wildly up at Peter.

'What's wrong?' he asked.

'I don't know!'

'Well, have another go, then . . .'

Kate tried again. Still nothing. The Tar Man's face betrayed no emotion.

Suddenly Gideon shot to the doorway. 'Someone's coming!' he called over his shoulder. 'Let us hope it is the Parson!'

Gideon stepped outside and Peter stood up in alarm, dragging Kate with him. When Gideon reappeared he did not need to explain. They all heard the sound of a crowd of people descending on them. Gideon hurriedly removed the key from the door, slammed it shut and locked it from the inside with seconds to spare. Someone threw themselves against the door. It happened again, only this time it was accompanied by oaths and shouting. Then they heard the sound of feet on the roof and a scraping noise as someone slid off a slate roof tile.

'Quickly, Mistress Dyer,' warned the Tar Man.

He meant her to set the machine off! . . . All at once there was a tremendous crash, so loud it hurt their ears.

'What was that?' cried Peter.

Two seconds later and there was another explosive *crash!*

'Quickly!' urged the Tar Man. 'They have a battering ram.'

Kate and Peter knelt down and Kate tried to key in her date of birth once more.

'I know what the problem is,' said Peter. 'Your fingers aren't strong enough to press the keys! Here, let me try. Tell me the code!'

Another terrifying *crash*. The Tar Man put his eye to the keyhole.

'They've ripped up a tree! There must be twenty of them, at least!'

Kate called out the numbers. Meanwhile Gideon and the Tar Man looked around for anything that they could use to block the doorway. There was nothing, nothing at all. Only themselves. Then, through a hole in the roof, an unseen hand pushed in bundles of hay that had been set alight. Kate screamed. Gideon ran over to the far end of the crypt and started to stamp on it but there was too much and more was being pushed down. Smoke filled the crypt and everyone started to cough.

'Please! Mistress Dyer,' spluttered the Tar Man. 'I am not fond of the smell of roasting flesh. Especially my own!'

Peter keyed in the last number.

Suddenly Kate dropped to her knees. She peered at a setting in a second display window.

'Pass me the candle!' she shouted at the Tar Man.

He thrust the candle at Peter, who placed it shakily on the ground next to the machine. The redcoats rammed the door again. This time the wood started to splinter. It would not survive another blow.

'Six point seven seven megawatts,' Kate read. 'I'm not making that mistake again! It's okay. We can go!'

The anti-gravity machine made a tiny beep. Some letters appeared in the digital display. Kate read: *Security Code accepted. Continue YES or NO?*

Peter selected *YES* and pushed the Enter key. Somewhere in the machine a procedure was initiated. A second sound was audible. The generator had started up. Kate and Peter looked at each other. Kate gripped Peter's hand tightly.

'Don't let go of me,' she said. 'I don't know what this will do to me . . .'

'I won't – I promise.'

There was another explosive crash. Kate heard hinges being wrenched from the heavy door frame. The Tar Man dived towards the machine. It was at that instant that Gideon realised that he was not meant to be going with them. He stepped away from the anti-gravity machine and pressed his back against the wall of the crypt. Peter looked from Kate to Gideon and back again in panic as the spirals started to fill his mind. They could see torchlight through the door and a scrabble of redcoats, like hounds baying at a cornered fox, sensing the kill.

'Gideon!' Peter screamed.

But it was the Tar Man who grabbed hold of his brother's arm and hauled him towards them . . .

The instant that Sir Richard's carriage drew up outside the crypt, Parson Ledbury jumped down and ran towards the commotion.

He bellowed at the soldiers to calm themselves and cease demolishing a tomb erected to the sacred memory of Lord Luxon's ancestors! But the redcoats were too roused to listen to a man of the cloth and they rammed the door yet again, the noise of it, like thunder, echoing into the night. Parson Ledbury started to push through them, determined to stand between the redcoats and the door of the crypt, if necessary. But all at once the redcoats did stop. Very suddenly and of their own accord. By the light of flaming torches, the now terrified foot soldiers saw their hands sink into the silvery trunk of the young birch they were using as a battering ram. The men pulled away from it in terror and stepped backwards away from the crypt, yet the tree trunk did not drop to the ground! The birch was dissolving before their eyes! Abruptly the whole tree trunk vanished. The redcoats stood there, shocked and afraid. The Parson walked past them and peered through the demolished door into the crypt. Thick white smoke billowed out of the gaping hole and escaped into the night. The Parson took out a handkerchief and put it over his nose and mouth. A galaxy of sparks glowed scarlet in the piles of blackened hay but there were no flames. Through watering eyes Parson Ledbury saw the candle lit in the sconce. There was no other sign that anyone had been here. He saw no trace of Kate nor Peter nor Gideon nor the Tar Man – nor of the anti-gravity machine.

He stepped into the empty crypt.

'They have gone home,' he murmured.

Parson Ledbury was torn between laughing and crying. He blew out the candle.

'Farewell, my friends, God speed you on your way.'

CHAPTER TWENTY-FOUR

That Bothersome Little Colony

In which Lord Luxon discovers that you should be careful what you wish for

Lord Luxon's sleep had been fitful. In his dreams he had battled to move forwards through icy winds towards a dark space haunted by the spectres of soldiers. As he drew closer, he perceived that the soldiers resembled his father and uncles, and all of them wielded sabres which they pointed at him. All the while, Sergeant Thomas's drooling hound snarled and tore at him ceaselessly with foam-flecked jaws until his clothes were soaking with his own blood. When he finally awoke, to the sound of William bringing in a breakfast tray, the sun was already high in the New Jersey sky. William helped him dress, as he always did, but today, just as the previous night when they had been forced, through necessity, to check into this downmarket, twenty-first century hotel, he was silent and refused to look his master in the eye.

'By the laws, William, I have had a bellyful of your sulking! The fellow wasn't a saint, he was a mercenary! And a mercenary paid handsomely for a job he failed to do!'

'Yes, my Lord.'

'For all his swaggering, Sergeant Thomas did not even have the bottom of that hideous hound from hell . . .'

'As you say, sir.'

Lord Luxon snorted angrily and threw down his napkin. 'Pray command me a carriage, William. I am eager to return to Manhattan to see the fruits of my labours.'

'A *carriage*, sir?'

'A cab, you impudent fellow! And, as there is no one else, I must charge you to stay in New Jersey and stand guard over the device until my return.'

'Yes, my Lord.'

William reached into his pocket and held out an envelope to his master.

'What is this?' asked Lord Luxon.

'I have sold your gold timepiece as you requested . . .'

'Ah. Capital. I trust you got a good price – I was fond of it. No matter – I shall buy myself another watch . . . or a hundred if I feel so inclined when I return to New York!'

Lord Luxon tore open the envelope and emptied a pile of banknotes and coins onto the palm of his hand. A smile slowly lit up his face. Instead of slim, green dollar bills he held up, one by one, larger paper notes, some blue, some green, some brown . . . and all with the British sovereign on the back.

'Five pounds! Ten pounds! A half-crown!' He picked out the largest note. It was tinted gold and bronze and had a fine silver stripe running through it. 'I promise to pay the bearer fifty pounds!' Forgetting decorum for once, Lord Luxon danced up and down on the spot, brought the notes to his lips and kissed them. 'America has come home!' he shouted. 'I have achieved what vast armies could not have done! Why, even my own father might have dropped his disapproving air for once and admired the genius of the plan, eh, William?'

'Indeed, my Lord,' said William flatly. Lord Luxon's father was dead by the time he came to work at Tempest House, but he was aware of his reputation and his ill-disguised contempt for his son. 'I am certain your achievement would have astonished him.'

William watched Lord Luxon's cab disappear out of sight and then stood looking at the sky for a long while. He thought of Sergeant Thomas and Sally. And then he wondered if this new America would have room for Michael in his bar off Sixth Avenue. Finally he returned to his room, put on his jacket and, with only the clothes that he stood up in, walked out of his employment towards a new life where, if nothing else, he could call himself his own master.

The cab was uncomfortable and hot, and the roads leading to New York were bumpy. Lord Luxon leaned out of the open window to feel the wind on his face and his blond hair escaped from its pigtail and blew into his eyes. It was a sultry, stifling day, and a thick carpet of lead-grey cloud was trapping the heat. A pity, he thought, that he would not be able to see the glorious island of Manhattan rising up out of the sea in brilliant sunshine that suited it so well. A pity, too, that he was not able to enter the city a conquering hero, carried on the shoulders of British redcoats, instead of arriving alone and in this shabby taxi.

It was early afternoon when the cab reached a stretch of water which was unfamiliar to Lord Luxon. He saw an island, or a peninsula – he was not sure which – and soon they entered a tunnel. When they emerged, Lord Luxon saw rows of municipal buildings of grand, if insipid, architectural design, that failed to compensate for the forest of factory chimneys that sent up plumes of smoke to the west. Also to the west was a small harbour or shipyard. Lord Luxon watched cranes swing giant crates out of rusting ships onto an empty quayside. The cab stopped behind a line of queuing traffic. Fumes filled the car from the ancient lorry in front of them. The line of cars did not move and soon all the drivers were sounding their horns, those of the big lorries booming over the water. Lord Luxon dabbed at his forehead with a violet silk handkerchief. The heat and humidity were becoming irksome.

'What *is* this city? *Must* we drive through it?' asked Lord Luxon ill-temperedly.

The driver turned around and looked at Lord Luxon as if he were a fool.

'But we've reached your destination, sir – *this* is New York.'

Lord Luxon bade the cabbie drive around the city until he told him to stop. He was shocked to the core of his being. What had happened to his city of dreams? Where were the skyscrapers? Where was the vibrant energy? Where was the crisp grid of streets? Where was his beloved Central Park and the great museums and art galleries! Where were the shops? Where were Saks and those irresistible boutiques in Greenwich Village and SoHo? Where were the bars, the luxury hotels, the restaurants serving cuisine from every nation that spilled out onto the side-walks? And why were all the faces a tediously uniform white? Why did everyone dress with so little panache? This town was . . . *dull*.

Lord Luxon's own face was the colour of putty as they drove through a succession of narrow, winding streets. His expression had set into one of deep despair. He mopped his clammy forehead repeatedly, closing his eyes each time and hoping that when he opened them some wonder would confront them. None did. True, there were some attractive little crescents, and churches, and there was an equestrian statue of George III in a toga that caught his eye in Bowling Green Park. There was also a tolerable statue of an English monarch called Queen Victoria set above a granite fountain on Wall Street. Most things he saw through the open window of the grimy taxi cab were distasteful to his eyes. He had not seen a single building above twelve storeys high. Where was the civic spirit whose pride and self-belief had built the man-made mountains of Manhattan? This New York was not the city which had made his imagination soar. This New York was a carbuncle on the face of America . . . What could have happened? Lord Luxon's heart sank. It then occurred to him that all the priceless treasures which he had amassed were housed in a street which did not exist and were guarded by men whose whereabouts in time and space he could not even guess at.

The overheated cabbie was becoming frustrated driving around and around with no definite destination. Every few minutes he would turn around and look at Lord Luxon questioningly, but his passenger would just indicate, with a sweep of his hand, that he should drive on. Eventually they entered a square where once elegant red-brick terraces had been converted into shops with rented apartments above them. Lines of washing hung from many of the wrought iron balconies. A cluster of enormous plane trees grew in a patch of sun-bleached lawn at the centre of the square. Beneath the trees, a life-size sculpture of a lady in Grecian costume stood on a plinth. A seagull stood on her head and one of her hands had dropped off. A vague memory of such a statue stirred in Lord Luxon's head but vanished again almost as quickly.

'You may stop here,' he said to the cabbie, finally accepting that he could not deny the evidence of his own eyes. This, whether he liked it or not, was what two and half centuries of British rule had done to New York.

When Lord Luxon asked if the café was air-conditioned, the waitress stared at him with such a blank look on her face that he did not bother to repeat the question, but went instead outside, and sat at one of the rough wooden benches overlooking the square. It was by now three o'clock in the afternoon, and the sun had burned away the cloud cover. The city was suffocating. The drains and the gutters stank. Hoping for a breeze which did not come, Lord Luxon stirred his cup of coffee. A large plane tree cast dappled shade but he did not feel any cooler. Opposite him sat a florid-faced man with neat white hair. He wore an immaculate white shirt with engraved cufflinks and he was reading through some documents, making occasional corrections with a gold-nibbed fountain pen. A pot of tea and a plate of scones stood in front of him on the bare wooden bench. When he asked Lord Luxon to pass him the sugar, he obliged, sliding over a half-empty bowl crawling with flies. Lord Luxon sighed deeply. He was already beginning to turn any remorse about what he had done into anger and disappointment at his fellow countrymen. What a lamentable lack of vision, he thought bitterly. What a terrible admission of mediocrity. Lord Luxon was all at once so angry he found himself about to thump the table. To stop himself, he clasped his hands together, very tightly, and put them on his lap. Absent-mindedly, he observed his whitened knuckles and the half-moons of his thumbnails. Something made him lift up his hands to examine them more closely. He looked at the fine gold hairs on the back of his hand and at the pattern of lines on the palms. He had the absurd, if fleeting, notion that his flesh did not look as solid as it normally did.

Lord Luxon took a sip of his coffee. 'Phwoah!' he exclaimed, spitting out the muddy liquid over the scrubby grass. 'Oh! *Oh!*' He wiped his mouth with a paper napkin and smacked his lips together trying to get rid of the taste.

The man opposite laughed heartily. 'You must be new in town to order coffee!'

'I shall not make the same mistake again,' replied Lord Luxon.

'Jack Grafton,' said the man, extending his hand.

Lord Luxon hesitated for a moment and shook it. 'Mr Luxon,' he said.

'*Luxon!*' laughed the man. 'How very appropriate.'

Lord Luxon wanted to ask why it should be so, but decided against it. 'Indeed.'

'I detect another Englishman by the sound of your accent.'

Lord Luxon nodded. 'You are correct in your assumption, sir.'

'Well I, for one, am counting the days until I can get back to London. I loathe New York, especially in the summer. Alas, I have an important client who insists on expanding his business into the American market. Be satisfied with Canada, I tell him. What's the point of battling with all that transatlantic red tape for a country with a population the size of Scotland?'

Lord Luxon gulped. 'Quite so.'

'And what about you? I presume you're here on business?'

'Yes . . .'

'What line are you in – if you don't mind me asking?'

'Oh, I came here to acquire a foreign property . . .'

'A holiday home, you mean?'

Lord Luxon smiled. 'In a sense.'

'Any luck?'

'No. You could say it has been a disaster.'

'I'm sorry to hear it. But perhaps it's a good thing – New York is a backwater. Property is cheap – but you can never be sure that it will retain its value. Personally, I don't think you can beat south-western Canada, particularly San Francisco. The climate is good and it's got a very European feel to it – King Louis XXIV of France has a holiday home there, I believe . . .'

'Really?' Lord Luxon raised his eyebrows and watched the gentleman spread jam and clotted cream on his scone.

'Forgive me, but what precisely *did* you mean when you said that it was appropriate that I found myself here?'

The gentleman smiled. 'Look up, Mr Luxon!'

He pointed to a street sign above their heads.

'Upon my word! Luxon Square! Do you, perchance, know the reason? Are there any famous Luxons?'

The gentleman looked at him, clearly surprised that he should be so ill-informed. 'With your name, how odd that you don't know all about them! The Luxon family is fabulously wealthy. They own half of London and great tracts of Canada and America besides.' He pointed up at the sign again. 'The most famous of them all, at least on this side of the pond, was this one, Lord Edward Luxon.'

Lord Luxon could barely disguise his delight. 'And why did they name a square after him?'

'The story is that he came to America incognito and assassinated some general, whose name I've forgotten, when the early colonists were causing trouble. He was certainly made first Duke of New York for his pains. Still doesn't ring any bells?'

Lord Luxon shook his head, biting his lower lip to stop himself laughing out loud in delight.

'And you see that?'

The gentleman indicated the statue of the lady in Grecian costume in the centre of the square. 'That is a reproduction of a statue you can see in the Luxons' family seat, Tempest House, in London.'

Lord Luxon swung his head around and scrutinised the statue. His eyes suddenly sparkled with recognition. Of course! It was the statue of Aphrodite that his father had commissioned for the fountain!

'Tempest House is in London?'

'Yes, close to the Surrey borders. It is *sublime*. If you've never been, you must go. They have regular open days. The gardens are spectacular – there are water gardens that cascade the full length of the valley. And as for the house itself . . . Are you positive you don't know what I'm talking about?'

'I do not, I assure you. Go on . . .'

'Well, the house easily rivals Versailles. It's enormous – but beautiful, too. An architectural masterpiece. And stuffed full of the most amazing artefacts. There's one wing of the house entirely devoted to timepieces. Thousands of the things. The children love it, of course. When the hour strikes, it's deafening.'

'Timepieces. Extraordinary!'

'I promise you that even if that sort of thing normally leaves you cold, you'll go around Tempest House open-mouthed. They say that Lord Edward Luxon bled America dry to pay for it . . .'

Lord Luxon stood up. 'Thank you for your company, Mr Grafton. Talking with you has brought on a sudden pang of homesickness. Upon my word, why tarry in America when Tempest House awaits?'

CHAPTER TWENTY-FIVE

The Luxon Wall

In which Kate demonstrates to Lord Luxon
the consequences of travelling at the speed of light

The Tar Man awoke to the sound of fountains and birdsong. His nose was buried in the sleeve of his jacket and smelled of burnt hay. He clutched at his skull, for his head was pounding worse than after a night at the Bucket of Blood. He shifted position onto his belly, groggy and unable to move, and felt the early-morning sunshine warm his back. He became aware of a pain in his hip and when he reached down to touch it, it felt tender and bruised. When he had summoned up enough energy to lift his eyelids, the Tar Man saw a multitude of rainbows in the dew-drenched grass. He heaved himself up onto all fours. The resounding boom of the battering ram suddenly came back to him, as did the clouds of choking smoke, and the redcoats with their flaming torches. The realisation suddenly flooded over him that he must have returned to the century that he had missed so much. He got to his feet to look out once more at the lie of the land. He closed his eyes and opened them again. Then he rotated a full three hundred and sixty degrees and burst out laughing.

How can this be? he thought. My Lord Luxon must have grown wealthier than the King himself. This is a wonder – never have I seen the like!

He directed a cursory glance towards his three companions, who were all still asleep or unconscious, and at the anti-gravity machine toppled on its side some fifteen feet away. At least they had not brought any redcoats with them! He picked up his three-cornered hat and put it on to shade his eyes from the sun. He viewed the landscape once more and let out a low whistle of admiration. His spirits soared: truly *anything* was possible in the future. But first he would get some rhino and some clothes. And then . . . then he would decide what to do next. There was certainly no point tarrying here.

All traces of the crypt and the cemetery had gone. As had the giant beech trees. Instead, there was an immaculate sweep of emerald turf as far as the eye could see. The Tar Man stood over his fellow-travellers and examined each in turn. His brother's face was buried in the grass and his back rose and fell in a steady rhythm. Master Schock lay on his back with his mouth open and the back of his hand over his eyes to shield them from the strong light. A veil tied around their wrists joined the children together. When the Tar Man looked more closely at Mistress Dyer his stomach clenched. He could have been looking at her through water. She is an abomination, he thought. She is damaged beyond the wit of man to repair. He looked down at his own flesh to reassure himself that time had not wreaked similar wounds on himself. He backed away from her, clutching his arms.

As for the device, it suddenly dawned on him that he was going to have to arrange some transport for it while he had the chance. He walked over to examine it and remind himself how heavy it was. As he drew closer he noticed something remarkable. The young birch tree, torn up by the redcoats and used as a battering ram, protruded from the dome of the anti-gravity machine. He crouched down next to it and put his hand on the cracked casing. Liquid was still oozing out onto the grass. Indeed, there was a wide border of blackened turf all around the device. His heart started to beat anxiously and he fumbled to find the on/off switch. He pressed the simple rocker switch. Nothing. He pressed it again. He heard a click but the read-out was dead. It was broken! That numbskull of a parson! If he had not arrived at precisely the wrong moment and announced their presence to the whole of Tempest House, to say nothing of an orchard full of soldiers, they could have slipped away with no one the wiser! As it was the precious anti-gravity machine had been demolished by a tree! The Tar Man consoled himself with the thought that at least the device had survived long enough to get him here. He consoled himself further by thinking that Lord Luxon had another, and, by the laws, he had more than one account to settle with him! He turned to look at his brother's blond head. Doubtless Gideon would feel duty-bound to care for these two innocents. Well, let him play the nursemaid if he so wished, but he did not have the stomach for it. The Tar Man did not even consider waiting until he awoke. He cared little for farewells and he cared even less to see the look of relief on Gideon's face at his going.

The Tar Man started to walk uphill and only looked back when he had reached a coppice just below the ridge. He observed his three travelling companions. From here, the tiny, prostrate figures, with their outstretched arms, looked as if they had fallen from the sky onto this bed of sumptuous green. There, in the distance, was the new Tempest House. From this angle he could clearly see its design. Little remained of the original building. Now it was built around an inner courtyard with formal gardens on all sides. There were paths of creamy gravel and rows of orange trees in giant containers interspersed with statues. In truth, this was not a house. It was a *palace*. Hundreds of people could comfortably live in such a massive edifice. An artificial lake in the form of a semicircle marked the start of the water gardens that stretched into the distance, almost as far as the eye could see. The Tar Man realised that Lord Luxon must have demolished all the cottages in the valley in order to build his park. He saw a line of fountains propelling jets of spray high into the cloudless sky; he saw canals of water flowing down the valley, shimmering like blue satin ribbons, and linked by rills and waterfalls; he saw the Corinthian arch that marked the end of the gardens. What a breathtaking vista! What astounding vanity!

He saw a road flanked by long lines of poplars and leading to a car-park. Two coaches were pulling up. There were already several cars and he could see people walking towards Tempest House. Even at this distance he could hear the crunch of gravel as the drivers manoeuvred their vehicles into parking spaces. The Tar Man frowned. Who were all these people and why were they here? But what did he care? He was not going to be around long enough to find out. He continued to walk along the ridge of the hill and when he came to a gap in the trees he headed north towards London.

Lord Luxon was trailing at the back of a line of wealthy Canadian tourists. They were being shown around by a guide, a bright young woman who seemed to know everything about everything to do with Tempest House and the Luxon dynasty. She wore late-eighteenth-century dress, as did all the other guides, and used her fan to indicate points of interest. There were *ooh!*s and *aah!*s as the group passed through gigantic double doors into the Hall of Mirrors.

'It is often said,' commented the tour guide, 'that Tempest House is only rivalled by Versailles, and in some ways surpasses it. This opulent stateroom was commissioned with the express intention of outdoing the original, in Versailles. And, well over two centuries later, it is still reputed to be the most beautiful room in England.'

There were murmurs of agreement.

'Innumerable treaties have been signed here, royal marriages arranged, wars declared . . . The great and the good from every country have feasted and danced and decided the fate of the world for over two hundred years on this very spot.'

Lord Luxon did as he was told and happily admired the ceiling painted in the manner of the Italian Renaissance, and the mirrors that lined the room from floor to ceiling. He craned his neck to view the priceless crystal chandeliers, and studied the exquisite mosaic floor which had taken Venetian craftsmen eighteen years to complete. Finally, he followed behind the troupe of visitors as they walked through French doors onto a paved terrace which allowed an uninterrupted view of the longest water garden in Europe.

Lord Luxon could not help smiling. How easily had he turned the great wheel of history! The American Revolution had failed; the French Revolution had failed; Britain had retained her colonies! Ah, Alice, he thought, if you could only have witnessed how your scholarly advice has sliced through history like a surgeon's knife! How I should have taken pleasure in entertaining you here. You, more than anyone, would have known how to appreciate it . . . He closed his eyes for a moment and tried to recall Alice's face that first afternoon on the boat in New York harbour. How amusing, how compelling he had found her conversation! But when he tried to picture her face all he saw was her look of horror as that Frenchman crashed into the floor of the museum. He dug his fingernails into the palms of his hands. When he realised what he was doing, Lord Luxon consciously made himself unclench his fists and realign his posture. He straightened his back and elongated his neck. He refused to allow the recollection of an unfortunate incident to sour this moment of triumph. Regret was pointless. Alice – just like the Manhattan he had seen rising in glory out of the sea – had never existed in this world. Save in his memory.

Lord Luxon felt suddenly very alone. He had known from the start that if he changed the course of history no one could be aware of it. How could they be? They had known nothing else. Yet, arriving back on his own soil, he had half-hoped, unreasonably, for some hint of patriotic gratitude. So it had been a bittersweet return. If only you knew, Lord Luxon would think, gazing into the eyes of strangers he passed on the streets of a world he felt *he* had created. If only you knew what I have given you. My actions have guaranteed this country's place in the world. He reached into his jacket pocket and touched the small pistol that had done the deed. Increasingly he felt the need to hold it, partly to glory in that pivotal moment, but also to convince himself that he had, in reality, won back America. In his mind the gun had become a kind of sacred relic, a talisman, something that justified his existence. He could not bear to be without it. And yet there was no denying that this solitary and self-satisfied gloating was a poor substitute for a triumphal march through the streets with a grateful crowd roaring its thanks. If only his father and uncles, at the very least, could have understood his achievement.

But his pale blue eyes drank in the splendour of the gardens and the house and he felt a little cheered. What a magnificent legacy he had left for his descendants to enjoy! The Canadian tourists were following their guide back into the Hall of Mirrors. Lord Luxon was about to follow them when an incident in the gardens caught his eye. People were gathered in a circle around something a little too far away for him to see properly. Perhaps someone had fainted. He lost interest and walked back into the house.

Tempest House's most famous treasure, the Luxon Timepiece Collection, which was housed in its own wing, was to be found at the end of a long, oak-panelled gallery. To his delight, as they moved along it, Lord Luxon spotted many of the portraits that he had grown up with – of his uncles and his father, and even one of himself, painted shortly before his father's death. As he looked up at it, the daughter of one of the tourists, a young girl with freckles, pointed straight at him and said for all to hear: 'Look at that man! He's in the painting!'

Everyone looked. Lord Luxon was striking his habitual pose in real life as in the painting. He did not have a cane today, but he kept one hand behind his back, held his back and neck very straight, placed his legs apart with one foot slightly forward. With his golden hair brushed back from regular features and with his fine blue eyes he was, without any doubt, a strikingly hand-some man. He heard everyone agreeing that it was an uncanny resemblance.

'Indeed,' he said. 'I am Lord Edward Luxon, come here to haunt you!'

Most people laughed, although he overheard one elderly man saying that he found jokes about ghosts somewhat tasteless when there had been so many time quakes of late.

'Lord Edward Luxon was certainly an intriguing character,' said the guide. 'Having acquired a lot of land in the American colonies, they say that he travelled there, incognito, to avert what could have turned into a revolution . . . Although there was a lot of mystery sur-rounding the episode and many historians dispute his involvement.'

'Is that so?' asked Lord Luxon sharply. 'And yet there is a square named after him in New York.'

'Well, I'm no expert – but that could be because he was created the first Duke of New York. Not that there was any great kudos attached to the title – as any of you who have visited the city can understand! But in middle life Edward Luxon acquired a reputation as a pathological liar. They say he had delusions of grandeur about what he had achieved in his life. He drank and gambled away several fortunes and the branch of the family who succeeded him took great care to distance themselves from anything to do with their embarrassing relation. He was a tragi-comic figure who died childless and alone.'

'But what about America?' spluttered Lord Luxon. 'Did he not overturn a revolution? Did he not assassinate the commander-in-chief of the Patriot forces?'

The guide looked at him with interest, clearly surprised that he knew so much about such a minor incident. 'Most historians agree that it was a British spy, a Welshman by the name of Thomas, I think, who was actually the hero of the hour . . .'

The guide was taken aback by Lord Luxon's expression.

'Some people,' she whispered to her neighbour, 'can't bear to be corrected.'

The guide looked at her watch. 'It's coming up for eleven o'clock. Can I ask everyone to hurry along to the next exhibit? We've got just under two minutes to take full advantage of the Luxon Timepiece Collection. It's worth the trip, I assure you!'

Lord Luxon tagged along at the back of the line of Canadian tourists, walking like an automaton, heart and mind numb with grief and shock.

*

Peter had roused Kate and Gideon with difficulty, having to practically drag them out of sight into the thicket of rhododendrons. They sat huddled together in deep shade on the fragrant, peaty earth. The odd arrow of sunlight pierced the evergreen leaves whose russet undersides had the texture of felt. This latest trip through time had done Kate no favours. When Peter had first seen Kate blur, so long ago now, at the bottom of the valley in Derbyshire, it had seemed as if she were flickering like a poorly tuned television set. She was flickering now. He held her firmly by the hand – even though he could scarcely feel her. He was avoiding looking at her. It was too distressing. He *had* to get Kate back to her parents. And as quickly as possible – which meant not attracting unwanted attention. A tall order in the circumstances.

Peter turned around to check up on Gideon who was holding his pounding head in both hands. The Tar Man seemed to have gone off. So much for blood being thicker than water. His friend did not look in great shape. With his bruised and battered face, anyone would have guessed he'd been in a terrible fight – which, of course, he had. All at once it came to Peter that as Kate and Gideon weren't capable of making any decisions right now, it was down to him to work out what to do next.

Peter went through the possibilities in his mind. As he did so he absent-mindedly pushed heaps of leathery, dead leaves into a pile and kicked them down again. He delayed worrying about how they were going to get Gideon back to his own time without an anti-gravity machine. All he could think about, all he wanted to do, more than anything in his whole life, was to save his friend. He knew, from what Kate had said, that he should actually be worried about the safety of the universe, rather than the well-being of one person. But how could he care about something so infinite and mysterious and incomprehensible? Kate had gone back in time to find him when he had been left behind – he wasn't going to let her down now. He squeezed Kate's hand in his own.

'Ouch,' said Kate. 'You're pinching me!'

'Oh. Sorry,' he said.

'Are you okay?'

'Yeah,' said Peter. 'Are you?'

'I'm okay, too.'

'I don't believe you.'

Peter pulled down a branch to get a better view of the commotion outside. The anti-gravity machine had attracted much interest from visitors to the water gardens of Tempest House. A circle of people stood around it, talking and pointing

'I'd like to hear what explanations people are coming up with,' commented Kate. 'Perhaps they think it's a sculpture.'

Kate's voice was as faded as her appearance looked. She sounded as if she were talking from the next room. He had to strain to hear her. He decided not to tell her.

'Do you think it can be mended?' he asked.

'It's got a tree through it! No, I don't. I think it's amazing we got here at all.'

Peter turned to Gideon. 'Do you think you might be able to walk yet?'

'The world is still spinning . . . but I think I trust myself to stand up.'

'All right. Let's go to the house and ask to use a telephone. I think the only thing we can do is telephone our parents and get them to pick us up here. With Kate looking the way she does we can't use public transport. We're just going to have to keep our heads down until they arrive.'

'It'll take hours to get to Surrey from Derbyshire,' said Kate. 'Are we going to be stuck in a rhododendron bush all day?!'

'It doesn't take long to get here from Richmond – if I can manage to get hold of my mum or dad, that is . . .'

'Oh,' said Kate, observing her faded arms. 'I'm not sure that I can face meeting your parents looking like this. Couldn't we wait until my mum and dad get down here? I'm not sure that I can—'

'Don't be daft, Kate, they won't mind what you look like . . .'

Kate's head drooped.

'Shall I see a tel-ee-fone at last?' asked Gideon, changing the subject.

'Yes, you will!' said Peter to Gideon. 'And then you'll see I haven't been making it all up!'

'Should we all go to find a phone?' asked Kate.

'I think we'll have to,' Peter replied. 'I can't let go of you and I don't want to leave Gideon by himself in a foreign century – just in case.'

'Shall I hear a police car crying *nee-naw, nee-naw*?'

This made Kate burst out laughing, which reminded Peter how long it had been since he saw her look jolly. 'I hope not!' she giggled.

When Gideon tried to get up he staggered and had to sit straight back down again. When he stood up a second time he managed to stay up.

'Poor Gideon,' said Kate.

Gideon looked at Kate and smiled at her.

'There is no need to be concerned on my account, I assure you. And soon you will be home, Mistress Kate, and all will be well.'

'I don't know how we're going to get *you* home, though,' said Kate.

'As Parson Ledbury would say, enough unto the day are the troubles thereof,' Gideon replied.

Peter raised an eyebrow at Kate. 'I think Gideon means that we can worry about that tomorrow.'

Peter and Gideon both donated their jackets to Kate. They placed Gideon's around her shoulders and put Peter's over her head. If anyone were to comment they would say that she had sunstroke and that they were keeping the light out of her eyes. As they were covering her up, a small child scrambled into the bushes in search of a good hiding place. She looked at the big people playing their strange game and backed away.

'It's all right,' Peter called out to her. 'It's all yours until we get back.'

They walked over the spongy turf and soon the shadow of Tempest House fell on them. They approached the west wing of the house marching three abreast with Kate in the middle, her form obscured by their jackets. Peter was delighted to see several guides in period dress as it had not yet occurred to him how they were going to explain away their strange clothes. Kate allowed herself to peep out from underneath her jacket and when she looked up at Tempest House, glorious in the sunshine, she noticed the roof terrace with its stone balustrades and corner statues. Her blood ran cold. *This* was the tall building where she saw Peter in her dreams. Suddenly she was overwhelmed by shadowy fears and lost her footing. Peter stopped her falling.

'Do you want to sit down for a minute?' he asked.

Kate consciously pushed away the images that crowded into her mind. 'No, no, I just tripped over something. Let's just make that call.'

'But what has happened to Tempest House?' exclaimed Gideon. 'It was always much admired but *this* . . . this is a palace fit for a king! Upon my word, Lord Luxon must have made several fortunes in the future . . .'

They entered through a glass side door which had *The Luxon Timepiece Collection* painted above it in copperplate script.

As soon as they walked into the cavernous hall with its tiered galleries on high, its sumptuous ebony panelling below, and its inlaid marble floor, Peter was aware of *ticking*. A lot of ticking. The air shivered with the marking of time. Rows of clocks studded the walls, there were half a dozen grandfather clocks placed at regular intervals, there were tables full of carriage clocks, cabinets where pocket watches lay on plush velvet, dress watches and miniature, bejewelled timepieces. At the centre of the lofty space was a golden water clock whose great wheel scooped up water and propelled a mechanism which both kept the hour and also rotated a baroque representation of Father Time. Everywhere pendulums swung and intricate mechanisms clicked and whirred. It was a veritable temple to celebrate the lie that time is constant and regular and can be tamed. Peter hated the terrible sound. The nightmarish tick-tock-ing was enough to send you mad. Then he noticed how all the people milling about in the room were not looking at the individual exhibits, but seemed to be waiting in anticipation.

Close to the door, a girl sat at a desk covered with piles of books and postcards and information leaflets. She was counting out coins. The three figures shuffled forward together in a line and Peter coughed gently. The girl looked up and a frown creased her forehead when she noticed Kate.

'Could I use a telephone please?' Peter said to her. 'I need to contact my friend's parents.'

The nervous girl looked from Peter to the person under the pile of jackets and back again. She spoke very quickly in a staccato voice. 'Sorry? . . . Are, are you tour guides? I didn't catch what it is you wanted – would you . . . would you mind repeating your question?'

Peter's face fell but he repeated the word all the same. 'Telephone? Could I use a telephone please?'

The girl shook her and looked even more anxious. 'I'm so sorry, I still don't understand. I only started this week. I'll ask my supervisor if you like – she might know what one is.'

'Never mind,' said Peter. 'It doesn't matter. Thanks anyway.'

Peter turned and walked away and the others followed his lead. His heart sank.

'Oh no,' he said under his breath.

He realised with a start that he could not feel Kate and checked to see that he held her insubstantial hand in his. But she was still there, her face shrouded by his jacket.

'What's going on?!' he whispered to her.

'I set it to the right reading, I know I did!' said Kate.

Peter scratched his head in exasperation. 'I don't know when they invented telephones but I'm sure it was a long time ago.'

'It must be Lord Luxon!' exclaimed Kate. 'He's done something. If there aren't telephones, he's done something to change the future!'

Peter put his head close to hers. He could only just make out what she was saying. 'But why would Lord Luxon want to un-invent the telephone?'

'I didn't mean that,' said Kate. 'And anyway, they might have telephones . . . they might just call them something else. What I meant was—'

Abruptly Gideon stepped in front of them and pointed. 'It's him! I am sure of it!'

Peter and Kate turned to look. Visitors were congregating in the large exhibition area and everyone seemed to be standing still in breathless anticipation. Indeed, people had even stopped talking so that Gideon's cry echoed over all the building.

'There is the man that destroys the world with his vanity and who pits brother against brother!'

Peter and Kate watched, open-mouthed, as Gideon started to sprint away from them as fast as if someone had set off a starting pistol. Kate clutched at Peter's arm.

'Oooh! Peter, look!' Kate screamed. 'It's Lord Luxon!'

It seemed to Kate that only one person in the entire room was not watching Gideon run through the crowds – and that was the solitary figure engrossed in his own thoughts next to the water clock, Lord Luxon himself. At the sound of such rapid footfall Lord Luxon looked up, startled, and the first thing he saw was Gideon, his face wild and fierce, charging at him from the other side of the room like a bull at a gate.

'*Gideon?*' he cried.

Instinctively Lord Luxon raised his arms to protect himself against imminent attack. But at the very moment that Gideon was reaching out to grab hold of Lord Luxon's shoulders, the hour *struck*. It was not for nothing that this collection was so renowned: hundreds of clocks all over the building were synchronised so that they all chimed the hour in perfect unison, like an orchestra coming to life in reaction to a tiny movement of a conductor's baton. It was so loud you could *feel* the vibrations. It was so loud it *hurt*. Without thinking, Peter, like so many others in the room, covered his ears with his hands, an action he regretted as soon as he had done it.

Kate's grip on her own time was by now so tenuous that she fast-forwarded the instant Peter removed his hand from hers. She tried to fight the distress that flooded over her as she held up a hand to see what more damage had been done. It was difficult to tell. This time the shapes she saw floating in the air around her were much clearer. In fact, if she compared her own flesh with the shapes, as she was becoming more transparent, they appeared more opaque.

She was convinced that they were alive. There must, she thought, be worlds whose very existence we don't even suspect because they move so much faster or slower than us, or because our senses just can't detect them. She wondered if the shapes were aware of her.

Unlike her own clothes, Peter and Gideon's jackets did not move when she did, so it was with relief that Kate found that she could just duck down and creep out of the stiff tent formed by them. She looked up at Peter. His face was screwed up and his hands were clapped over his ears. The jackets floated next to him, the contour of her own head and shoulders still clearly visible. Kate realised how much easier it was to move in this world now, as if her body was better adjusted to life at this speed. She also realised how much effort just walking or keeping upright had been taking.

She looked over towards Gideon. It was a striking scene. Every eye in the room was trained on the two figures, frozen in a dramatic tableau in front of the water clock. Kate's experience with the Tar Man had made her wary of touching anyone, so she wove a very careful path between the visitors to Tempest House. She wafted the indistinct and floating shapes out of her way as she went. Did they remind her of thistledown or butterflies or jellyfish? She wasn't quite sure.

When she reached the water clock she saw that Gideon was in full flight and that neither of his feet was actually touching the ground. He was reaching out to grab Lord Luxon with both hands. Lord Luxon was gawping at him in alarm from behind arms crossed defensively in front of his face. Poor Gideon, thought Kate, looking at his bad eye. It was still very swollen and red, with a halo of purple and yellow bruising. Kate slowly circled Lord Luxon as if he were a statue in a museum. She had never come across a man who took this much care of his appearance. How vain he must be, she thought.

Lord Luxon's ivory jacket was hanging open. It was lined with matching silk, and a small black object, protruding from an inside pocket, caught her eye. It wasn't a wallet. It was made of metal. Being extremely careful not to touch Lord Luxon, Kate drew closer. It couldn't be a gun, could it? Not that she had ever seen a real gun, but it seemed to Kate that it could potentially be the barrel of a small gun. Taking a step backwards, she scrutinised Lord Luxon's body language – was he preparing to reach for a weapon? It was possible, she supposed. She decided that she had to investigate. If Gideon was in danger she could not take any chances.

Kate stood uncomfortably close to Lord Luxon. Very slowly she placed thumb and forefinger around the small metal cylinder and pulled as hard as she could. It was to no avail. Then she tried pulling with two thumbs and two forefingers but she still could not budge it at all. The object might just as well have weighed a ton. She felt frustration and panic in equal measure. If it *were* a gun and Lord Luxon *did* intend to use it she would not be able to warn Gideon in time. By the time she had touched Peter and stopped fast-forwarding and shouted to Gideon to be careful, he could already be shot and bleeding on the floor.

What should she do? Or, rather, what *could* she do in the circumstances? It then occurred to her that this was not only about Gideon's safety. If Lord Luxon got away, and continued to use the anti-gravity machine, there would be more parallel worlds and more time quakes until . . . who knows what might happen. The weight of responsibility on her shoulders made her feel tearful and afraid. She looked at her hands again. Didn't she have enough to deal with?

Kate observed the water clock and at the ropes of sparkling water pouring off the top of the golden wheel and hanging in mid-air. She sat down next to it and patted the spongy surface of the water. The memory of the Tar Man's horrified face when she had grabbed hold of him by the Thames was still vivid in her mind. And though she recoiled at the thought, this *was* a possibility . . . If she frightened Lord Luxon enough, it would give her a few more precious seconds to warn Gideon about the gun. Meanwhile Gideon would be able to grab Lord Luxon and wrestle him to the floor – and then Peter could help, too . . .

But such a course of action made her anxious and Kate procrastinated for a while. But then a calmness fell over her and her courage returned. Suddenly it seemed that this was the way it had to be. If Peter had not taken his hand from hers at that precise moment they would all be in a much worse position. She searched her own future again and still saw nothing. She searched Peter's future and still saw him distraught at the top of this very building. There were no easy answers for her, there were no instructions to be plucked out of the sky. All there was to rely on was her own intelligence and her own judgement. Her father always told her to trust herself and that was all she could do. If anyone else had tried to stop Lord Luxon, they had clearly failed. She now had a chance to stop him – and she was not going to turn away from it.

Kate marched straight up to Lord Luxon and, without hesitation, grabbed him by both wrists. Nothing happened. His flesh felt hard and smooth. She stared into his face.

'Come on,' she cried. 'Surely you can feel that!'

She carried on gripping him, indeed, she gripped him for so long that she grew bored, but then, all of a sudden, she realised that his hands had grown soft and then she saw his face crease in a violent spasm. Lord Luxon's eyes, already open wide, opened even wider, and he turned to look at her. He opened his mouth to cry out but no sound came. Although she had willed it to happen, now that it had, she had the impression that a corpse had come to life. But when Kate tried to remove her hands from his wrists she could not. The two of them were stuck together like opposite poles of a magnet. She pulled and tugged and shook her hands and soon Lord Luxon was doing the same. When she looked down she saw that not only was her flesh transparent, now, so too was Lord Luxon's. Her Law of Temporal Osmosis had proved all too accurate – she and Lord Luxon were accelerating through time together. Both of them struggled uselessly against invisible forces that fused them together.

'Why can't I take my hands away?' cried Kate.

It seemed to her that they were travelling through time faster and faster, and faster. Soon they were surrounded by a carapace of light. Lord Luxon tried to run away from Kate and his terror was so great he could not stop even though he saw that he was pulling Kate along with him.

'Stop it!' Kate screamed. 'I can't keep up with you!'

But he continued to stagger sideways, dragging Kate alongside him when she lost her footing. They knocked into people and clocks and tumbled into the long gallery where Lord Luxon's father and ancestors stared down at him from their portraits, as disapproving as ever. Now they were moving much faster than the floating shapes, and the crackling light that emanated from them was growing more intense. Around and around they went, leaving the long gallery and entering the Hall of Mirrors. Kate no longer had the strength to struggle against Lord Luxon and allowed herself to be carried along in this macabre dance. They were spinning around now at much greater velocity, though whether this was due to Lord Luxon or the force that held them Kate could not tell. Slowly but surely Kate was beginning to lose consciousness. Slowly but surely Kate sensed that she was drifting apart. Through half-open eyes Kate saw their dazzling double silhouette reflected from one mirror to another in an infinite crescendo of light. The Hall of Mirrors started to fade. Soon it disappeared altogether. Now they were lost in an unfathomable darkness. Kate struggled to keep awake for she was beginning to sense a change in the force that held them together. Lord Luxon must have felt something, too, and as he stared in horror into Kate's eyes a final time, the force abruptly *stopped*. Lord Luxon fell away from her into the void. Her eyes followed his trajectory. He was a spark from a bon-fire that rises into the night sky, caught by the wind, swirling, falling, burning more brightly for an instant, and then vanishing for ever in the velvet blackness. Kate's eyelids closed. It was over.

CHAPTER TWENTY-SIX

A Perfect Day

In which all is lost for Kate

The diaphanous shapes floated by. Sometimes a cluster of them would gather around her and she had the impression that they were tasting her, much as butterflies might sip nectar from a flower. Soon she would have so little substance that she doubted even she could see herself. She felt her eyes sliding shut.

Then the memory came to Kate like a benediction. It was so strong it blotted out everything else. It was during those carefree days when the door of the future was still closed to her. It was the last day of the autumn half-term holiday, only a few weeks before the day that Peter Schock arrived in her life.

She was perched on the narrow bench in the back of the ancient Land Rover, squashed up between Sam and Sean. She was so cross at being dragged off on a family outing when she had already made plans of her own. Kate felt every jarring stone and pothole as the Land Rover juddered up the rough track towards the main road, throwing her brothers and sisters around so that their shoulders thumped one against the other. All Kate's friends had proper cars with springs and everything. Why did *her* family have to ride around in this bone-rattler?

She had been feeling put upon all week. As the eldest, she felt she had done more than her fair share of the chores and the boring stuff and she had tons more homework than anyone else. Somehow, being deprived of her freedom on the last day of the half-term holiday before school started again was the final straw. She had upset Sam by stomping off up the stairs and slamming her door. Sam could not bear it when Kate and their mum fell out. They were each as strong-willed as the other so that when Sam tried to get them to make up, mother and daughter just got cross with him as well. Kate felt bad about it but was definitely not going to say sorry. She was entitled to her own personal space! Anyway, it was no big deal. Just a family squabble. A case of people getting on each other's nerves. But now that Kate's temper had cooled she was starting to feel miserable.

'But it's such a beautiful day!' Mrs Dyer insisted as she drove them out of their valley. 'Just look how blue the sky is. It'll be winter soon. Let's not waste this lovely sunny day. You never know how many days like this you've got.'

'Don't say things like that!' exclaimed Sam. 'I hate it when you say stuff like that!'

Kate looked at him. He had tears in his eyes. The twins rolled their eyes theatrically towards heaven.

'Poor 'ickle Sammy, he's *so* sensitive,' said Issy.

Sam reached over and slapped her hand hard. 'Shut up!' he shouted.

Issy burst into tears. He had hurt her.

'Calm down, for goodness' sake, Sam,' growled Dr Dyer. 'We do *not* – even when provoked – hit each other in this family.'

Kate's dad had not felt like a trip out either. He was in the middle of emailing a NASA colleague with some complicated data but he had come along because he did not want to disappoint Kate's mother.

Issy sniffed and Kate passed her a tissue.

'For goodness' sake!' exploded Mrs Dyer. 'I only wanted all of us to go on a family outing for a change. Is that too much too ask?' No one answered. 'Clearly it is!'

The path that led from the gardens at Chatsworth House to the Hunting Lodge was very steep. Dr and Mrs Dyer walked ahead, holding hands and talking. Sometimes Mrs Dyer rested her head on her husband's shoulder. Kate was on sheepdog duty, as usual, rounding up the four younger ones and giving Milly a piggy-back when she needed it for she was going through a stage of refusing to sit in the buggy. The atmosphere was still tense and Sam, who would normally help her, was dragging behind looking sad. Kate put her baby sister down and stood still for a moment to get her breath back. She looked down at how far they had climbed. She was beginning to feel better despite her mood. Her cheeks had turned rosy. Below them Chatsworth dominated the valley. The trees were fast losing their leaves and had turned shades of yellow, red and brown. The great fountain gushed forth a plume of white water high over the lake and, beyond, a silver river slid under the arched stone bridge.

Suddenly Milly, exhausted from the climb, sat on her bottom and refused to budge. She started to cry. Shrill, piping sobs echoed through the woods and the whole family stopped in their tracks and looked over at the tiny figure, her golden curls blowing in the breeze, her red corduroy trousers bulging with a nappy that no doubt needed changing, her podgy arms raised in the air waiting for someone to pick her up and make her feel better. There was a slight pause and then, moving inwards like the spokes of a wheel, everyone approached the toddler at the centre of the circle. Dr and

Mrs Dyer started to jog towards Milly, Sam slid off the iron cannon at the foot of the Hunting Lodge and the twins and Sean abandoned their game of tag. Kate reached her tiny sister first and picked her up, holding her soft, wet cheek against hers. Mrs Dyer got there next and Kate realised that, inexplicably, tears were running down her own cheeks, too.

'Oh, Kate,' said her mother. 'I expect so much of you, don't I?'

And Mrs Dyer put her arms around Kate and Milly and then Sam joined them and they all opened their arms to let him join the circle and the next moment they were all there, clinging silently on to each other, their hearts brimming over with some unnamed emotion. It only lasted a moment.

'Why's everyone crying? This is very silly,' said Sam, sniffing.

Dr Dyer laughed and ruffled Sam's hair. 'Human beings *are* very silly. Didn't you know?'

Mrs Dyer squeezed Kate's hand. 'I knew this would be a perfect day.'

And then it was over. Sam and Sean and the twins went off to clamber over the cannon and Milly wriggled out of Kate's grasp and started to crawl over the damp clover. With the last ounce of her strength Kate willed the memory of that moment to return and she felt the clutch of arms and warm breath on her cheeks and hard chins resting on her hair. And with the power of her imagination, for that was all that was left to her, she placed Peter, who she knew was so often lonely, and Gideon, who had lost so many brothers and sisters, firmly into the centre of that circle of belonging, too. Just for a moment. And then, as the scene started to slip from her grasp, she said goodbye to the people that she loved and who loved her, for she knew that she was now beyond help. *Goodbye*, she said. *Thank you. I love you.*

*

Kate was going in and out of consciousness. 'BELIEVE!' whispered Dr Pirretti. 'Remember what the Marquis de Montfaron said. Nothing is ever lost . . .'

Kate murmured something which Dr Pirretti could not catch.

'We did not mean to invent time travel,' said Dr Pirretti. 'Who would have wanted to open such a Pandora's box?'

Kate wanted to reply. She wanted to say that after Pandora let out all the evils of the world, Hope still remained. But she did not have the strength.

Dr Pirretti's voice was unsteady. 'I swear that I shall not rest until I have undone the harm we have done to the universe. I shall never forget your sacrifice. Can you hear me, Kate? Kate? KATE!'

But by now the only sound that Kate could hear was the faltering murmur of her own heart beating in her temples. And soon, too weak to resist any longer, even that was lost to her as the precious, unique structure that had been Kate Dyer was swept away by the ungovernable waters of Time.

CHAPTER TWENTY-SEVEN

Mr Carmichael's Homework

In which the Tar Man lends some welcome
support and Peter is reminded of the usefulness
of homework

No sooner had he put his hands to his ears than Peter realised what he had done. He stood on tiptoe, trying to see Gideon. He immediately held out his hand for Kate again.

'Sorry!' he shouted over the clocks. 'Give me your hand. We've got to help Gideon—'

But out of the corner of his eye he saw the two jackets they had draped over Kate drop to the floor as if balloons had been pricked beneath them. Peter froze, his hand still extended for her to take. Then he slowly picked up the heavy jackets one by one and stared in disbelief at the empty floor. He ignored the commotion coming from the other side of the room and searched frantically all around him for any sign of Kate. The air was thick with the chiming of an army of clocks whose relentless pendulums swung, measuring out the seconds since he had last seen Kate. He ran wildly through the crowd, pushing people out of the way, continuing to call out for her, yet all the while somehow knowing he had lost her. An invisible bond had been cut, a candle blown out. But, of course, he could not accept it.

'Kate!' he screamed, not caring what people thought. 'Kate!'

He ran towards the water clock hoping to find that she was helping Gideon with Lord Luxon. People were in a state of high agitation.

'Did you see it? Am I dreaming?'

'He just vanished! He vanished off the face of the earth!'

'Should we call the police?'

'Has a crime been committed?'

'He said he was the ghost of Lord Luxon come back to haunt us!'

'Did you know him?' a woman asked Gideon. 'You looked so angry!'

Gideon was backing away. Peter stood next to the water clock trying to take it all in. Kate had gone. Lord Luxon had gone. Gideon glanced at Peter and immediately understood that something terrible had happened. Peter's face was ashen. He needed to get him away.

''Twas a magician's trick, that is all,' Gideon called to the crowd as he pulled Peter towards the long gallery. 'He has good timing, has he not, to vanish at the very moment the hour strikes? Doubtless he will be back soon to beg for your pennies . . .'

Gideon took hold of Peter's arm and led him firmly out of the crowd before anyone got any ideas about stopping them. He marched Peter through the long gallery and then into a corridor and then, when they came across a narrow wooden staircase, roped off and labelled *No Entry* he unhooked the rope and pushed Peter through. They climbed up five flights of stairs to the top of the building and found themselves on a vast roof terrace that stretched the breadth of Tempest House. There was a carved stone balustrade and Peter slumped onto the floor and rested his elbows on the sun-warmed stone, panting a little after all the stairs. Gideon sat down next to him.

He waited for Peter to speak. From the movements of his back Gideon could tell he was crying. Suddenly Peter started to hit the balustrade with clenched fists.

'I let go of her!' he cried. 'And now she's gone . . .'

He felt Gideon's hand on his shoulder.

'Then we will look for her,' said Gideon.

'How can we do that when she's moving so fast she's invisible?'

'Then . . . Mistress Kate will have to find *us*.'

Peter sat up and looked directly at Gideon, his eyes red from crying. 'She would have found us by now!' he shouted. 'Don't you understand? For her, it's probably been a hundred years since she disappeared. If she was going to come back she would have done by now. I promised not to let go of her . . . and I did. It's all my fault!'

Gideon looked taken aback by Peter's outburst and covered his own face with his hands for a moment. Peter saw that the truth of the situation had sunk in. Gideon's blue eyes had misted over.

'So Mistress Kate is lost for ever? She is beyond our help?'

Peter nodded. 'And wherever she's gone, I think she's taken Lord Luxon with her.'

They both looked out through the gaps in the balustrade. The sun shone down on the water gardens and on a vast London neither of them recognised. Time passed. The two of them felt punch-drunk, overwhelmed, unable to take in the desperate reality of their situation. The hum of conversation drifted up to them. Sightseers enjoyed the warm weather and admired Tempest House and its magnificent gardens. After a while two uniformed attendants appeared on the lawn and Peter and Gideon watched them knock canes into the turf around the anti-gravity machine and tie striped tape around them. The two of them began to get thirsty, but still they did not move. For a while Gideon looked in fascination at the cars moving in and out of the car-park but finally grew tired of it and lay flat on his back, preferring to stare at the cloudless sky instead. Peter sat cross-legged looking towards London. This isn't my home, he thought. Once, in another world, I lived in south-west London in a house overlooking Richmond Green, with my mum and dad . . . And I had no idea how lucky I was.

More time passed. It was Peter who broke the silence first. 'Gideon, look!' he exclaimed, pointing beyond the great arch that marked the end of the gardens towards London.

Gideon heaved himself off the ground and stood up painfully. He scanned the cityscape that stretched as far as the eye could see. Peter heard Gideon's sharp intake of breath as he saw it.

'I had hoped never to see such a thing again . . .'

A glowing, billowing mass pulsated over perhaps a quarter of the city on the eastern side. The sky had grown very dark over London, even though here, at Tempest House, all was blue sky and sunshine.

Below them they heard frightened cries and when they looked down at the people on the terrace, they saw that everyone was looking in the same direction.

'Another time quake!' someone shouted.

People began to hurry away from the house. They heard the sound of engines revving and tyres crunching on gravel. Soon there was a mass exodus and the drive was full of visitors and staff. It was not long before the car-park had emptied and the gardens were deserted. On the horizon, lurid green lightning streaked across the city like a skeleton's fingers. As Peter watched, a strong sense of unreality came over him. He did not even feel frightened any more.

'Kate was right,' said Peter. 'We've damaged Time – and who is going to mend it? Even if Lord Luxon can't cause any more damage, the time quakes aren't going to stop. It's too late.'

Gideon looked as sad as Peter had ever seen him. 'Come,' he said. 'I grow weary of this place. I need to find you food and water and a roof for your head.'

What's the point? Peter was about to say. We might just as well lie down now and wait for it all to be over. We're all alone, with no means of getting home, in a world that's falling apart in front of our eyes! What's the point of doing *anything*? It'll only prolong the agony . . . But he bit his lip. He felt suddenly ashamed. For the first time he considered what Gideon might be feeling.

'*We* need to find food and water and a roof for *our* heads,' said Peter.

The time quake was still raging over London. The strange wind that emanated from it came in violent gusts that blew the hair from their faces and, although it was early afternoon, there was so little light now it seemed more like dusk. They had left an empty Tempest House and now not a soul was to be seen in the gardens. Even the birds had stopped singing; the only sound was that of the splashing of fountains and an ominous roaring, like an angry tide, rolling towards them from the city. Gideon suggested that they walk away from London, deeper into Surrey. Perhaps Abinger Hammer, the village where Gideon had lived as a child, still existed in this world. Gideon suddenly stopped. He wheeled around and stood, alert and watchful. Peter looked at him. He was put in mind of a fox sniffing the air to see if hounds were on its trail.

'What is it?'

Gideon pointed. A large white vehicle, a van of some kind, had come into view at the opposite side of the park. It was heading towards the house. It was still some way away and, unwilling to draw any attention to themselves, Gideon pulled Peter behind the nearest cover, which happened to be a large barrel. It was painted white, and contained a clipped bay tree. They crouched down behind the barrel and peeped out. The van approached the house, drove right past it and continued onto the lawn.

'They're heading for the anti-gravity machine!' said Peter incredulously. 'But why? Why do they want to shift a broken machine now, when they don't even know what it is and when half of London is in meltdown?'

Gideon started to smile. 'I know who it is.'

Peter looked at him, puzzled, and then the penny dropped.

'Do you really think he'd come back?'

The Tar Man jumped out of the van and ordered the driver to direct his headlights at the anti-gravity machine. From their hiding place, some fifty metres away, Peter and Gideon saw him kick over the canes, take hold of the trunk of the birch tree, and drag it away. Then the Tar Man called to the driver to help him. They picked up the heavy weight between them and loaded it onto the back of the vehicle. The driver got back into the van and started up the engine.

'Surely you're going to tell him we're here?' hissed Peter.

Gideon put his finger to his lips and continued to watch.

The Tar Man did not get in the van but slowly turned around in a full circle. Then he stepped into the yellow beam of the van's headlights, so that he was spotlit for all to see, cupped his hands to his mouth, and shouted: 'Gid-e-on! Gid-e-on!' till it echoed all around the valley.

Gideon laughed out loud. 'Upon my word, Peter, Nathaniel is full of surprises!'

'*Nathaniel?*'

'It is his name.'

Gideon leaped up and hollered. 'Here!' he cried.

The Tar Man ran forward to meet him. Peter thought he looked very pleased to see them, or pleased to see Gideon, at least, yet he stopped short of actually greeting him.

'I wagered you would have need of my help.'

'Greetings, Nathaniel! What has brought you back to Tempest House? Is blood thicker than water or was it the device that you sought?'

'Do not flatter yourself, Gideon, I have come for the device.'

'I did not doubt it,' said Gideon.

'It is broken – yet I may find someone to mend it in this strange future.'

Gideon pointed to the amorphous, semi-luminous mass over London. 'You have seen the city?'

'Do you think I am deaf and blind? Yes, I have seen the city. It seems that Nature is angry, in this century just as in our own.'

'I fear that Lord Luxon has made much use of the device,' said Gideon.

'Yes, damn his eyes! He has changed the future and I do not care for it! I scarcely recognise his London!'

'Yet you contrive to get what you need,' said Gideon, indicating the van and the driver.

'Human nature is the same no matter what the century. Besides,' the Tar Man said, patting his pockets, 'all the panic in the city has made for easy pickings. But it does not please me here. Would that the machine was not broken, I would—'

'How can you talk like that?' burst out Peter. 'Can't you see that the universe is disintegrating around our ears because of time travel? How can you think about easy pickings when the earth is about to end?'

The Tar Man looked directly at Peter for the first time.

'Peter speaks the truth, Nathaniel,' said Gideon.

'By the laws, Gideon, do not think to lecture me! The world is strong enough by far to survive such things. Fear begets fear, has life not taught you that, at least? I recall that when I first lived in London I felt a tremor beneath my feet. 'Twas strong enough to cause a few fish to leap out of the Thames and to cause some plates to fall to the floor. I heard of no injuries to speak of, yet it struck so much terror into people's hearts that it sent half of the city scurrying into the countryside like frightened mice! How I laughed to see the crowds creeping back the next morning, all foolish, when another day had dawned . . .'

'There'll be no countryside to scurry back to, you stupid man!' exclaimed Peter.

'Hold your tongue, you impudent young—'

The Tar Man raised his hand, but Gideon caught hold of his arm.

'He is distraught . . .'

The Tar Man shook his arm away.

'And where is your young friend, Master Schock?' asked the Tar Man. 'I do not see her.'

'Mistress Kate is lost to us,' said Gideon quickly. 'We believe that Lord Luxon is . . . lost also.'

The Tar Man drew in his breath. 'Ah. Then, I am sorry for it, Master Schock. And you say Lord Luxon, too?'

'Yes,' said Gideon. 'Lord Luxon, too.'

'Upon my word . . . And how did this occur?'

'In truth, we do not know. Lord Luxon and Mistress Dyer

vanished at the same instant. Neither has returned – and we must fear the worst.'

The Tar Man's face revealed his shock. He rubbed his arms where Kate had touched him. Presently he said: 'And Lord Luxon's device, do you know of its whereabouts?'

'Is that all you care about? Why can't you get it?' cried Peter. 'It's using the anti-gravity machines that's caused *that*!' He pointed towards the time quake. 'Isn't it obvious, even to you, that the world can't cope with any more time travel?'

'I'll thank you to control your young friend,' said the Tar Man to Gideon.

He looked over at the city, beginning to pace up and down as he did so. It seemed to Peter that the time quake was beginning to recede.

'Suppose for a moment that I accept that we are doomed – which, I have to say, I do not – what can be done, Master Schock, to tear us back from the brink of disaster?'

'Nothing! It's too late!'

But even as he said it, Kate's premonition came back to him. She said that she could not see a future for herself, but she also said that *he* would be all right, that when the time came he would know what to do. A spark of hope awoke within him, a glimmering of something stirred . . .

'In which case, Master Schock, it can surely matter little to you what *I* do with the time I have left to me?'

'Unless,' said Peter, 'unless we really *could* stop the very first time event happening . . . But we'd need to find Lord Luxon's anti-gravity machine—'

'Stop the *first time event*?' repeated the Tar Man.

'The one that you and Gideon witnessed – when Kate and I were in her dad's laboratory one minute and the next we were in the middle of nowhere in 1763. If we had not gone to help Kate's dad that day, maybe the accidental discovery of time travel would not have happened. Or not in that way, or it might have happened later, or something.'

'But *you* could take us back, could you not, Nathaniel?' exclaimed Gideon.

'It is possible, I suppose . . .'

'What do you mean?' exclaimed Peter. 'How?'

'Nathaniel uses objects to take him to another time . . .'

'*That's* what you were doing with Kate's trainers!' cried Peter triumphantly.

'Ha! They were useless to me. They were made of too many parts – it confuses what I can sense. I need simple objects . . .'

The driver got out of the van, wanting to know what was happening.

'Patience, my friend,' the Tar Man called. 'You will be well rewarded, I assure you!'

'And you could take us with you?' asked Peter.

'Nathaniel took *me* back in time,' said Gideon.

The Tar Man looked non-committal. 'Why should I help you do such a thing?'

'If you do not, I fancy you will soon have cause to regret it,' said Gideon.

'How can I believe you?'

'You cannot.'

Peter suddenly grabbed hold of Gideon's arm. 'If the first time event did not happen, Kate would still be here!'

Gideon shook his head. 'How can I understand the workings of time? I do not know . . .'

'But even if I were to agree to help you,' said the Tar Man, 'it is a crude method. I cannot navigate time like a ship on the high seas.

I cannot set a course. I am at the mercy of whatever object I have at my disposal.'

Slowly, Peter reached into his pocket and took out a crumpled piece of paper. *Thank you, Kate*, he said silently. Where the paper had been folded it was worn and grubby.

'On the last day of term, Mr Carmichael handed this out. It was our English homework for us to do over the Christmas holidays. It was the next day that I met Kate and we went to visit her dad's laboratory and got catapulted back to 1763.'

Peter held out the piece of paper to the Tar Man but then took it back again.

'What's wrong, Peter?' Gideon saw the happiness fade abruptly from Peter's face.

'I don't know if it will work . . . Lord Luxon changed the future. I don't know if we can get back to that time . . . Perhaps it never happened.'

The Tar Man took the piece of paper from Peter's hand.

'Do you remember being given this piece of paper?'

Peter nodded.

'Do you remember the first *time event*, as you call it?'

'Yes.'

'Then, can you doubt that it happened?'

The Tar Man held the piece of paper between the palms of his hands and Peter and Gideon watched him as he concentrated. Peter watched open-mouthed as the Tar Man started to fade. After a few seconds he looked opaque once more and looked up at them. The Tar Man threw back Mr Carmichael's English homework to Peter.

'*If* I am minded to help you, the object will do,' he said.

Peter grabbed hold of Gideon's arm. 'But we'd have to go to Derbyshire . . .'

Chapter Twenty-Eight

Derbyshire

In which Peter takes an important telephone call

It was early afternoon on Saturday, the sixteenth of December, the first day of the Christmas holidays. In a valley in Derbyshire, three figures waited next to a narrow track, out of sight of the farmhouse, in a frozen field where black and white cows grazed on hay. They listened to the biting wind whistle through the hawthorn hedge that screened them from the road, and they listened to the rooks cawing in the wintry sky. But then they heard what they had been waiting for. The sound of an engine carried over the crisp, cold air. Their arms were linked, Gideon standing between his brother and Peter. They had fallen silent for, as the Tar Man had repeated, there was only one way they would find out what good – if any – might come of this final effort to put matters right. Now that the time had nearly arrived, Peter felt very calm. He could only suspect what might happen to him and he was ready to take the risk. He looked up at Gideon.

'Whatever happens next, I wanted to say thank you – while I can – for staying with me and Kate when you could have walked away.'

Gideon did not reply but tightened his grip on Peter's arm. Then Peter leaned forward to look at the Tar Man. 'And you, too, Nathaniel. Thank you for doing this. I know how you feel about it . . .'

The Tar Man indicated the approaching vehicle with his thumb. 'It is time,' he said to Gideon.

While the Land Rover juddered along the farm track that was always so full of potholes in winter, Gideon got ready to take aim. Peter peeped out through a gap in the hawthorn hedge. The Land Rover was spattered with mud. He saw Dr Dyer at the wheel. Behind him he could make out Molly, Kate's Golden Labrador, and then – his heart skipped a beat – he saw a flash of red hair and a pale face. It was Kate! As the Land Rover drove past, Peter saw the final passenger in the car. For the briefest of moments he was allowed to gaze on himself, on Peter Schock, this boy who was here for the weekend against his will, who wished he was not going to have to spend the day with Kate Dyer, whose mind kept brooding on the worst argument he had ever had with his father. How could so much have happened to him since that day? He wanted to pull open the car door and pound on his own chest and tell him: Don't you realise how lucky you are? Don't you ever feel sorry for yourself again! You've got everything! Everything!

The Land Rover drove past. Now they could hear Mrs Dyer running up the track holding a phone in her hand.

'Andrew! Wait!' she shouted after them. 'Wait! It's Peter's dad on the phone . . .'

'Now!' said Peter.

Gideon took aim. Suddenly the Tar Man grabbed hold of his brother's arm.

'One last chance, Gideon – what if this takes everything away? Do you truly wish to go back to how things were?'

Gideon struggled with his brother. 'Each day brings a new dawn, Nathaniel. Changing the past will never change that! You make your life each day, whatever happened yesterday . . .'

The Tar Man seemed to relent a little but by now the Land Rover was some twenty metres away. Mrs Dyer had almost reached them. Peter grabbed hold of the pebble from Gideon's fingers and for an instant their eyes met. Suddenly Peter was overwhelmed at the thought of what he was about to lose. And he would not even know it. Gideon returned his gaze and nodded at him. Peter turned and threw the pebble with all his force at the rear window.

'What was that?' asked Dr Dyer.

Kate looked round. 'It's Mum! Oh dear,' she giggled. 'Look what's she's done to the glass. It looks like a bullet hole. I think you'd better stop, Dad.'

Dr Dyer stopped the Land Rover and everyone got out. Dr Dyer inspected the rear window and tutted.

'Did you have to throw a stone?' he complained to his wife. 'This had better be important!'

'I didn't throw a stone! And I don't know about important, but it's Peter's dad,' panted Mrs Dyer. 'Here you are, dear.'

Peter took the phone that Mrs Dyer offered to him.

'Well, somebody did!'

'Don't make a fuss,' said Mrs Dyer, 'it will have just been thrown up from the road.'

'Dad?' Peter held the phone to his ear and listened.

Mrs Dyer put her mouth to her husband's ear. 'Peter and his dad had a bit of an argument this morning – he's talking about driving up this afternoon. He's cancelled a meeting or something.'

Dr Dyer looked over at Peter whose face had lit up as he listened to his father.

'Why don't I go over to the lab on my own – there's nothing much there to interest Kate and Peter, in any case.'

'All right, love – don't be too long, though, lunch is nearly ready.'

Behind the hedge, Gideon and the Tar Man exchanged glances – the Peter they had grown to know had gone. The two brothers were alone.

'The deed is done,' said the Tar Man.

Gideon peered out from the hawthorn hedge.

'Come,' said the Tar Man.

Gideon sensed that they were already fading.

'Not yet! Wait!'

Gideon ran out of the field onto the road, dragging his brother with him. The wintry light passed through them. The two brothers had scarcely any substance left in this world.

'Wait, Nathaniel! Just a little longer!'

Gideon reached out a hand to Kate who was throwing a stick for Molly, her cheeks rosy and her eyes sparkling. He reached out as if to touch her hair.

'How good it is to see you well and whole, Mistress Kate.'

'Gideon! Do not resist me!'

'One moment more!'

Gideon stood behind Peter as he talked to his father on the phone, smiling as if all the cares in the world had just lifted from his shoulders.

'Farewell, Peter, be the man I know that you can become.'

Peter turned, and looked all about him, but saw only the wind rustling the sparse leaves of the hawthorn hedge.

Afterword

When Dr Dyer arrived at the research laboratory on that Saturday in December he was met by a security guard. He asked Dr Dyer to come with him straight away. Someone had broken into Tim Williamson's laboratory. The anti-gravity machine which Dr Dyer had come here to adjust now lay scattered in a thousand pieces over the floor. He surveyed the scene of destruction. Nothing else had been touched. Who would want to do such a thing? he asked himself, and, more to the point, *why?*

The Universe contains mysteries we cannot even dream of, and it is right that its mysteries push us ever onwards. Who knows what echoes will resonate through the world on account of our accidental discovery of time travel. Ordinarily, we can only ever truly know our own stories, and are rarely allowed more than a glimpse of those of others. I have been privileged to tell the stories of those characters who, as you have seen, in their own ways, and within their own limitations, pulled us back from the brink of an apocalypse.

As for the two brothers, the last remaining witnesses – along with myself – of these remarkable events, how will they go on to live their lives? What will Gideon and the Tar Man do with the knowledge that they gained and the memories that they still possess? As for me, I have not forgotten the promise that I – or rather an alternative version of myself – made to Kate as she was overcome by the ravages of time. I no longer hear my voice from a parallel world – how could I? For at the instant that Peter's stone hit the window a multitude of universes calmly winked out of existence. Now I must learn to live with the ghosts of parallel worlds and the paradox that I can remember events which have not happened. I have become a witness, a living testimony to something that must not be. So I remain ever vigilant – for who knows how long it will be before Time itself is threatened again by our curiosity – or our greed.

Yet as I write these final sentences, I can safely say that Peter Schock and Kate Dyer go happily about their daily lives; that the Marquis de Montfaron never ceased conducting his experiments nor corresponding with the great and the good; that the professors of Princeton continue to conjecture about the What If's of History; and that the sun still shines down on the many castles of Manhattan. Indeed, I believe that I can say – or at least for now – *that things are as they should be.*

Acknowledgements

I first had the idea to write *The Gideon Trilogy* in June 2000 and said my final farewell to the characters I have grown to know so well in February 2009. Along the way these books have brought me into contact with people on both sides of the Atlantic whom I count myself privileged to have met and whom I would not have encountered otherwise: readers, publishers, agents, booksellers, writers, teachers and librarians.

I should firstly like to express my gratitude to the Arts and Humanities Research Council without whose support this project would have stalled in its early stages.

My profound thanks are due to Caradoc King, for his impeccable judgement and enthusiasm, and to all at the incomparable literary agency, A. P. Watt: Christine Glover, Elinor Cooper, Louise Lamont, Linda Shaughnessy, and Teresa Nicholls.

Much of the trilogy was written whilst undertaking research at the University of London and I shall always associate it with Goldsmiths College – my thanks to Professor Blake Morrison, Professor Chris Baldick, fellow novelist, Emma Darwin, and, above all, to the poet, Maura Dooley. It was during conversations with Maura that my approach to writing the trilogy was shaped. I am also very grateful to David Hunter, Imelda and Isadora for their timely and insightful notes. Thank you.

I have been privileged to work with editors from Simon & Schuster's offices in both London and New York. A huge thank you, for their keen editorial eyes, to David Gale and Venetia Gosling. Many thanks, also, to Navah Woolfe for her editorial input, to Matt Pantoliano for introducing me to Fraunces Tavern in 2006 (and thereby planting the idea of sabotaging the Revolutionary War in the first place) and to David Gale and Laurent Linn for diagrams and advice on how to murder one of my favourite characters in the Metropolitan Museum of Art in New York.

I am indebted to Professor John M. Murrin, of Princeton University, who responded so generously to my question: 'If you wanted to sabotage the American War of Independence (Revolutionary War), how would you go about it?' Professor Murrin was good enough to propose several options for my counterfactual endeavour. Any historical errors and inaccuracies are, of course, wholly my own responsibility. I also owe a debt of gratitude to the Grafton family: to Professor Anthony Grafton for his advice on the sartorial habits of Princeton students, to Louise Grafton for showing me where General George Washington crossed the Delaware, and to Anna Grafton for giving me my first American history lesson at the NFT in London.

I am grateful to Dr Adrian and Christine Fowle for their advice and support, and to Heather Swain for her initial encouragement and for reading the first draft of *The Time Quake*. My thanks, as ever, to my friends at G.W. for listening to the work in progress: Stephanie Chilman, Jacqui Lofthouse, Louise Voss, Kate Harrison and Jacqui Hazell. And the final 'thank you' must go to R., L. and I. without whom there would not have been a story in the first place.

L. B.-A.
London, February 2009